Shinju and the Master of Tides

Shinju and the Master of Tides

CHARISA NORRIS

This is a work of fiction. Names, characters, places, and incidents either are the product of the author's imagination or are used fictitiously. Any resemblance to actual persons, living or dead, events, or locales is entirely coincidental.

ISBN 978-0-578-29184-0

Printed in the United States of America

For Papa.
Thank you for telling me to never give up on this dream.

Kanju Shima
The Golden Sea
Fundai Province
Kuishi Province

re
mo
The Black Harbor
Imperial City
Itshino Province
Iotake
rovince
Coast of Kumato
The Sea of Stars
Manju Shima
Mayaki Province

PART ONE
A Collision of Fates

1

I *AM A GHOST. I am a whisper. I am one with the shadows.*

Quiet as a mouse, Shinju tip-toed lightly down the corridor that connected to the kitchen, repeating the mantra in her head.

Just around the corner, she could hear the servants talking and laughing while they worked. Delicious smells drifted through the air, and Shinju grinned, knowing that amongst the many delectable foods being cooked for the evening meal were the ever-coveted dumplings.

Short for her age, and slight, Shinju frequently made a habit of practicing stealth by visiting the kitchen to swipe her favorite snacks. She did not necessarily need secrecy to obtain food whenever she wished, but it was more fun this way.

The fact that she also liked hiding from her handmaids contributed to her desire to be able to sneak through the castle unseen.

Keeping to the wall, Shinju quickly stole inside the kitchen, hiding behind some stacked crates of oranges. Plucked chickens and ducks hung from the ceiling on racks, waiting to be baked or fried. Negi onions simmered in oil on a pan atop a great stove. Here, the smells of garlic, ginger, and spices were almost blindingly fragrant.

With the servants as busy as they were in dinner preparations, no one took notice of the little figure darting from hiding spot to hiding spot, working her way towards the platter of fresh pork and vegetable dumplings, perfectly fried to a golden brown. Shinju's mouth watered.

She had just scooped a handful into a spare scrap of paper wrapping when the first cook spotted her.

"Shinju-sama! What are you doing? Stealing again!" Myako marched over, waving a spoon threateningly and drawing the attention of the other servants.

Shinju bit her lip to keep from laughing and darted away, heading for the back door. The cooks shouted after her half-heartedly as she made her escape out into the little yard behind the kitchen, where chickens pecked the dirt and vegetables were grown in neat gardens.

There were perks to being the daughter of a daimyo; she couldn't be punished for her mischief by the servants.

Rounding the buildings that housed the servants' wing of the castle, she giggled at her success and popped a hot dumpling into her mouth, almost regretting her haste as it burned her tongue.

Mouth full of savory pork and crunchy vegetables, Shinju

headed towards the courtyards, nodding at the various samurai or officials who passed her by. Scholar pages walked swiftly along the stone pathways, their large sleeves billowing in the wind like birds' wings, armed with papers instead of feathers.

She wound her way through the maze of courtyards and small gardens that added a sense of calm and harmony to the castle grounds. Shinju arrived at the entrance to the samurai training yards; here she hoped to find Akira.

Her best friend stood in a small sparring square reserved especially for the children when they trained. Already lanky, with a mop of dark hair and knowing chocolate eyes, Akira swung his staff made of bamboo in practiced arcs.

Shinju grinned and gave a loud squawk, surprising Akira out of his concentration. He missed catching the pole and it whacked him on the head.

"Ow!" he moaned, rubbing the offended spot. "Thanks for nothing, Shinju-chan."

"Sorry." Shinju giggled, then revealed the stolen dumplings to soften her prank. His wound forgotten, Akira quickly grabbed a couple of them, tossing one into his mouth.

"Aren't you supposed to be in lessons?" he asked around his chewing.

Shinju shrugged, finishing off the last dumpling. "Osamu-sensei has been particularly boring lately," she told him. "I want to learn about yokai and kami and legendary battles, but all he ever wants to talk about are family trees and important years that I'll never remember."

"You are the daimyo's daughter. You have to learn all that stuff," Akira said. Two years older than Shinju, he was a ward of her father, Io Harigoshi, the daimyo of the Itshino Province. Raised alongside the noble family, Akira had been allowed to choose what he wanted to be in life: a scholar or a samurai, as a favor to his deceased parents who had been close to the Harigoshi family.

At twelve years old with a hunger for knowledge, Akira decided to pursue becoming a scholar. "Someday, I'll serve the Emperor in the Palace by the Sea," he would tell Shinju. "I'm going to learn everything I can, even the details most people ignore."

Shinju slightly envied him for his freedom. As the only child of the daimyo, her path in life was clear: she would become a lady of the Imperial court and marry into a noble family. Her husband would most likely be another daimyo, or even a general.

As a result, her days were spent in practicing courtly manners and learning the names of important relatives and officials. Shinju's desire to honor her parents drove her to achieve success in these areas, but she could not help but wish she too had a choice.

Shaking away thoughts of her currently neglected duties, Shinju suggested a sparring match with Akira. They took up bamboo poles and began their usual exercises: swipe, dodge, roll, come together, swipe, dodge, again.

The clacking of their poles echoed around the yard, and a few lower samurai paused to watch. Not keen on performing for an audience, Shinju faltered in her steps and Akira's pole grazed her shoulder.

She grit her teeth and stepped back to recover, eyeing him carefully. They were always taught to assess their opponent, find out their tics, their weak spots, their emotions.

Shinju lunged forward, making as if to strike his head, and when Akira lifted his pole to block, she switched directions and aimed for his legs. Grinning as her pole made a satisfying whack against his shins, Shinju leapt back from Akira's outraged swipe.

"Tired yet?" she asked.

Akira stuck his tongue out at her, and their poles met again with a resounding clack. Ten minutes later a handmaid came looking for Shinju and scolded them for getting their fine clothes dirty and torn. She whisked Shinju away to bathe and change while Akira was told to report to his own room in the scholars' wing.

"Soon you will need to give up these childish games, my lady," the maid told Shinju as she dressed her in an airy kimono of green silk, much finer than her play clothes.

"You are the daughter of a daimyo. The more time you spend preparing for court, the better."

Shinju gave a sigh of exasperation as the maid moved to comb her hair into an elaborate bun.

"I am only ten years old, Fuji." The maid had been with the family for many years, previously as the personal handmaid to Airi, Shinju's mother. Ever since Shinju's birth, Fuji had been assigned to her instead.

This also meant that Fuji was given an extra amount of freedom to speak on things that most other servants could be punished for uttering.

"All the same, you will be a young woman before you know it." Fuji had watched Airi grow up in the court and had come with her to Harigoshi castle when she married Io, so Shinju knew the woman to be correct in her statement.

Still, to Shinju, court life might as well be a hundred years away. Why should she waste all her time learning how to use a fan when she could be sparring with Akira, or riding a horse, or doing any number of more interesting activities?

She kept these thoughts to herself, of course. Shinju had no wish to get in trouble for arguing with Fuji. She already dreaded the lecture she was sure to receive about Osamu, her tutor. He would no doubt give her parents a full and detailed report of how she had once again run from lessons.

The afternoon would be spent sewing with the other high-ranking maids who served Airi and Lady Hono, Airi's sister, or important guests. They were discussing the Festival of Lanterns, a day celebrated throughout Horitamo, for which even the nobility would mingle with the peasants. Thousands of lanterns would be lit in the city, and people would write wishes on small paper squares to place on the lanterns.

According to legend, the wishes could be granted only during the festival, so it was important to think of a good one and write it down before the night ended.

Shinju's work today consisted of mending her red kimono, which she had torn climbing trees. Fuji took up the usual station at the back of the terrace, a private space with marble floors and pillars. Peach trees grew near the railing, allowing the wind to brush the blossoms' fragrance into the terrace.

"I hear Lady Hono has a special surprise this year," one maid commented. "She is always so thoughtful during the festival season."

"Indeed," added another. "Perhaps she is announcing an

engagement."

They glanced at Shinju, as if hoping for confirmation, but Shinju only stared at them blankly. She had not the slightest clue about her aunt's personal affairs; she rarely saw her anyway.

"What do you think, Shinju-sama?" the first maid prompted. "Have you seen any suitors fluttering about our dear Lady Hono as of late?"

"No, I haven't," Shinju replied. "But I don't think she wants to get married."

That much Shinju knew. She had overheard arguments between her aunt and Airi about Hono's refusal to accept any suitors that came to the castle. Shinju did not particularly care about courting and wooing, so she had not bothered to pay more attention.

"Ah, well," said the second woman, looking over her needlework. "Lady Hono is a free spirit."

"Perhaps a mysterious man at the festival will catch her eye!"

The ladies returned to gossiping about eligible lords and landowners and Shinju tuned them out until the subject turned to the recent raids of villages in their region.

"I heard this morning from a samurai that there was another raid last night."

"This time they set the village aflame."

The women murmured in dismay, and Shinju lowered her sewing to her lap, her head spinning. Why hadn't she heard about this yet?

"Did they catch them?" she blurted out, before realizing how it looked for her to be asking questions. Thankfully, her youth excused her.

Imeko, Lady Hono's personal assistant, gave her a polite though slightly condescending smile. "The daimyo's samurai were able to prevent more damage to the village, but I'm afraid these…criminals that have plagued the land managed to escape."

Shinju swallowed her disappointment and tried her best to keep a neutral face. Something she had learned in her lessons about court life was that emotions could be used against you, especially if they were visible.

"Well, I am sure it is only a matter of time." She returned to her sewing as if she had merely discussed the weather. "No samurai are better than ours."

The other women agreed heartily, nodding their heads and spouting assurances that the samurai of Itshino Province were indeed the best, even better than the emperor's guard.

Shinju's thoughts raced. This was the fourth village that the bandits had attacked. Dressed in black, they moved swiftly through the night, stealing whatever they could and leaving the village in destruction, always disappearing before the samurai could retaliate.

What would their next target be? Shinju knew her father cared deeply about the peasants that lived in their province and would not want them to be harmed. No doubt he had a plan to catch these criminals once and for all, after what had happened last night.

She had the chance to ask her parents about the raid during the evening meal. Though always busy with the affairs of Itshino, Io and Airi always made sure to take mealtimes with their daughter.

Shinju tried not to fidget on her cushion as servants placed bowls and platters of food around them. The plate of dumplings set nearby almost distracted her, but once the servants stepped back and her parents picked up their chopsticks, Shinju used the gap in conversation to bring up the subject.

"The maids mentioned another raid last night," she said, picking at some rice. "Are the villagers going to be alright?"

Airi and Io looked at one another. "Daughter, this isn't the time or place to discuss this," Airi told her gently.

Shinju squirmed. Her mother was the perfect lady, never a hair out of place, and her dresses were always perfectly clean and in order. Shinju admired her greatly for her grace and wisdom, but right now, the desire to know more about the raids conflicted with her obedience.

"Our samurai will be stationed at every village," Io commented after a pause. Airi shot him a glance, but he simply shrugged. "Can I begrudge my daughter for asking questions about her birthright?"

Shinju struggled not to beam at these words. It was very rare that she had the opportunity to discuss the province and its functions with her parents. Normally those things were reserved for her lessons with stuffy Osamu-sensei.

"Who are these men who keep attacking us? Why would they do so?" Shinju asked.

"I am sure we will discover their identity soon enough. As for their motive, they are simply criminals who are trying to take advantage of a peaceful region," Io explained.

Shinju nodded slowly, wanting to ask more questions, but the tired lines around her father's eyes and the worry on Airi's forehead stopped her. She could ask Akira if he knew anything later; he was always listening to the scholars or the samurai talking amongst each other.

The meal continued with no further discussion of the raids, and soon it slipped from Shinju's mind completely.

2

O*KAASAN*, WILL YOU TELL me a story tonight?" Shinju asked her mother.

She sat on the edge of her bed, gazing out the open win-dows of her room, while Airi brushed Shinju's long hair. Over the sounds of trees stirring in the evening breeze, Shinju could hear the faint, lulling roar of the sea miles away.

Harigoshi castle sat at the edge of a forest, and beyond that, to the west, lay the coastline that bordered Itshino Province. Shinju had only seen the sea once, and it left an unforgettable mark on her.

Since then, she always longed to hear stories about the sea and what lay beneath it. And her mother's stories were the best of all.

"Yes, but only one story tonight," Airi assented. "Which one would you like to hear?" She finished combing and quickly plaited Shinju's hair.

Shinju turned and crawled up the bed to her pillows so she could lean back. "Tell me about Ryūjin-sama."

"Ah, the great dragon who lives beneath the sea." Airi's eyes twinkled as she drew herself into a comfortable sitting position. "Very well. Let's see..." She tapped her chin thoughtfully.

"Once, very long ago, there was a poor fisherman. He struggled to survive and thought that because he did not catch many fish, he must have done something to anger Ryūjin.

"The fisherman decided to sail his boat far out to sea and find Ryūjin so he could ask him what he had done to offend the dragon. When he reached the middle of the Golden Sea, he took out his flute and began playing it. Attracted by the music, all creatures of the sea gathered to hear him play."

Shinju smiled, imagining the scene: a fisherman on his tiny boat, surrounded by whales and fish and turtles.

"He played for three days and nights, barely stopping to eat or drink or sleep. Finally, even Ryūjin deep beneath the surface in his palace heard the fisherman's music. The dragon rose from the depths and asked the fisherman what he wanted.

"'Oh, great Ryūjin,' the fisherman wheezed. 'At last you have come to my aid. Please, tell me how I have offended you so. As you can see, I am a fisherman who cannot catch fish.' Ryūjin had pity on the poor man, and told him, 'You have come all this way with nothing, but you will not leave empty-handed.'

"Ryūjin then gave the fisherman a net, one that could not be cut or torn, and told him that as long as he cast the net on the right side of the boat, he would also have fish. 'But take care that you do not use it for greed,' the dragon warned. 'If you do, the net will turn to seaweed, and you will not catch fish again.'"

"That was a very good gift," Shinju interjected. "Yes, it was," Airi agreed. "The fisherman was overjoyed. He thanked Ryūjin, and as he sailed home, he cast the net over the right side of the boat. Just as the dragon said, the net filled with fish, and the fisherman returned home with more than enough to eat and sell.

"But the hearts of men easily forget difficult times, and the fisherman soon grew greedy with his net. He bragged to his friends and fished more than he should have, leaving nothing for them. One day he threw the net over the right side of the boat, and it did not catch a single fish."

"What did he do then?" Shinju asked, even though she knew the story.

"He grew angry, shook the net, and demanded that Ryūjin give him a better one. The net turned to seaweed in his hands, just as the dragon said. The fisherman, ashamed, left his town in the night, and traveled to the country to become a farmer."

"I bet he didn't make a very good farmer," Shinju replied as the story ended. Airi laughed. "No, he probably did not. Now, it is time for you to be in bed. Tomorrow, you will go to your lessons and apologize to Osamu-sensei for running off again, yes?"

Shinju winced and sunk down into the blankets. "Yes, *Okaasan*."

"Good night." Airi kissed her forehead and blew out the bedside candle, leaving just the glow from the brazier for Shinju to see by. "Good night, *Okaasan*."

After her mother left, Shinju stayed awake for a long time,

watching the shadows play across the walls and ceiling, imagining herself adrift on the wide sea in a boat, with the shadow of a dragon swimming beneath her.

On her way to her lessons the next morning, Shinju crossed paths with her aunt, Hono, in the hallway. She quickly bowed, feeling a little nervous, as she always did, around the stern and beautiful woman.

"Good morning, *Oba*."

"Good morning, Shinju-chan," answered Hono in her usual low, cool voice. "Will you walk with me in the gardens? It has been a long while since we have spent time together. I do not want to be accused of neglecting my duties as your aunt."

There was something in the undertone of her words, but Shinju was not sure what it could be. "I am supposed to be attending my lessons…" she answered uncertainly.

"I am sure Osamu will understand that family comes first," Hono replied smoothly. Shinju could feel Fuji shift behind her, as if preparing to disagree. "You may go," Hono spoke first, shifting her eyes to the maid.

Waves of displeasure rolled off Fuji as she bowed and gave Shinju a warning glance before shuffling away.

Hono gestured down the hall, and they continued to walk side-by-side, heading for the gardens located just outside the castle's east wing.

It was a quiet, peaceful place. Bonsai and bamboo grew in

carefully planted spots, and a stone path wove through them to end at a koi pond. A bridge painted in bright crimson arched over the pond, connecting the two halves of the garden. A cherry blossom tree grew near the bridge, the pink and white flowers just beginning to bloom.

"How are you getting along with your lessons, Shinju-chan?" Hono asked as they paused at the edge of the pond. The fish swam in lazy circles below, occasionally bringing their mouths to the surface in search of food.

"They are fine." Shinju squirmed at the question, wishing they could talk about something other than lessons. "How have you been, Aunt Hono?"

Her aunt sighed, and replied softly, "I am well, though I cannot say the same for our people." Shinju glanced up at her in surprise. She'd never heard Hono say something like that before. "Why is that, Aunt? Is it the raids?"

Hono lifted an eyebrow and toyed with the sleeve of her kimono. She always looked perfect, not a hair out of place.

"You are an observant child. Yes, I worry about the raids. They are growing worse. I fear that if we don't come to a resolution soon…" She seemed to check herself and gave Shinju an indulgent smile. "But I would not wish to worry you, dear Niece. You have other matters to occupy yourself with."

Shinju swallowed, disappointed. She wanted to continue discussing the raids and not be treated like a child. "Come, I will walk you to your lessons," Hono said after a few minutes.

They left the garden and walked through the halls of the castle until they reached the room in the scholar wing where Shinju and Akira spent much of their days.

"Oh, one last thing, Niece." Hono bent low so Shinju could see her face clearly. She gave a slightly abashed smile. "As I am not supposed to discuss the raids with you, I would appreciate it if you kept our conversation a secret. Is that alright?"

"Of course, Aunt." Shinju breathed in the scent of water lilies and something earthier as her aunt straightened, satisfied with her answer, and floated away down the hall.

Shinju took a deep breath and pulled open the sliding paper door to the study. Akira looked up from where he was copying notes on a scroll, and his eyes widened at her appearance. At the front of the office stood Osamu, and Shinju stifled a sigh as the man's sharp eyes scrutinized her.

"Good morning, Shinju. I am glad you finally found your way." Osamu had served as a scholarly advisor to the Harigoshi family for decades and accepted his appointment to instruct Shinju and Akira in their studies with rigidity and resolve.

Knowing etiquette might shorten her lecture, Shinju gave him a bow and moved quickly to her desk. "Good morning, Osamu-sensei. Forgive my tardiness, I was talking with my aunt in the gardens."

Osamu's eyes narrowed and he slowly placed his hands into the sleeves of his black *haori*. "Very well. I shall have to remind her of the time lessons begin, so that any future talks in the garden may not interrupt our delicate timetable."

Akira caught Shinju's eye and they almost laughed as Osamu turned towards a map on the wall. "We were just learning about the Western War, led by Emperor Shudan."

He droned on about locations and dates of battles. Akira wrote furiously on his scroll, barely lifting his brush in his haste to note every detail. Shinju slowly wrote a few names down, then her brush took on a mind of its own, creating the sweeping tail, then body of a dragon, intent on eating up the emperor and his armies.

3

THE DAY BEFORE THE festival, Shinju felt strange, as if something dreadful loomed on the horizon. The feeling did not dissipate as she moved through her daily routine of lessons and etiquette training.

She thought she was simply excited for the festival; she'd spent a long time that week deciding what wish she wanted to place on the lanterns. But the hard knot in her stomach seemed to prove otherwise. It resembled the anxiousness she felt when she got in trouble or had to recite a long lesson to Osamu-sensei when she had not paid attention.

Even her dreams had been different, filled with dark and murky figures, knives, and horrible laughter.

It was a relief to receive word that her parents wanted to partake in a tea ceremony with her that evening. Between raids on various villages and preparation for the festival, Shinju had not seen much of her parents in many days, and she looked forward to the valuable time she would get to spend just with them.

Shinju made a beeline for the kitchen, followed by Fuji, in a mission to select all the needed equipment herself. As usual, the servants graciously offered to help Shinju gather everything, from the various tea leaves to the different pots that would be used.

"Shinju-sama, Niko will assist you in the preparations for your tea. I've been told she is quite knowledgeable about tea," Myako instructed.

The servant, whom Shinju could not recall seeing before, bowed and murmured a greeting. She had a narrow body and sharp, exact eyes that darted like a bird's. "Which teas do your parents enjoy most?" Niko asked in a low voice.

Shinju studied the selections before her, all carefully labeled and sorted into small pots. Together, they chose green teas with notes of jasmine, and an orange tea created from the castle's own trees.

The most enjoyable part of these preparations involved creating the *namagashi*, little sweets made from fruit jelly that are carefully crafted by hand into flowers or animals to be eaten before the tea ceremony. Shinju could not help but sneak one into her pocket to consume later.

Stars twinkled high in the night sky when Shinju entered the small room in the family quarters that was used for tea ceremonies or private discussions. She bowed to her father and mother and they bowed to her as well, smiling as she giggled.

They kneeled on the tatami floor and a servant helped

Shinju arrange the tea equipment. At one end of the room, large latticed windows with the curtains pulled back provided a beautiful view of the moon, partially hidden by ghostly clouds. Candles had been lit in high, round paper lanterns, washing the room in a pleasant yellow glow.

At Shinju's back was an alcove, where a vase of cherry blossoms had been carefully arranged, and a scroll hung on the wall above them, written in Shinju's own hand about the good tidings they expected the festival to bring: hope, fortune, and guidance.

"This all looks lovely, Shinju-chan," Airi complimented with a loving look at her daughter.

"Indeed, it has been too long since we have had a tea ceremony together as a family," Io added, his eyes eagerly moving to the plate of *namagashi*. He shared a grin with Shinju: they both shared a weakness for sweets.

As befitting a tea ceremony, the conversation remained light: no mention of raids or samurai movements. Shinju glowed with the appreciation of her parents as they drank the first tea, a thick green herbal blend.

"Your skills have improved, Shinju-chan," Airi said. "I have no doubt you will be a shining star in the court when the time comes." Shinju had a harder time smiling at that compliment. She didn't want to think about the future, she wanted to enjoy this moment.

"Ah yes, it won't be long until I will have to assign an imposing samurai guard to ward off the incessant wave of suitors." Io gave a long-suffering sigh, much to Shinju's amusement.

"I can take care of myself," she replied, retrieving their

bowls and preparing the next tea.

"I suppose you mean all the times you sneak into the sparring yard with Akira," Airi mentioned, folding her hands into the sleeves of her kimono. Shinju winced, knowing that her mother did not exactly approve of her waving around a bamboo pole and getting bruises.

"Well, I need the exercise," she explained lamely. Her father covered up a laugh with a cough, and even Airi pursed her lips to hide her smile. "Be that as it may, it is not proper," she continued.

Shinju nodded to show she understood, not that she agreed. She hoped her parents would not impose more restrictions on her; losing her sparring time with Akira would be a rule she wasn't sure she would be able to follow.

She enjoyed the physical activity, the demand that fighting had on both her body and mind. It felt good to move and be adept at something other than bowing and waving a fan correctly.

Shinju set aside the new tea mixture and waited for it to reach the proper temperature on the brazier, then she poured it into each of their bowls. As tradition dictated, the guests would drink before their host. Shinju watched as her parents smelled the tea's aroma and each took a long sip, before they lowered their bowls and smiled at her.

She started to reach for her own tea when the bowl suddenly slipped from her mother's hands, crashing to the floor.

Airi leaned forward, clutching her throat and making a terrible choking sound. Shinju froze, staring in horror. "Airi, what is it?" Io exclaimed, placing his hands on his wife's shoulders.

Suddenly his own face turned dark red, and his eyes bulged as he too began to cough and clutch at his throat.

"*Okaasan*? *Otousan*?" Shinju leaped to her feet and rushed around the tea set as her parents collapsed to the floor, gasping for air.

"Help!" she cried. Rolling her mother to her back, she stared as Airi grasped the front of Shinju's tunic, clawing desperately for air as she managed to wheeze out one word. "...Tea..."

"Hold on, Mother," Shinju begged, tears welling from her eyes and streaming down her cheeks. She cried out again for help, wondering where the guards and servants were.

Airi gave a final lurch, then lay limp in her arms, her eyes open and unseeing. Ice gripped Shinju's heart as she turned to her father, who grew still, his arm falling from his throat to hit the floor with a thump.

"No...please..." Shinju shook her father, then her mother. The door to the room slid open, and soft footsteps brushed against the tatami floor. Shinju whirled desperately around to meet the pale and horrified face of her aunt Hono.

"What have you done," whispered Hono in a voice full of ice.

"Please...*Oba*...you have to get help. Something is wrong," Shinju begged. Tears splashed onto her hands and wetted the clothes of her parents. Hono took a few steps forward, bringing a hand to her mouth as she stared at her sister and brother-in-law.

"It is too late," she gasped. The words slammed into Shinju like a punch to the stomach, and her mind refused to accept it. "No...no...they can't be," she sobbed.

"What did you put in the tea?" Hono demanded, her voice still deathly quiet.

"Nothing! I prepared it like I always have!" Shinju couldn't understand why her aunt made no move to get help, and she opened her mouth once more to cry out.

"You've killed them," Hono whispered, kneeling down to bring her face level with Shinju's.

The call died in Shinju's throat as she gazed at her aunt's white face in shock. "W-what?"

"The tea. You put something in it, and you killed them."

"I…I…didn't…it…" Shinju's eyes raced between the tea equipment and her parents, unable to make sense of this. She had not done anything to the tea, she was sure!

"I would never do this," she pleaded, Hono's terrible words stirring a flurry of fear in her chest. "It was an accident…someone else must have done this…"

Hono cocked her head, then shook it with a long sigh. "No, Shinju-chan. You prepared the tea yourself, did you not? An accident…yes, perhaps. You are only a child, after all."

Fresh tears blurred Shinju's vision as she sank, reaching for her parents' still warm hands, silently begging them to wake up.

"You must go," Hono said after a moment. Shinju blinked up at her uncomprehendingly.

"W-what?"

"You must go. When they find out what you've done, you will be executed," Hono explained in a shaky voice. She reached out and placed a hand on Shinju's arm. "Leave this place. Go through the window there. Quickly now!"

Shinju's head spun, the realization of her parents' deaths

and her own part in it crashing over her in waves of terror. She was sinking, drowning in the shock, but somehow, she managed to lean down and kiss first her mother, then her father. "I'm sorry," she gasped in a strangled voice. "Forgive me."

"Hurry," Hono hissed, casting her eyes towards the door. The word sprung Shinju into action. She hurried to the windows and threw them open. A trellis extended from the wall down to the balcony several feet below her.

She gave one last look at her parents, and at Hono, who watched her with wide eyes and trembling lips. Then she clambered onto the railing and hooked a foot into one of the holes in the trellis. It held fast, and she carefully maneuvered her body over, trying not to look down.

Thinking of the trees she and Akira climbed in the gardens, Shinju forced her way down the makeshift ladder and reached the balcony below.

The room here beyond was dark, but Shinju did not pause to check if it was unoccupied. She searched around for a further escape route, and spotted an oak tree that had grown large, the nearly bare branches extending just over the castle wall.

Shinju bit back a fresh onslaught of tears. Any moment now, Hono would alert the guards and they would be searching for her. Maybe she should let them catch her…maybe she deserved to die.

Whatever motivated her to slide off the balcony and down the wall, Shinju did not pause to figure it out. She bolted for the tree and climbed as quickly and quietly as she could towards the wall. Shouts rang out behind her, and Shinju almost lost her footing.

They had discovered the dead daimyo and his wife.

She reached the final section of branches that hung over the wall, and Shinju scooted carefully to the edge, looking down. She knew that samurai patrolled the outer walls of the castle, but with a call raised to aid their daimyo, she had a short window of opportunity to make a run for it.

Taking a deep breath, Shinju dropped down from the branches and hit the ground hard, the impact knocking the wind out of her. Pain shot up through her legs and she tried to roll like she had seen Akira do when he fell, but she ended up only clumsily landing on her face.

With a groan, she pushed herself up, trying not to cry out at the scrapes to her hands and knees.

With only the iron lanterns on the corners of the castle walls to light her way, Shinju stared into the black abyss of the land around her, trying to orient herself. She was on the east side, so…the Dark Forest was not far away. If she could get there, she could hide and then…Shinju shook her head.

Do not think of the future just yet. One step at a time.

Limping, she turned in the direction of the forest and left the castle behind as shouts and the sound of steel filled the air.

4

SHE BURST THROUGH THE undergrowth, the bushes whipping against her limbs and causing red cuts to appear against exposed skin. Shinju paid the stinging no mind. All she could see through her tears was her mother and father's dead bodies. All she could hear was the cold, low voice of her aunt saying, "You killed them."

How did this happen? Shinju's thoughts were jumbled as she tried to understand; her heart was beating so madly that she knew she must stop to catch her breath or she would collapse.

Leave this place.

The echo of those words rang in her ears as she halted by a clump of bamboo, her breathing ragged and mixed with hiccups. Snot ran down her nose, and she wiped at it aimlessly with her sleeve. The sight of her dress stopped her, its color vibrant in the otherwise dimly lit woods. Her special dress, the one meant for grand occasions. The one her mother had helped her sew.

More tears poured from her eyes, and Shinju gagged at the bile rising in her throat. She gripped a nearby tree, her stomach threatening to empty its contents.

The sudden but distant sound of voices shook her from the haze of nausea, and she tensed, straining to hear.

"I know she came this way," said a raspy voice. "She's left a trail all over the place. Can't be far."

Trembling, Shinju crept as quietly as she could behind the tree. She didn't know who was looking for her, and as the voice was unfamiliar, she wanted to see who it could be before announcing herself. She half hoped, half dreaded, that it was samurai from the castle looking for her.

"This way," said another voice; this was one deep and menacing. Shinju bit her lip, wondering if she should stay put or run.

"Come on, little girl, come out wherever you are," the first voice hissed. The hair rose on the back of Shinju's neck, and she took a step back. A strange laugh rang through the brush, and a moment later she caught a glimpse of three figures dressed in black, slinking into the clearing. They carried katanas, and they each wore a black face covering, but the red sash on their arms gave them away. Fear coiled her stomach. She knew who they were.

Akira had told her that the raiders of the villages wore this kind of clothing, according to the conversations he had overheard from the samurai.

And now they were looking for her. But why? How had they known she would be here?

One of them paused to look around, and with a sickening jolt, Shinju looked into his dark, dead eyes.

She knew then that if these men found her, they would kill her. She had to escape before they discovered her hiding place.

Glancing around, she saw a pinecone on the ground by her feet. Picking it up, she aimed for the other side of the clearing, praying that they wouldn't notice as she launched it into the air. It hit the brush with a crash, and the figures whipped around, hurrying over to investigate. Shinju turned and ran as hard as she could.

She did not know where she was going, and the forest was growing darker the deeper she went, but she would take the dangers of the foreign trees over the raiders. From behind, she heard shouting, but refused to turn and look. There was only her and the forest, and she begged silently for it to protect her. *Conceal me, don't let them find me.*

A cold wind blew, and a sudden downpour of rain pelted the earth. Shinju wiped at her face as water streamed into her eyes, almost blinding her. She tripped, and with a cry she fell down a steep slope. Her arms flailed for purchase and scraped against roots, rocks, and undergrowth. With a hard thump, she rolled and slammed against a tree.

She must have stumbled across a drop-off in the forest and missed the ledge. Groaning, she managed to rise on her knees.

Shinju was hurting all over and so, so tired, but she pulled herself to her feet and began limping. The rain grew worse, but it felt oddly good against her bruises and cuts. She hoped that the water would cover her tracks.

It wasn't long before she was soaked through, not to mention muddy from her fall. She was shivering too, and her empty stomach continued to roil from lack of food and the horrors of the evening.

As the shadows grew longer and the rain continued to fall in a thick curtain, Shinju knew she had to find shelter somewhere. She paused and took in her surroundings. Everything looked much the same, except that the trees looked larger and older than she had ever seen, and it was oddly quiet, save for the dance of raindrops. She supposed most animals would be hiding too.

A few more steps, and through the trees she glimpsed a faint, silvery light in the distance. Shinju wrinkled her brow., wondering what it could be?

She walked towards it as quietly as she could. The trees grew thinner, and before she realized it, she stumbled out into the open.

The edge of the forest ended on a cliff that sloped down to a beach. The silver light she'd seen had been the moonlight shimmering on the waves of the sea.

Momentarily distracted from her predicament, Shinju breathed in the salty air and looked around her. Pulled up to the shore were rows of fishermen's boats, their sails and tackle gathered neatly to await the next day's fishing. No one was in sight.

A shout rang out behind her. "There she is!"

Panicked, Shinju crouched and began sliding down the slope covered in sand, stones, and thick grass. In her haste, she lost her footing and stumbled once more, rolling down the rest of the way. Every bone in her body felt rattled when she landed at the bottom with a thud, sinking into the cold, hard-packed sand.

Get up! Whimpering, Shinju pushed herself to her feet and scrambled towards the nearest boat, a small but sturdy-looking vessel. She had no idea how to sail, or even swim, but she didn't have much of a choice.

With every last drop of strength she possessed, Shinju pushed on the boat, sliding it off the beach and into the water. The figures in black were behind her now, making their way down the slope.

A *shuriken* raced through the air and whizzed past her scalp, taking a few strands of her hair with it. The raiders called to her mockingly, but Shinju persisted, continuing to push the boat until the tide brought it further into the water.

She climbed in and found an oar. A knife flew by her this time, even closer than before, and she ducked, trying to paddle as best she could with the oar, which was much larger and heavier than it looked.

Shinju peeked over the edge of the boat and saw that the figures had stopped on the shoreline, watching. She expected them to grab a boat as well, but they did not.

"You'll die out there!" one of them called to her, his voice harsh and cruel. "The sea monsters will get you!"

Shinju paddled furiously, trying to put as much distance between them as she could. Perhaps they could not sail or swim either?

The waves carried the boat farther out to sea, and as the

minutes passed, the beach and the figures in black grew smaller and smaller. Shinju was sure their weapons could not reach her now and she straightened, pausing in her paddling to breathe.

The only world she knew disappeared into the night.

For hours Shinju floated in the boat, not even bothering to paddle. She had no idea of where to go, nor did she care. Her heart had shattered, and she lay curled up in a ball on the boat's small deck, sobbing until her throat grew raw.

Over and over, her mind replayed the memory of her parents' deaths, until Shinju fell asleep with exhaustion, her tears leaving a burning trail on her cheeks.

She awoke to a rush of cold water splashing over her. With a start, Shinju realized the wind had picked up, as well as the height of the waves. What had once been a gentle sea now looked terrible and deadly.

Waves beat against the sides of the boat, causing it to tip wildly side to side. Frightened, Shinju grabbed the paddle once more and tried to steer, but hopelessness clawed at her futile actions. There was nowhere for her to paddle to.

As far as she could see, there was only the water and the sky, filled with dark clouds that covered the stars. The wind blew again, accompanied by rain.

Desperate to find land of some kind, Shinju paddled uselessly against the waves. Water sprayed against her with icy fingers, and she was drenched within minutes.

Shivering and chattering, Shinju felt tears prick her eyes again. She should never have taken the boat. Now she would die out here, and no one would know what had happened to her.

Sitting in the bottom of the boat, her arms curled around her knees, Shinju shivered and wished with all her might that she was back home, in her warm bed, with her mother combing her hair and singing songs, or telling her stories. Perhaps this was all a terrible dream.

The boat lurched and rocked atop the waves, knocking her to the side. "Ow!" Shinju rubbed her arm, sniffing. Then her eyes caught something in the water.

Grasping the railing, Shinju lifted herself up, searching the waves. "Oh!" A flash of scales appeared, then they were gone.

Shinju gulped. Thoughts of sea monsters invaded her mind. Or maybe it was a yokai. Shinju had read stories about such creatures that would attack sailors and eat their boats whole. *I wish Akira were here. He wouldn't be afraid.*

The water around her suddenly calmed, and even the wind blew less. Shinju smoothed her hair back, looking around her in surprise. She didn't know much about the sea, or storms, but it seemed odd that the weather could change so quickly.

A gentle, slight rain still spattered on the boat and clung to Shinju's eyelashes. She turned back to the waves, and gasped.

Scales appeared again just under the surface of the dark water, stirring into white foam. The moonlight reappeared, giving the scales a nearly pearlescent sheen. Shinju held her breath, watching with all her might as the scales twisted and turned, keeping in line with the boat.

She leaned her chin on the railing, the gentle rocking of the boat soothing her. The creature, whatever it was, did not seem intent on attacking. Perhaps it was merely a curious serpent, or a large fish.

Shinju briefly wondered if it could even be the great dragon himself. "Ryūjin?" she whispered. Nothing changed in the movement of the scales, or the body they belonged to, but Shinju felt an overwhelming sense of peace at the thought of the Kami Dragon of legend watching over her.

"If it's you," she continued to whisper, her eyes drooping, "please, help me."

As her vision blurred the foaming water, Shinju thought she briefly caught sight of an enormous eye watching her, but the boat rocked again, and a heavy sleep eased her into unconsciousness.

5

SOFT MORNING LIGHT WARMED her face, chasing the darkness away. The rocking had stopped, as well as the sound of waves rushing against the sides of the boat.

Shinju moaned and swallowed; her throat was as dry and hoarse as sandpaper. She was still sore, but no longer cold, at least. Rubbing her eyes, she glanced blearily around her, and froze when she spotted a little tray on the ground nearby.

A simple pot of tea and a small cup sat on the tray, along with a bowl of what looked like broth. A whisper of steam rose from the teapot, and a fragrant scent reached Shinju's nose. *That* definitely had not been there before…

Shinju froze, every part of her tensing. She wasn't on the boat any longer. Where was she?

Closing her eyes tight, then slowly reopening them, Shinju took in her surroundings. She lay on a soft futon, lumpy but comfortable, in a small but clean room. It was empty except for the tray, and a bamboo plant in the corner. One papered window was responsible for the sunshine she'd felt.

She panted, trying to grasp what had changed. Had she found land at last in the night? Whose home was she in? Why was she here?

Her hands…they were bandaged.

The memories rushed back to her, and Shinju gulped a deep breath, squeezing her fingernails into her palms as she willed herself not to cry. She wasn't sure if she had any tears left in her anyway. Carefully, she approached the tray on her hands and knees, then spotted the open doorway.

Someone sat a few feet away from her on the smooth wood floor, his back to her. He wore a wide straw hat, and a trail of smoke floated from a long pipe held in one hand. He was dressed in simple yet well-made clothes, dyed a dark blue color Shinju had never seen before. Long black hair streaked with gray fell down his back, unbound. An intricately carved staff lay on the floor next to him.

The man sat very still, and Shinju wondered if she should pretend to go back to sleep. It was obvious now who had provided the tea, but why? Had he also been sailing on the sea and found her?

Shinju's eyes narrowed as she quietly picked up the pot of tea, still hot to the touch. This could be a trap. The man could be a yokai who had shape-shifted into a human form, or maybe even one of the criminals that had chased her last night, wearing a disguise.

As she tiptoed closer, the man spoke without turning

around. "I hope you are feeling rested." The voice, low and soft and kind, held a tinge of humor to it, as if he knew what Shinju was doing. Embarrassed, Shinju stuck her chin out stubbornly and marched out before him, raising the teapot towards him defensively.

"Who are you?" she demanded. The bowed head turned and lifted, peering at her from underneath the brim of the hat. Shinju met a pair of kindly brown eyes set in a slightly weathered and tan face. A neat goatee that matched his hair was the only other distinguishing feature about the stranger. He looked perfectly normal, but Shinju was not quite ready to let down her guard, not after all she'd been through.

"My name is Takumi Tsoma," answered the same calm voice. "You have no need to fear, young one. You are safe now. Please, sit and have some tea, it will help you recover."

Slightly abashed, and desperate for a kind word, Shinju slowly lowered the pot back to the ground, then went and fetched the tray she had left behind in the room.

The stranger did not move, seeming content to sit there and smoke his pipe, the smoke curling out through the open doorway of the little house. Shinju set the tray before him and sat down opposite, crossing her legs.

Takumi watched her with a vaguely amused expression, but also a searching one, and after a moment Shinju lowered her eyes to the tea. "*Arigato*, Takumi-sensei, for all this," she said, gesturing towards the tray and then placing her palms together with a little bow.

Takumi simply nodded in return. Shinju poured herself a cup and one for him as well, remembering her manners despite her brain feeling like a gnarled bunch of string.

The tea had a very light fragrance, lemongrass and something else Shinju could not identify. She took a sip, and the warmth filled her, easing away the tight ball of fear and worry that had gathered in the pit of her stomach. She sighed, and the man smiled. "Better?" he asked.

"Y-yes."

"Good. Now, suppose you tell me your name?" Takumi prompted. "I am…Shinju. I live…lived…not too far from here, I think. I'm not sure where I am now." She paused, taking in the man's appearance once more. "Where are we?" she asked.

"This is my home, on an island called Kanju Shima," Takumi answered. A soft breeze tickled Shinju's face as he spoke. Outside she could hear birds chirping, and voices far in the distance. An island?

She tried hard to remember all the island villages and towns mentioned in her lessons, but her thoughts were too groggy. "I've never heard of it," she responded awkwardly.

"I did not think that you would. It is very far from Horitamo." Takumi took a sip of his tea.

"H-how did I get here?" Shinju asked weakly.

"Your boat washed up on the beach very early yesterday morning," Takumi replied. "I went down to the beach to check my traps in the lagoon and found you. You were soaked to the bone and running a fever."

"Yesterday morning?" Shinju couldn't believe it. She had really been asleep all this time?

"Indeed. Some of the village women came to bandage your wounds and change your clothes." With a start, Shinju realized she was indeed wearing something other than the kimono she'd fled in.

She smoothed her hands over the layers of the soft *jinbei* set. "Thank you," she whispered. Takumi nodded, then fixed her with a more serious gaze.

"Shinju, what are you doing so far from home? Where are your parents?"

A hard lump rose in her throat at the thought of her parents, lying still and cold. Suddenly the tea did not seem as appealing, and with a trembling hand she quickly lowered the cup, memories of the night before returning to her hazy mind.

"They are dead," she whispered. For a moment she warred internally over whether to tell Takumi everything, but in the end she only added, "I'm alone."

Takumi's brow furrowed with concern and he slowly lowered the pipe. "How did they die, my child?"

Flashes of the tea ceremony came to Shinju's mind, and she fought back bitter tears. *I can't tell him. I don't know him, or this village. They might send me back!*

"They…got sick. There was no time to get help. It all happened so fast." She stared at her shaking hands in her lap. Shinju had never been good at lying, and while her words weren't false, she fretted over whether Takumi would see through the halting words.

He stayed quiet for a long time. "It is a hard thing to lose the ones we love, especially family." A few moments passed before he continued. "Why were you in that boat on the open sea?"

"I-I ran away. Some bad men were chasing after me. I did

not know what would happen…" The words failed, and she started to sob, wringing her hands in her clothes.

"There now, it is alright. You do not need to speak any more of it at this time," Takumi said, laying a gentle hand on her head. "I think I understand."

How could he possibly understand? Shinju thought sullenly, trying to collect herself.

"Where will you go?" Takumi asked after her sobs began to cease.

"I don't know…I can't go back home…" Despair clouded her brain. Where *could* she go? She had nothing, knew no one. Eventually the Harigoshi samurai or the bandits could find her, and she would be dead either way once everyone knew what she'd done.

"What should I do?" she whispered, hating the tears that formed again in the corners of her eyes.

Takumi carefully put his pipe away in a small box at his side, then he stood with a fluidity that she wouldn't have expected. "For now, you are somewhere safe," he said. "My clan are a peaceful people, but we have a very important duty. If you wish to stay, I will tell you more."

Shinju regarded him warily. "Why would you help me?" she asked in a small voice. "You are a stranger."

Takumi looked down at her, a sadness entering his eyes. "I am no stranger to loss, Shinju-chan. I too have lost my family. And you are but a child."

A gentle breeze tugged at Shinju's hair, causing the bamboo outside to creak in rhythm. Takumi closed his eyes as he felt the wind, and Shinju watched him curiously.

"You have much sorrow and guilt in you, child, and if you let it fester, it will consume you. We could teach you another way. But the choice is yours."

6

SHINJU BLINKED, SCRAMBLING TO understand his meaning. He sounded as though he truly cared, and desired to help her. Still, that did not mean this man was a friend. Or that he wouldn't be repulsed if he learned the truth.

As if guessing her thoughts, Takumi slowly raised a hand, turning it palm up. "I am not your enemy, Shinju-chan. If you wish to go home, I will escort you there safely. If you wish to take another path, I will advocate for you to remain here. But know this: whatever way you choose, eventually, we must all come to terms with our past, the good and the bad. Which way will you choose, Shinju?"

Shinju regarded him for a long time, thinking. "There is nothing for me back there," she said in a small, trembling voice. "If your clan will not forsake me, I would like to stay here, Takumi Tsoma."

The man nodded. "Please, eat and rest. There is plenty of time for you to see the island and learn more about us."

Shinju humbly accepted his direction and drank her broth, now cold, and crawled back into the cocoon of the futon.

Every day she felt a little stronger. But the anxiety and grief curled in her stomach like a poisonous serpent; she feared being found by the bandits, and the only things that could distract her were Takumi's stories.

He described to her the wondrous things that the island held beyond the little house: it was a place of magic, he said, and thus some rare creatures lived there, basking in its beauty and the harmonious nature. "What kind of creatures?" Shinju asked, thinking about yokai and ghosts.

"Most are forest kami and spirits," Takumi answered. "But we have some birds and animals that migrated here from other islands long ago."

He told her of how his clan had lived here in isolation from the rest of the empire for hundreds of years. He would not tell Shinju what it was the clan guarded, only that it was something very special and valuable.

The assurances of safety and the peaceful environment around her did little to ease the ache of her loss. Remembering her parents' absence burned, like the time she had picked up a tea kettle the wrong way and singed her hand. The pain had seemed never ending, and so too did this.

She wondered sadly about her friend Akira. What was he doing now? Was he angry with her for running away? She wondered about her aunt as well, burying the only family she had left, and the guilt would slam against her chest so hard she could barely breathe.

At night, trying not to wake Takumi, Shinju would cry silent tears, and the knot of grief in her stomach turned and twitched. Why couldn't she have done more? Had she really done something so terrible to the tea that it had caused their deaths? Should she have left their sides while they choked and run for help?

Regrets filled and haunted her every moment of the day. If only she had been stronger, or older, maybe she could have done more. The worst thought of all was the one that whispered with a poisonous snarl, *It's your fault.*

One morning, Takumi looked at her red eyes and told her gently, "Shinju-chan, it is alright to cry and miss those you love. You do not need to hide it."

"I…I didn't want to bother you," Shinju admitted hesitantly, looking down at her feet.

"Death, grief, loss, these are natural parts of life and we all feel them in different ways. You should have seen me when my wife, Niko, and my daughter, Umeko, passed on from this world."

Shinju perked with interest at the mention of his wife and daughter. She had wondered why he lived alone.

"How did it happen, Takumi-san?" she asked, hoping her question would not be too personal.

"Niko loved the water, and she spent as much time in her little boat as she could," Takumi stated after a few moments of silence, gazing into the brazier glowed with embers, strands of gray smoke spilling listlessly into the air.

"One day while she took Umeko out sailing. A giant *Umi*

nyōbō attacked the boat. They are rarely seen in the waters by our island, but when they are, we drive them away because they are very dangerous. Niko fought to stay afloat, but the beast turned the boat over, and they fell into the icy water. By the time we reached them, it was too late."

How terrible, Shinju thought with a shiver. "I am sorry, Takumi-sensei."

"That was many years ago," he continued. "I was younger then, rash, and angry at what I had lost. And so I set out to kill the *Umi nyōbō*. I almost perished as well."

"And did you kill it?" Shinju asked eagerly, leaning forward. Takumi sighed and nodded. "I did. And then I shut myself up in my home and did not come out for weeks. The elders finally had to break in and address my behavior."

His dark eyes slid over to meet Shinju's. "I had gone to a very dark place, Shinju-chan. I do not want that for you. So, grieve your parents, feel their loss, and remember them, but do not blemish their memory with anger or regret. Do you understand what I am telling you?"

Shinju nodded slowly, feeling heat rise in her face. He knew what she had been thinking, somehow. "I understand, Takumi-san." *But doing so is another thing entirely*, she thought.

By the fourth day, Shinju insisted that she felt better and Takumi suggested that they go for a walk. A couple of women from the village had checked on her, and though they had been kind, they had not said much.

"We are not used to outsiders here," Takumi explained. Shinju was given a tunic to replace the *jinbei*, as well as a pair of new shoes, which were much sturdier than her slippers.

The day before, Shinju sat on the porch at the back of the house, gazing out into the gardens and jungle beyond. The island even had a mountain peak, rising green and proud to the sky.

This place was so different from Harigoshi Castle; Shinju had never seen such bright fauna, not even in her home gardens. While the castle grounds were carefully designed and meticulous, they lacked the wild beauty of the island.

Takumi led her down a little winding path from his house to the village. Growing a little nervous now, she moved closer to his side. Would the Tsoma Clan accept her? Young as she was, Shinju could feel that this was a very special and sacred place, something to be treasured. How would they feel if an outsider came in? Would they send her away?

All these questions were banished from her mind when they entered a clearing scattered with flowers and longer grass that brushed Shinju's ankles. The ground continued to slope upwards, leading to thatched roofs of the buildings ahead. As they drew near, Shinju could see that the houses and shops of the village were scattered up the path, winding and climbing further up to the island's peak.

At the very top of the path, she could see a taller building, the roofs curved with lacquered tiles. A large, fire-red bird she had never seen before sat preening its feathers on one of the corners. It had a long tail that brushed against the bottom of the balcony, and when it raised its head, Shinju thought she could see that it had the most wonderful golden eyes, even from so far away.

"What is that, Takumi-san?" she asked, pointing.

"Ah, that is Hōō. Beautiful, is he not? He enjoys sitting up there in the mornings."

Before Shinju could inquire further, they entered the village. People were carrying out their daily tasks: gardening, cooking, washing or mending clothes. Young children played in between chores, laughing and chasing each other.

Life here was not so different from the peasants Shinju saw in Itshino Province. She stared in wonder, taking in the blue and white lanterns that ran between the buildings on strings, the scrolls that hung from doorways, both painted and embroidered, the chickens and livestock that added their voices to the villagers' conversations.

A few people paused in their duties to watch their approach, then more stopped and looked, nodding to Takumi and regarding Shinju with curiosity.

She swallowed and half-hid behind Takumi, feeling shy and even more of an outsider.

The children also stopped their games and openly gawked at her, whispering to each other. A couple waved at her and smiled, which Shinju returned gratefully.

They were greeted by another man who left the rest of the gathering villagers. He strode forward and gripped Takumi's forearm. "I see you've finally brought our new friend out to meet us, Takumi!"

He had a kind face despite the large scar that spread from

his forehead down to his cheek. His eyes, dark chocolate and warm, fell on Shinju. She smiled back tentatively.

Takumi glanced at Shinju then patted the man on the shoulder. "Come, Saburo, there is much to discuss." To Shinju, he placed a hand on her shoulder.

"Shinju-chan, I need to go speak with our daimyo, Yuudai-sama, and the elders. I will take you with me, and we will continue our walk after. Is that okay?" Shinju nodded mutely, wondering if they were going to talk about her and whether she could stay. Her hands grew sweaty and she hid them inside the long sleeves of her tunic.

They continued their walk through the village, heading for the taller building Shinju assumed must be the home of the daimyo. Her heart twisted as she took in the peace around her. Back in Takumi's house, she'd felt as though there was some hope for the first time since her parents' deaths. But fear plagued her thoughts.

What if Takumi was commanded to take her back to Horitamo? What if they put her back in her boat and exiled her back to survive on the sea alone?

The path ahead was lined with stone lanterns, leading up to the castle. It was not nearly as large or grand as Harigoshi castle, but Shinju could sense that it was a place that still demanded respect. She craned her neck back to see the top, and on the three balcony levels she could see samurai guards.

Sounds to her left broke through her thoughts, and Shinju looked around to see a group of children, some as young as her but mostly older, standing in a group where a bamboo grove had been cleared.

They were all holding long poles, and an instructor was in the process of demonstrating various moves with his own pole, twisting and swinging it through the air. Shinju came to a halt, forgetting Takumi and Saburo, and watched as the children followed suit, recreating the movements with their poles with precision.

They are all training, she realized. Just like she and Akira had done.

Her chest felt a pang as she thought of her friend. What must he be thinking right now?

The instructor gave a nod of approval, then began to go through other forms. Sensing she'd fallen behind, Takumi stopped and turned towards Shinju.

"Are you all warriors?" she asked.

Takumi grinned. "Every Tsoma is trained in the basics, and some choose to continue their training. So in a way, yes we are, though we fight no wars, save only those that may come to our doorstep," Takumi answered. "We always train and prepare for the possibility of attack."

"Why, Takumi-san?" Shinju asked, regarding him and Saburo with even more respect.

"Your questions will be answered soon, I hope," was all he said, and gestured that she come along.

At the front door to the castle, Shinju got a closer look at the Tsoma samurai. They wore light armor of black and gold and blue, with the standard helmets that covered their necks. One of them gestured towards another flight of stairs across the room. Takumi and Saburo bowed and entered.

Shinju followed them up so many stairs and through so

many corridors that she wondered if they were going all the way to the top. The decor was simple and calming, dark wood and plants and paintings adorning the walls and corners. Here and there they saw other guards, who merely glanced their way before continuing their duties.

At last they arrived at an intricately carved door, and the guard stationed outside slipped inside. Shinju took the opportunity to study the door.

The image of a mighty dragon emerging from the sea covered almost the entire door, the water and foam carved around its body looking so realistic that Shinju wondered if it might not be truly wet. Above the dragon's head floated two orbs.

Before she could take in more, the door reopened, and the guard asked Takumi alone to come inside. Shinju was told to remain outside until she was summoned.

Kneeling outside the door, Shinju waited with increasing suspense. The minutes passed and she tried not to fidget. Saburo had walked farther down the hall to speak with a guard in low tones.

After some time, Shinju could hear raised voices in the room beyond. She inched a little closer and strained to listen to the muffled sounds.

"We do not know where this girl has come from. She could bring trouble to this island," said a stranger.

"Her parents are dead, she claims to have no one else," Takumi argued. "There must be a reason why she landed on our shores."

"Did it occur to you that her presence here could bring more people? How do we know for certain that no one is looking for her?" asked the first voice.

Takumi answered, but Shinju could not make it out. Sweat dripped down her forehead and coated her hands. The other man, who she assumed must be the daimyo, seemed suspicious of her. Shinju prayed that Takumi would convince him that she meant no harm.

Eventually the door opened once again, and Takumi stood on the other side. He looked a little weary, but he smiled and gestured for her to enter.

The room beyond the door was surprisingly light and airy, with the open balcony allowing the sea breeze to move freely in and out. Plants, mostly bamboo, were growing abundantly in here as well, and the mat beneath her feet was soft. A silk curtain hanging in front of the balcony was pulled aside, and Shinju saw a man standing there with his hands behind his back, looking out.

"Shinju-chan, this is Yuudai-sama, our clan's daimyo," Takumi told her. Shinju bowed and waited, her heart pounding.

After a few minutes the man turned and padded softly over, sitting as well. While everyone else in the village wore tunics and kimonos of various shades of blue and silver, this man wore long robes of the deepest midnight, and in the knot of his hair he wore a pin shaped like a dragon's tail.

His eyes bore into Shinju's own, contemplative and serious. She stared back, feeling as though this was some sort of test.

"Please, have a seat." The daimyo kneeled before a small low table, where a pot of tea and cups rested. Relieved to sit down, Shinju folded her knees and rested her hands in her lap, lowering her eyes respectfully.

Reaching for a cup of tea, the man spoke. "I'm sure you have many questions, Shinju." He calmly and patiently poured some honey into his cup and stirred. Shinju tried not to fidget or betray her nervousness. After seeing this beautiful place, she was determined to be allowed to stay.

"Do you know that you are the first outsider to set foot in this village?" the man continued, his gaze returning to her, though less intense than before. She shook her head.

"The Tsoma Clan have occupied this island for hundreds of years. We remain apart from the rest of the world as much as possible, for we have something very important to protect, as Takumi has told you." Shinju nodded at that, confirming that she remembered what her companion said when she'd awakened.

"There is magic here," she added, completely forgetting her manners.

"Indeed." The man threaded his fingers together and looked at her intently. "Tell me, Shinju, what your first impression of this place is."

She blinked in surprise, then chewed her lip, casting her mind about for a good answer. "It's unlike anything I've ever seen before," she offered. "It's beautiful. Everyone seems so happy and…" Furrowing her brow, she tried to think of the right way to describe the feeling this village evoked.

"It feels more alive than anywhere else I've been."

The two men shared a look and the daimyo smiled. "You are very perceptive, Shinju. Takumi has told me all about you." A shadow of sadness flickered over his face. "I am sorry to hear of your parents' fates."

Shinju bowed her head, whispering, "*Arigato gozaimasu.*" Her face grew hot, wondering if the daimyo had figured out who she really was, and what she had done…

Seeming to sense the conflict of emotions on her face, the daimyo leaned closer. "What has happened has happened, Shinju. You cannot change it, but, when the time is right, I believe you will be able to face it."

Shinju raised her head, searching his eyes for a clue to understanding those words. "You should not want me here," she whispered, once more battling the desire to unburden herself of the truth or continue to keep it hidden.

There was a small silence. Takumi shifted closer next to her. "Shinju-chan," he began softly. "What happened to your parents was not your fault. In time, you will see that we are right. Do not punish yourself any longer."

"But what if there was something I could have done?" Shinju asked, hot tears rolling down her cheeks. She wiped at them angrily with her sleeve.

"There would have been nothing within your power to do so," Takumi answered gently.

Shinju felt a small flicker of uncertainty break through the cloud of guilt. She thought back on the tea and all she had done to prepare it. It had been a busy day in the kitchen, maybe someone had…

She gritted her teeth, remembering Hono's words. Somehow, Shinju had played a part in her parents' deaths, and that would not be something she could forget.

The daimyo was the next to speak. "Takumi will explain more of who we are to you. If you choose to become one of us, you will no longer be who you were, but a Tsoma. We will teach you to move beyond your past life, to find healing, so that you will be ready to face it when that time comes. You will be a part of something much larger, and it will require your full devotion. Consider all that he tells you carefully before you make your decision."

They were dismissed. Back out in the corridor, Takumi gave her a half-smile.

"Come, Shinju-chan, I want to show you something." He led her down a couple of floors until they stood before a wall Shinju had not noticed before. It was covered by a large painting of swirling colors, the shapes creating a story. Amidst it all, reappearing over and over, was a dragon.

"Many generations ago, when the islands were young, and the kingdom of Horitamo was not yet realized, the great Kami Dragon Ryūjin created two magical jewels, the Kanju and the Manju. These jewels were a gift to our empire, which was struggling to gain its footing on lands surrounded by dangerous and wild seas. The jewels allowed one to control the tides, so that we could voyage, fish, and explore safely."

He gestured to a part of the panel, where people seemed to be living in harmony, holding two jewels. Shinju smiled: the story was like the ones her mother used to tell her.

"But people could not always be trusted to use the tide jewels wisely. They argued over who should be allowed to wield them, who should be master of the tides. Clan leaders and warlords fought for their power, and many used them to conquer other lands rather than live in peace."

The scene on the painting changed, depicting a fierce battle on both land and sea. "Because of their greed, Ryūjin reappeared and took the tide jewels back, seeking a place where they could be guarded safely and no longer used for ill."

Takumi looked down at Shinju. "Our first daimyo, Fumihiro Tsoma, earned the great dragon's respect. He was a good man, and a wise one. And so Ryūjin gifted him the Kanju, the tide-ebbing jewel, with the responsibility of protecting it. He guided Fumihiro and his family to this island, in the path of the sea known only by those who have sailed it before, and they settled here, creating a new life with a new purpose."

Shinju listened wide-eyed, understanding sank in. The stories, the legends, they were all true. Her heart raced excitedly with this knowledge.

"What about the Manju?" she asked.

"It was decided that the jewels be kept separate in case the Clan was ever invaded," Takumi answered. The painting depicted a man and woman, each holding a jewel, with Ryūjin looking down on them. "The Manju was given to Fumihiro's sister, Kasumi, and she went to another island far to the east to keep it safe."

He turned and walked out onto a nearby balcony. Shinju followed, and gasped in delight at the sight before her. The sea sparkled beneath them, midnight blue with the sunset casting a golden light across the waters. It stretched out as far as she could see, speckled here and there by rock formations. Waves lapped gently at the shoreline below.

"The Kanju is still protected by the Tsoma Clan," Takumi continued. "We have spent the last three hundred years guarding it. Its magical nature has emitted an essence that causes this island to become more beautiful and pleasant than anywhere else.

"As I mentioned before, many creatures who would be killed or used for entertainment have flocked here, drawn by the call of magic that flows through them and the world around us. We are all bound to it, Shinju-chan. Our very lives are intertwined with the tide jewel."

He dropped down on one knee, taking Shinju by the shoulders and peering into her eyes. "Shinju…you will be allowed to stay here, and become a part of the Tsoma Clan, if you wish. I…I will raise you myself. It's all arranged." He gave a shy, sad smile. "It would be nice to have a family again."

Tears pricked at Shinju's eyes as she nodded. She still missed her parents so much it hurt to breathe, but neither could she deny the appealing offer of comfort and safety from Takumi.

"Yuudai-sama said I had a decision to make," she said slowly. Takumi nodded. "Yes. If you choose to stay, Shinju, you must take the vow we all take."

"What is it?"

Takumi gathered her hands in his own, speaking very clearly. "You must vow to protect the Kanju at all costs. If it were to ever fall into the wrong hands, it would mean destruction for our clan, and the empire would be at risk of war. The ocean would only be navigable by the one who controls the jewels. They could cut everyone off from the water, or send it to destroy all."

Shinju swallowed, wondering who could ever want to do something so terrible.

"But Ryūjin-sama would stop them, wouldn't he?" she

asked.

Takumi hesitated. "We have not seen Ryūjin in a long time. He is a kami, after all, with his own path. He has not emerged from his palace beneath the sea in a very long time."

"Have you ever seen him?' Shinju asked eagerly.

Takumi smiled. "I thought I did, once. On a clear morning, when the sun had just barely risen, I saw a flash of scales upon the water, and they were gone in the next instant. It might not have been him at all."

Shinju chewed her lip, thinking over the story. She looked out over the calm sea and the village. A memory, as if from a dream, briefly crossed her mind: she too thought she had seen the flash of scales in the water the night she'd fled the bandits.

Her hope slowly restored itself. Maybe here on this island, she could truly have a family again, like Takumi said. Maybe here she could forget what happened and become someone else. Her heart gave a longing tug, and she nodded. "I will take this vow, Takumi-san."

She knelt to the floor in front of him, taking his weathered, leathery hands in her own this time. "I vow to protect the Kanju with my life, and if it were ever to be stolen, I would not rest until the thief was found and the tide jewel restored."

Takumi's mouth trembled and he placed a hand on her head. "I, Takumi Tsoma, accept your vow. Welcome to the Tsoma Clan, Shinju."

7

AKIRA FLINCHED AS THE man cried out in pain. No one moved to stop the beating, for fear of their own punishment. Fear was all anyone seemed to have these days.

"Please, my Lady," the man groaned. "I know nothing of these rumors. I beg you!"

Hono, the new daimyo of Isthino Province, watched emotionlessly from her throne of plush red cushions. For the past few weeks, she had spent considerable efforts on rooting out the bandits and anyone else whom she deemed a participant in the assassinations of her family.

In a short time, the Great Hall of the Harigoshi Castle had turned from a place of union between the daimyo and his province to one of interrogation and suspicion. The daimyo's council members murmured uneasily at this new way of ruling, but no one had the courage to defy her.

The morning after the deaths of Io and Airi, Lady Hono had announced to the region that they had been murdered by poison, and the assassins had kidnapped Shinju. These were the same criminals that had plagued the villages in Itshino, and they must be crushed.

Given free reign by the Shogun, Hono began bringing in new samurai, and dismissing those who previously served Io. "You are a disgrace to the Code of Bushido," she'd hissed at the dozens of men who knelt before her. "You allowed the murders of your daimyo and have failed to capture those responsible, as well as retrieve my niece from their clutches."

The samurai, now ronin in the eyes of the empire, left in anguish.

Lady Hono's new legion of samurai, led by one Lord Hotaka, were cold and cruel and calculating. Akira did not trust them at all.

He had done his best to stay out of the way during Lady Hono's investigations. His grief over the loss of Shinju, his best friend, not to mention the two people who had been like parents to him, still felt raw. He kept to himself, mourning the darkness that had overtaken Harigoshi castle.

He had never liked Lady Hono. Something about her eyes made him think of a snake: cold and calculating and sly. And now that she was in power, he knew he'd been right to be wary of her. She never regarded him as anything more than an insect, a plaything for her niece and another irritating child underfoot in the castle.

Osamu was the only one who did not forget about Akira, and he stood by him now, quivering with distress over this public beating. Akira and Osamu had formed an unexpected alliance; gone was the tutor and student divide. Now all that mattered was making sure neither of them gave any reason to join the suspects on the marble floor before the daimyo.

Lady Hono stood, her kimono sweeping softly against the steps as she descended upon the beaten man, who lay in a quivering heap. Dressed in black and red, she looked like a giant vulture about to descend upon its prey.

These public beatings and interrogations were meant to bring full shame to the guilty as well as a warning. Akira privately wondered if she just enjoyed making a spectacle. At the funeral for Io and Airi, Lady Hono had not cried.

The daimyo grabbed the man's shaggy hair and pulled his head back so she could look into his face. Her private guard stood nearby, as well as the samurai who had brought the peasant in. She studied the man's face, coated with blood and sweat and tears, and her mouth curled in disgust.

Akira swallowed, his nails digging into his clenched fists. How could she be so cruel?

"I believe you," she spoke at last, releasing the man's hair with a flick of her wrist. He collapsed before her, panting. "You don't know anything about the rumors concerning my missing niece."

"Th-thank you, my Lady," the man sobbed.

"That does not mean you don't know anything about the murders," Hono continued in a deathly tone. "Take him away for questioning later." The guards seized the man up, and he began to shake and bellow, "No! No, this is a mistake! I didn't do anything!"

He was dragged off, his cries echoing through the hall. Lady Hono returned to her throne as if nothing happened, and sat with a sigh. "I fear we shall never be done with this," she said so softly Akira wasn't sure she even meant for them to hear her.

No further announcements were made, and the session was concluded. Courtiers hurried away, eager to be out of the presence of the daimyo. Akira turned to Osamu.

"Something has to be done," he whispered. "Someone has to do something!" Osamu shook his head at him and glanced towards the raised dais where Hono sat. "Not here, boy. Too many ears and eyes."

Frustrated, Akira bit his tongue and waited for the people to disperse so he could slip away. Lately he had been spending all of his time in the scholar wing or Shinju's room, which had been left untouched. Dust was beginning to gather on her belongings, and Akira tried to keep it that way in case her room was ever visited by the servants.

He would sit on the ornate rug with scrolls and books before him, trying to lose himself in other matters besides the terror happening within the castle walls.

Lost in his thoughts, Akira did not notice he was being herded by the courtiers into the open, in clear view of the throne. "Akira," called the daimyo in a kind tone. He froze, and Osamu froze with him.

"Come here, child." Hono beckoned to him with a finger. Akira hesitated, then slowly walked to the dais, where he knelt and bowed. Osamu stood rooted to the marble floor behind him.

"*You* may go," Lady Hono commanded in a harsher voice.

Akira glanced up at her, but realized she was addressing Osamu. The old man paused, glancing anxiously at him, then bowed and shuffled away.

"Now then," the daimyo resumed, turning her attention back to Akira. "I have not seen you much these past few days, Akira. I hope you have not been feeling neglected."

Akira swallowed. "Not at all, my Lady. I know you have a great many matters to attend to." *What does she want?* he thought miserably.

"Indeed, I do, but I cannot forget our family's ward." She leaned forward, hands gripping the armrests of the throne. "You must miss our dear Shinju-chan terribly."

Akira did not know how to answer, so he simply nodded. It was the truth, after all. "It is a sad time for us all," Hono reflected, not sounding sad at all. "But we must persevere, mustn't we?"

"Yes, my Lady," Akira responded, doing his best to keep his tone neutral. "I hope that you can come to me with any concerns you may have, Akira." He looked up into her black eyes rimmed with kohl. "You may, after all, be the closest thing to family I have left."

Once dismissed, Akira left the hall feeling sick to his stomach. He missed Airi and Io. He missed Shinju. How he wished she was here; she would have put a stop to the beatings, the unjustified interrogations. Shinju, with her tangled hair and fiery eyes, should be daimyo instead.

But his best friend was missing; there were already whispers that she too was dead.

A hand grabbed the sleeve of his *haori* and yanked. With a

startled yelp, Akira found himself being pulled behind one of the large pillars in the corridor. "Shush!" Osamu hissed. When he seemed assured that Akira wouldn't make a sound again, he jerked his head down a side passage. "Follow me and stay silent."

Akira curiously followed the older man, wondering at this strange new kinship between them. Osamu had never treated Akira any differently because he was an orphan and a ward of the daimyo, but neither had he been warm or fatherly. It seemed that the recent circumstances gave them little choice but to rely on each other for support.

Osamu led him down several passages in the East side of the castle. These were the chambers and rooms of the scribes, scholars, and pages. Akira knew them all. But when Osamu pulled out a ring of keys and opened a hidden door behind a tapestry, Akira's pulse quickened as he realized the old advisor was letting him in on a secret.

Stone steps led down into some unseen chamber. A single oil lamp rested on a small shelf in the wall. Osamu shakily lit it and continued forward, stepping carefully. "What is this place?" Akira whispered. Surely it was safe to speak now.

"An old passageway for the Scholar wing, in case of an attack on the castle," Osamu answered. "The daimyos of old wanted the educated to be able to have an escape plan. As these walls have not been breached in hundreds of years, most have forgotten the existence of these passages. But not all of us."

Before Akira could respond, the steps ended and the lamp revealed a rounded room filled with dusty supplies, pots, and a table covered in scrolls. At the far end of the room another doorway yawned into complete darkness.

Akira swallowed and looked around, noticing that while the shelves lining the room were dusty and the bags of supplies were covered in cobwebs, the rocky floor had footprints and scuffs in the dirt, and the scrolls on the table looked fresh.

He looked at Osamu's serious face. "Why did you bring me here, Osamu-sensei? I am only a student scholar."

Osamu placed the lamp on the table, then folded his hands into his robes. "The time has come for us to have a place to meet in secret. Akira, you were Shinju-sama's closest friend, and like a son to the daimyo and his wife."

The advisor took a shaky breath. "I am entrusting you not only with the location of this place, but also with the knowledge that there are those of us who do not support Lady Hono's recent actions, as well as her appointment as the daimyo by the Shogun."

Akira felt a jolt of surprise. "W-what do you mean?" "I mean," Osamu said patiently, "that though Lady Hono may have a claim to the title by being next in the family line, I believe the province of Itshino, and this very castle, have been compromised."

Akira braced himself on the wooden table. He thought about the recent events: the murders, the new samurai, the interrogations. Lord Hotaka and the way he always kept close to Lady Hono.

"You...you don't think she had something to do with their deaths, do you?" he croaked.

Osamu sighed. "I do not know, Akira. But her choices have been suspicious, and I do not like this Lord Hotaka and his new samurai. Lady Hono claims he is from the Fundai Province and that she met him at the Imperial court a year ago. But I have been searching through the Empire's records and have not been able to find any mention of a Lord Hotaka in the past one hundred years."

Akira chewed his thumbnail. "Did they think no one would find this out, and question him?"

Osamu shrugged. "I think Lady Hono is counting on us to be too afraid to do anything about it if we did. She has disrupted the running of this castle and province and has been allowed to do so by the Shogun. We must be very careful."

"What can we do?" Akira asked. He felt fear crawling up his back. "Could we send word to the Shogun, and ask him to listen to our concerns?"

"You mean the concerns of an old man and little boy? We have no real evidence, or reason to suspect Lady Hono's involvement in the damiyo's death. From all appearances at the funeral, she did exactly as expected of her, and she satisfied the Shogun."

He sighed. "We continue to gather what information we can. We will keep our heads down and our ears open." Osamu grasped Akira's shoulder. "It is very important that you give Lady Hono no reason to suspect you. You have access to rooms in the castle due to your status as ward of the daimyo's family. It would not be unusual for you to be seen in the family's private chambers."

"You want me to spy." Akira felt his stomach clench. He and Shinju had often played at being ninjas spying on warlords many times; never had he thought he would have to put their games to real life. He suddenly felt much younger than he was, longing to crawl under the table and disappear so the adults could handle these matters.

Osamu looked unhappy too. "In a sense, yes. You don't need to change your routine or go out of your way to search for things. Just keep your ears and eyes open for anything unusual." With another sigh he added, "If you don't want any part of this, I understand. You won't be approached again or have anything expected of you. I would only ask that you keep this place and our conversation secret."

Akira nodded and licked his lips. "And if I say yes?" Osamu searched his eyes. "Then you may be able to help bring justice to an entire province."

8

I DON'T KNOW ABOUT this." Shinju eyed the boat warily, thinking back on her frightening voyage on the sea at night. The calm waters looked nothing like they had now, but she couldn't quite forget her fear just yet.

"You will be perfectly safe, Shinju-chan," Takumi assured her patiently from his spot in the boat. "Tsomas live on the water. It is important for you to learn how to sail and fish."

He extended a hand to her on the shore. "I will be with you the whole time."

Shinju smoothed a few loose strands of hair behind her ears, chewing her lip. She'd arrived on Kanju Shima weeks ago, but Takumi had yet to convince her to join him in the boat.

"Okay, I'll do it," she said, forcing herself to be brave. *You are a Tsoma now, Shinju. Act like it!*

Taking his hand, she stepped into the boat and sat down

quickly. How she had ever done this on her own all those nights ago, Shinju did not know. It was as if another force entirely had guided her actions.

She watched as Takumi pushed the boat off the shore and began to use the lines to adjust the faded blue sail. Below them, the water was crystal clear, and she could already see little fish darting out of their wake.

Sweat coated her palms and she gripped the sides of the boat, looking around. Other boats dotted the sea, occupied by the Clan men, women, and even children fishing and enjoying the water.

A stronger wind caught the sail, and they began to move faster, smoothly cutting through the water. Despite her previous fear, Shinju laughed. "It's like flying!" she exclaimed. Takumi smiled at her, the water sending a salty spray onto his face.

For a while they simply sailed around the island. Takumi pointed out various large fish that leapt through the surf, and where a family of dolphins preferred to hunt near the lagoon. Shinju observed sea turtles, aquatic birds, and jellyfish, gasping in delight at the strange creatures she'd only ever seen in painted scrolls.

Farther from the island, the current was stronger, and Takumi focused on steering them along with the lines and rudder; at one point he even put down the sail and used only the paddle to show her how they navigated in rougher waters.

The swirling water splashed against the boat, spraying them with a salty mist, and despite a little measure of fear returning, the thrill of being thrust along something as wild and untamed as the sea was stronger.

Shinju even stuck her hand in the waves, feeling the icy water push against her fingers, and laughed. No wonder the Tsomas loved this so much!

Takumi eventually brought them back towards shallower water and began to show Shinju how he fished. He demonstrated using both a line and hook, and spear. Together, they caught octopus and various rainbow-colored fish that flapped unhappily in a basket.

Shinju wrinkled her nose about touching the slippery creatures, but after a couple of hours, she could slip their mouths off the hook as smoothly as Takumi, and she no longer squealed when a fish leapt from her grasp to flop around the boat's floorboards.

"Will you teach me to sail next?" Shinju asked eagerly when they set off for home. Her face was burned, and her arms ached, but she hadn't been this happy in a long time.

"Of course!" Takumi wiped a bead of sweat from his brow before settling his pointed straw hat back on his head. "You begin your lessons with Kyo-sensei tomorrow as well."

Shinju nodded, growing quieter. She would be training alongside the other children, and the thought made her a little nervous. From what she had observed of the sessions, the Tsoma children were far more advanced in their techniques than she and Akira were.

I can do this, she resolved silently. *I am a Harigoshi, and now a Tsoma too. I will catch up!*

They reached the beach, and Takumi leapt out into the thigh-high water to pull the boat up onto the sand. Shinju helped him unload their catch for the day and watched as he showed her how to clean the fish, scraping the scales and gutting them.

"I think I like catching them better," Shinju remarked. "This is gross."

Takumi laughed. "It is a necessary part of enjoying what we are blessed with. Now, you try." He handed her his filet knife, and Shinju squatted on the sand to work on the fish before her.

"Takumi-san," Shinju asked later as they carried the basket back to their house, "Will you take me to see the Kanju?"

From what she'd been told, the tide jewel was kept at a shrine on the path to the mountain and was guarded by samurai day and night. Ever since Shinju learned of its existence, she'd been plagued with curiosity about this magical object that held the power to control the tides.

A jewel created by Ryūjin himself.

Takumi considered this. "Yes, I will take you tonight after dinner. It is right that you should see it." He gave a rueful smile. "We are so used to living with the Kanju in our midst that sometimes I think we forget just how special it is."

Excited, Shinju rushed through her chores and preparations for dinner. Takumi seared the fish over a fire pit outside, and Shinju rolled rice into little balls and fried them with eel sauce and seaweed.

Everything tasted delicious, but Shinju could hardly wait until their meal was over and Takumi picked up his staff, signaling that they had a long way to go.

The palm trees swayed in the evening breeze as Shinju followed Takumi up a now familiar path through the village, climbing higher until they left the daimyo's castle behind them.

"There are other ways to reach the shrine," Takumi told her, "but I prefer this one for the view."

Shinju had to agree with him. The path rose higher and higher, winding through the jungle, and far below she could see the village spread out like doll's houses; and beyond them, the ocean in all its glittering majesty, bursting with fiery orange as the sun slipped lower on the horizon.

"That is how it earned its name." Takumi pointed the head of his staff towards the ocean. "The Golden Sea."

"It's beautiful," Shinju whispered. Not even at the castle had she seen sunsets like this.

Presently, they arrived at a torii gate. A plaque in the middle of the arch indicated that this was the entrance to the Kanju Shrine.

Fireflies floated in lazy circles around the gate. In the undergrowth, Shinju could hear the shuffling of small creatures. "The magic here is strongest," Takumi explained in a hushed voice. "You may see some of the forest spirits; they are most active at night. We live in harmony with them, but they still keep their distance, and we shall keep ours."

"*Hai!*" Shinju agreed with a nod, shifting a little closer to him even as she kept her eyes alert for any spirits. She'd never seen one before.

They passed under the torii gate, continuing the path until they reached the shrine. It was small, with a curved tile roof that matched that of the daimyo's home. Two lanterns swung on either side of the shrine's entrance, and to the right was a large suspended gong, moss and ivy growing over the frame that held it.

As Takumi had said, samurai guarded the shrine, one stationed at every corner; Shinju could see more of them at their posts around the clearing.

"Ho there, Takumi," one of them called. "Visiting the shrine tonight?"

"Yes, Kichirō. I wanted to show Shinju-chan the Kanju."

The samurai nodded and gestured towards the open doorway of the shrine. "Go on in."

Takumi bowed, and Shinju quickly mimicked his movements. They left their shoes outside and stepped into the quiet space.

Covering the walls were intricately painted scrolls, all depicting the Kami Ryūjin and the stories that featured him. Shinju was surprised to see that she even recognized some of them. But what truly caught her attention was the podium at the far end of the shrine.

Resting on a pillow atop the podium was a large pearl, glowing with a blue-green light that pulsed every few seconds. Its surface was smooth and solid, and yet Shinju thought she could detect movement swirling within.

Her heart raced, drawn to the jewel. The air within the shrine filled with an air of something she could not name, but it felt the way she had earlier on the boat: wild, free…uncontrollable.

Takumi kneeled a few feet away from the podium, leaning on his staff. Shinju kneeled as well, never peeling her eyes from the jewel.

"The Kanju," she murmured. "It's…it's…"

"Overwhelming?" Takumi asked with a smile.

"Mhm." Shinju stared at it, questions racing through her head. "Have any of the Tsomas used it before?"

"When they first came to this island, the jewel's magic was used sparingly. But as the Clan settled and built the shrine, it was decided that no one should use it unless in dire circumstances. They feared that we would argue amongst ourselves about who could use the jewel and when."

"What kind of dire circumstances?" Shinju asked. "An attack on the island, or if some other calamity were to befall us," Takumi answered. "Thankfully, neither of those things have happened. It seems that the rest of Horitamo has forgotten all about the tide jewels."

9

HEAD BENT AGAINST THE icy wind, Akira walked briskly from the east end of the Scholars' wing across the courtyard. He carried a bundle of scrolls and papers with him, intending to spend the rest of the afternoon indoors reading by the warm fire.

He'd grown taller over the past year, but that did not keep him from staying out of sight, and out of mind, from the daimyo, as well as her samurai who skulked through the castle corridors with arrogant swaggers.

Akira nearly reached the kitchen entrance when a servant ran towards him brandishing a summons in her cold fingers. "Lady Hono wishes you to attend to her immediately," the girl huffed.

Tensing, Akira slowly took the summons and read it, then crushed it between his fingers. So much for keeping a low profile, he thought miserably. Hopefully, the daimyo would require nothing of him but idle conversation.

Hurrying now, he flew down the hallways to his room, where he tossed the scrolls onto his cot and quickly smoothed back his hair and straightened his jacket. He'd been given hand-me-downs from some of the older scholars; there was no one else to attend to any of his personal needs.

It won't matter soon, he told himself again as he splashed water on his face and thought about the news Osamu gave him earlier that week.

If all went well, Akira would be joining the next caravan of merchants on their way to the Imperial City. Osamu had written to the head scholar in the Emperor's palace, and Akira had been accepted to join them as an assistant. He could finally escape this place.

Moving briskly through the halls, Akira reached the chambers of Lady Hono. The doors were guarded by her personal samurai, and they regarded Akira with poorly disguised contempt.

Akira grit his teeth and stood his ground. "Lady Hono requested my presence," he said without preamble.

The samurai glanced at each other, then one grumbled, "Wait here." He stopped inside the chamber while Akira waited, ignoring the glare from the other samurai, until he was told he could enter.

The study was warm from a crackling fire in the hearth. Lady Hono sat behind a wide mahogany desk, bent over some papers. Akira bowed and remained silent, waiting for her to acknowledge him.

With a start, he realized a figure stood behind Hono, near the windows. Lord Hotaka. What was he doing here?

"Please, have a seat, Akira," Hono said, gesturing towards a cushion on the floor before her desk. "You must be cold from your walk." Akira hesitated, then knelt, trying not to appear nervous.

"You know Lord Hotaka, of course." Akira nodded towards the man, who simply watched him with a detached expression, his eyes hard as flint.

A servant entered, bringing a tray of tea. She served them quickly and bowed out of the room. Akira wished he could leave as well. The heat of the room was beginning to stifle him.

"Thank you for coming to see me so quickly," Lady Hono said, daintily sipping her tea. "I noticed you passing by outside the window here, and I realized that it has been some time since we've spoken."

Akira didn't know what to say, so he simply bowed his head again.

"Now, I simply must know what papers you were carrying so protectively," she added sweetly.

"Oh...it is simply research, my Lady. For Osamu-sensei."

Hono nodded, her eyes narrowing slightly. "I see. You are a very diligent and studious young man. A credit to your parents. I'm sure they would be proud of you," Hono answered, watching his reaction closely. He gave a nod of thanks and shifted uneasily. Why was she talking about this?

"You are close with Osamu, are you not?"

"I suppose so, my Lady."

"And are you…unhappy here at the castle, Akira?"

His head snapped up, unable to hide his surprise. "Unhappy, my Lady?"

Hono folded her hands and gazed down her nose at him, waiting. Akira licked his lips nervously. "No, my Lady, I am not unhappy." The lie came easily enough, but Akira couldn't fight the heat that rose into his cheeks as he said it.

"I wondered," Hono continued, "because I have received this scroll from the Head Scholar that requests my approval for your transfer to the Imperial City."

Sweat gathered on Akira's forehead and his fingers clenched his pants. So she *had* summoned him here to talk about.

"Do you wish to leave Harigoshi Castle, your home, Akira?" Hono asked, her voice growing soft, but a thread of steel ran through it. Akira had learned to be very wary of this tone after hearing its likeness in the Great Hall while she interrogated suspects.

"It has been my dream to become a scholar, my Lady," Akira answered shakily. "Osamu-sensei felt that I would be an asset to the Emperor and the royal scholars at the Palace by the Sea."

Hono smiled, slow and satisfied. "Of course, and you've done very well as a page from what I understand."

She stood up, walking around her desk towards the fire, holding the scroll in her hand.

"The former daimyo was very indulgent towards you," she said thoughtfully. "However, it is my desire that your talents are better used here in service to Itshino province."

Akira felt his heart come to a stop. "M-my Lady?"

Without a glance in his direction, Lady Hono tossed the

scroll into the fire. Akira gasped, instinctively reaching towards it. He controlled himself just in time as Hono turned and swept towards him.

With long, cold fingers, she leaned down and gripped his chin tightly. "You will not be going to the Imperial City. You will no longer study to be a scholar, or report to Osamu. Starting tomorrow, you will report to the garrison to begin your training as a samurai."

Akira felt every part of his body grow numb as he stared up into her dark, cruel eyes. With just a handful of words, his hope of escaping Harigoshi Castle drifted away to join the smoke rising from the scroll's flickering remains.

10

Ten Years Later…

YOU’RE DISTRACTED AGAIN,” TAKUMI said. Shinju barely dodged the swipe of the practice blade, but she used the momentum to land a crack at his knees. He stepped out of the way just in time and she fell forward, managing to roll out of the way of his next attack.

“I’m focused,” she protested; it was not exactly a lie. Shinju just had a lot on her mind at the moment. She gritted her teeth, trying to bring her head back to the present.

She adjusted her grip on the sword she held and flew at Takumi. They parried, turning in circles in the muddy yard. Swipe, dodge, duck, swipe. The morning air filled with the sounds of their swords cracking together.

Shinju allowed Takumi to get close, then she rammed her

fist into his chest and brought the hilt of her sword up to knock his chin back. Takumi grunted and kicked at the back of her knee.

Shinju clenched her legs quickly to bear the impact, but it was enough for Takumi to recover and move at her again, faster this time. She parried off with him once more.

An image of two children cracking their staffs together in a training yard flashed before her eyes, and Shinju gasped, losing her footing. Takumi disarmed her and the sword fell to the ground.

"Not focused," he breathed, holding the sword to her neck. Shinju grimaced and shoved it out of her way. "You know I prefer hand-to-hand combat," she mumbled as the thoughts dispersed from her mind like a flock of birds taking to the skies.

Takumi nodded. "I do, but you must continue to practice in the areas you are not as strong in. I have no doubt you could improve." The end of his sentence hung in the air, and they gazed at each other in silence. Shinju knew what he meant: she could improve if she wasn't getting in her own way.

"You must clear your mind," he advised. "If you are ever in a real duel, you cannot allow doubt or fear to hinder you." His eyes searched hers, trying to discern whether she understood him. Shinju gave him a small smile.

"I am trying, Takumi. There's just something about using a weapon that does not feel as natural to me."

He sighed as she stood up and brushed herself off. "Well, that is true. And you are still young." He returned her smile with one of his own. "And you are the most gifted among the others in close combat."

Shinju glowed with his praise. When she had begun training with other children in the Tsoma Clan many years ago, she had felt far behind. Her sparring matches with Akira seemed silly and childish compared to what she was faced with in the training yard outside the village. It drove her to work harder and longer than the others; at night she would beg Takumi to teach her more.

Eventually, her preference for her fighting style emerged. Shinju loved the technique of close combat, of being able to use her hands, arms, feet, and legs against an opponent, even one who was armed. Takumi and the other sensei indulged her desire to learn, and oftentimes their lessons went beyond the training fields.

Shinju would be going about some task, when one of the sensei would appear and attack her. She would have to ward off the surprise using only her fists and feet; in some cases, the fighting would move away from close combat to using props to defend herself, everything from a fishing pole to a fan to a folding screen.

"Use everything at your disposal," Takumi told her. "Trust your instincts, and do not let pride prevent you from wielding a weapon if it comes to that."

She devoured these lessons eagerly, longing to prove herself. Shinju was at one other disadvantage compared to the rest of the Clan: magic. While she had learned to feel, understand, and know when magic was around, she could not wield it the same way the Tsomas could. For them, magic existed not only in fighting, but in simple everyday life.

Shinju had watched in astonishment as Takumi first showed

her magic in combat: gliding through the air on invisible steps, levitating and manipulating nature around him to match his movements; it was like a dance, and though she learned the steps, magic did not bend with her, not matter how much she tried.

Sensei Kojo told her it was because she had not been born a Tsoma on the island. Their very lives were connected to the magic that poured out from the Kanju, seeping into the island. Since she was an outsider, the same abilities granted to other Tsomas may never come for her.

This had been difficult for Shinju to swallow early on; Takumi found her crying once, off alone in the forest, because the other children had been calling her a "False Tsoma" when she could not levitate a bowl of rice.

"Do not take their words to heart, my child," Takumi had said, holding her close. "You came to us in that boat for a reason; you are here for a reason. You took the same vow, yes? You are just as much a part of us as if you had been born here."

Takumi raised her as his own daughter, and the other villagers accepted her as such. She had been quite a novelty in the beginning, and the women in the Clan took her under their wing as if she'd always lived there. Eventually the other children grew to admire her determination in training, and they became friends. Her loneliness eased as the years passed.

Now, Shinju rarely tried to remember life outside the island. This was her home now, and memories of the past, painful as they were, remained behind a locked door in her mind.

A squeaky bark brought a grin to Shinju's face as she turned to see Peiku, a small and mischievous tanuki that had decided on being Shinju's near constant companion. He had wandered out of the woods a couple of months ago, and upon finding Shinju, he did not seem in a hurry to rejoin his family.

"Hello, Peiku, what have you been up to now?" Shinju asked, picking up the furry raccoon-like creature. He held a glint in his eyes, which made Shinju sure that her friend had been into some mischief.

"I'm sure I'll find out soon enough," she chuckled as Peiku wiggled around in her arms, wanting his belly scratched.

Takumi shook his head with a resigned grin. "I suppose that's all for training today." He picked up Shinju's practice sword and nodded to her. "Go on, the morning is still early, and you have time for your walk."

"Hai! *Aregato*, Takumi-sensei," Shinju answered brightly, and bowed to him. Peiku jumped from her arms and sprinted down the path that ran parallel to the village below, looking over his shoulder for her.

Shinju laughed. "I won't be long!" Handing Takumi her sword, she jogged to catch up to the tanuki. Together they walked across the hill and down to the other side, heading for the western half of the jungle and the beach beyond. It was a ritual of Shinju's to go exploring after a training session. The quiet sounds of the island, the breezes shifting through the palm trees, and the waves of the ocean provided a calming environment for her to ease down from training.

And today, she very much wanted to be alone in her thoughts.

They reached the beach, and Peiku immediately became interested in the hermit crabs that scurried over the sand. He snarled playfully, following one as it sidled away in a hurry.

Shinju slipped off her shoes and wiggled her toes into the cold wet sand at the edge of the surf, giggling when the water rushed forward and licked around her skin.

As far as she could see, the sparkling sea stretched unending. The day was warm and the wind low, and the water was as still as a painting, save for the small waves that ceaselessly lapped the shore.

With the sky a mixture of gold and turquoise, and barely a cloud to be seen, Shinju could understand why Ryūjin and Fumihrio Tsoma had chosen this place to hide away the tide jewel. Its seclusion from the world, as well as its beauty, had much to offer in exchange for a lifetime of guardianship.

There was always plenty of fish in the lagoon and the sea itself, while deer and boar populated the jungle that made up most of the island's landscape. Crops grew plentifully, and the Tsomas practiced careful conservation of the island's resources. As long as the magic in the island did not falter, they would always have what they needed.

Squinting at the horizon, Shinju studied, as she always did, to see whether she might finally catch a glimpse of Ryūjin. She longed to see the great dragon in all his glory ascending from the depths to take note of the humans who were protecting his gift.

No one had seen the dragon in hundreds of years. At night, when she couldn't sleep, a faint thought would cross Shinju's mind, of scales and an eye watching her from beneath the water. But it would vanish like smoke before she could hold on to it, leaving her to wonder if it was simply a dream or an actual memory.

"There's no way it was Ryūjin-sama," she muttered. "I must be imagining it after hearing so many stories."

Peiku joined her and wrinkled his nose at the water, fluffing his tail indignantly as a wave crept a little close for his comfort.

"Come, Peiku, let us head back," Shinju told him, and as she turned around to collect her shoes from a higher spot in the sand, a tingle of alarm ran up her spine, freezing her in place.

Taking a few breaths, Shinju slowly looked back over her shoulder, expecting to see something on the sea behind her. The water was still smooth and undisturbed, but instead of feeling peaceful, it now felt…as if it was holding its breath.

The calm before the storm.

Her hair stood on end as Shinju crouched into a ready stance, casting her gaze all around her for the source of discomfort, but there was nothing.

She hastily put on her shoes and trudged back up to the grassy bank, and after one more look, decided that it must have been her imagination.

Letting Peiku lead the way, she tried to ignore the tension settling into her stomach. It was the same feeling of apprehension that had haunted her ten years ago.

11

Every year, the Tsomas celebrated the day their ancestor, Fushimara, first arrived on the island bearing the Kanju. For a whole evening, they would put aside their work and participate in games, cooking, and listening or telling stories.

Children made colorful paper dragons attached to strings, and as they ran the dragons would lift into the air, fluttering wildly. A makeshift stage was erected for the purpose of the storytelling, including the one that had created their community. It was one of Shinju's favorite times of the year.

She had fully intended to find Takumi and tell him about the strange feeling she'd had, but when she arrived back at the village, preparations for the celebration had begun, and she set her worries aside.

Nothing should cast a shadow on this night, she decided, and joined in the laughter and smiles of the children, who she was rather fond of.

"Shinju-chan! Shinju-chan!" a group of them cried, running to meet her. "Where have you been?" one boy asked.

"I was down at the beach with Peiku," Shinju told them, grinning as she gestured to the tanuki at her ankles. Peiku, who of course was a favorite with the children, allowed a few pats on his shaggy fur, before the stimulation was too much and he sauntered off, sniffing at the smells of food already wafting from the makeshift stalls.

"Are you going to tell a story this year, Shinju?" one of the little girls asked, taking Shinju's hand as they walked. "I have no stories to tell," Shinju answered. "But I bet Takumi-sensei will." The children oohed and ahhed at that, for Takumi's stories were often the most adventurous.

They reached her house, and Shinju waved the children goodbye. "I'll get ready quickly and join in the festivities," she promised. "I'll save you a dragon!" one of them yelled as they scampered off. With a chuckle, Shinju pushed open the sliding door to enter her home.

Built much like the other houses in the village, an open common room with floors of polished wood greeted her. The small table they ate at was clean and the mats were rolled up underneath. On the paneled walls hung scrolls and some paintings done by Shinju in her youth.

Shinju slipped out of her shoes and left them by the door before padding lightly across the floor to her room. Inside, her festive attire waited for her, already set out by herself that morning. Glancing down at her hands and training Gi, she grinned. "I should probably wash up first."

Grabbing a towel and a robe, Shinju left the house through the back door and headed down the little path in the yard to where the pools were. Surrounded by rocks and brush, the pools would normally have afforded little privacy for bathing, but short, thatched walls had been erected around some of them to allow for such occasions. The water, pure and clear, flowed down from a waterfall, then snaked out under the ground to the ocean.

Rejoicing when she found one of the pools unoccupied, Shinju quickly undressed and slipped in. The water was cooler than she expected, but still warm thanks to the heated vents under the island, and she washed quickly but thoroughly, humming along to the music she could hear in the village.

Back at home, Shinju brushed out her waist-length hair and carefully pinned it back, then dressed in her blue and silver kimono, the colors of the Tsoma Clan. Leaves and blossoms embroidered the sides, and a silvery dragon ran alongside her shoulders. It was a beautiful piece of clothing, sewn by women in the Clan, and given to Shinju when she turned fifteen.

She patted and smoothed the material lovingly, then pulled on the long white stockings that were worn with wooden sandals.

There was one tiny mirror in the house, and Shinju left her room to stand before it now, stepping back and forth to survey her appearance. A young woman with almond-shaped eyes stared back at her, tentative but bright with excitement. Her skin had grown tan from a life spent outdoors in the sun, giving it an almost golden glow.

Shinju grinned. "Still short, but you look like a proper

young lady now, not like a wild jungle girl." The words were echoes of one of the elder women's criticisms of Shinju's often fly-away appearance as a child, and she and Takumi still joked about it.

The sky had turned into a palette of fiery orange and pink by the time Shinju left home to join the celebration. The other Tsomas were also clad in blue and silver, strolling up and down the village street, eating special treats. Shinju took a deep lungful of the sweet and savory smells floating from the village center where the food stalls were, and her mouth watered.

A few minutes later, balancing two plates of dumplings and small round pastries, a bowl of noodles, and a cup of fragrant tea, Shinju found a spot with her friends, Haru and Izumi, at one of the blankets set along the sides across from the stalls. Her companions chuckled at her enthusiasm as she set down her food.

"Shinju-chan, are you really going to eat all that?" Haru asked, raising an eyebrow. He'd been one of the children first to greet her when Shinju first arrived at the island. They'd formed an easy friendship, and he loved to tease her about how much she ate.

"Just watch me!" Shinju told him with a wink. She pushed her sleeves up and hummed, trying to figure out which food to sample first.

Dumplings. Definitely dumplings.

Chopsticks were fished out of her *obi*, and she proceeded to pop one of them into her mouth. Haru rolled his eyes but smiled, returning to his own plate of shrimp.

As twilight fell, the stories began. One by one, Tsomas took to the wooden stage to tell their audience old favorites or new tales. Shinju, finally stuffed, moved closer, eager to hear and see the performances.

Shadows, puppets, and even magic were used to tell these stories. Peiku emerged from under a table, his fur full of sticky sauce and looking quite pleased with himself, to curl up at Shinju's feet.

After traditional legends were told, the most important story began: Tsoma Clan's beginning. Shinju straightened and listened intently as one of the elders took to the stage. The light from the torches cast eerie shadows on his solemn face. He even wore simpler clothing, and carried staff. The audience quieted, giving their full attention and respect to him.

Softly, the beat of dreams echoed from behind the stage. "Three hundred years ago," began the elder, "the realm now known as Horitamo was in chaos. Many people had perished in battle as the warlords fought over the sacred tide jewels."

He pulled a round polished stone from behind his back. It was not the real Kanju, of course; that was kept safe in its guarded shrine. "The tide jewels had been gifted to mankind by Ryūjin-sama, the great dragon. The Master of Tides."

A large paper dragon dyed blue and green appeared behind the stage, floating in the breeze. Shinju smiled as the children in the audience pointed with excited gasps.

"Whoever used the Kanju and the Manju was able to control the tides," continued the elder. "They were intended to help mankind flourish and travel the dangerous waters around Horitamo."

"Ryūjin was saddened by man's inability to use the jewels for peace, and so he emerged from the ocean depths and retrieved them from the war lords. But he wanted to prove to the other kami that man could still be trusted, and so he searched all of Horitamo for one who would value the tide jewels and keep them from being used for wicked purposes."

Another man took the stage, humble in appearance, his face partially hidden by a straw hat. Shinju knew instantly that it was Takumi.

"Ryūjin found a man named Fushimaru Tsoma. The man's heart was pure and honest, and so Ryūjin gave him the Kanju, the tide-ebbing jewel, and to Fushimaru's sister, Kasumi, he gave the Manju, the tide-flowing jewel." The elder handed the stone to Takumi, and then pulled another one out of his robes to give to a woman who joined them on the stage.

"In order to keep the jewels safe, the Tsoma siblings asked Ryūjin to guide them to a place where their families could survive and protect these gifts. Ryūjin led Fushimaru to this island, bestowing honor on him by choosing a location on the sea above the dragon's palace. For Kasumi, Ryūjin plucked a star from the waters and flung it into the sky, and where it landed, he told her that would be where she could go to protect the jewel. Kasumi took her family and left, and Fushimaru settled here."

The audience gave a slight murmur of approval towards the elder's version of the familiar tale. "This island welcomed our ancestors with open arms, and the magic of the Kanju spread to every corner. We have flourished and grown strong, and so has our home."

He gave a quick gesture, and a long tapestry was unrolled on either side of the stage, revealing a simple yet elaborate painting of the island.

Shinju clapped and cheered with the others, drinking in the beautiful tapestry. "We have remained largely removed by the outside world, dedicating ourselves to the guardianship of the Kanju, training and preparing should a day ever come that we are attacked."

His sobering words hushed them all. The elder looked down on his listeners from the stage, his eyes drifting slowly across each face.

"In more recent generations, we understood that this life of exclusion may not be for every Tsoma. And so, every year on this day, we present an offer to anyone who has just turned of age: if they desire to leave the island and build a life on the mainland, they may do so. But they can never return and are bound by an oath to never speak of this place or the jewel to anyone."

No one spoke. The night's conclusion had arrived: in a moment, the young men and women who had just turned eighteen would be allowed to step forward if they wished to leave the island. Shinju's turn had come two years ago; she had stood by Takumi's side and held his hand, lifting her chin. She wasn't going anywhere.

In the days leading up to the ceremony, Takumi had told Shinju that if she wished to leave, he would not hold it against her. Shinju had stared at him in shock.

"Of course I'm not going to leave, Takumi! This is my home. You are my home. What else could I want?" Takumi had simply nodded with tear-filled eyes, and she could tell he'd been both happy and relieved to hear her words.

Now, the elder bowed to the crowd and backed away. Yuudai, clothed in brilliant blue robes, stepped onto the stage. He bowed to them, and they in turn bowed to him. "My friends; my family. Tonight is the Choosing Ceremony. You have heard our history, and your duty. If you are of age, you may choose to step forward, and go a different path. Your choice will be respected, and you will be given what you need to journey to the mainland."

He paused, studying them all. "If you do choose to leave, you will take an oath. This binds you under magic to never speak of this place or the tide jewel, lest those words be heard by the wrong ears. In this way, you fulfill your first oath you took as young children, which is to keep the Kanju safe."

Shinju swallowed, glancing around her. The Clan was not very large, despite being on the island for a few hundred years. It was not hard to find the people who were of age, just twenty in all. After this night, if they chose to stay, they would not be permitted to leave the island unless it was under extreme circumstances.

Yuudai bowed again, then waited quietly. People looked around and shifted in place. It was not very often that someone chose to leave, but it did happen. Shinju had only ever seen it once in the ten years she'd been there.

A few minutes of silence went by, and no one stepped forward. Yuudai brought his hands together and clapped once, twice. A collective breath was released, and everyone returned to chatting and laughing. The ceremony was over.

Shinju joined Haru and Izumi in a dance when the drums began to beat again, accompanied this time by *sanshin*, a three-stringed instrument. They took thin strips of wood with long, colorful flags tied to one end, and moved in tandem to the beat, waving the banners to the side and above their heads.

The rest of the evening was filled with song and dance, and it was not until a late hour when Shinju finally stumbled back home and fell into bed, her head swimming with colors and laughter and the plum wine that Izumi convinced her to drink.

She kicked off her shoes and undressed quickly, then lay down again, listening to the sounds of the night, and she drifted off into a contented sleep, forgetting completely about the foreboding feeling she'd had on the beach.

12

THE INTRUDER CREPT QUIETLY up from the shore and moved noiselessly through the brush. Clothed all in black, he was a part of the night itself. An invisible figure, a phantom. Just a few more steps, and he would achieve his goal.

At the top of the hill, he crouched down, looking at the shrine. The shrine that held the tide jewel. Slowly, carefully, he slid his knife from its sheath, the blade glistening in the moonlight, before it left his hand and found its mark.

Shinju sat up, sweat pouring down her face. She gulped deep breaths, trying to slow her heart. The dream was already fading from the edges of her mind, but…it had felt real, and left a disturbing presence behind.

She sat back on her hands and listened to the crickets chirping outside the house, and Takumi's snoring in the room next to hers. Shinju had been exhausted from the celebrations, but now, sleep seemed completely out of reach, especially after that dream. She pulled a shuddering breath and pushed the blankets aside to stand up.

The air was chilly despite the low fire burning in the brazier, so she took up her robe to wrap around her sleeping gown. She splashed some cool water on her face from the little basin in her room, hoping that it would also wash away the growing trepidation in her chest.

Shinju slid open her door and padded quietly over to the back door. In automated movements, she slid on her boots and slipped out of the house. A walk was what she needed, she decided. A walk to clear her head and exhale some of the energy she'd awoken with.

The village was quiet as Shinju left it behind, taking one of the many paths that wound through the island. The festivities had finally ended and the lights were extinguished, except for a few lanterns burning very low in front of a few homes. The stark contrast of the night's silence to the evening's earlier mood caused a shiver to run down Shinju's spine.

It was almost too still.

The jungle was dark, leaves whispering in the wind as Shinju trekked up the hill. The sensations of dread she'd had at the beach were returning, and her mind grew more awake and wary. Doing her best to remain quiet, Shinju pushed on for a long time until she reached the torii gate that guarded the entrance to the shrine.

This was a familiar place to her now, though it'd been some time since she last visited. The shrine was maintained by a select few of the Clan and guarded heavily by their best samurai at all hours of the day and night.

The curved roof of the shrine shone in the hazy moonlight, and Shinju caught sight of the guards: dark, unmoving figures in the shadows of the shrine's corners. There were fewer of them tonight because of the festivities.

She opened her mouth to announce her presence, but the words died in her throat.

Two torches were always kept lit at the entrance to the shrine, no matter the time of day. Right now, the torches were extinguished.

Shinju paused, then crouched down, reaching for the small knife she kept in her right boot. Blood pounded in her ears as she peered through the inky blackness at the guards, waiting for them to rotate positions, move their heads, anything. But the seconds crawled past, and none of them moved.

She took a careful look around, then crept out into the open, heading for the closest guard. At this angle, he seemed to be standing oddly, as if…Shinju raised her hand to muffle the cry that broke from her lips. The guard had been propped against the shrine wall. His throat was cut clean open, dark blood bubbling out and spreading down his neck and chest.

Whirling, Shinju held her knife out defensively, searching for the attacker, then hurried around to the other guards.

All dead.

"No…" she whispered, her hands starting to shake. "This…this can't be..."

One of the guards had fallen to the ground with his limbs splayed out. His sword was still in one hand, while the other clenched something tightly. Trembling, Shinju pried it out of his fist.

It was a piece of torn black fabric. With the lack of light, Shinju could just make out the partial symbol of a red crescent moon sewn into the material.

She gasped. The samurai must have fought the attacker and managed to tear it from his clothing.

A fresh wave of fear consumed her, and Shinju rushed around the shrine and pushed on the doors. They swung open silently, and in the dying moonlight, Shinju saw the pedestal that held the Kanju was empty.

Horror swept through her, and instead of freezing her in place, it propelled her to action. She flew from the shrine and grabbed the mallet that hung from the gong. She hesitated for only a moment. The gong had never been rung in all of the Tsomas' long history, and now she struck it with all her might.

A deep, resounding clash answered, vibrating through the clearing, shaking the moss from the gong's frame. Shinju rang it twice more, then dropped the mallet. Relighting one of the torches, she held it over the ground around the shrine, searching for footprints.

There. A faint but distinct track in the loose soil. It led away from the shrine, through the jungle, and towards the north-eastern beach.

Shinju returned the torch and grabbed one of the fallen guard's bow and arrows as she ran towards the beach. An intruder, a thief, could only come by the sea.

Shinju had never run so fast in her life, and it was a miracle she did not trip on tree roots or stones, as the path was dark, the moon now completely hidden in the clouds. Within minutes she arrived at the tree line that gave way to the beach, and she halted, trying to take deep breaths as quietly as she could.

Slowly, she crept forward, and peered out at the water, not wanting to be seen. Who knew how many there were? She knocked an arrow and moved closer.

A lone boat floated on the sea, not far away yet, but the wind was quickly filling its sail. The vessel was painted black as well as the sail, which rippled in the breeze, showcasing the same red crescent moon symbol. She could only make out one figure on the boat, and that was enough. With a growl, Shinju leaped onto the beach, pulled the arrow back, and let it fly.

It soared through the air towards its mark, and just missed the black-clothed figure. He turned as she was already fitting another arrow and running towards the water for a closer aim. "Stop!" she cried. "Thief!"

Almost too late, she saw something flash through the air, and she threw herself to the sand to miss the *shuriken* that embedded itself into a palm tree behind her.

Angrily, Shinju pushed to her knees, and released another arrow. But the thief was too far away now; the wind had filled his sail and sent him speeding away. Her arrow struck the water harmlessly.

"Stop! Please don't take it!" she called out to the figure as he grew smaller in the distance. "You don't know what you're doing!"

There was no response, and the thief, with the Kanju, sailed farther away.

Shinju watched in despair for a moment, then remembered

the guards. The village. She had to make sure they had heard her alarm. They could still stop him if they got to the boats in time.

Air burning in her chest, Shinju trekked as quickly as she could back through the jungle paths and up to the shrine. The gong had proved to be effective in its purpose as far below her, Shinju could see lights flickering to life in the village at the bottom of the hill.

Within minutes, samurai burst into the clearing, katanas drawn. Some had their armor on as they had been patrolling other parts of the island, but most were still in their nightshirts. They caught sight of Shinju and stared in surprise.

"The Kanju has been stolen!" she shouted to them, suddenly aware of tears rolling down her cheeks. She stumbled towards them, pointing in the direction of the beach. "We have to go now! He escaped by boat, but we can still catch him!"

No one moved at first, stunned by this news. Then Masao, captain of the samurai, strode forward. Plated fingers grabbed her arms roughly and shook her.

"Where? When? Speak, girl!" he growled. "Moments ago," Shinju answered, shaking off his hands. "I tried to stop him, but he was too far on the water to be hit with the arrows."

More villagers began pouring through the trees, holding any weapon they had. Lanterns were lit, and everyone's faces looked grim in the flickering orange glows. They had been trained for moments like these, but it had never happened before, and the reality that the time had come caused even the strongest warriors among them to look pale.

"Why were you in the shrine of the Kanju? How did you come to find our fallen guards?" Masao demanded. Some of the samurai had begun assessing their fallen comrades, and shortly after, family members began to cry out as they realized they were dead.

Shinju pushed him away, pointing again towards the beach. "There's no time!" she yelled. "He's getting away! We have to go to the boats!"

Takumi appeared at her side, dressed in his armor, katana sheathed but ready. "Listen to her," he told the crowd. "However it happened, we are wasting time. If we hope to catch this thief, we must act now." There was a pause. Masao nodded curtly and began shouting orders. Samurai surged together and the crowd parted to let them pass.

Together, Shinju and Takumi followed them. "What happened?" Takumi asked her quietly as they ran. "I had a dream that the Kanju was stolen…it was so real that I woke up and…" she shivered, remembering the crawling feeling on her skin, the sweat on her brow, the thundering of her heart that told her something was wrong, that something terrible had happened.

"I knew something was wrong with the Kanju. I don't know why, but I had to go see for certain whether all was well. When I reached the shrine, the guards were…fallen. And the Kanju was gone from its pedestal."

"Did you see who it was?" Takumi asked. They were running past the village now, its inhabitants awake and scurrying like ants. They ignored them, hurrying farther down the mountain to the beach where the boats were kept.

"No, it was too dark, but from what I could tell, it was just one person," Shinju explained in a ragged breath. Takumi did not answer, but from a fleeting glance she could tell he was very troubled by her words.

They reached the section of beach where the longboats were stored. Longer than the regular, every day fishing boats, these had been hewn and crafted especially for any fighting they may have to participate in at sea, built to hold multiple samurai in their armor and weapons. Training took place in these boats, but never had they been seriously used in combat against an enemy.

The animal hide tarps were thrown off the vessels and they set to work at pushing them into the water, untying rope, and readying the sails. Shinju joined Takumi at one of them, determined to come along. Hurry, hurry, she wanted to yell again, but they were doing their best. It would not do to set out unprepared. The thief had been just one, but who knew if he had comrades waiting for him across the water.

A low roll of thunder in the distance paused their movements. The wind died suddenly, eerie in its stillness. It was early morning now, but dark clouds were rolling quickly across the sky, shielding any chance the sun had of giving them light.

"A storm?" Shinju wondered, staring out at the sea. Takumi did not answer, but he looked even more worried than before.

As quickly as it died, the wind revived itself with a great force, whipping across the beach and blowing so hard Shinju had to grab onto the side of the boat. It caused the lanterns to swing violently and banners to flap wildly. Palm trees began to creak and bend over. The gentle sea around them started to churn, waves growing higher than usual, their white crests racing to pound at the shore.

"What's happening?" Shinju asked, reaching for Takumi at her side. "The magic," he breathed, his eyes wide with alarm. "The magic on the island has been disrupted from the removal of the tide jewel."

Branches and debris snapped and were flung through the air. With sickening cracks, the masts on some of the boats broke. People cried out as the heavy wood poles were tossed to the ground like twigs. Beneath their feet, the earth trembled, knocking some of them down.

"Get to higher ground!" Masao barked, and the samurai abandoned the boats to follow him, helping other villagers along the way.

"But the tide jewel!" Shinju protested when Takumi took her arm. "Look at the sea!" he shouted over the wind. "There's no way we will be able to sail on that!"

He was right; the water was churning furiously, waves crashing into each other with an intensity Shinju had never seen before. Reluctantly she followed her guardian, her arm braced over her eyes.

It was soon clear they were heading for the daimyo's home, the most fortified building on the island. The homes in the village were already being evacuated; some roofs were lifted away or smashed in by the wind and debris. Children were crying, and adults yelped and clung to each other desperately.

The earth shook with several tremors, and a great crack opened up at the top of the mountain, spreading rapidly down towards them. It devoured everything in its path: trees, animals, buildings.

Frightened and confused, the orderly line of people

shepherded by the samurai broke. They fled in every direction, trying to escape the angry chasm. "This way!" Takumi shouted, tugging Shinju with him. She stumbled and nearly fell, catching her foot on a stone. In the back of her mind, she wondered where Peiku was.

And then, a roar such as they had never heard before echoed from deep in the ground. Roots, vines, and tendrils burst from the dirt and grass, grasping at ankles and tugging people down. Shinju watched, horrified, as a man next to them was completely encased by the earth, his cries muffled until he was entombed.

One by one, the ground latched itself onto the fleeing villagers. Samurai drew their katanas and tried to fight, but more vines were simply sent towards them, or cracks opened beneath their feet and they were swallowed.

"Takumi! Why is this happening?" Shinju cried as they ran, slashing at roots that pulled at them. "The island has been derived from its magic!" Takumi panted, cutting several roots in two. "I think…I think it is trying to hold on to what is left, which is us!"

"What do you mean?" Shinju dodged and ducked, then slashed at a vine that had gotten too close. Back to back, they headed for an outcropping of rock near the beach, watching helplessly as more of their clan were claimed by the island.

"The Tsomas are connected to the magic of the tide jewel, remember?" Takumi told her. "Without it, the balance of this place has been thrown off course, and the island is searching for any magic left. It's embedded in our very beings."

More vines and roots headed for them, the ground rising

like a wave on the sea. Shinju cried out when vines wrapped around Takumi's ankles and tugged him off his feet, dragging him away.

"No!" She ran after him, but the earth shook again, and she lost her footing, falling to the ground hard. "Takumi!" she screamed as she watched her guardian become enclosed by the vines.

"Takumi!" Panic grabbed at her heart as she crawled along the ground towards him, begging for the island to stop its raging. And suddenly, it did.

The air became still and quiet, and the wind eased to only a gentle breeze. Dark clouds still swirled overhead, but the rain and lightning ceased. The cracks in the earth stopped spreading, and the ocean quieted but still churned with larger than normal waves.

Not a sound was heard: no birds, animals, or people. Shinju's heart sank as she pushed strands of hair out of her face and slowly rose to her knees. When nothing stirred, she crawled to Takumi.

His body was almost entirely covered by the vines and roots and dirt. Shinju pulled at them desperately, then grabbed her knife and began hacking at the thick cords, trying not to cry as despair crashed over her.

She managed to tear off a clump of roots covering his face, and Takumi blinked slowly up at her, his face calm and serene. The effect startled Shinju so much she paused at hacking.

"Shinju," he said softly. She stared at him in confusion. "It's alright," he said. "You will be okay. You can help us."

"What?" she choked out, uncomprehending. "You were not

born here, Shinju-chan," he told her tenderly. "You do not have the same connection to the tide jewel that we do."

"I…I don't understand."

"The island did not take you," he breathed. "I wondered… if it would."

He was right, she realized with sudden clarity. Of all the inhabitants on this island, she had remained untouched. The revelation did not do much to calm her fears.

"I won't be okay, not without you," she sniffed. "Please don't leave me. I can free you."

"Yes, you can. But not like this," Takumi wheezed. His eyelids started to droop, and tendrils began to grow and recover his face. Shinju batted them away, angry tears pooling down her face.

"Find it, Shinju. Bring it back, and break this curse," Takumi whispered. "I…always knew I had found you for a reason. You came to us for a reason."

Shinju gripped the roots where his hands should be. She knew now what he was asking her to do. What she had to do.

"I will hunt down this thief and take back the tide jewel. This is what you have trained me for," she vowed, willing her voice not to shake. "I will not lose my family again. I promise, Takumi."

Takumi searched her eyes, his own revealing a level of emotion that Shinju had not seen often.

"Shinju-chan," he whispered. "Trust in Ryūjin-sama. Even if you do not see him, the dragon will guide you. Do not despair." He gave her one last smile, and then his face was hidden from her once more.

13

After murmuring a prayer over Takumi, there seemed to be nothing else to do but go on. Shinju walked to the spot where Takumi's katana had fallen and she picked it up, slid it into her belt, then headed down to the village.

Shinju expected to see damage from the storm, but the sight that greeted her froze her in her steps. Trees had been ripped up by the roots and flung like a toddler playing with flowers. Palm fronds covered the pathway and lawn, and debris from the forest had found its way onto every surface possible. A lump grew in her throat as she took in the destruction. Everything had changed so quickly.

Not a single Tsoma had been spared by the island's wrath.

According to the Tsoma legends, the tide jewel magic kept their home in perfect weather and living conditions. It rained when it needed to, grew cooler when it needed to, and they had learned to adapt and prepare. Never had they experienced a storm like this though.

Even the sturdy wood homes, built to withstand the strong winds that sometimes came down from the island's peak, had fallen like children's playthings. Shinju looked out over the sea, which seemed to watch her warily, like it was holding its breath and waiting for her next move.

The air felt still, listless, as she picked her way down to the village, heading to her house where some much-needed supplies were. Thankfully, their home seemed to have taken lesser damage. The roof had caved in, and the paper windows had been torn, but it was not unmanageable.

Shinju searched through her room for her warmer garments. She wasn't sure how long she would be gone, and it could get bitterly cold on the sea. She rolled a blanket and some clothing into a woven pack. In the kitchen, she was able to scrounge up some fruit and dried fish to pack, as well as some rice and root vegetables. It wasn't much, but it would have to do.

Next to her provisions, she stored Takumi's carefully copied notes about the tide jewels and Ryūjin from records at the daimyo's home. She knew their history by heart by now but having the familiar words would bring her comfort. She also found his compass; the glass face was cracked, but the needle pointed correctly.

At the doorway, she paused, eyeing her personal katana from its place on the wall. Then she looked down at Takumi's, already sheathed and ready at her side, and she made her decision.

Her next destination was the beach to find a boat that was

still in good condition. Daytime finally brought a hazy, gray light to the island, so she was at least able to see where she needed to go.

The destroyed boats were flung haphazardly across the beach, many of them smashed beyond any quick repair. A few still bobbed in the shallow water, but all leaked water except for one: Takumi's. His had been tucked under an alcove of rock, and instead of being flung against the stone and broken, the boat had used the rock as a buffer to protect it from the waves.

"Well, that's some good news at least!" Shinju exclaimed, feeling slightly more hopeful. Repairing a boat would take a long time, and she had never done one on her own before. Quickly, she set about inspecting the small vessel, checking to make sure there were no leaks, dumping out water that had managed to slosh inside, and examining the mast and sail.

When she was satisfied, Shinju untied it and paddled out from the rocks and onto the beach, pulling the boat up onto the sand so it wouldn't drift away. As she began to load her supplies, a furry object raced out of the trees nearby and nearly knocked her over.

"Peiku!" Shinju cried, hugging the excited tanuki. "I'm so glad you're alright!" She gave him a few good scratches under his chin, relieved that she was not completely alone. "The island must not have taken the animals, then," she wondered aloud as Peiku extracted himself from her arms and began sniffing at the boat.

"Or it just didn't want you," she teased. The tanuki gave her an eye roll and hopped into the boat, settling himself down with authority. "I guess you're coming with me. Are you sure?" Shinju asked him, doubtful. “It’s going to be dangerous!”

Peiku ruffled his fur, gave a short bark, and scampered off the boat, hiding behind Shinju. “It’s okay. Look, I need you to stay here. I don’t want you to get hurt out on the mainland. I don’t…I don’t know what will happen.” She sunk her fingers into his fur and stared into caramel-brown eyes.

“I’ll miss you. Keep an eye on things while I’m gone, okay?” she whispered. Peiku seemed to accept this, as he turned and burrowed into the sand to watch her leave.

Shinju gave the island a final look, then pushed off on the beach, letting the boat float out on its own before she took up the paddle. Keeping near the shore, she paddled around the island to the portion of beach where the thief had escaped. There were some things she needed to collect.

Shinju carefully pried the throwing star from the deep gash it had made in the palm tree. It was unremarkable to her eyes; nothing about the shuriken stood out to her besides the razor-sharp blades. She shuddered, remembering how close it had come to sinking into her flesh.

She wrapped it up in a cloth and tied it carefully, then she headed up the slope and towards the shrine. Shinju did not know what she expected to find, but she hoped for another clue that could tell her more about this thief.

At the shrine, the dead samurai were gone, claimed by the island like the rest, Shinju supposed. It saddened her that they hadn't been able to give the warriors a proper burial.

Brushing those thoughts out of her mind, she focused on the task at hand, combing through the rubble of the shrine: it had not been spared in the tremors.

Righting what she could along the way, including the stand where the Kanju had rested, Shinju's hand brushed against something foreign, and she dug it out from under the stone and dirt. It was a dart: small, black, with a pronounced point and red feathered tail. A small symbol was painted on the side: a crescent moon again.

Shinju held it at arm's length by the feathered tail, studying it with revulsion. A small dart would not have hurt a samurai on its own; no, it must have been poisoned. This too she wrapped up safely and decided that this was all she would be able to find. Time was running out; she needed to set out in the boat if she had any chance of catching up to this thief.

The hazy light of day did not strengthen as she returned to the beach and tucked away her findings. With one last look behind her, Shinju pushed off on the boat, and began paddling out into the open water. The churning tides sucked at the small vessel, guiding her along as she steered it towards the direction the thief had taken.

Shinju was now forever grateful that because of the long, hard sailing lessons from Takumi, she felt confident enough to navigate even these dangerous waves that prowled around her.

As she paddled into the channel that would bring her farther out to sea and towards the mainland, Shinju could not help but wonder how the thief had found them in the first place. The island was far away and well hidden, and yet this thief had managed to reach them in the dark through difficult waters.

The thought made her uneasy. Had they not been as secretive as the clan thought? Had a clan member who left long ago found a way to break their oath and give them away?

No, Shinju told herself. A Tsoma would never do such a thing. This thief, whoever they were, had discovered where they were and what they were protecting through some other means.

Shinju gripped the rudder of the boat tightly, the weight of her mission growing heavier as she sailed farther and farther away from home. She had to find the tide jewel and restore balance to the island to save her clan, but also prevent the Kanju from being used for evil purposes. *I must not fail. I cannot lose my family again.*

Gradually the dark clouds that hovered over the island and surrounding water dissipated, and a clear, blue sky greeted her. Gulls floated lazily above the boat, calling to each other. Shinju was glad for the more cheerful weather: she needed something to distract her from her gloomy thoughts. Exhaustion pulled at her eyelids, the handful of hours of sleep the night before not nearly enough.

The rocking of the boat did not help either. Shinju blinked furiously, squinting as the sun danced on the waves and cast a bright glare into her eyes. "I wish I had brought a hat," she mumbled. Her stomach growled next, unused to skipping breakfast, so she reached into her pack and produced an apple to munch, using one hand to steer.

This was the first time she had ever sailed through the tiny islands that dotted this area of the sea, but Shinju felt confident of the way after studying the few maps the Clan had drawn many years ago.

It was strange to think that ten years before she had come through this very channel as a child without crashing the boat and had slept through the entirety of the experience.

As the water remained calm for her journey, Shinju reflected that this must mean the thief had not used the tide jewel, not yet. She wondered again for what purpose he had stolen it: perhaps he did not realize its importance, or perhaps he had taken it out of desperation.

Well, she would find him and explain to him very sternly that what he had done was wrong and she was there to take it back by any means necessary. "You might have shuriken," she told a black bird that landed on the prow of the boat, pretending it was the thief. "But I have a katana and a pair of flying fists!"

She thrust a closed palm through the air to illustrate, and the bird squawked crossly and flew off.

In a few hours she spotted the mainland, dark green against the blue of the sea. Shinju sailed towards it, spotting a beach. The thief could have gone anywhere, but she had to start searching somewhere. Perhaps he had landed here.

From her recollection of the maps, this would place her around the Fundai Province. If she was lucky, there would be no one at the beach to question her arrival.

As she drew closer, a dark shape on the sand caught her eye, and she leaned forward, urging the boat along as quickly as it could with the wind.

The dark shape was a familiar vessel. With a gasp, Shinju immediately lowered her sail and crouched down, using only the paddle to guide her. It looked abandoned, but she could not take any chances. The thief might be hiding in the brush beyond the beach, watching her.

Slowly, she floated a safe distance away into an outcropping of rock and used a rope to tie the boat securely, then she placed her pack around her shoulder, drew her katana, and crept out, scanning the beach.

All was quiet; there were no movements except for a couple of birds pecking for lunch and tiny crabs scuttling sideways in search of their own meals.

Once she was convinced there was no ambush, Shinju sprinted to the other boat and examined it. There was nothing left behind in its bottom, and besides being a sleek, well-made vessel, nothing distinguished it to her. Frustrated, Shinju searched along the tackle and lowered sail, frowning at the crescent moon symbol painted on the fabric. This had certainly belonged to her thief then.

Walking around to the prow, she spotted a faint set of footprints leading away from the boat and up to the forest beyond. "Aha!" she huffed. "Not so sneaky, are you?" Setting her shoulders, Shinju followed the prints and marched into the forest.

14

SHE WAS LOST, AND she knew it. With a groan, Shinju stopped to lean against a tree to catch her breath and wipe her face. With the sun blazing high overhead, it was warm even under the canopy of the trees. And she was dressed in a thick tunic and pants, better suited for a cooler climate.

Water was also nowhere to be seen, and Shinju was beginning to get worried about the flask in her satchel that was growing lighter and lighter as the hours passed. She was still hungry too, but she didn't want to eat anything for fear of making her thirst worse.

Hoping for some guidance, Shinju took out the compass again. She had been heading east, but the forest turned out to be much larger than she had thought. With no marker, she had no idea how much farther she had to go.

The thief could have gone anywhere at this point. After

following the footprints on the beach, Shinju had simply headed in the same direction as much as possible. It was her only lead. Now she felt desperation beginning to kick in.

"What did you expect, Shinju," she told herself crossly as she continued onward. "That the thief would just be waiting around for you in a clearing?"

After another hour, Shinju stopped again and sat on the forest floor, frustrated. She had climbed a tree at one point, trying to peer above the forest for a landmark to go by, and saw what looked like a rise many miles in the distance that she could head for.

She was thirsty, and hardly any water remained in her flask. She was no closer to finding the thief than she had been hours ago, and he could have gone a completely different direction than this.

She unbraided her hair from its bun and sighed, combing her fingers through the long locks and trying to think. "Let's see, if I was a thief who had just stolen a tide jewel, what would I do next?" she asked a beetle that investigated her shoe.

Then it hit her. "Oh!" Her cry frightened the beetle away. "That's it!" Excitedly, she unrolled the scroll that contained the story of the tide jewels.

"Of course," she whispered, tracing her finger across carefully written text. "One tide jewel is good, but two are even better." The thief, and whoever he was working with, would probably want both jewels if they were searching for real power. Shinju guessed that they would be heading for the location of the Manju.

Of course, the thief may have already stolen that too...but

it was all she had to go on. The revelation still lifted her spirits and gave her something to focus on besides her overwhelming thirst.

Changing direction and hoping to be closer to getting out of this forest, Shinju hurried on with renewed determination. She squeezed every last drop from her flask, hoping it would be enough.

The sun had finally lowered in the sky when she spotted the trees thinning ahead. "Finally!" she gasped. Shifting her pack and katana, she pushed through the brush and ducked under branches. Just as she was nearing the forest's edge, a voice rang out.

"Help!" it cried. Shinju paused, looking around. "Please, someone help!" The voice sounded truly distraught, and Shinju headed in its direction, gripping her katana. She couldn't ignore a cry for help, no matter that she was on a mission.

The cry led her a little farther from the tree line, then out of it. Before her stretched open land and a road that wound its way out of sight. Off to the side stood a peasant in a worn travel tunic, worrying over an overturned cart. Vegetables had spilled out and over onto the ground, and he was struggling to push the cart back on its wheels, which Shinju noted were not in the best condition. No wonder it had turned over!

"Excuse me," she spoke, and the man whirled around, startled. "I heard you shouting for help."

"Where did you come from?" the man demanded, wringing his hands. He looked her up and down, noting the katana with confusion.

"Oh, I'm just a traveler, and took a shortcut through the

woods," Shinju answered lightly. She did not want to lie, but she couldn't very well tell this peasant where she was really from.

"I see…" he answered faintly. "Well…my donkey ran off as I was making some adjustments to the cart, and he knocked it over! I have a bad back, you see, and I cannot lift it on my own."

He looked down at the cart with despair. "If I can't find my donkey and set the cart back in place, I won't be able to go into the nearby town and sell my vegetables. I need the coin to buy medicine for my sick wife." He sobbed and blew his nose on his sleeve.

Shinju was touched. *Poor man*, she thought, and came closer. "I can help you," she told him.

"You?" he replied doubtfully. "Oh, yes. I'm stronger than I look!" she assured him cheerfully. "Don't worry, we will fix your cart. And I'm sure your donkey can't have run off too far."

Setting down her pack and sword, Shinju walked around to a corner of the cart. "Now, you take that other side, and we will lift together. It won't be as heavy with the two of us," she said.

The man scrambled over to help, and just as Shinju had braced her legs to begin lifting, an awareness tickled the back of her mind, one she had always been taught to acknowledge. Dropping the corner of the cart, she spun around and just missed the heavy club aimed at her head.

It thudded against the side of the cart, and Shinju stared wide-eyed at the beefy arm connected to a large and dirty, not to mention ugly, man. He had not been prepared for her to dodge his attack and he reacted slowly, giving Shinju the precious seconds she needed to gather herself and bring her knee up into his gut.

He grunted, nearly dropping the club, and Shinju sent several hard punches into his chest and face, causing him to stumble backwards. She gave him a kick to the stomach, but this time he swung at her again and she had to dodge the club once more.

"Why are you attacking me?" she demanded, backing into a defensive crouch.

Then something hard slammed into the side of her head, and the world went black.

15

SHINJU AWOKE WITH A start and felt her head immediately throb painfully in response. With a groan, she gingerly felt the sore area where she'd been struck. There didn't seem to be any blood, but the bump was very tender. She blinked a few times, trying to focus on her surroundings, and slowly sat up.

She appeared to be in some sort of prison cell, if the iron bars blocking her exit from the tiny room were any indication. She'd been unceremoniously dumped in the corner on top of a smelly, moldy blanket, and the ground was filthy with dirt, straw, and other things Shinju did not want to examine more closely.

A grime-covered bucket sat in another corner, and that was the extent of her accommodations. The smell was almost unbearable, and Shinju swallowed down a wave of nausea in response.

Placing her hand on the uneven stone wall to steady herself,

Shinju searched around uselessly for her belongings, but of course the men who attacked her had taken them. Her pack, sword, and anything else on her person that could have been used as a weapon or tool to escape, were gone.

Muttering a curse in frustration, Shinju kicked the filthy blanket and balled her fists. How could she have let this happen? She had been a fool to let her defenses down so easily, but even worse, she'd barely even had a chance to fight back. All her years of training, and to be taken out by a couple of bandits? It was humiliating. What would Takumi say if he saw her now?

"I can't believe this!" she groaned, raking her hands through her hair. "How dare that man pose as a helpless peasant!"

There was no telling when someone might come to check on her, and Shinju knew she had to find a way out of here and fast. She didn't have time to wait around in a cell: the clan was depending on her to find the Kanju and return it.

She took a deep breath to calm herself, willing her senses to gather and focus on the task before her. Even if she had to search every inch of this cell from top to bottom, she would find a way to escape.

Brushing off her clothes, Shinju's eyes landed on the iron bars again, and beyond them she noticed another cell, which was also occupied. Moving closer, Shinju peered through her bars; only a narrow passageway separated the two cells, but at this angle she could not see much farther to the left or right. Her attention landed back on her fellow prisoner.

A man lay on the ground, one arm behind his head, while the other arm was flung across his face, and a leg was drawn up over his other knee. He was…snoring?

Shinju gaped at him in disbelief. How could he be sleeping in a place like this? She squinted at him between the bars, trying to get a better look.

Even laying down, she could tell he was a tall man, and powerfully built like a warrior. His biceps strained against the sleeves of his plain, woven tunic, and though most of his face was hidden by his arm, Shinju could spy a hint of stubble on his chin.

Dark hair spilled over his shoulders in tangled strands. While the rest of his clothes were lacking in any kind of ornamentation, and were simple shades of brown and gray, the gauntlets around his forearms told a different story. The leather straps were simple enough, but the silver plating shone even in the dim light of the prison. From her position, Shinju could not quite make out the design or symbols engraved in the plates.

Who was he? she wondered. How did someone like him get thrown in here? He didn't look like the sort of person who would be easily overcome in a fight. Perhaps he could tell her more about where they were and what she was up against.

"*Sumimasen*!" she hissed at him. "Psst!"

The low snores stopped, and the man shifted slightly, but otherwise he did not respond. "Excuse me," Shinju tried again, keeping her voice low. "I'm sorry to disturb you, but I need to ask you some questions."

A resigned sigh emitted from the stranger. "Ask your questions, girl, so I can go back to sleep," came his answer in a rough, raspy sort of voice. Shinju bristled at his use of the word "girl" but refrained from arguing the point. She bit her lip, gathering her thoughts.

"Where are we?"

"In a prison," the man retorted.

"I know that!" Shinju exclaimed, her patience running thin. "I mean, *where* are we? Is this a thieves' hideout? Is it part of the slave trade? Is it some sort of cage where they keep us to be fed to a bear?"

The man snorted at her last guess. "You have a very vivid imagination, girl. Don't you know already? We are being held by the Kasuda Gang, criminals who run trade to the Black Harbor."

The Kasuda Gang? Shinju thought hard, trying to recall if she had heard the name before. It did not feel familiar at all, but, if they were associated with the Black Harbor, then these were terrible people indeed. There were no depths they wouldn't sink to, especially if the price was right.

The Black Harbor was well-known, even to the Tsomas. A harbor to the north, slaves were purchased and sent across the sea, as well as counterfeit goods from this empire or lands beyond Horitamo. Some daimyos and Shoguns had tried in the past to shut down the business, but too many others, including some closest to the Emperor, were involved in lining their pockets with coin funneled through the harbor, and so it remained a dark stain on the empire.

Blood thundered in her ears. Was this gang connected to the thief who had stolen the Kanju? The two men she encountered earlier did not seem to be in the same league as a skulking ninja who had taken out some of their best samurai. More than likely, they were just ordinary criminals.

Not that that made her feel any better.

Somewhere above them, muffled voices rose and fell, followed by laughter. Shinju felt perspiration gathering on her forehead in the hot, stale cell. "How did you get in here?" she asked the other prisoner curiously.

"They claimed I cheated in *shogi*, and I was drunk, so I let them have their fun and throw me in here. I got some sleep at least, until *someone* woke me up."

Shinju wrinkled her nose. *Not a very respectable man then.* But she had not missed his choice of words. "You *let* them?" she questioned, more to herself than to him. "Why didn't they take your gauntlets? They look valuable."

"Oh, they tried. I broke an arm and several noses before they decided to give up," he rumbled, and in the shadow of his arm she detected the slight curve of a smile.

An idea began to form in her mind. A terrible idea, probably, but her options were slim. Summoning her most persuasive voice, she addressed him again.

"I'm sorry to keep you from sleeping, but I really need to get out of here. I'm on a very important mission and time is of the essence. If you can help me escape, I'll…reward you."

The man did not respond for a long moment. Then he threw his arm off his face and slowly got to his feet, turning as he did so that she still could not see his face. Shinju felt her mouth drop open; he was even bigger than she had thought. Definitely a warrior, she affirmed in her mind, taking in his broad chest and sturdy legs hidden beneath rough spun trousers. Then she realized she was practically ogling him, and her face grew warm.

"What makes you think I can help you escape," the man

asked as he rolled his shoulders.

"You don't seem too concerned with being in here. And you seem familiar with these...people." Shinju tried to choose her words carefully. If this man could not help her, she would not have much time to think of another solution. Someone was bound to come check on them soon. "That makes me think you're pretty confident of getting out. Which means that you could help me escape and..."

The man finally turned to face her fully as she was talking, and her words faded. She did not notice the other features of his face at first, for it was his eyes that paralyzed her.

They were a brilliant mixture of deep gray and blue, like clouds that gathered above the sea in prelude to a thunderstorm, and...they were *glowing.*

Shooting through the irises with white-hot intensity were flashes of silver, like the gauntlets he wore. They pierced through her sharply, as if reaching for her very soul.

His eyes were like looking into a bolt of lightning as it struck the earth: powerful, wild, and unpredictable.

Shinju barely registered her sharp intake of breath as she stared into those eyes, her mind blank of anything but the tingling feeling that spread all throughout her body, even causing her hair to stand on end.

The man drew closer to the bars of his cell, staring at her just as hard as she was him, and thrust his arms through the spaces to hang out lazily. "So this is how I get you to stop talking," he said with a low chuckle. "Just flash my pretty eyes at you."

His words snapped Shinju out of the trance she'd been

under, and she shook her head slightly to clear it.

"I just...um, wasn't expecting…that," she replied lamely, feeling another blush spread through her cheeks. What was the matter with her?

He snorted, and she returned it with a glare, determined not to be frozen by those eyes again. The rest of his face was rugged, handsome, with high cheekbones and arched brows, and like her, he was dirty from the cell and his own encounter with the gang.

Shinju tried to focus elsewhere as she continued her previous speech. "Like I was saying, if you help me escape, I'll reward you."

He raised an eyebrow, taking in her appearance doubtfully. "What kind of reward?" he asked in the same grating, raspy voice. Shinju thought quickly, wondering what she could promise him that was actually desirable.

Her clan was not wealthy: they didn't even use money on the island. Everything was made by hand, and they bartered with each other for anything they needed. She knew some precious stones had been found on the island, as well as pearls from mollusks, but she wasn't sure any of that would be appealing.

"What do you want?' she blurted in an effort to give her time to think. Instead of laughing at her like she expected, the man seemed to consider her question seriously.

"Something I don't think you could give me," he answered, the words accompanied by a wry grin. Shinju furrowed her brow at that, but before she could ask what he meant, the sound of footsteps echoed in the corridor.

Shinju gave him a pleading look, and he stared back. "I saw

what they took from you when they brought you in here. That katana. Why deprive you of the chance to pay back what they did to you?" He nodded at the bump on her head. "Let's see what you're capable of. Unless the sword is all for show?"

Shinju gaped at him in surprise, then grit her teeth as the steps drew closer. *He wants to see what I can do? Fine, then.* She thrust her chin in the air stubbornly, and the man only smirked in response.

A man appeared at their cells, dressed in black garb that had seen better days judging by the frayed edges and various holes. He smelled of sweat and his face was streaked with it too. His hair was pulled back in a loose tail, complimented by an equally shabby black scarf.

He surveyed the two prisoners with an arrogant manner that plainly told Shinju he thought he was above them. "Nice of you two to finally join the living again," he mocked, giving the stranger a quick glance before moving closer to Shinju.

"Well, Missy, better pack your things, the boss has booked you a nice little trip to the Black Harbor." He laughed rudely, spittle flying from his mouth.

Shinju recoiled in disgust; the thought of being carted off to the Black Harbor to be sold was more than she could bear.

"I'm not going anywhere except to continue my mission," she told him. "I demand that you release me and return my belongings, or you'll be sorry."

The bandit stared at her in surprise, then laughed again, this time tipping his head back with the effort. "Oh ho, my lady demands it, does she? Well, we will just have to see about that." He ran his tongue over his bottom lip, looking at her in a way that made Shinju's skin crawl, but she was determined to stay calm. Her plan was working.

"Looks like you could use a little preview of what awaits you at the Harbor," he slurred, and took a sip from a sake jar in his hand. With the other he reached for inside his tunic and withdrew a ring of keys.

Shinju stuck her chin out, backing away a little from the bars. "I doubt you could do much," she taunted, slowly relaxing into her stance.

The man growled at her and angrily stuck a key in the lock, turning it. The door creaked open on rusty hinges, and he stepped towards her, arm raised for a back hand.

Now! Shinju struck forward, fast as a snake, and chopped him in the throat with the side of her hand. The man gasped and stumbled backwards, choking, and Shinju quickly kicked his legs out from under him. He fell with a hard thud, his head cracking against the stone floor, and lay still. Shinju leaned down quickly to check his pulse, then snatched the keys from the ground.

She turned and met the gaze of the man in the other cell, who had watched the entire exchange in silence. He gave a short, barking kind of laugh that startled her. "Ha! I knew it. And you said you needed my help to escape."

Shinju shrugged, feeling a sense of satisfaction for defeating her opponent. "It's not over." She stuck a key into his cell door, but it did not turn, so she searched for a different one.

"You're letting me out?" he asked, still chuckling.

"Yes. There's bound to be more guards, and they'll have weapons." She found the right key and his door opened. The man filled the entrance, looking down at her, and Shinju swallowed, suddenly feeling even smaller than she usually did. She avoided his eyes, which bore into her with a studious intensity.

"What's your name, girl?" he asked, his voice softer than before.

"Shinju. Shinju Tsoma. Pleased to meet you." She placed her hands together and gave a short bow, as she had been taught when introducing herself.

He regarded her with a hint of amusement on his face, then reached up and rubbed his chin. "Well, Shinju Tsoma, I accept your offer." He cracked his neck and rolled his shoulders, casting his gaze down the corridor towards the dark stairway that led out of the jail. A grin spread across his face, hungry and almost feral. "This should be fun."

"Wait!" Shinju exclaimed as he began to head in that direction. He paused and glanced back over his shoulder. "I…don't know your name," she faltered, searching his face and trying to reconcile the foreign, otherworldly eyes with the rest of him.

His mouth twitched. "Raiden."

16

THE RUMBLING SOUND OF his name seemed to echo off the stone walls around them. Shinju tested the word silently in mind. *Raiden.* Did he have a connection of some kind to the Kami Raijin? It suited him, she thought. Almost too well. His name referred to thunder and lightning, matching the storm within his eyes.

No ordinary man had eyes like that.

The sake bottle that the bandit had been drinking from now lay on the floor in pieces, the liquid soaking into the dirt. Raiden gave a shake of his head at the sight. "What a waste," he muttered. "Could have used something to wet my throat."

Shinju rolled her eyes. "You need to have your wits about you if we are going to fight our way out," she admonished. "It's a good thing it broke."

"Well, are we leaving or not?" Raiden prompted and

gestured towards the stairs. "After you, my lady." Shinju shot him a dark glare as she moved past him, stepping as quietly as she could. At the top of the stairs was a wooden door with a ring in it, as well as another keyhole. "Guess we are using these a little longer," she told her companion, lifting up the ring of keys she'd swiped. He only blinked in response.

After a few tries, Shinju found the right key and turned it quietly, then she opened the door with just a sliver to peek through. A larger room seemed to be on the other side, with a low table, musty-looking cushions, and kegs shoved in one corner. Two men sat at the table, and with a start, Shinju realized they were going through her belongings.

She closed the door again and looked at Raiden, who had climbed the stairs behind her. "Only two men that I could see, both distracted. I can get my things back," she whispered with a smile at the thought.

"Hmph," Raiden grunted with annoyance. "They only left two to guard us? How insulting."

His eyes seemed to glow brighter in the darkness, and the tingling sensation returned to her skin, as well as a crackling sound in the air. Before Shinju could react, Raiden pushed the door open and lunged into the room.

What happened next was something that Shinju had never in a thousand years expected to encounter, even though she had spent most of her life raised to believe in magic and the unusual.

With wide-eyed shock, she watched as Raiden grabbed the two men by their throats, effectively cutting off the beginnings of their yelps. The air in the room filled with static, and ribbons of lightning formed around his hands, traveling all the way up his forearms.

The men struggled in Raiden's grasp, but there was no escape. The lightning surged through his arms, around his fists, and into their bodies. They shook uncontrollably for a few seconds, their faces a grotesque mixture of terror and pain, and then they grew limp.

Raiden tossed them down like they were rag dolls. The lightning still licked at his fists, as if the death it had achieved were not enough to satisfy its hunger. Raiden turned to look at the table, then back at her.

Shinju could only stare at him, then at the men on the ground, whose bodies were burnt and smoking. "What…what have you done? What was that?" she asked hoarsely, unsure of whether she should flee or keep this mad alliance with him.

"You'll thank me later when these fists fight our way out of here," he told her calmly. He cast a disgusted eye towards his victims. "Those men are murderers, rapists, and thieves. They deserved to die."

Shinju winced; perhaps he was right. She had not considered until this moment that she might have to kill her way out of this place.

But the way he had just ended them…

Shinju had never seen such a thing, even though the Tsoma Clan were familiar with elemental magic on the island. Trembling, she stumbled into the room, unable to tear her gaze away from his hands. There was no question who he was now.

"How are you able to do that?" she asked anyway.

"I'll tell you later if we both survive," Raiden responded impatiently. "Grab your things and let's get moving. I doubt that we've gone unnoticed."

Shinju closed her mouth, trying to withhold further questions, and examined the contents of her pack, which had been strewn across the table. Luckily nothing seemed to be the worse for wear, and she began stuffing everything back in the satchel.

"I don't see my katana," she commented worriedly. "I can't leave that behind." Raiden stalked up to the other door across the room and was looking through the small window cut into it. Shouts echoed outside and Shinju almost froze her movements.

"More are coming," Raiden told her. He grinned and the lightning on his fists crackled with a frenzy.

Searching around her, Shinju spotted the used knives in the sheaths of the two dead men. With a grimace, she forced herself to crouch over them and drew both out. The blades were nicked and poorly made, but they were better than nothing. She swung her bag over her shoulder and secured the cord, then braced herself with one of the knives and nodded to Raiden. "I'm ready."

He nodded in response. "Let's dance."

Together they emerged from the room and entered the courtyard of a crudely built fortress that was filling quickly with other gang members, all carrying various weapons. Most held katanas, but some held large chains with a spiked iron ball at the end, and a few held shuriken and kunai.

Shinju drew closer to Raiden, taking in their opponents. She doubted these would be as easy to pick off as the man she'd knocked out, or the two Raiden killed. She knew nothing of their technique either, making them unpredictable and more dangerous. Her eyes bounced from person to person, weighing their movements, looking for any weakness.

Her palms were sweaty as she gripped the knives. She had fought against human opponents before, but that had always been training, against someone she knew, and you held yourself back.

This would be a fight of life or death…and she might have to kill someone.

One of the bandits stepped forward from the group that had gathered, positioning themselves throughout the courtyard. "Put down your weapons," he ordered. "Surrender. You cannot win." A scar zigzagged over his left eye, which was covered by a patch. His hand rested on a katana at his side, and with a start, Shinju recognized it as Takumi's. *The nerve!* she thought furiously.

Raiden chuckled in response, lifting one of his hands to showcase the lightning coursing over his skin. "I'm not the surrendering type," he said. "So I guess it is you who should put down your weapons. Let us go, and you'll keep your lives."

The leader sneered and nodded to his men. "Kill the freak," he ordered. "Leave the girl to me." The bandits moved forward, weapons moving in response.

Raiden smirked. "I thought you might say that." He whipped around and plunged his fist into the face of the bandit closest to him. The man flew back, knocking down several others. Raiden batted away a spiked staff from another thief as if it were a butterfly, then kicked him squarely in the stomach.

With shouts of outrage, the men surged towards them. Shinju launched a knife into the leg of one bandit, then used the other to meet a katana swinging down towards her head. The man was skilled, meeting her swipe for swipe. He had the advantage of a longer weapon, but he had clearly underestimated her from the beginning, and Shinju used that to her advantage.

Ducking under one of his thrusts, she spun close and stabbed him in the stomach. Blood spurted out from his tunic, and the man fell with a cry.

One of the men holding the ball and chain approached, swinging his weapon in a wide arc. Shinju ducked to the ground, narrowly missing the spikes.

Adrenaline pumped through her, making every detail sharper. She launched to her feet when the ball cleared overhead and charged at the attacker. He hurried his swing, and Shinju managed to catch the chain in her hand, digging in her feet against the momentum.

With a twist, she yanked hard and the man stumbled. The movement was enough to bring the ball back around, and Shinju dodged, yanking the chain at the same time, and the spiked ball collided with the bandit, knocking him down.

Two down, she thought, and glanced over to see how Raiden was fairing. Most of the bandits had rushed him, deeming the man wielding lightning to be a bigger threat than she.

Raiden stood in the middle of a circle of men, delivering blows and kicks with ferocity, no matter how many came at him at once. Lightning crackled and snapped into his opponents, blowing them back through the air when his fists connected with them. The weapons used against him appeared almost useless, bouncing off or being used as extra conductors of his magic. From the wild grin on his face, Shinju had the feeling he was enjoying this fight.

Another man attacked her then, wielding a katana. Backing up to avoid the blade, Shinju tuned out the other noises of battle, but kept her focus on her surroundings. Takumi and the other masters had taught her to use everything to her advantage in a fight, even her small stature. "Size does not matter as much as speed and agility," Takumi's words floated to her from a distant memory of her early teachings. "Wear them out and use their strength against them."

Resorting to defense, Shinju ducked and dodged, twisted and turned, until she could see he was growing too confident in overcoming her, and she used a moment of distraction to quickly slam her fist into his wrist. He dropped the blade in surprise, and Shinju smashed her foot into his face, following that up with punches. He reeled back, howling as blood gushed from his nose.

But the victory was short-lived; more opponents took his place. One by one Shinju met their attacks head on, using every move she knew to disarm and wound them. Her hands, arms, and legs were burning, and blood and sweat made her skin slick. The haze of battle put her in a trance-like state as she punched and kicked, jumped and rolled.

Arrows began to fire in her direction as she started to leave a trail of fallen gang members, and she turned to race up the flight of stairs to the upper level of the courtyard where two archers were stationed, the second firing arrows at Raiden.

She flew at them, slamming her forearm into their throats and then sriking them in the face. They collapsed, howling, and she grabbed one of the bows and aimed it at them in warning.

In the courtyard below, Raiden was still wielding lightning

bolts, but they seemed fainter now, as though he was tiring, and the smell of burnt flesh and clothing began to fill the air. Glancing over the edge of the railing, Shinju spotted a stack of barrels in a corner, and realized they had a chance to make a distraction and escape.

"Raiden!" she called down. "The barrels!" She pointed so he knew where to look. He glanced up at her with a frown, then struck another bandit in the face before turning to see the barrels. Understanding crossed his face, and with a deep breath, he unleashed a bolt of snapping white power directly at the barrels.

They caught fire immediately, then seconds later an explosion rocked the courtyard, sending men and pieces of wood and powder flying through the air. Men screamed as smoke and fire swept furiously throughout the buildings, quickly devouring anything it could.

Shinju coughed and held her arm up as a shield. The plan had worked a little too well, but now was not the time to second guess her actions. She quickly swung over the edge from the second level and dropped to the ground, peering through the haze of billowing dark smoke.

"Raiden!" she called. A man, blood running down his face, lurched at her, but she quickly grabbed his wrist, twisted his arm behind him, and tossed him to the ground.

A large hand grabbed her by the arm, and Shinju immediately swung her leg around to kick her opponent in the chest. She met the flashing eyes of Raiden, and he held up a forearm, blocking her kick. Her mouth dropped open as she pulled back.

"I could have hurt you!" she admonished. Raiden rolled his

eyes. "Unlikely. Let's leave this place before they regroup." He turned away and headed towards the gates, the smoke closing around him.

"No, wait!" Shinju glanced around and shuddered, seeing the dead men scattered around the courtyard. Raiden turned back, looking irritated. "What now? I thought you wanted to escape."

"I do, but I need to find my katana. It's important to me." Scanning the smoke and the fallen, she spotted the scarred man who had addressed them before. He was leaning against a pillar, holding his hand to his side where blood slowly oozed around his fingers.

Shinju turned and headed towards him, with Raiden soundlessly stalking behind her. She knelt a couple of feet away, catching the attention of the man she guessed to be the leader. His one eye glared at her with unconcealed rage. Takumi's katana lay in his limp hand.

"That belongs to me," Shinju told him, and she wrenched it from him, hating that such a terrible man had touched Takumi's sword.

"Stupid girl," the man growled. He eyed Raiden and spat at the ground. "Kami demon offspring," he hissed.

Shinju didn't need to turn to know the deadly currents were winding around Raiden's hands again as he stepped forward. "You," she addressed the man, "what do you know of this?"

She reached into her bag and pulled the torn fabric from the special pocket, raising it up so he could see the crescent moon clearly. "Did this come from one of your men?"

The man blanched and drew back from her, disgust mixing

with the pain from his wound. "Are you an idiot? Don't you know better than to brandish the sign of the Otami?" he growled.

Shinju's brow furrowed. "The Otami?" she repeated. "Who are they?"

"A deadly ninja clan," Raiden answered. She spun to look at him. "They specialize in assassinations and reconnaissance."

"And I don't need them to come here, wondering why a foolish girl is asking questions about them," the gang leader spat. "Get lost and take this demon with you."

Otami, Shinju thought, stuffing the piece of cloth back into her pack. So, they were ninja. Now she at least had a name to associate with her thief.

"Alright, let's go." She started to walk away but stopped when she saw Raiden approaching the scarred man, lightning flickering around his arms. "Raiden-san?"

He cast his glowing eyes at her. "If you leave him alive, he will hunt you down," he warned. The currents snapped around his hands, eager for another victim. Shinju swallowed, looking from Raiden to the scarred man.

"That is true," she answered slowly. "But there has been enough death today. Please, leave him alone."

Raiden glared at her, then clicked his tongue and the lightning faded from his arms. "Fine."

Peering through the smoke, Shinju found the gate that trapped them inside this hideout. "That way," she pointed, and they headed for it, ignoring the Kasuda leader's curses that followed them.

17

"WELL, I'D SAY THAT could have gone worse," Shinju commented cheerfully as they left the Kasuda Gang's hideout behind. The sun was now dipping low in the sky, setting it aflame with oranges and pinks.

So much time has been wasted, Shinju thought with a sigh. She must have been knocked out far longer than she'd thought.

Raiden remained silent during their short trek on the road that led into another forest, unreceptive of her few attempts at conversation. Now he folded his arms over his chest and planted his feet apart, staring down at her with the same searing look he'd given in the prison cell. "Alright, time to pay up, girl," he announced.

Shinju rolled her eyes at him and placed her hands on her hips. "Why does everyone insist on calling me 'girl' instead of my name? It's *Shin-ju.*" She drew out her name slowly, like she was explaining it to a small child.

His eyes narrowed. "You don't have anything to reward me with, do you?"

"Um." Shinju scratched the back of her head, grinning sheepishly. "Well, not exactly…"

Raiden stepped closer, his eyes growing darker. "But you did help me escape," she added quickly, holding up her hands to placate. "And I will reward you, just as soon as I…complete my mission."

"Is that so? Well then, you can tell me what your so-called mission is." He shot her a sharp grin. "I think it's the least you could do."

Shinju hesitated. She would be breaking every rule to tell him, but…this man was connected to the Kami. He carried lightning in his fists and was capable of incredible strength. She was convinced that he had ties to Raijin, the Kami of storms. If anyone could respect what her mission meant, it would be him.

Perhaps he could help her. Perhaps they were meant to meet. What were the chances that she would be thrown in the same prison as this man? *There are no coincidences*, Takumi's voice echoed in her mind.

"It's a long story," she finally admitted.

"I've got time," he rasped stubbornly. "What's so important that you're traveling alone and end up being captured by the likes of the Kasuda Gang, not to mention the Otami?" He quirked an eyebrow at her nervous expression. "I've traveled the land extensively and have heard many things. The name Tsoma is not unfamiliar to me." He leaned forward, closer than ever, and Shinju almost gulped at his proximity.

"Whatever you're looking for, it is something special isn't it? According to legend, the Tsomas are rumored to be guardians of a relic given from the Kami."

The clan would be mortified to know that someone had heard so much about them, Shinju thought. But then again, this was no ordinary person.

She lifted her chin defiantly. "I know who you are, you know. I know why that man called you a…well, why he called you that."

Raiden's eyes flashed dangerously as he curled his fists, taking an intimidating step forward. "Oh?" he questioned. "Do you now?"

Barreling ahead, Shinju nodded, determined to stand her ground. "You're related to Kami Raijin. That explains your powers and your name. Is he…your father?" she guessed.

"I suppose you're not as stupid as I first thought," Raiden retorted. "Though you still don't know much. You think announcing your name to someone like me is a good idea? What if I told someone about you and your little mission?"

Shinju crossed her arms stubbornly. "You wouldn't if you had any honor," she said. "Ha! Honor?" Raiden chuckled and shook his head, turning to go. "Honor is a fairytale, girl. No one has real honor in the world." An undertone of bitterness laced his words, and Shinju frowned curiously. What did he mean?

"Wait, where are you going?" she asked as he turned and began to walk. "Away from here," Raiden responded, not glancing back. "I've wasted enough time with you."

Shinju bit her lip, watching as he moved farther away, before jogging to catch up. "Wait," she requested, jumping in front of him with her arms stretched wide. "Get out of my way," he growled.

"Just listen, please!" She took a deep breath, hoping her instincts were not steering her wrong. "You're right. I am looking for something special, and I think you can help me with that." He rolled his eyes.

"Where have I heard that before? Forget it." He started to brush her aside.

"I'm hunting down the Kanju!" The words blurted out of her mouth, and Shinju could barely believe she had just divulged that secret. But she was desperate, and…something about Raiden made her feel that she could trust him.

Despite his words about honor, he had helped her escape. And he had not hurt her in any way…yet.

Raiden's eyes widened at her admission. "The Kanju?" he repeated slowly. "One of the legendary tide jewels? That's what you're after?"

Shinju nodded. "Yes. The Tsoma Clan have been in charge of guarding it for hundreds of years. But yesterday someone found our island and stole the jewel." The memory of that horrible night, and all that followed, flooded her vision.

"Didn't do so good of a job guarding it then," Raiden snorted. Shinju glared at him. "The thief had to be a very skilled ninja to get past our samurai. Someone who may have even been familiar with the clan."

That theory hurt the most, that someone could have betrayed them like that. To break the oath would be the highest form of betrayal. Shinju still hoped that suspicion was wrong.

"So if it is so important, why are you the only one looking

for it?" Raiden questioned, his expression turning thoughtful.

"The removal of the Kanju affected the magic in our home," Shinju explained. "After so many years of magic seeping into the island, the Tsoma Clan's lives have been intertwined with the magic of the Kanju. Everyone was…cursed, taken by the island in its desire to hang on to any magic left." She swallowed, her eyes burning as she thought of the terrible screams and panic and the very ground opened up and swallowed the Tsomas.

"I was the only one who could leave because I was not born there like everyone else."

Raiden's eyebrows rose at that, but he didn't ask about it further. Shinju drew a little closer, beseeching his help with her eyes. "I don't know how much time I have before…before it's too late. I know they are still alive, but I need to find the Kanju quickly, not just for my clan, but to protect it. If it should fall into the wrong hands, it could be used to wreak terrible things in the kingdom. Whoever controls the tide jewels holds unspeakable power."

He didn't answer right away, his face unreadable as he looked at her. "I don't know who I am up against, but I have an idea of where they might go next," Shinju continued. "I could really use your help."

She gave him a small smile when he still didn't respond. "Earlier you said there was something that you wanted, that you didn't think I could give. If you were to help restore the Kanju, we would reward you, but maybe Ryūjin-sama himself will rise from the sea and bestow a gift upon you!"

At that, he scoffed. "Don't count on the benevolence of a

Kami, no matter who they are." He stared off into the distance, scratching his chin. His eyes had a faraway look, like he was thinking of something other than their conversation. Shinju held her breath, waiting for his response.

"Fine," he finally said, folding his arms. "I'll help you find the Kanju."

"Oh, thank you, Raiden-sama!" Shinju placed her palms together and bowed, her heart light. This was going to be so much better than traveling alone, no matter how cranky this man was!

"Enough with the Raiden-sama business. Just Raiden is fine," he grumbled.

"As you wish," Shinju told him brightly.

"Well, where are we heading then?" he asked. "We should get out of the open, it won't take long for the gang to regroup and start searching for us."

Shinju smiled, pointing east. "We head that way, towards the next place this thief is likely to go."

"And where is that?" Raiden asked, squinting at the mountains rising in the distance. Shinju smiled.

"The location of the other tide jewel."

18

PUTTING AS MUCH DISTANCE between themselves and the gang's hideout was the most important objective at this point. The girl pulled out a wrinkled scroll and consulted it, her tongue sticking out of the corner of her mouth in thought. Raiden observed silently.

This young, unassuming girl was an enigma. Not only had she assisted in his own escape from the prison cell without a second thought, but she had also shown mercy to the gang leader, a man Raiden knew to be cruel and unyielding. And despite seeing his powers and knowing what he was, she had asked him to accompany her on her quest.

She was a fool. Yet he had agreed to help her, so maybe he was a fool as well, even if he had reasons for doing so.

Raiden had been tempted to knock her out of the way when she blocked his path and started babbling out nonsense about her clan, but the moment she mentioned the Kanju he froze.

He knew about the Kanju and the Manju, the legendary tide jewels created by the Kami dragon Ryūjin, bestowed upon mortals. They had disappeared so long ago that most assumed they had either never existed, or were lost, or that Ryūjin had taken them back to his palace under the sea.

Like most children, Raiden had heard the stories when he was young, and a memory of another time, when he was a different person, floated out of the haze of his life. A woman, pretty and simple, had held him tightly and whispered fantastical stories to him at night with only the light of a candle to see by. He'd held on to every word, not wanting the tales to end, and always begging for one more.

The memory cut like a knife through his heart, and he quickly shut it out, lest his face betray him. He had glared down at Shinju, her eyes hopeful and determined, and accepted her offer.

The girl was foolish, he thought again as she rolled her scroll up and directed their path into the forest. She knew almost nothing about him and chose to trust him. Sadly for her, she would learn the hard way what a mistake that was.

They walked in silence for some time, the girl occasionally glancing his way curiously, her gaze bouncing to his gauntlets. Raiden hoped she wasn't the talkative type. He'd been alone for a long time and liked it that way. No need to fill the space with useless jabbering.

"So!" she began, and he barely suppressed a groan. So much for no idle chit-chat.

"Where are you from, Raiden-san?" He bristled at the

formal address, but there was no point in correcting her. "Nowhere worth mentioning," he muttered. "I am, however, interested in where you come from."

He eyed her intently, taking in her appearance. She was petite, with long dark hair that fell to her waist. Her clothing, dirty from her time in the cell, consisted of a solid blue kimono, a gray obi, and pants tucked into simple boots.

Her golden skin was smooth and flawless except for a sprinkling of freckles, evidence of a life lived in the sun. It was a stark contrast to the ivory skin most women in Horitamo craved.

She was pretty, he thought, his mouth twitching. She walked with a kind of grace that didn't match that of a peasant's gait; more like a lady's. But she seemed completely ordinary. Nothing like the guardian of a magical object like the Kanju.

"How did you become a part of the Tsoma Clan, if you weren't born into it?"

"Takumi Tsoma found me after…my parents died," she answered quietly after a moment. "He offered me a new life, and it was that or trying to survive on my own. I chose the Tsomas."

Raiden nodded, mulling over her words. She was clearly leaving a lot out, but he could understand that. "And they taught you how to fight, or something like fighting."

She shot him a look of shock and irritation. "Excuse me? I beat just as many bad guys as you back there. And yes, they taught me to fight." She scowled and Raiden chuckled. She was too easy to rile up.

"You're not bad," he allowed, locking his hands behind his head. "But you've never had to fight for your life before, until then. Am I correct?"

She pouted. "Actually, I have fought a few yokai. It is part of our training." She cast a look behind them. "But that was my first time fighting other people…outside of sparring." A shadow passed over her face, and she fiddled with the handle of her katana.

"It gets easier," he told her. She blinked at him in confusion. "What does?" He smirked. "Killing."

The girl looked horrified and shook her head. "I don't believe that. I don't want to kill more people if I can help it."

"You may have to in order to get the Kanju back," he warned her. *You might have to kill me. Or you can try, at least.*

Her shoulders slumped. "I know. But I must get it back, no matter the cost." She clenched her fists and continued to march forward determinedly, and Raiden followed silently.

They trekked through the forest for a couple of hours, keeping to their own thoughts. The girl finally stopped, leaning against a tree. Raiden cocked his head, wondering if she was tired already.

"I'm sorry," she said bashfully. "I can't remember the last time I ate, and I'm sore and tired. What about you?" Raiden shrugged, unperturbed by such things. He'd gone a long time without food before, though the thought of a drink sounded good after the day he'd had.

"There's a town not far to the north," he mentioned, jerking his thumb in the right direction. "We could stop there and refresh supplies."

"Perfect!" she exclaimed, beaming up at him. She started to stretch, rolling her shoulders and raising her arms up and down.

"I'd like to have a bath there," she added in a dreamy voice.

"I'd like that too. You stink," Raiden deadpanned.

She reached out and slapped his arm, her cheeks growing red. "That's so rude, Raiden-san! You don't smell like a cherry blossom tree yourself, you know!" He laughed and walked away, letting her be the one to follow him now. She had spirit. He had to give her that.

The forest eventually thinned at the edge of a busy town. Lights shimmered from lanterns strung between the houses and shops, and the streets were bustling with peasants and merchants.

"It's so pretty," Shinju gushed, clasping her hands together as they neared. "This was a good choice, Raiden-san." He grunted, uncomfortable with her bubbly attitude. Was she always like this?

They followed the natural flow of the crowd until they reached an inn, marked as such by a banner decorated with cherry blossoms and sweeping writing in black paint. Raiden tugged at the sleeves of his tunic, pulling them down lower over his gauntlets. He didn't want to draw more attention to himself than he already would, with his eyes and stature.

Shinju watched his movements but didn't comment, instead heading for the door of the inn.

Inside, a few patrons sat on cushions at low tables, drinking and eating. A pleasant chime sounded as they entered, coming from a jade charm hanging above the door.

"Ah, welcome, welcome, travelers!" A little man met them, bowing multiple times. Shinju smiled and greeted him cheerfully, also bowing. Raiden took stock of the room as the innkeeper babbled: a few people turned and glanced their way, met his eyes, and looked away quickly, cowering over their food. Good, it didn't seem as though they would have any trouble here.

"Oh! Raiden-sama! It is you…again," the innkeeper babbled, straightening the tiny spectacles on his nose and beginning to tremble. "W-we are…always happy to have your…ah…p-patronage. You would like a room, yes?" he asked, sounding as though he hoped they would say no.

"Um." Shinju glanced at him and she blushed. "I'm sorry, Raiden-san, but I don't have any money. We don't use it on the island. I should have asked before we came…"

Raiden arched his brow. The Tsomas didn't use money? Curious.

He held up a hand, silencing her apologies. "It's fine. I have plenty."

He turned to the sweating innkeeper. "A room and baths for us both, as well as food. Whatever you have is fine. And a jug of sake." He handed the man a few coins, and he bowed and bobbed like a bird. "Thank you, thank you, my pleasure! Of course, Raiden-sama, whatever you wish! If you please, come this way."

As the innkeeper guided them to the upper levels of the inn, Shinju leaned back and whispered to Raiden, "The Kasuda Gang didn't take your money?"

He smirked and showed her the small bag of coin he'd tied to the inside of his tunic. "They did, I just took some back on our way out." Her eyes lit up with understanding, and she giggled. Raiden tried to ignore the warmth in his chest at the sound.

They were led to different washrooms, a maid taking over for Shinju. The innkeeper showed Raiden to a room with a large tub. A maid was pouring in some steaming water. On a little stool rested a bar of soap and a pinch of lavender petals.

Raiden nodded his thanks and quickly stripped down, eager to get the bath over with. It wasn't that he didn't like to be clean, but he hated feeling vulnerable in any way; naked in a tub where anyone could burst in was not high on his list of places to be caught unawares.

As he scrubbed the dirt, blood, and sweat off his skin, Raiden's thoughts wandered back to the girl. He led a solitary life, preferring to avoid people as much as possible, and they avoided him. His eyes, the gauntlets, and the power he wielded, not to mention his name, made him a cursed man. People were either afraid of him, or they blamed him for ridiculous things like their failed crops.

It was beyond his understanding why the girl would want him to accompany her, even with the advantage of his skills aiding in her quest.

He dunked his head under the water and shook the hair out of his eyes like a dog. Better to stop trying to figure out Shinju Tsoma, and focus on what he had to do, which was to steal the tide jewels at the earliest opportunity.

19

The bath was wonderful. Shinju had never washed harder in her life, trying to remove any residue of the prison from her flesh. Thankfully, when she had taken her bag back, her change of clothes had still been untouched. She put them on gratefully, making a mental note to stop somewhere along the way to wash her other ones.

The maid from before arrived as Shinju was running a comb through her hair and offered to assist her in putting it up or braiding it. Shinju thanked her shyly but insisted on doing it herself.

"You are lucky to have such a fearsome man," the maid commented as she led Shinju out of the washroom. "Raiden-sama is a most intimidating warrior."

"Oh! Um, er, yes," Shinju stuttered, taken aback by the girl's comment and blushing face. Was this how people talked on the mainland? She supposed Raiden was rather handsome, and imposing, but she had been trying not to think about it; they'd been fleeing for their lives after all.

The girl pouted, unimpressed with Shinju's response. Likely she'd been hoping for some tantalizing gossip to share with the other servants.

They entered another small, private room, and Shinju's stomach immediately growled at the sight and smell of food on a low table. Bowls of rice, vegetables, and a teapot wafted delicious scents her way. Under the table spread a comfortable rug with two worn but plump cushions.

"*Arigato,*" Shinju told the maid, giving her a bow. The maid giggled and bobbed before leaving.

Shinju approached the table and sat, wondering how long she should wait for Raiden, when the man in question slid the paper door open. His hair was still wet and hung around his face, water droplets falling onto his tunic. His eyes immediately met Shinju's and she smiled, trying to avoid getting sucked into them again.

"*Konbonwa*, Raiden-san," she greeted. He gave a noncommittal grunt and sat across from her, reaching for a pair of chopsticks. Shinju followed suit, and they ate in silence for a few minutes.

"So," he ventured after a few minutes. "How did this thief you're tracking defeat your strong samurai?" Shinju tried to ignore the slight mocking edge to his voice. "He used knives and some kind of poison dart."

Raiden paused in his eating.

"This dart," he said. "Show it to me."

"Um, okay." Shinju stuffed some more rice into her mouth, then reached into her bag, careful not to touch the tip of the dart as she drew it out and handed it over to him.

He held it in his large hand, twirling it slowly and thoughtfully. "How many of these had been used to take down the guards?" he asked.

"I'm not sure. I only found that one. But some of the guards had their throats cut or were killed in other ways." She shuddered, not wanting to remember that terrible scene.

"The ones that were killed by the dart…the poison must have worked its way quickly through their systems before they noticed anything." Repeating the events of that night brought a pang of sorrow to her chest. She had grown up knowing those samurai just as well as any other member of the clan. She still couldn't believe they were gone.

"I recognize this," Raiden announced. Shinju blinked at him in surprise, then placed her hands on the table and leaned forward excitedly. "Really? You do?"

He nodded. "I once took a job with an Otami ninja who used darts like these. Very skilled."

"You did?" Shinju's eyes grew wide. "Do you know why he would steal the Kanju?"

"Obviously he was hired to do so," Raiden explained, laying the dart on the table. "Back when we worked together, the man was in the employ of the daimyo of Itshino Province."

Shinju tensed at the mention of that place. Truth be told, it had been far in the back of her mind this whole journey. As focused as she was on her mission, Shinju couldn't deny that the thought of her old home had crossed her mind since returning to the mainland.

"Oh?" she asked, hoping her voice did not sound shaky as she picked at her vegetables.

"It's possible that the daimyo may know who hired your thief, or where he is. Either way, it may benefit us to go there and find out," Raiden added.

Shinju considered this. He had a good point. If they could catch the thief, or Otami, whoever he was, in Itshino, then there would be no need to travel further to try to find the location of the other tide jewel, and she could return home sooner to restore the Kanju.

But going to Itshino would also mean an encounter with her past life. A life she had tried to put behind her.

Trying to act natural, Shinju reached for another bite of food. "What is the name of this daimyo?" she asked.

"Lady Hono."

Chopsticks clattered to the table as Shinju stared at Raiden in horror. "Lady…Hono?" she repeated in a strangled whisper.

He raised an eyebrow, taking in her reaction. "What is it?"

A familiar wave of fear washed over Shinju as she struggled inwardly with this revelation. For years, Takumi and the other elders had coached her in letting go of her grief and guilt about the death of her parents. Holding on to these feelings would only bring misery and restrain her ability to gain clarity and peace in life.

Shinju thought she had succeeded in burying her past and become reborn as a Tsoma. So then why did the mention of her aunt's name stir such trepidation in her stomach?

Shinju had assumed long ago that the Shogun would have

chosen a new daimyo for the province, but she had never considered that Hono might be placed in that position. And why would her aunt associate with a clan like the Otami?

"Hey!" Raiden clicked his chopsticks together in front of her face, bringing her out of her thoughts. "Where'd you go?" he questioned, looking at her oddly.

Shinju ran a hand through her hair, taking a deep breath and trying to calm her beating heart. "*Gomen*, Raiden-san, it was rude of me to just withdraw like that. It's just…I did not expect you to say that name."

Raiden furrowed his brow and studied her skeptically. His eyes were glowing a deep silvery blue in the dimly lit room, and they seemed to grow even more intense in color. "You know Lady Hono, don't you?" It was more of a statement than a question.

Shinju hesitated, then nodded, swallowing hard. If they were to work together, she would have to be honest with him. "Yes. She is…my aunt."

That certainly surprised her companion. He straightened, even lowering his chopsticks and ignoring the next bite of food. "Your aunt, huh?" He scratched his chin, mulling over this information. "But that would mean you're the niece of a daimyo. Why didn't you live with her when your parents died?"

Shinju shifted in place, her fingers idly tracing the grain in the table. "It's complicated."

"Hm. Family is always complicated." He said it lightly, but Shinju glanced up in time to see him look away, his jaw hardening as he too seemed to slip into his thoughts.

"Anyways," Shinju continued after a moment, "I doubt

she'll want to see me. I don't think we'll have a chance at getting an audience with her."

"She might. If not for you, then for me. She will remember me," Raiden replied.

Shinju swallowed hard, considering the possibility of seeing her old home again…of seeing Hono again. Her eyes burning, Shinju tilted her head back and blinked, staring up at the ceiling. "I really don't want to."

The words, spoken so softly, sounded loud in that small room. "I never thought I would go back there," she added. They sat in silence for several minutes as Shinju fought to collect herself. Finally, she looked back at Raiden with a sad smile.

"I'm sorry again, Raiden-san. It is not right for me to burden you with my problems. There is something more important happening now, and if you think my aunt may know something that could help us find this thief, or assassin, then I must face her."

The man across from her nodded slowly, looking slightly confused. Shinju cocked her head curiously. "What kind of work did you do for Lady Hono?"

"It was some years ago," Raiden responded. "Lady Hono wanted to send a message to someone she had a…disagreement with, and the coin was good." He shrugged. "I cared nothing for the politics or the grievances between them. I hired myself out, did the job, and left."

Shinju chewed her lip, mulling over his words. Her aunt sounded like a stranger, and nothing like the reserved, perfect lady that Shinju had known in her childhood. How much had changed in the past ten years?

A thought occurred to her, one that chilled her blood. "You…you don't think Aunt Hono is the one who sent the thief to the island to steal the Kanju, do you?" she questioned, dreading his answer.

Raiden shrugged, shoveling in another mouth-full of food. "I don't know, but you should be prepared for that possibility."

Shinju leaned her head in her hand. Things were getting more and more complex. She felt as though she knew even less than when she left the island. Unfortunately, it seemed that her best option was to go see Hono and discover what she could.

Reaching for her food, even though it had lost some of its appeal, Shinju glanced at Raiden.

"So…you're a sellsword," Shinju stated slowly. Raiden cracked a sideways grin. "I'm whatever gets me by at the time, girl. Like I told you before, I'm not someone you should be around."

He spoke in a confident, honest way, but underneath the timber of his voice, Shinju detected something else that sounded a lot like bitterness.

"I see. Well, you still don't scare me, Raiden-san," she told him brightly, pouring a new cup of tea.

He snorted, shaking his head and reaching the mug of sake. "Yet."

20

IT WAS FULLY DARK when they left the inn. Raiden had grown restless after their meal. He didn't like to spend time in larger populated areas very often. Someone like him attracted attention, and he doubted the patrons from the inn would keep his presence to themselves.

Shinju seemed just as eager to leave as he did. They paid their respects to the innkeeper and returned to the streets, which were just as active now as they had been earlier in the day. The girl gazed around them in delight at the music, swinging lanterns, and food carts that wafted delicious smells through the town. Most of the provinces were celebrating the Festival of Lanterns all week.

Raiden couldn't help but think about Shinju's face earlier when he mentioned Lady Hono's name. The pain and sorrow in her eyes told him there was some unspoken conflict between her and her aunt over her parents' deaths, but he couldn't imagine what. She'd said before that the Tsomas found her and took her in…why? How had she ended up on a remote island hundreds of miles from Itshino?

He shook his head. He shouldn't concern himself with her and what this meeting with Lady Hono might mean. It was none of his business. Caring for others was a weakness and had only brought him misery. The girl would have to handle the situation herself; she was no longer on her island where everyone lived at peace.

Truth be told, he wasn't too keen on encountering the daimyo of Itshino again either. Raiden had no doubts that Lady Hono would be willing to see him. She had, after all, told him when they last met that he knew where to find her if he ever wanted work again. She'd hinted at a few other things too, things that convinced him to never take her up on the offer.

They reached the edge of the town without incident, few people noticing them in the midst of the festivities. The ones that did could not meet his gaze for more than a few seconds.

Cowards.

Raiden flexed his arms; he was growing irritable, and when he grew irritable, the kami side of him began spoiling for a fight.

The girl was unusually quiet as they left the town behind and continued on the dark, winding road. No doubt she was thinking about seeing her aunt again and coming to terms with that part of her past.

Grinding his teeth, Raiden pulled the sleeves of his tunic over his gauntlets as moonlight from above cast them in an eerie glow. No need to flash those around out here, attracting bandits to slow them down; they were on a tight schedule after all.

As soon as they found the tide jewels, Raiden could continue his purpose in life: hunting down and slaughtering the man who had taken everything from him.

And the girl walking next to him would not get in his way.

21

THEY JOURNEYED ON THE road for some time, passing no else. Their path was lit by the bright moon above, seeming to bless their mission. Shinju yawned and rubbed her eyes. She had not slept since being knocked out by the Kasuda Gang, and a full stomach was making her sleepy.

"Want to rest a while?" Raiden asked, glancing at her as she yawned again. She sighed, feeling torn between pressing on or taking a break.

"I want to keep going, but I don't think I'll be able to if I don't get some sleep," she admitted, hating that she couldn't stay awake longer. But she hadn't slept in almost two days and had had to fight her way out of a throng of murderous bandits. She would not be fit to stop the thief and protect the tide jewels in this condition.

Raiden didn't look tired at all. She wondered, being part

kami, if he ever slept, or felt exhaustion the same way regular humans did. His eyes were still glowing, though much dimmer than before, as he scanned the land around them.

Her companion led her off the road and into the shelter of a grove. They found the remains of another traveler's fire and in a few minutes, Raiden had a small blaze crackling before them.

Shinju leaned against a tree, wrapping her long sleeves around her as she hugged herself. She found herself studying Raiden, who sat on the other side of the fire, legs and arms crossed as he glared into the flames. The shiny plates of his gauntlets drew her attention as she smothered another yawn.

"So," she began. "Do you get your lightning from your gauntlets? Is that why you never take them off?"

Raiden's eyes narrowed for a moment, as if trying to figure out her motive for asking. She gave him a smile and he snorted. "Come on, who am I going to tell?" she prodded. "I'll keep it a secret. I'm really good at keeping secrets."

"That sounds like something someone who doesn't keep secrets would say," Raiden answered drily. "But, no. The lightning…I channel it from the air around me. My fists are like a conduit for the charge. These," he held up his arms so that the silver glinted in the firelight, "help me control the lightning. Without them, my powers are unpredictable, and I don't like feeling unbalanced in a fight."

Shinju nodded, pleased that he had told her. She was curious about his life, what it must be like being part kami. "Did you make them?" she asked. "They are very beautiful." He didn't answer for so long she thought he was going to ignore her.

"Someone gave them to me," he finally said.

"Wow," she murmured. She wondered if it had been Raiden's father, Raijin-sama, who had made the gauntlets. If so, she didn't understand why he did not say that.

"I've never met a half-kami before," she mentioned thoughtfully. "What is it like, being one?"

Raiden glared at her, then he gave a sharp, mocking laugh. "Oh, it's a real privilege," he snarled. "You want to know what it's like, being treated with revulsion wherever you go, because with one glance people can tell you're not quite human, that you're dangerous, that you're worth only what for what you can give them?" He shook his head.

Shinju gawked at him, stunned by this sudden flood of words from the warrior who had barely spoken until now.

"I'm sorry, I didn't mean to offend you," Shinju apologized humbly. "I was just curious. But it was rude of me to pry." The man across from her only snorted and turned away, looking off into the woods.

"I'm sorry that you have been treated that way by others." He was like a mean dog, she realized as she studied his sour expression. A mean dog who bit and growled at everyone after too much abuse.

"I don't want your pity, girl," Raiden turned his eyes back to her, and they glowed even brighter. His jaw was clenching and unclenching. "Spare me your polite sorrys."

"I don't pity you," she argued softly. "Is it wrong for me to feel sad about what you've endured?"

He blinked, still glaring, but now looking a little unsure. "Why should you?" he asked.

"Because you matter, Raiden-san. And I don't care if you're

half-kami or not." She smiled, and after a long moment he looked away, as if uncomfortable.

"Whatever helps you go to sleep faster," he muttered. "I'll take the first watch."

Shinju nodded, and for a few minutes she watched the firelight dance as her eyelids grew heavier and heavier, and her head began to nod. She settled further against the tree and murmured, "I am glad you are with me, Raiden-san. I…don't think we met…by accident…"

Her eyes closed and she drifted towards sleep, and she never knew if he answered or not.

The water flowed around her, caressing her skin with cool fingers. She gasped for air, then realized she had no difficulty breathing. The current pushed her along, paying no heed to her flailing limbs.

Down she shot toward the murky depths. Everything grew colder and darker. Bubbles danced up from her body, swirling towards the diminishing light above. Shinju wondered how much farther she must go. When would she reach the end of this never-ending descent?

Then, something flashed below her, growing larger with every second. The gleam of spires in a pearlescent glow broke through the midnight water, so bright that Shinju had to squint and blink, waiting for her eyes to adjust. Seaweed waved in long, tall towers surrounding the structure. As she grew closer, Shinju could see the walls and spires were covered with shells and pearls and colorful coral.

She realized then where she was. The palace of Ryūjin, the great dragon Kami of the seas.

How had she come to be here? Why? The questions swirled in her mind as the current brought Shinju along, slowing slightly as she reached a large opening in the palace.

Her heart stuttered as she gazed into the gateway to the dragon's home. She had been told how large he was through stories, but…

All thoughts vanished as two eyes the size of islands appeared in the dark haze, blinking at her. They were green and blue and gold, and the pupils were shaped like slits as they took her in. Steam rose from between the eyes.

A shudder passed through her as a voice, deep and ancient and terrible, whispered her name. "Shinjuuuu Tsomaaaa."

Shinju gasped and started from her sleep, almost falling sideways into the grass. Heart in her throat, she scanned her surroundings, blinking in the firelight. Raiden still sat across from her, watching with an amused expression.

"Bad dream?" he asked. Shinju took several deep breaths as she righted herself, letting her head fall back with a *thunk* against the tree. "Not exactly," she mused, thinking back over what she had seen.

First the dream about the thief, and now this? What did it mean?

"Have you ever had a dream so real that you really believed it?" she whispered. Raiden thought for a moment. "Yes." He studied her closely. "You must have had some dream. You're shaking." Then he gave a devilish smirk. "Was it something naughty? Maybe about me?"

Shinju shot him a withering glare. "You wish," she

responded, trying to ignore the heat flooding her cheeks. He only chuckled and stood, stretching his arms up in the air. "We should move on, if you're awake," was all he said.

The night had begun to lighten into the early gray hours of dawn. Shinju rose to her feet and stretched as well, feeling the sore muscles from fighting the day before. That was good though; it reminded her of why she was out here. For a few minutes she followed her morning routine of stretches and then spared a little water to wash her face with.

Raiden had tramped off somewhere into the forest, and just when Shinju had begun wondering where he went, he returned to the fire, a pair of small rabbits dangling from his fist. "I'll skin and roast these quickly and we can eat as we walk," he told her. Shinju nodded and, not wanting to partake in that messy business, excused herself to tend to personal needs.

As she searched for a spot a short way from camp, she mulled over the dream that lingered in her thoughts. The last time she'd had a dream like that, it had come true. Could this be the same? Would she really go down to the palace of Ryūjin himself? It seemed too fantastical. No human, as far as she was aware, had ever done such a thing.

Once she finished, she walked slowly back to Raiden, where he was turning the rabbits over the fire with sticks. "Not long now," he said. Fat sizzled and dripped off the rabbits, and Shinju's stomach gave a loud rumble. Digging into her pack, she withdrew some rice balls purchased from the town. Her other food had disappeared at the gang's hideout.

She offered Raiden a rice ball, and in exchange he gave her one of the rabbits. They stamped out the fire, swept over their footprints with a branch, and headed back to the road, munching on the meager breakfast.

"How far are we from Itshino province?" Shinju asked as she licked her fingers. The rabbit was unseasoned and a little bland, but the meat was tender.

"A couple of days' worth of walking," Raiden replied, tearing off a large chuck of rabbit with his teeth. "I would start thinking about what you're going to say to Lady Hono."

That dampened Shinju's mood a little as they kept to the edge of the trees, following the road from afar. She didn't want to think about that, but he was right. "Hello, Aunt, it's me, back from the dead," she muttered, kicking a rock. "What if she asks why we want to know about the thief?"

Raiden shrugged. "Make something up or stick as close to the truth as you can. Doesn't matter to me as long as you get the information you need."

"What was my aunt like when you worked for her?" Shinju wanted to know. Raiden shot her a glance with his piercing eyes, the glowing colors more subdued this morning. "She's nothing like you," he answered simply, and turned away to continue eating.

22

THE LANDSCAPE SLOWLY DIPPED and changed as they neared the province of Shinju's birth; instead of wooded areas, the terrain turned flat with long, waving grasses. Memories of her child-hood continued to trickle into the front of her mind, escaping past the doorway she'd carefully kept them locked behind.

Takumi and the other elders of the clan believed that she had accepted that her parents' deaths were accidents, and Shinju allowed them to by playing her part. She repeated all the right words and behaved as she should. But deep inside, the little ten-year-old girl was still there, struggling with grief and guilt over Io and Airi's deaths.

She still blamed herself, and no matter how many times she went over that day in her mind, trying to figure out how she could have chosen the wrong ingredients in the kitchen, how a poison could have slipped in; nothing became clear to her, and the lack of closure on how they could have been poisoned ate away at her heart.

It was not the clan's fault, she knew. They had done what they could for her. But how could they truly help, when she hadn't even told them the truth?

Fear kept it a secret. Fear kept her from spilling her soul to the man who'd been like a father to her. It choked and withheld the words, until Shinju decided she would simply try to forget, and began to separate her old life from her new one.

The locked door in her mind had held for a long time, but now, having returned to the mainland of Horitamo and only a day or two's journey from Itshino Province, Shinju struggled with the flood of internal fears and uncertainties that seeped past her mental defenses.

Would Aunt Hono recognize her? Would she be angry that Shinju had returned?

Raiden remained silent, leaving her to her thoughts. Shinju tried to focus on the reason she was even here to distract her. Not knowing exactly who or where the thief was provided an endless fountain of anxiety, and more than once she considered if they should just forget going to see Hono and instead head for the other tide jewel.

How could she make the right decision when there was so much she did not know?

"I wish Peiku were here," she whispered, missing the furry tanuki's calming presence. When she held and pet him, her worries grew more bearable.

"Peiku?" A voice interrupted her thoughts. She glanced up

at Raiden, who watched her with narrowed eyes. "Who is that?"

"He's kind of my pet tanuki," Shinju explained, stepping carefully around a pothole in the road. Now that they were farther from any towns, Raiden thought it would be safe enough to travel on the Emperor's Road, which stretched across Horitamo.

"A pet tanuki?" He shook his head. "Of course you would have one of those."

"What does that mean?" Shinju inquired.

"You're an odd girl. It fits that you would have an odd pet," Raiden answered with a smirk.

Shinju batted his arm. "I'm not odd! Besides, Peiku is great! Even if he does steal food and chase the chickens sometimes."

Raiden rolled his eyes. "Sounds like a trouble-maker. I would turn him into a snack."

Shinju gasped in dismay. "Absolutely not! Peiku is not for eating! How can you even suggest it?"

Her companion laughed, a deep, grating sound that sent a funny flutter through her stomach. "I'm guessing they don't teach sarcasm on your island."

It was Shinju's turn to narrow her eyes and she crossed her arms with a huff. "Well, it's not exactly common practice to tease someone about eating their pet there."

"Hmmm, not sure I'd fit in there then," Raiden commented, then he clenched his mouth closed quickly, as if he'd said something he hadn't meant to.

"Actually, you would! There's a lot of rules, almost all of which I've had to break on this journey, but it's a beautiful place full of magic!" Shinju gushed, forgetting her previous irritation.

"I don't like rules," Raiden countered. "I'm not going to be confined." A glint entered his strange eyes.

Shinju regarded him thoughtfully. She'd almost forgotten that he was half-kami, an anomaly. Not only that, being the offspring of Raijin clearly meant he had inherited the wild unpredictability of his sire.

It should frighten her, she supposed. Raiden had reminded her several times now that he was dangerous, something that most people did not want to be around. Just how much of him was more kami than human?

She remembered how he fought the Kasuda Gang, using his lightning to turn them into charred remains. And he'd laughed as he fought, enjoying himself. She shuddered. Yes, she should be frightened.

Instead she found herself growing more curious about him, wanting to know more, like a moth drawn to flame. Besides, it kept her distracted from her own problems.

"What were you doing before you were thrown into that cell by the Kasuda Gang?" she asked, ignoring his last comment.
"Looking for a job," Raiden replied, giving her a wary glance.
"More mercenary mischief?" she asked with a raised brow.

He let out a huff. "Something like that."

"It's a good thing we did meet, after all," Shinju affirmed. It could not be a coincidence that they had crossed paths, she thought satisfactorily.

Raiden scoffed at that. "Not sure about that, yet. This better be worth my time."

"Because you were so busy before, playing shogi and getting thrown in cells," Shinju couldn't resist saying, adding a slight edge to her tone. He scowled at her and she smiled innocently. "What, don't they teach sarcasm where you're from?"

"Nice," he growled, but the side of his mouth turned up as he slid his gaze towards her. "So what else do you like to do?" Shinju asked casually. She reached down, plucking a small flower that grew bravely next to the wheel cart path that had made indentions in the road. She twirled it near her face, smelling the fragrance.

"What do you mean?" he asked.

"I mean, what do you do for fun? You can't work all the time, right?" Shinju thought wistfully about the games the Tsomas would play on the island.

"I don't have fun," he rasped. "Unless you count the occasional fight. But not many people are a big enough challenge for me."

"You don't have fun?" Shinju repeated in shock. "How can you not have fun, Raiden-san?" She moved in front of him on the road, walking backwards so she could look up into his face.

He frowned at her. "I just said fighting is fun." "Yes, but that can't be all," Shinju protested. He rubbed his chin, staring down at her. A slow grin spread over his face. "Well, there *is* something else that's fun," he drawled.

"What is it?" Shinju asked, taking a quick glance behind her to make sure she wasn't going to trip over anything in the road.

He chuckled. "You sure you want to know?" "Yes," Shinju replied, puzzled. "Why wouldn't I?"

He bit his bottom lip, slowly dragging it out from between his teeth. "Maybe I'll show you one day," he said, his voice deepening into a husky timber that sent a trail of shiver up and down Shinju's spine. She blushed and turned back to walk forwards again.

"You're a horrible flirt, Raiden-san," she told him, dismissing the conversation with her hand.

"Not the worst thing I've been called," she heard him snicker behind her, but he dropped the subject as well.

By the time the sun hung high overhead, beating upon them with stifling rays, Shinju grew hot and tired and thirsty. She unplugged the little canteen of water in her back and drank carefully, not wanting a single drop to go to waste.

"How long have we been walking?" she wanted to know. The terrain had not changed much; the road wound through flat, grassy land and dipped occasionally through valleys. In the distance to the east she could see a mountain range wreathed in fog. They must be the Kyosho Mountains, which divide the eastern coastline from the rest of Horitamo.

"A few hours," Raiden replied. "It would be faster if we had horses or a cart, but we don't have enough coin for that."

Shinju sighed, reaching her arms up to stretch. She hadn't walked so far at once in her entire life. At this rate, she worried they wouldn't reach her aunt in time to stop the thief before he handed the Kanju over to whoever had hired him.

A voice drifted towards them from behind, and they both tensed. "Hya! Let's go!" it said, followed by the faint slap of reins.

"Go behind these trees," Raiden told Shinju, moving off to the side of the road and clenching his fists. "What? I'm not going to hide!" she protested. "Fine," he sighed. "Just be ready in case it's the Gang."

After a few minutes, two brown heads appeared over the rise. Horned, with large, watery eyes, the oxen mooed and trod diligently down the road, pulling a cart. Above them rode a weathered farmer, his straw hat pushed back on his head and a tune whistling from his mouth.

Shinju relaxed, replacing her fighting stance with a friendly wave. "*Konichiwa*!" she called out. The farmer turned to look at them in surprise, then pulled on his reins to bring the cart to a stop.

"What are you doing?" Raiden hissed. "Getting us a ride, obviously," Shinju whispered. She strode forward to greet the farmer. "Excuse me," she said with a bow. "My companion and I have been walking a long time. If it is no trouble, would you be so kind as to give us a ride in the back of your cart?"

The farmer stared down at her, then shifted to look at Raiden, who hung back. "Ah, I suppose so," he answered slowly. "Where are you heading?"

Shinju told him, and the farmer nodded. "I'll be stopping at a village not far from there. I'm afraid there's not much room in my cart as it is filled with turnips."

Shinju peeked over the edge of the cart, noting the mountain of white and red vegetables. "That's alright!" she answered cheerfully. "I'm sure we will be very comfortable. Thank you for your hospitality." She bowed again, and the farmer shook his head with a bemused expression. "Er, okay."

"Let's go!" Shinju called to Raiden, who finally trudged forward reluctantly. They climbed into the back of the cart, settling in amongst the vegetables.

Raiden scowled at Shinju, who only smiled. "This is much

better than walking," she whispered. Raiden flicked away a turnip that had rolled into his lap. "I hate turnips," he said.

Shinju rolled her eyes. "Why am I not surprised?"

The farmer clicked his tongue and the oxen moved forward again. Over the rough road they bounced and shook, listening to his whistling and the huffing sounds of cattle.

Ignoring Raiden's irritation, Shinju settled back and closed her eyes, allowing the rocking of the cart to lull her to sleep.

23

A LIGHT DRIZZLE WOKE Shinju from her nap. She'd slept longer than she'd expected, and when she opened her eyes, gone were the sun's rays, replaced by dark, somber rain-clouds.

She wiped at the water on her face and glanced over at Raiden. He had fallen asleep as well, it would seem. His chin dipped low, resting on his chest, and his arms were folded over his crossed legs. *Even when he sleeps he looks cross*, Shinju thought with a grin.

Muscles sore and stiff from sitting in one place for so long, Shinju stretched as best she could, then looked out at the road ahead of them. Past the farmer, she could see a village rising out of the gloom. It didn't look like much, she thought, taking in the sad row of houses and shops, shuttered and wilting under the rain.

"We are almost there," the farmer sang out, glancing over his shoulder. "*Arigato*," Shinju told him, then she turned to wake up Raiden.

"Pssst, Raiden-san," she said, and when he didn't stir, she picked up a turnip and tossed it at his chest. It hit him with a thump and instantly startled him from sleep. His eyes snapped open and his arms uncrossed, tense and ready to fight. He fixed his glare on Shinju, who was laughing behind her hand.

"I'm sorry," she giggled. "That…that was so funny!"

"Tch!" Raiden relaxed slightly and glowered at her. "There are nicer ways of waking a man up, you know." He yawned and reached his arms up to stretch. Shinju blushed as she watched his biceps flex, and she looked away, suddenly very interested in the turnips piled around her.

The cart ambled on into the village as the rain started to fall harder. Shinju squinted at the houses, wondering where everyone was. Even on a rainy day, people should be out working. Not a soul was in sight, not even a stray dog or chicken.

An eerie feeling crept over her as she studied the closed doors and windows they passed.

A glance at Raiden confirmed that he felt similarly. His eyes flicked around the quiet village with mistrust.

The farmer pulled up to a house near the end of the narrow street and jumped down. "Well, here we are!" he announced. Was the smile on his face genuine? Shinju gave him a shaky one in return and climbed out of the cart.

"We appreciate your generosity," she told him. "I'm afraid we wouldn't be able to pay you much for the ride." The farmer looked at them both with a strange expression, as if weighing something in his mind.

"We should go now," Raiden huffed behind her.

"Go now? But you'll catch a cold, walking in all this rain! Come, come, you must enter my home and dry yourselves and wait for the skies to clear," the farmer insisted. He sounded nervous, Shinju thought, watching as his eyes darted between them and the hut.

"Thank you, but we are in a hurry," Shinju answered, backing away a few steps.

"You can't!" the farmer cried out hysterically, his hands reaching for her. Shinju reared back, placing a hand on her katana. Raiden snarled at her side. "Out of the way, peasant, or you'll regret it," he spat.

"You must pay tribute!" the farmer insisted, wringing his hands. "All must pay tribute to her."

Frowning, Shinju cocked her head. "Who?"

"Doesn't matter," Raiden snapped, grabbing her arm and starting to drag her away. "This place is wrong; can't you feel it?"

The farmer suddenly reached into the cart and withdrew a rusty but wickedly shaped sickle, aiming it at them. "I can't let you!"

"*Baka*! You think you can stop us?" Raiden growled. Static filled the air around them, raising Shinju's hair on end despite the dampness. Lightning began to flicker around Raiden's fists and his eyes flashed menacingly.

The farmer gasped and began to shake. "You're… you're yokai," he stammered. Raiden scoffed, planting his feet apart. "Not even close, peasant, but you'll still regret crossing me."

"Why are you trying to stop us from leaving?" Shinju asked.

Regardless of the man's intentions, he seemed desperate, and she didn't want to kill him if they didn't have to.

"*She* will demand tribute," he muttered, his eyes white and wild. "Who?" Shinju demanded.

"Me, of course," came a soft voice from the hut. They spun around, and Shinju gasped.

A tall, thin woman dressed in red stood before them, leaning one delicate hand on the doorway. Her skin shone pale in the rain. Her eyes were large and dark, her lips bright red. She gave a slow, spreading smile as she looked Raiden up and down.

"My, my, what have you brought me today, Korin?"

The farmer went to his knees, bowing low in spite of the mud. Shinju watched nervously, unsure of what to make of this woman and her eyes that made her skin crawl.

The lightning did not fade from Raiden's fists. "It's no concern of yours what we are," he told the woman. "We are leaving."

The woman kept smiling, but her gaze sharpened. "Oh, I don't think so. You heard my servant, after all. A tribute must be paid." She seemed to flicker, almost as if she wasn't really there, then suddenly she launched herself at Raiden, mouth open wide in a blood-curdling scream.

Shinju drew her katana and stepped forward as Raiden grabbed the woman's wrists, holding her back as she tried to scrape him with long, cruel nails. With a roar, he shot a blast of lighting at her, and she flew backwards, landing in the mud.

Korin got to his feet and approached Shinju with his sickle, raising it above his head. Shinju knocked his attack aside with her katana, edging backwards as she tried to keep an eye on both him and the strange woman.

"What's going on? Why are you doing this?" she demanded.

The woman, growling, raised herself up on her arms, and to Shinju's shock, one side of her face tore away, revealing the skeleton beneath. "She's a Hone-onna," Raiden growled. "A yokai that preys on the lifeforce of men."

Her tongue flicked over her red lips as the woman rose upright. "How insightful of you, my dear. And to think, my next prize will be the offspring of Raijin himself!"

Raiden smirked, fresh lighting flowing across his gauntlets. "I'm no one's prize, yokai scum. You might hold this village in your grasp, but I'm the one to be feared here."

With a scream, the Hone-onna threw herself at him once more, and Shinju was kept occupied by the farmer's swinging sickle. He screamed at her, his face contorted by fear. Shinju knew he must have been a good man, once. He probably brought travelers to his village to give to the Hone-onna so she wouldn't kill him and the other villagers.

Shinju ducked a wide swipe and then brought her katana down, slicing the sickle out of his hand. The man screamed, falling to the ground and clutching his bleeding hand.

Behind them, Raiden and the yokai fought, the half-kami shooting lightning at her, but she was quicker this time, dodging his attacks, trying to get close. Shinju turned back to the sniffling farmer.

"Don't try to stop us," she told him. "We will defeat this yokai and your village will be safe again." She kicked the sickle farther away from his grasp, then turned to the other fight.

Raiden panted, wiping the rain and tendrils of hair out of

his face as he confronted the yokai. Shinju wondered why he did not draw his sword; it seemed as though he was having a hard time hitting her with his lightning.

With an angry shout, Raiden suddenly raised his arms above his head, the lightning spiraling up down his fists and intertwining in the air. Thinking she had an opening, the Hone-onna pulled herself into a crouch, then sprinted towards him, another terrifying scream bursting from her throat.

Shinju started forward with a shout, raising ker katana, but skidded to halt when Raiden yelled, "No, stay back!"

A giant bolt of pure, white-hot lightning erupted from the clouds above, streaking its way downwards. It struck the yokai head-on as she leapt through the air, and her scream faded as her body burnt. Within seconds, only a charred remnant remained, disintegrating into the muddy street.

Shaking, Shinju ripped her eyes from the Hone-onna's corpse to Raiden, who slowly lowered his arms, then fell to his knees. "Raiden-san!" She hurried towards him. Static still clung to her, and when she reached him she felt a strange heat rippling through the air.

"Are you alright?" she asked, dropping to her knees as well. She wanted to help him, but little tendrils of lightning still lingered around his arms, and she wasn't sure if she would be shocked.

"Fine," Raiden grunted, still panting. "Just give me a minute." Shinju glanced over at the yokai, wincing at the horrible scene. "That was scary," she whispered. "I've never seen one like that."

"We need to get out of here," he repeated, and with a groan

he pushed to his feet.

"Yokai! Demon!" The farmer was gasping, pointing at Raiden with his bloody hand. Faces began to appear in windows, and a few doors cracked open as the villagers peered out in fear.

Shinju rounded on him. "Are you crazy?" she exclaimed angrily. "We just saved you and your village from a yokai! You should be thanking us!"

But the farmer was too overcome with fear. "Get out of here!" he shouted, grabbing a handful of mud and throwing it in their direction. "Hey!" Shinju yelped.

"Let's go," Raiden growled, and he spat into the earth. "This place smells of cowards."

Keeping her hands nearby to catch him just in case he stumbled, Shinju followed Raiden slowly out of the village. She wondered wearily what else would be in store for them by the time they reached Itshino.

24

RAIN CONTINUED TO FALL in a dreary curtain as they plodded across a giant field, the long grass swiping at their ankles. Raiden was slowly regaining his energy; he could already feel the power strengthening, coursing through his body.

He felt annoyed that he'd had to resort to such an attack for a minor yokai. Perhaps he was getting soft. It had been too long since he'd had a real challenge, a chance to test his limits.

Glancing at the girl walking beside him, Raiden reflected silently on the way she had defended him at the village. With no thought to her own safety, she charged the yokai with her katana, then yelled at the farmer who cursed them out of the village.

No one, except for his mother, had ever stood up for him before. The experience unsettled him.

When he was a boy, Raiden had believed there were good

people in the world. After all, his mother had been one. She was sweet, kind, and beautiful, but fierce when she needed to be. Which was often. She had protected him, told him that there was nothing wrong with him.

"Why do people call me a demon spawn?" Raiden asked her one day when he was five, old enough to know when adults were talking about him.

His mother had been outraged, but she held back her anger by taking him into her arms and telling him a familiar story.

"Once upon a time, a great and powerful Kami left his realm to see what humans were doing upon the earth. He flew across the sky, leaving thunderstorms in his wake. Sometimes he would stop and play tricks on the unsuspecting humans."

Raiden snuggled closer, listening to the words pouring from her gentle mouth. "The Kami saw a woman fend off a yokai, and he was impressed by her bravery. He decided to shapeshift into a human and approach her. The human woman and the Kami fell in love, but their passion was cut short, because the Kami could not remain on the earth as a human. And so he returned to the skies and the realm of kami."

"But he left the woman with a precious gift." Here, his mother would ruffle his hair. "A son, to remember him by. The little boy had eyes like his father, and could do great, wonderful things. And so the woman was not sad, because she had gained more than she had lost."

Raiden swallowed, his childish mind thinking over the story. "You see, my son, you are not demon spawn, and those who say so are ignorant fools. You are different, yes, but special, and I love you."

Her words had soothed his fears for the present. As long as he had his mother, nothing would harm him, and it didn't matter if he had unnatural eyes or could turn clouds to gray when he became angry.

The father he'd never known barely crossed his mind after that.

They lived in their own little world, hardly going into the village, preferring to stay around the snug home in a cozy clearing a mile away. They had everything they needed, for his mother was clever, and her skills as a seamstress earned them enough coin to live on.

The customers had been wary of Raiden at first, but they grew used to him, and many of them would bring little toys or treats to keep him occupied while his mother sewed.

When he was seven, a stranger came to the door of their home. He claimed to be the messenger for a feudal lord, who had heard of Raiden's mother's sewing skills, and wanted her to come to his home to create some beautiful garments for his new wife.

Surprised but pleased by the offer, his mother accepted, but hesitated when the messenger told her to come alone, without Raiden. "I am sorry, but I cannot leave my son alone here," his mother said.

Raiden could tell this was important, and so he assured he would be fine on his own while she sewed the clothes. "Think of the coin you'll make, Okasan," he told her. "It will only be for a day or two. I'm old enough now to take care of the house."

His mother had been reluctant, but after Raiden's insistence and the compliments of the messenger, she relented and went away with her needles and thread.

Two days passed, and Raiden did not hear from her, but he knew she must be busy, and so he tried hard to take care of their goats and chickens and the house for her return.

After the fourth day, he grew worried. Why hadn't she come back, or sent a message? Something felt wrong, but he didn't know what to do.

A week passed, and Raiden decided to go find his mother. They had never been apart this long, and he was afraid something had happened to her.

The night before he would leave, the first significant rainfall of the season arrived. Raiden always loved storms, and he awoke to listen to it.

Over the sound of raindrops dancing atop the roof, Raiden picked up on another sound, and he sat up in bed. Grabbing a stump of candle, he quickly lit it and opened the front door. A figure was approaching the house, limping slowly through the rain.

A rush of cold fear fell upon him, and Raiden ran out to meet his mother. "Okasan!" he cried out. His mother doubled over, holding her stomach and clinging to him. Somehow, he managed to half carry, half drag her into the dry house.

She collapsed on the floor. "My son," she whispered faintly.

"I'm here, Mother, I'm here," Raiden told her, sniffling as tears streamed down his face. What was wrong with her?

He helped turn her over onto her back, and his heart clenched. Blood seeped through her dress, soaking the hand that was held over the wound. Her face was now lit by the candle, and Raiden could see bruises and swelling distorting her pretty features. Her lip was torn and bleeding, and darkened blood caked her head as well.

"Mother," he sobbed, frightened. "What happened? Who hurt you?" She gave him a soft, sad smile, and reached for his face with her other hand. "You must be brave, my son," she managed in a low, rough voice he barely recognized. "I…am sorry…I could not…"

Her words faded, and she took her last breath with a rattling, choking sound. The hand on Raiden's face fell, hitting the floor with a sickening thump.

Time stretched into eternity as Raiden stayed kneeling by her side, staring at his mother's open but unseeing eyes. A million thoughts raced through his mind as he grasped to comprehend the terrible truth that his mother, his world, was gone.

Then they crystallized into one feeling, an emotion that swelled larger and larger, like a never-ending wave rising from the ocean. The house began to shake, the little tea set near the brazier began to rattle. The rain intensified, and a low roll of thunder echoed overhead.

Raiden clenched his fists, breathing hard. Fury like he'd never known or imagined filled every pore, every fiber of his being and with a scream he unleashed it all at once. Lightning poured from his fingers, striking at anything it could reach. It broke through the walls and windows of the house, shattering their few possessions.

He didn't care. All that mattered was this power, this unyielding, great and terrible rage that consumed him. Bolts of lightning shot down from the sky, striking through the roof of the house.

When he finally came to, the home was destroyed, smoking and charred. Only Raiden and his mother remained untouched by the lightning.

His powers had awakened that night, as well as the realization that the world was not as good, that people were not as good, as he'd believed. How could they be, when they had killed his mother?

From that day on, Raiden carried only one goal, one desire in his soul: find the man who had murdered his mother and kill him as slowly and painfully as possible.

25

As night fell, the rain cleared, and a couple of miles away Shinju could see the lights flickering from the city. They were almost there.

Raiden had fallen into a moody silence ever since the fight with the Hone-onna, not that it was much different from his usual personality. Shinju had watched him anxiously for a while as they walked, but slowly he seemed to regain his strength and shake off the weariness that attached itself to him after he called down that lightning bolt.

If she wasn't so worried about what lay ahead, she would not have been able to resist asking him more questions about his abilities. As it was, she did not feel much like talking.

She needed to think of something to say when they requested an audience with Lady Hono. Shinju had no idea what had changed in the city since she left, and felt it was unlikely that they would be permitted inside the castle, even with Raiden's assurances.

The city gate was closed for the day, and the guards posted on watch were not easy to convince to let them inside. "We've been traveling all day," Shinju pleaded. "It's dangerous out here at night."

"Not our problem," one of the guards told her shortly. "You should have stopped somewhere else."

Raiden, who had kept his eyes lowered and head turned for most of the exchange, now joined in. "You'll have to answer to Lady Hono then, as to why her guests were made to wait until dawn to enter the city."

The guards stared at him, startled, exchanged uneasy glances. They were lower samurai, Shinju could tell, but they were apparently familiar enough with Raiden to recognize him. "You are expected by the daimyo?" one of them asked, gazing at their wet and muddy clothing.

"Of course," Shinju assured them, drawing herself up in an attempt to look important and official, and less like a drowned rat. "She sent for us on an urgent matter."

After some deliberating, the samurai shook their heads. "Our orders are clear. No one is to be allowed into the city after the gates are closed for night. You'll have to wait until dawn."

Shinju groaned in frustration. They had lost so much time already. Raiden turned to her, waiting to hear what she wanted to do. It was her mission after all.

Taking a resigned breath, Shinju knew what she had to say. They must get inside the city and speak with Hono.

"Please," she addressed the guards again. "Can you send a

message to the castle, and let Lady Hono know that her niece has returned?"

Their eyes practically bulged from their sockets as the samurai gaped at her. "Niece?" one of them sputtered. "But-but you cannot be. Lady Hono's niece died many years ago."

That was strange, Shinju thought, but she supposed after so long, it was only reasonable for people to assume she had died.

"I am she, and not dead, as you can see. Please, it is most urgent." "How do we know you're the real Shinju Harigoshi?" the other samurai asked, peering at her through the darkness and rain.

"I don't know how I can prove it to you, but my aunt will recognize me," Shinju replied. "Do you want to be known as the guards who would not let Shinju Harigoshi back into her city until morning?"

"We could also be punished for letting a lying peasant inside, no matter who her companion is," the first samurai muttered with a distasteful glance at Raiden. But Shinju's words seemed to work, and he walked over to a door in the gate and opened it. "One of us will escort you to the castle to ensure your word is true."

"Thank you!" Shinju exclaimed with a bow. She stepped through the door, Raiden following her, and entered the city for the first time in ten years.

A flood of memories washed over her as Shinju looked around at the familiar streets. The city was small, but still bustled with activity despite the rain. Lanterns swung sleepily, casting faint orange glows on the buildings. Peasants wearing broad straw hats to keep the rain off their faces pushed carts or carried sacks and barrels.

Despite that, something about the city seemed off, as though its soul had been quenched. As they walked, the houses looked more worn, the clothing more threadbare; and there was no laughing or singing or music, like Shinju remembered. Instead, everyone kept their eyes down, their faces set in stern, closed off expressions.

The contrast between the city now and the one of her childhood filled Shinju with confusion. What was happening? Why were the people not celebrating the festival, like the other towns and cities were? Why did everything feel subdued, even gloomy?

She caught sight of samurai stationed at almost every corner, watching, patrolling. That wasn't too unusual for the cities of daimyo's but never had there been so many. She wondered if something had happened recently that inspired more samurai presence in the streets.

The guards tipped their heads to the samurai leading Shinju and Raiden and looked at her with some flicker of interest. Shinju was disheartened to discover she recognized none of them.

Following their guide, Shinju and Raiden reached the entrance of the castle. Torches lit either side of the outer gate, which was also patrolled by samurai. "What's this, Kenzou?" one of them questioned.

"They claim to be sent for by Lady Hono," the guide said with a bow to the superior officer. "I brought them here to ascertain if it was true."

The higher-ranking samurai surveyed Shinju with a puzzled

look, then his eyes roved to Raiden and widened. "Why, Raiden-sama, this is an unexpected pleasure indeed! I was not aware that Lady Hono had requested your presence."

"She told me I could return any time I needed work," Raiden answered gruffly.

"I see. And who is this?" the officer asked, regarding Shinju.

"She claims to be Shinju Harigoshi," Kenzou supplied.

The officer was visibly surprised, then he scrutinized Shinju with a calculating look she did not like, but she held her shoulders back and chin high, refusing to back down.

"Well, well, this is turning into a most interesting evening," the officer said, stroking his chin. "Of course, you must come in. Lady Hono will be more than happy to see you."

Shinju gazed up at the looming castle as they were led through the gates and into the courtyard. In the dark of night, lanterns glistened from the many windows beneath the pointed roofs that extended from the fortress.

No one strolled through the gardens or lawns, enjoying the fresh air after a hard rain and feeding the fish in the small ponds that dotted the property; instead, samurai patrolled and watched them silently as they were led up the steps to the doors of the receiving hall.

A tremor coursed through as they passed under the entrance. Tears pricked at her eyes and she blinked them back rapidly, trying to focus on where they were being led, rather than be distracted by the all too familiar interior.

The polished wood floors and marble pillars were just as she remembered from the depths of her mind. She could not help but notice the changes in decoration here and there; where her parents had preferred light and flora to enhance the natural beauty of the stone and woodwork that was used to build the castle, Hono had evidently chosen to replace those things with dark draperies, sumptuous gold statues, and cold, glinting weaponry.

This had been Shinju's home once. She expected to be overwhelmed, to feel a sense of belonging…but rather, her heart felt empty, as if a hole had been dug and could never be filled again.

Her parents had died here. And in a way, a part of Shinju had too.

She wondered if Hono would recognize her. Shinju had to admit she looked quite different from the little girl who had dressed in fine silks and braided hair. Despite herself, she glanced down at her dress and pants that were spattered with dirt and grime, and wished she wore something a little finer to be presented to her aunt for the first time in ten years.

No matter. She was who she was, and clothing could not change that.

The samurai officer led them down a few corridors, then paused outside a set of heavy doors. "Wait here," he told Shinju and Raiden, before he opened the door and slipped inside.

Behind them, the additional samurai guards shifted slightly, their armor making metallic clinks that sounded loud in the quiet hallway. Raiden leaned towards Shinju slightly. "Alright?" he asked.

Shinju thought about it. "Yes and no," she whispered back. "It's strange, being here after so long…"

She didn't get to finish her thought, as the door reopened.

The officer stood on the other side and waved them. "Have a seat, the daimyo will see you shortly," he told them.

Inside the room they were greeted with beautifully woven tatami mats, with soft zabuton cushions dyed in red and woven with gold patterns. Small candles flickered in bowls set carefully in a row alongside each side of the mats. Otherwise the room was very dark.

A black lacquered lattice shoji wall on the other side separated them from another room beyond, where Shinju suspected Hono had vanished in order to prepare for their greeting.

Shinju took a seat on one of the zabutons, grateful to give her shaking legs a rest. Raiden sat beside her, his eyes flicking around the room with disinterest. She wondered if this was where he had been received before, when he had worked for her aunt.

Suddenly Shinju wished she had asked Raiden more about that. Maybe she could have been more prepared to meet this woman that sounded more like a stranger than a family member.

The shoji slid back, revealing the slim figure of Lady Hono.

Draped in an elegant black silk kimono embroidered with flying cranes, and holding a fan in one hand, Hono gazed upon them with all the air of an empress. Shinju stared at her in astonishment for several seconds, before remembering her manners and bowing low over the mat. Her heart was thundering in her chest, and she wondered if Raiden could hear it.

"My goodness," came the soft, lilting voice from Lady Hono. "Is it really you? Stand up, child."

Shinju obeyed shakily, raising her face to meet Hono's eyes again. Her aunt drifted a little closer, and Shinju took in the painted face, the delicate cheekbones, the high hairstyle dripping with pearls. Hono had always been more extravagant than Airi, but this was excessive even for her. Surely this had not been for their benefit.

Hono came closer, raking her eyes up and down Shinju's body, taking in the worn clothing, then her face. She reached out a hand, taking Shinju's chin. For a long moment they stared at each other.

"Tell me truly, are you my niece, Shinju Harigoshi?" Hono asked softly, almost breathless. "I am," Shinju answered. To her surprise, her voice did not shake.

"Oh," Hono gasped, and then she slowly, carefully, as if Shinju might break, hugged her.

26

AKIRA CREPT QUIETLY THROUGH the underbrush, his senses on high alert. Already he could hear the distant chatter of soldiers and the creaking of the wagon on the rough road.

He glanced to his right, noting the position of one of his companions. Like him, he was dressed in green and brown, wearing a mask that covered the mouth and nose and dark paint that covered the rest. Like Akira, he too was focused on their mission, but he gave Akira a slight nod.

Since the beginning of his training as a samurai, Akira had often thought about the samurai dismissed by Hono. He heard rumors of the ronin residing in the Dark Forest beyond the city. Once when he had a free day, Akira ventured out into the forest.

The former samurai knew him, and greeted him into their camp, though they were wary. Akira assured them he had no intention of causing them trouble but believed that Lady Hono had unfairly charged them.

As the years passed, Lady Hono's rule of the province constricted, squeezing out higher and higher taxes from the peasants. The farmers and merchants struggled to support themselves, much less pay the daimyo what was due.

Akira thought it cruel.

The Itshino ronin agreed with him.

The wagon drew closer, jarring Akira from his thoughts and he scolded himself for letting his mind wander at such a crucial moment. He tightened his grip on his sword and peered through the brush as the wagon began to roll into view, escorted by a half-dozen guards. Akira pursed his lips and brought fingers to his mouth and whistled, imitating a bird call.

An arrow shot from the trees above and buried itself into one of the guards' chest. He gave a strangled gasp and fell, his foot catching in the stirrup of his horse. The horse whinnied and tried to buck, rolling its eyes in fear. The distraction was enough for the ronin to emerge and begin their capture of the wagon.

Akira dodged a swipe from one of the guards and parried the sword with his own, shouting directions. Two of the ronin climbed up on the wagon and engaged with the two drivers. The rest fought the still mounted guards.

Akira sliced his blade along the leg of the guard barreling down on him and dodged another swipe of his sword. Cursing, the man fought for control over the horse and looked wildly around for Akira, who was stepping lightly behind him, staying out of reach.

Akira took that moment to slap the horse's rump, causing it

to whinny and rear violently, tossing the guard from the saddle. He let out a yell as he hit the road with a smack, and Akira was over him in an instant, blade pointed at his throat.

"Don't move," he warned. "Give us no trouble and we will let you live."

The soldier scowled at him in return. "You might as well kill me," he retorted. "The daimyo will kill us all for losing another wagon to you thieves." Akira could see the fear in the man's eyes, and he hesitated.

"Ghost! Let's go!" one of the ronin called. They had disarmed the other guards and tied them to a tree. Their heads hung, clearly knocked unconscious. The rest of the ronin in their party now rode the remaining horses and the wagon. They needed to get moving.

Akira looked back at the guard on the ground. He was not much older than himself. "You could join us," he said. "You know what we do."

The guard shook his head in disgust. "You're traitors. You bring dishonor to the Code of Bushido. I will not dishonor my family, and my daimyo, for your *noble* cause, Ghost." He spat into the dirt.

Akira frowned. "Suit yourself." He swung the handle of his katana at the man's head, and with a crack, the guard slumped over. "Tie him up with the others," Akira ordered one of the rebels.

As they neared the village on the outskirts of the city, water was passed around to wipe their faces clean of the paint and dirt and sweat. They needed to look inconspicuous; there were often soldiers even in this small village, which was becoming more like a refugee camp every day.

Homes had been ransacked by Lady Hono's samurai not long ago as part of collecting taxes, and now the people scraped by in broken huts and tents, barely surviving on the scanty vegetables and rice they managed to grow. It was here that Akira decided they would unload most of the supplies. People in the city suffered as well, but not so much as these poor souls.

They stashed the wagon in a grove to retrieve later, stripping it of any insignia of the Kvishi daimyo, and carried the goods on foot. Word would soon spread of the theft, and the sooner they got these supplies to those who needed them, the better.

Akira could not help but smile as the village children recognized them; some ran to their homes to tell their parents, others trailed alongside them, peppering them with questions about what was in the bundles they carried, and how they got them this time.

"You know the rules," Akira chided them good-naturedly. "No one can know how we got these. It's top secret!"

They covered ground quickly, and the villagers knew the protocol by now. Food was stuffed into walls and holes in the ground. Clothes that were meant for the castle were cut up and stashed for sewing into tunics and pants for the children later.

They tried to give everyone an equal share, and even though the villagers were grateful and thanked them a dozen times, Akira still felt the uncomfortable pull in his stomach that they weren't doing enough.

The children's eyes were hollow despite the spark brought on by the promise of more food for a time, their bones jutting out beneath rags. The parents were suffering from bent backs and hunger as well as they toiled away in fields for Lady Hono, treated little better than slaves.

When would it end? he wondered impatiently as they began to head back to the city. They could not raid wagons forever. Akira was risking much to disguise himself and sneak out of the city to join the ronin. If he was caught, it wouldn't be exile for him, but death.

He had become so adept at sneaking through the forest undetected, that the ronin gave him the nickname of "The Ghost of Itshino." It helped to have a moniker, Akira decided. Among the castle inhabitants, he was quiet, dutiful, obedient, and competent. The perfect samurai.

No one could suspect that he was not who he appeared to be.

Akira wished he could do more. Something needed to happen; something that would bring them hope.

He bade farewell to his companions after retrieving his samurai armor and horse from the forest. Rain was falling hard now, and he squinted through the water running down his face as he rode to the city gates.

The samurai guards glowered at him but opened the gates to let him pass. "You're out late, Akira," one of them commented.

"*Hai*! Patrol took longer than I thought," Akira answered.

He guided the horse through the narrow streets of the city,

trying to keep his eyes ahead and distant so he wouldn't see the peasants scurrying through the rain. He still did not trust many of the other samurai he saw patrolling the city; they seemed to take pleasure in reporting any acts of kindness from Akira to his superior officer, who in turn would make sure he was punished in some way.

It was so unlike the samurai code Akira had learned as a boy that he'd been horrified at some of the things he would witness when he began training with the new samurai acquired by Lady Hono, courtesy of Lord Hotaka. He'd had to learn quickly to keep his head down and not draw attention to himself.

In the castle stables, Akira wiped down the horse himself, trying to delay going to his superior to report on the patrol he was supposed to have been on. The stable was quiet and warm and peaceful, a place where he could, for a few moments, escape the depressing life he knew.

"*Konbanwa*, Akira-san," a servant greeted him, carrying a bucket of oats. "Just got back?"

"Yes." Akira acknowledged the servant with a nod.

"There's some talk throughout the castle," the servant continued, lowering his voice. "About a visitor who just arrived not long ago."

Akira furrowed his brow. What visitor would cause the servant to speak so?

"Indeed?" he asked. "Who is it?"

The servant licked his chapped lips and glanced around. "I only heard a whisper of a name as I was walking across the courtyard, between Lord Hotaka and one of the samurai."

Akira placed the brush down and turned to face the man

fully. “What name?”

The servant glanced around again before leaning forward and whispering, “Shinju Harigoshi.”

27

WHERE HAVE YOU BEEN all this time, niece?" Hono asked in that same soft voice as she sipped her tea. She had beckoned them to sit once more, and a servant entered bearing a tray of tea and small cookies. For once in her life, Shinju was not hungry, but she accepted the hot tea gratefully, if nothing more than to have something to do with her hands.

"I've been living far away from here," Shinju replied. "On an island." She did not feel quite ready to share more just yet.

"An island? My, how primitive," Hono tittered. "And did Raiden-sama find you and convince you to return home?" She fluttered her eyelashes at the man in question, who simply frowned.

"Ah, no," Shinju managed, unsure of what to make of her aunt's behavior. She seemed happy to see her, but that hadn't been what Shinju expected, and now she felt off-balance. "I met

Raiden-san on my journey here."

Hono's eyes sharpened slightly and she tapped a fingernail against the side of her cup. "I see." Silence settled for a moment as they stared at each other. Then Hono gave a funny little laugh.

"I must say, Shinju-chan, you have truly startled me. I did not expect…" She took a deep breath. "I did not expect to see you again. After that night…"

Shinju clenched her jaw. The door in her mind that had held back her memories had been opened, and she tried to reign in the flurry of emotion that threatened to choke her. "I did not expect to return," she answered honestly.

Hono leaned forward. "But why not? Why did you never send word that you were safe? Why did you not come back a long time ago?" Shinju shifted uncomfortably, gazing down into her tea.

"I…I did not think I should, after what happened," she admitted. "I was afraid. So I ran…" The memory of her aunt, cold and angry, telling her to leave the castle and her dead parents, flooded into her mind, leaving a bitter taste in her mouth.

"....like you told me to," she whispered finally.

Hono settled back immediately, blinking. "I did not think you would actually leave the castle," she countered. "I meant for you to leave and return to your room, perhaps."

Shinju's mouth dropped open.

"You must know, you caused quite a lot of panic and confusion here, when we discovered you were missing. I thought you had been taken," Hono continued.

Shinju felt cold all over. Had she really made such an

enormous mistake? Could it be true that she had misunderstood her aunt's intentions? She had been young and frightened… perhaps her memory was not as good as she thought.

"B-but…" "But, the important thing is that you are now here again," Hono interrupted, setting down her tea. "Where are my manners? You must be exhausted from your travels." She rose, and Shinju clumsily rose as well. Raiden, ever silent and dark, stood and folded his arms.

"I have already requested rooms to be prepared for you," Hono told them as she rang a little bell. "You must wash and rest. There will be plenty of time to discuss the future later."

Bewildered, Shinju's thoughts scattered like birds as she tried to reconcile this conversation with what she had expected, and what her purpose in even coming here was.

"Wait, please," she blurted. Hono arched an eyebrow. Shinju licked her lips, then dug into her pack. "I need to ask you a question. It's very important."

"Very well, my dear, what is it?" Hono questioned, sliding her hands into the sleeves of her kimono.

Shinju withdrew the poisoned dart and held it into the light. "We are looking for the person connected to this. Raiden-san told me he worked with a man under your employ who used darts like these."

Hono's eyes widened, and for a moment she looked as if she'd seen a ghost. Then she turned to Raiden. "Raiden-sama, have you been naughty, spreading my secrets?"

Raiden sniffed irritably. "Should be more careful with who you tell your secrets to," he ground out.

Shinju waited, still holding the dart. "So, you do know him," she prodded. "If so…why?"

Hono sighed. "My dear, when you are a daimyo, sometimes you have to work with unsavory folk for the good of the empire." Her eyes roved over the dart. "I have not seen this man for a long time, but I will ask my associates about him. Why is this so important to you?"

Shinju decided to stick as close to the truth as she could. "This dart killed a friend of mine. I want to know who is responsible."

"My condolences," Hono said, not sounding too sorry. "Well, I will inquire about the location of this *assassin* of yours. But come, it is late and you must rest."

Another servant entered the room and bowed low. "Meiko will escort you to your rooms and see that you have everything you need. We will speak more in the morning."

Hono paused, then reached her hand out again to touch Shinju's face. "You look like her," she muttered. Then she drew back and disappeared behind the shoji door once more.

"Alright, what in all the kami was that?" Raiden demanded as they were led to their rooms, keeping a purposeful distance behind the servant.

"What?" Shinju asked absently. She felt as though she had just had an out of body experience.

"You know what I mean, girl. What happened?" he hissed. Shinju nodded at the servant. Raiden huffed and folded his arms, scowling.

Meiko led them through the upper corridors to the daimyo's family quarters. Shinju broke out in goosebumps when she realized where they were. Not even different interior decorations could make this part of the castle unrecognizable to her.

They stopped in front of a door, and Meiko bowed. "The daimyo thought you might like your old room, my lady," the servant spoke in a hushed tone. Nails digging into her hands, Shinju stared at the door as if it might come alive. She did not want to go in there. But she also did not want to insult her aunt.

"Th-thank you," she mumbled. Next to her, she could sense Raiden absorbing everything, storing up his questions. "I'll see you later," she told him, and slipped inside the room, shutting the door before he could answer.

Alone, she observed the space before her, and raised a trembling hand to her mouth. Everything had been kept exactly the same as it was when she left. Even more, it was clean and well-kept, instead of covered in white cloth to keep dust off the furnishings.

The beginnings of a headache throbbed in her temples as Shinju stumbled to the basin and splashed her face, hoping the cold water would wash away this place and she would be back home on the island. Maybe this was all a long nightmare. It certainly resembled one.

Why on earth would Aunt Hono think Shinju wanted to stay here? Clearly, they were not on the same page. Whereas Shinju wanted to learn what she needed and leave, Hono seemed to think Shinju had returned to stay for good, to pick up where she'd left off.

She gazed at her reflection in the now dusty water. A tired, strained face peered back at her. She raked a hand through her messy braid, then crumpled to the floor, gasping for air. *I can't do this, I can't do this*, paraded through her brain. She needed to get out. The walls of the room were closing in on her; she could hear the accusations echoing from them. *You killed them. It's your fault. Why did you come back?*

A knock on the door startled her out of her spiral into blurry darkness. Shinju quickly rubbed her face with her hands and stood, wondering who it was.

"Come in," she said weakly. Meiko and another servant entered, bearing a large tub and buckets between them. "Pardon us for the interruption, my lady," Meiko told her. "But we have your bath ready."

They set it in front of the lit fireplace and filled the tub with steaming hot water. Shinju watched them, dazed. Meiko sprinkled some jasmine flowers into the tub, then set aside a brush and some cleaning cloths. She glanced at Shinju hesitantly.

"Would you like help with your bath, my lady?"

"Oh…no…thank you," Shinju answered faintly. The servants bowed and backed out of the room, bowing once more before they closed the door. Shinju sighed. They probably thought she was crazy.

The bath smelled wonderful and looked inviting, so she tugged off her smelly travel clothes and katana and sunk into the water with a grateful sigh. Whatever else this visit brought, at least she could face it with a clean body.

She set to work scrubbing every inch of herself until all the dirt grime were removed, then washed her hair. The water grew cloudy and less warm by the time she finished. After rising out of the tub and using a drying cloth, Shinju looked over her old clothes with a wrinkled nose. Maybe she should have given them to the servants to wash.

She was about to dump her clothes in the bath water and sit around in the drying cloth when she noticed a robe and a soft kimono spread out on the futon.

With damp fingers, she reached out and fingered the fabric, biting her lip. It was fine, luxurious clothing, befitting the niece of a daimyo.

Shinju did not care. What mattered was that they were clean. She slipped into the undergarments, followed by the kimono, wrapping the sides around her. She finished the look with a scarlet obi. There were even matching silk slippers on the floor by the futon, and she put those on as well.

Her aunt had accomplished a great deal in a short amount of time, preparing for her to stay, Shinju thought curiously. She approached the small and familiar vanity: crafted of wood and painted a deep fiery orange, with detailed gold trees spreading their limbs across the single drawer.

The paint was faded, just as she remembered. A piece of her mother's childhood passed down to Shinju.

She drew the tips of her fingers across the vanity's surface, lightly touching the brushes and combs arranged neatly. As if no time had passed, as if Shinju had always been there, as if she had just returned from a long trip and all her possessions were waiting for her.

It was too much. Shinju needed to escape the room, to walk and think. To breathe. She'd been keeping her emotions about this place bottled up for too long.

She burst out into the hall, gasping. After a quick search up and down the corridor, she headed in the opposite direction of where they'd come, hoping to find a place of solitude where she could process the day's events.

No one stopped her as she walked. In fact, hardly anyone seemed to be around. Not even servants or samurai. Shinju puzzled over this for a moment before waving it away. She couldn't compare how things in the castle were run now to her parents' preferences.

Without really thinking about it, Shinju found herself leaving the current wing and heading for the family crypt, which lay across the courtyard on the northern side of the castle. They would be there. Her mother and father.

This would either be a terrible idea, to go see the place where their bodies eternally rested, or, as Shinju hoped, it would bring her some measure of peacc and balance.

The cool night air bit at her skin underneath the thin kimono when she exited the castle. Shinju gulped it in, walking down the stone steps and entering the courtyard, which broke off into various gardens. A couple of cranes minced slowly across the lawn, placing one foot down slowly in front of the other. They eyed her with disinterest, but Shinju was glad to see another living creature in this place.

Ahead, she could see the torii gate that arched over the entrance to the shrine and family burial ground. She paused at the gate to wash her hands, then bowed her head respectfully for a few moments before moving forward.

The lanterns outside the shrine were enough to light the

short pathway. Bamboo that grew on all sides of the buildings creaked slightly in the breeze. The sound did nothing to calm Shinju's beating heart as she drew near.

Stone dragons on the other side of the shrine guarded the doorway, and Shinju could not help but smile sadly at the irony of that. *Ryūjin,* she thought as she walked past the shrine and to the crypt. *I wish you could have truly guarded them.*

The crypt was surrounded by a high, square shaped wall. In its center rose the stone structure signifying the family crypt and burial plots. Shinju's ancestors were buried in the center, their family lineage spread out around the yard.

Wishing she had brought something to place at their graves, Shinju walked along the rows until she found the markers for her parents. Two tiny tea lights lit their names on the headstones. Someone remembered them enough to light those.

Warm tears crept down Shinju's face as she kneeled in the dirt. She placed one hand on her father's grave, then her mother's. "I'm sorry," she whispered. "I'm sorry I didn't come sooner. I'm sorry I tried to forget you."

She shivered and sighed, gazing down at their graves for several long moments. A twig snapped behind her, and Shinju instantly tensed. Slowly she stood up and turned, expecting to see Raiden, furious as a storm cloud that she'd wandered off while he had questions.

Instead, a samurai stood at the opening to the graveyard. In the darkness, she could not make out much of his features, except that he was young, maybe about her age. He wore the armor of a lower official, but she could tell that he wore it with some pride.

He didn't speak. Shinju wiped her face and tried to collect herself. He was probably a guard, sent to make sure nothing happened to her…or to make sure she hadn't run away again, she thought drily.

"Can I help you?" she asked after the samurai continued to forgo announcing himself.

He took a couple of steps forward, studying her with a strange intensity. Shinju tensed again, wondering what he wanted.

"It's really you," he spoke in a voice so low she barely heard him. She squinted, taking a few steps forward herself.

He seemed familiar… "Who are you?" she asked. He smiled sadly. "Don't you recognize me, Shinju-chan?"

28

SHINJU IMMEDIATELY STARTED TO say no, of course not. But she hesitated, studied his face: young like she thought, and hand-some, but wearier than she would have expected for a youthful samurai.

Then she looked at his hair, pulled back into a neat knot, a few strands escaping it to hang in his face. An itch in the back of her mind told her this was not a stranger to her.

"Shinju?" he whispered again and took another small step forward. They were now only a couple of feet away from each other.

Shinju felt a ringing in her ears as she examined his face harder. As if knowing her thoughts, he raised his hand up and smoothed the messy black strands of hair from his face and smoothed the stubble on his chin. He suddenly looked bashful.

She swallowed and wavered in place, trembling at the

impact of emotion and recognition that slammed into her like a tidal wave.

"Akira?" she exclaimed. A wide grin that was familiar enough to both bring joy and sorrow to her heart, split his face. "Yes! Shinju-chan, it is me!"

For a moment they simply stared at each other, letting the revelation sink in. Then Akira swooped forward, grabbing her into his arms. "Shinju!" he cried. "I can't believe it! You're... you're…"

"I'm being squished!" Shinju protested, too stunned to really care about his sudden physical contact. Akira. Her best friend...he was here, but why?

"Oh, sorry!" He quickly set her down, laughing like a boy. "I just can't believe it! How can this be? When I heard the others talking about how you had returned, I had to know for certain."

He looked around, realizing where they were standing, and sobered. "I thought you might have come here," he added sympathetically.

"Yes," Shinju breathed, giving him a grin. Then she frowned. "But, you! You're a samurai? I thought your dream was to go to the Imperial City to be a scholar?"

Akira winced and absently placed a hand on the hilt of his katana. "Things…changed after your parents passed, Shinju," he said. A shadow passed over his face, leaving Shinju to wonder what that meant.

"Tell me everything," her old friend said, startling her from her thoughts. "How is it that you are here? How are you…" He swallowed and looked down at his feet. "How are you *alive*?"

Shinju gestured for them to walk and leave the graveyard.

Together, they strolled back towards the shrine. Her heart hammered, with both fear and joy. How much did Akira know about what had happened?

Akira gazed at her closely and Shinju shifted uncomfortably, wondering if he could guess her thoughts. "You don't look as happy to see me," he told her, his voice tight. Shinju's head snapped up and she met his eyes with a stab of guilt.

"Of course I'm happy to see you, Akira," she stated sincerely. She moved a little closer to his side and placed a hand on his armored arm. "I guess I am just...in shock, that's all."

"Yes, I think I know the feeling," he said with a wry smile. Shinju mirrored it, looking over his face. He had truly grown into a good-looking young man, though there was a haunted look in his eyes. What had he been doing all these years?

She realized she hadn't answered his questions. "That night…I ran away. I've been living on an island far out on the sea."

Confusion danced in his dark eyes as Akira observed her. "I can't tell you all the reasons that I've returned. I wish I could." Would it really be wrong of her to confide in her old friend about her mission? Shinju had already told Raiden, and Hono might find out as well. How many more people would she have to break the rules for?

"I don't understand," he responded after an awkward pause. "Why wouldn't you be able to tell me?" Then he shook his head. "You know what, it doesn't matter. I'm just glad you're alive!"

He lowered his voice and pulled her to a halt by the shrine. Water tinkled from a fountain, splashing onto the stones below their feet. "Shinju," he whispered. "You have to be careful around here. You can't go wandering around by yourself anymore. It isn't safe."

Shinju wrinkled her brow. "What does that mean?"

Akira winced again and glanced around nervously. "This isn't the place," he muttered. "We are too exposed here. Just…listen to me, okay?"

"Don't worry, Akira, I'll be fine," she assured him, still unclear about his warnings. Why wouldn't it be safe for her here?

"No, you don't understand," he began. The sound footsteps echoed on the path to the shrine. Akira spun, whipping his katana out of its sheath and taking a protective stance in front of Shinju.

A large shadow fell over the stone walls of the shrine. Raiden stood on the path, halting a few feet away from them. He too had changed into fresh clothing, but still wore his gauntlets and light armor. He crossed his arms and looked scornfully at Akira.

"Put that away before you hurt yourself," he sneered.

Akira scowled, not relaxing his stance. "You," he spat. "What are *you* doing here?"

Shinju stepped forward, tapping Akira's shoulder. "It's alright, Akira."

Her friend shot her a puzzled expression, then his face darkened. "Don't tell me you came here with him," he demanded.

Shinju cocked her head, looking between the two men. "How do you know each other?"

"We've had the unfortunate occasion to meet once," Akira replied with disgust, but he sheathed his katana.

"Looks like someone is still bitter," Raiden snickered. Even matched against Akira's samurai armor and dual swords, the half-kami made an imposing figure in the dark of night, with shadows playing over his features and his eyes glowing silvery-blue.

"I would never waste such emotional effort on someone like you," Akira retorted venomously.

"Ouch, I'm wounded," Raiden said sarcastically.

"Okay, okay," Shinju cut in, raising her hands in a symbol of truce. "I guess I don't want to know, after all."

Akira crossed his arms, glaring at Raiden with narrowed eyes. "Why is he here with you?" he asked Shinju.

"He's helping me," Shinju answered lamely.

"With what?"

"None of your business," Raiden interrupted.

"I didn't ask you!"

Raiden ignored him and addressed Shinju. "What are you doing out here anyway?"

"I just needed some air," Shinju ground out, starting to feel annoyed that both of them were chastising her. "I wanted to see them. My parents. I mean…where they are buried."

Raiden's eyes flickered, and his face softened slightly from his usual scowl. "Oh."

"If you don't mind, Shinju and I were in the middle of an important conversation," Akira quipped, still glaring at Raiden.

"I do mind, actually," Raiden replied, taking a few steps towards them. "In fact, Shinju and I were going to have an important conversation as well about what happened earlier with her aunt."

"Would you both shut up!" Shinju scolded, checking their surroundings. "Any more of this and everyone in the whole castle will know what's going on!"

The two men stared at her in surprise. "She's right," Akira affirmed. "We need to go somewhere more private." He stressed the last word while casting a pointed look at Raiden.

"Fine, we will go back to my room. If anyone asks where we've been, you were both escorting me to the shrine to pray," Shinju stated. She could feel her headache coming back.

Glaring daggers at each other, the men followed her back into the castle and through the corridors to the Harigoshi family quarters. When they stopped at Shinju's room, Akira recoiled. "She gave you this room?" he hissed. "Yes, now hush," Shinju told him.

They walked inside, and Shinju found that her dirty clothes had been taken away, as well as the bathwater and tub. The blankets on the futon had been turned down, and her bag and katana were resting on the bench where she'd left them. Candles had been lit in addition to the small crackling fire in the hearth.

She suddenly felt shy. The room seemed smaller than before with two warriors filling up the space, looking everywhere but each other.

"Um, you can sit," she told them, gesturing towards the cushions on the floor. Akira shook his head. "It would not be proper for me to sit in front of the daimyo," he said.

Raiden's head whipped around from where he'd been examining a wall painting. Shinju froze in the middle of sitting down on the futon.

"W-what?" she stammered.

Akira regarded her calmly. "With your return, you are the true daimyo of Itshino," he stated. "When your parents passed, you would have inherited the position when you came of age, which you are now. Lady Hono no longer has a claim to it."

Shinju had never even considered that. Akira, shifting his weight slowly, went on one knee before her. "I should have done this earlier," he said. "But I was just so shocked to see you, to find you after all this time."

He pulled his katana out of its sheath and held it towards her with both hands and bowed his head. "I serve the daimyo of Itshino. My life and my katana are yours."

"Akira," Shinju whispered, both horrified and moved by his actions.

"As touching as this is," Raiden growled from the other side of the room, "would either of you care to explain what Ryūjin's name is going on?"

Shinju frowned at him. "Raiden-san, that's not very respectful."

"None of this concerns you," Akira added, rising to his feet. Before Raiden could retort, Shinju jumped in with, "Actually, Akira, it does."

She sighed and drew a pillow to her chest. Raiden folded his arms and waited. Akira stood by, hand on his katana hilt.

In slow, faltering words, Shinju told Raiden that she was the daughter of the late Itshino daimyo, and what had happened the night she had run away from this castle, including how her parents died after she served them tea, her face heating with shame.

As she spoke, Akira grew more and more tense, and rubbed his face, looking disturbed. Shinju wondered if he might regret pledging himself to her once he knew the truth.

When she finished, no one spoke for several seconds. Raiden had begun pacing the room like a caged tiger as she spoke, clenching his fists tightly. For a moment, Shinju thought he might start creating lightning.

Now he turned to her, thoughtful but still on edge. "So, the Tsomas found you in your boat and kept you on their island."

Shinju winced. "Ah, yes."

"Tsomas?" Akira questioned. "Who are they?"

"You mean you don't know?" Raiden shot back, feigning surprise.

"Please," Shinju begged. "Akira, like I told you before, there are things happening right now that I can't tell you about. I'm not even going to ask you to trust me. Just, please, don't speak about any of this to anyone."

Akira shook his head. "Of course not, Shinju-chan. But…" He hesitated, then continued. "Your version of events that led to your parents' deaths…that is not the story we were told by Lady Hono."

Shinju's brow furrowed. "What do you mean, Akira?"

Akira stepped closer, his earnest face begging her to listen. "I mean that the morning after your parents died, Lady Hono told us all that they had been killed by assassins, and that you were kidnapped. Every samurai we could spare had been sent out, searching for you. She blamed it all on the outlaws who had been raiding the villages. When no one found you, she dismissed many of the samurai."

Shinju gasped, covering her mouth. "No! She…she turned them into ronin?" Ronin were former samurai, disgraced, with no masters. They were shunned by most society, regarded as men without honor.

Akira nodded gravely. "After that, she began accusing some of the peasants for being in collusion with the raiders or disguised as the criminals themselves." He swallowed hard. "Things began to change here. The Shogun recognized Hono as the next in line as daimyo, and she was granted the position. They thought keeping a member of the family in place would prevent unrest in the province.

"Hono began to acquire new samurai. Men we had never seen before. She took on an advisor named Lord Hotaka, whom none of us had heard of. And those of the household who asked questions were punished. It's as if the deaths of your parents drove her to madness."

Shinju gripped the edge of the futon, hardly believing what she was hearing. How could this all be true?

"Osamu-sensei suspected something. He did not trust Lord Hotaka. He asked questions too." A streak of pain crossed Akira's face. "Not long after I began my training as a samurai, he was found at the bottom of a flight of stairs, his neck broken."

Tears stung her eyes at the thought of her old sensei, a grumpy, rigid man Shinju had not even given much thought of as a child. He had cared enough about her and her family to seek the truth. And now she could never show him that she lived.

"By that time, everyone thought you were dead, and Hono fueled that theory. Eventually she called off her hunt for the outlaws. Then she informed me that I would not continue my studies as a scholar in the Imperial City. I was to begin training as a samurai. As a ward of the Province, I had no choice."

"Oh, Akira." Shinju reached out and took his hand, her lips trembling. Her poor friend…while she had been wracked with grief but taken care of by her new family, Akira had been forced to change the course of his entire life, with no one to watch out for him. She couldn't imagine how lonely he must have been.

The weight of his revelation reopened the wounds of her guilt. "This is all my fault," she whispered. "If I hadn't left…if I had come back sooner, maybe this would not have happened."

"Or you could be dead at the bottom of a staircase too," Raiden interjected. Shinju blinked at him with watery eyes. "You-you can't mean to insinuate that Aunt Hono played a part in my parents' deaths…she must have lied to protect me…she didn't want people to think I had something to do with it."

"You were a child!" Akira exclaimed. "Does her behavior not seem odd to you, Shinju? The things I've seen take place within these walls…your parents would never have done what she has."

"There must be some mistake," Shinju protested weakly. "She-she couldn't have…you weren't there!" Her head swimming, she pushed off the futon and lunged for the chamber pot, her empty stomach turning over.

"Shinju-chan!" Akira cried. Raiden quickly moved to her side and scooped her hair out of the way as she heaved. "Make yourself useful and get some water and something for her stomach," he barked at Akira. The young samurai hurred from the room, careful to shut the door securely behind him.

"I'm sorry," Shinju groaned, her face red and flushed from the heaving and embarrassment of being seen like this. The stench from the chamber pot made her gag again.

"Don't try to speak yet, just do what you need to," Raiden told her in an oddly comforting tone.

When the moment passed, Raiden poured fresh water into her basin and helped her walk over so she could rinse her mouth. Akira returned, bearing a small jug of water, a pot of tea, and three cups on a tray.

As he set them down on a low table near the hearth, Shinju gazed at the teapot, a strange tingling of discovery working its way through her mind.

"Akira," she croaked.

"Yes, Shinju-chan?"

"What did Aunt Hono say the assassin used to kill my parents?"

Akira sat back on his heels. "Oh, *gomen*, Shinju-chan…I forgot that part. She said it was poison. Poison from two darts to their necks."

29

THINGS WERE GETTING COMPLICATED. And Raiden greatly disliked complications.

He was a simple man, with a simple focus in life: find the feudal lord who killed his mother, kill him, and then nothing mattered after that. He did not make attachments with other people; people annoyed him, and after all, why bother when they could disappear from his life as quickly as they'd entered it?

After wandering the Kuishi Province for days after his mother's murder, Raiden had thought he'd found a clue to the location of the lord. But when he'd arrived at the fortress, it was abandoned, and had been for a long time by the looks of the crumbling walls and rotting wood.

Filled with renewed rage, he headed in no particular direction, simply determined that he would search every last inch of Horitamo until he found his target. Peasants fled from him when he entered villages, afraid of the unpredictable lightning that coursed through his fists and the air around him.

Despite his anger, Raiden did not want to truly hurt anyone else. The peasants, as much as they could not stand him, were not responsible for his loss. And so he vanished into the forest, a deep, dark, ancient place where kami dwelt, and there he met ronin who had formed their own small clan.

Cast off, like them, Raiden's story and powers intrigued the ronin, and they took him in, training him to fight. They were bitter, disenchanted warriors, disgraced for failing their sovereigns, and the only work they could get was that of an unsavory nature: escorting counterfeit goods, guarding a hold, beating someone who did not pay their dues.

Raiden did not forget his mother and his vow to avenge her; when he was old enough he left the ronin and continued his search.

Everything had been very simple indeed, until he met this girl with soft eyes and a kind but stubborn disposition. She reminded him of his mother.

The similarities in their lives did not escape his notice. The pain, the confusion, the fear that clouded her face and broke her spirit…he knew what that was like.

She lay on her futon, a cold wet cloth to her forehead, while the samurai brat (Akita? Akira? Raiden didn't really care which) fluttered around her like a mother hen.

"I am sorry, Shinju-chan," the samurai said, staring at the dart produced from Shinju's bag. "I should have known when you said you'd thought something had been wrong with the tea…I should have said something right away about the darts…"

"It's alright, Akira-kun," Shinju whispered. She was staring at the ceiling, her eyes unfocused. At her chest she clutched something she'd taken from her obi. Raiden caught a glimmer of gold, but otherwise it was hidden by her hand.

"Nothing is what I thought," she continued hopelessly. Slowly she sat up, ignoring Akira's hands that reached out to help her. Raiden nearly snorted. The boy was treating her as if she was made of glass. He hadn't seen her fighting spirit yet.

Shinju settled her eyes on his face, and they looked at each for a long moment. Raiden wondered what she was thinking. Akira glanced between them, a frown tugging at his mouth.

With a sigh, Shinju fiddled with the cloth. "I have to know the truth," she said at last. "I have to find out how Hono is connected to these darts…and what role Lord Hotaka plays in all this."

Raiden shifted from his spot on the floor. "You'll have to be careful," he warned. "She will expect your questions. No doubt she already knows that you and the samurai here have reunited."

Akira cursed. "I should have been more careful when approaching her at the graveyard."

"Yes, you should have," Raiden agreed, noting with amusement that the boy's face colored angrily. "But what's done is done."

"We still don't know where the assassin is and whether he has…*it*," Shinju mused wearily.

"Are you still not going to tell me what you're after?" Akira pleaded. Shinju sighed again, looking torn. "I suppose I should. You deserve the truth too, Akira-kun. But, you have to promise to keep this a secret," she told him very seriously.

"Of course, Shinju-chan!"

Raiden rolled his eyes at the samurai's eagerness. He had a feeling if Shinju asked him to roll over and fetch, the boy would do it.

Shinju told her friend about the tide jewels, the thief, and what had led her and Raiden back to Itshino. Akira stared at her in surprise and awe, but did not seem to disbelieve her story. Perhaps his loyalty to her kept him from showing any doubt he might harbor, Raiden thought.

The girl seemed even more exhausted after she spoke of her new family and the daunting mission she'd taken on. Dark circles had formed under her eyes, and she sipped a cup of water absently. For the first time in a long time, Raiden actually felt a twinge of guilt.

He had only decided to help her so he could steal the tide jewels too. What kind of person did that make him? This seemed like a new low, even for him. He'd never really cared before what others thought about him, but the thought of seeing her face when he revealed his true reasons for accompanying her twisted his stomach.

After she had been through so much, could he really betray her too?

I don't owe her anything, Raiden argued internally. *I warned her about me.*

But in spite of that, in spite of all she's seen you do, here you are, fueling her confidence in you, a little voice whispered back.

Akira's voice broke through his musings. "Shinju-chan, I think you need to drop this quest," he was saying. "We need you here. You can challenge Hono. If you reveal yourself to the Shogunate, and tell them all that has happened, we can remove her as daimyo and begin to set things right. You will have the backing of all the ronin."

He spoke feverishly, as if this had been the moment he'd waited for and could barely contain himself. "With you as the true daimyo, you can restore our samurai and bring prosperity back to this province."

Raiden looked at Shinju. She stared at her friend with regret. "Akira-kun, I cannot do this," she replied. "I am not here to become daimyo. I will discover the truth of what Aunt Hono has done, but I cannot put aside the Tsoma Clan and my search to retrieve the Kanju."

"Shinju, please," Akira begged. "Once you become daimyo, you'll have all the resources you would need to find this thief. We just need a little time."

Shinju shook her head. "Time is exactly what I do not have, Akira."

"Look around you!" Akira exclaimed, forgetting to keep his voice low. "Did you not see the city when you came to the castle? The people are working too hard and receive very little in return for their labors. They are barely able to live. The farmers and merchants have buckled under the weight of Hono's unfair taxes. You could change all this, and yet you're throwing it away to chase a fairytale."

Shinju stared at him, stricken. "I am sorry, but the tide jewels cannot wait. It is no fairytale, Akira. This has been my life for the past ten years. I made a vow."

She sighed, her shoulders slumping. "If the jewels fall into the wrong hands, the entire empire will be at risk. Anything I could do here will not matter by then."

"So you're just going to do nothing? I thought we were your family too," Akira ground out, clenching his fists.

Shinju rose to her feet, looking up at her friend with the most serious expression Raiden had ever seen on her face. "Do you think this is easy for me? Do you think it's easy for me to come back here and face what happened that night, a night that has haunted me for the past ten years? Do you think it is easy for me to swallow the suggestion that my own aunt was involved?"

She spun, her long hair flying out behind her as she stepped over to the window to look out, her shoulders shaking.

Chastened, Akira lowered his head. "I am sorry, Shinju-chan," he whispered. "It was rude of me to push you like that. I just…your return gave me hope again. And I don't want to lose you a second time."

Shinju slipped off the futon and walked to him, putting a hand on his shoulder. "You've become an amazing young man, Akira. I am glad to have been able to see you again. Your parents, and mine, would be proud of you."

Raiden crossed his arms. "So, what is your plan now? Lady Hono was not very happy to see that dart you have. It's possible she already suspects that you know what she's done. I doubt we will get any information from her about your thief."

He watched Shinju's face pale, but she pushed her shoulders back determinedly. "Akira, how quickly could you contact the ronin?"

PART TWO
A Reckoning of Seas

30

COME IN, COME IN!”

Hono graciously welcomed Shinju and Raiden into the private apartment. Shinju tried to ignore that this room had once belonged to her parents.

After a restless night’s sleep, Shinju had awoken in the morning with a sense of impending doom. There seemed to be no positive outcome to what lay ahead. She could only hope that their suspicions would prove to be false, and that they could discover the location of the thief.

She was told by servants that Lady Hono would be busy with appointments all morning, but had requested that she and Raiden-sama join her for a tea ceremony in the evening.

That had nearly snapped Shinju’s last nerve. Surely her aunt meant to insult her, to rub salt in her wounds, by suggesting a tea ceremony. But she would go, and be brave. Too much depended on this moment.

Shinju bowed and kneeled on the mat before her, trying to keep a composed expression. She hoped Hono wouldn't notice that Shinju was wearing her old clothes again. Raiden ignored propriety and took a seat in the corner, his eyes watchful but his face cold and still, almost detached.

Hono did not seem to mind as she arranged the tea tools. "I hope this isn't too painful for you to participate in," she cooed, gesturing towards the teapot. "But tea ceremonies are still performed at Itshino castle, and I'm sure your parents would still want you to find some joy in that tradition, wouldn't you agree?"

Shinju's neck and face burned hotly at Hono's implication, the insult hidden under false sincerity. The suspicions aroused within her by Akira were growing too strong to ignore.

But she could not show her emotions just yet. With a faint smile, she bowed her head and accepted the tea, being careful to only let the hot liquid touch her lips and not enter her mouth.

"Raiden-sama, wouldn't you like some?" Hono asked the hulking warrior, fluttering her eyelashes at him. It took all of Shinju's willpower not to pull a face at her aunt's flirting.

"I don't like tea," was Raiden's curt answer. "How odd," Hono giggled, treating his rudeness as simply a quirk.

Shinju took a deep breath after she faked another sip of tea. "Were you able to discover anything about the whereabouts of the assassin?" she began, lowering the cup and hoping her aunt wouldn't notice that the liquid had not lowered.

Hono hesitated, her eyes narrowing slightly. "Well, my dear, these things take time. I couldn't possibly provide you with any news so soon." She began to mix a new tea together.

Shinju chose her next words carefully. "Aunt Hono, about the night…the night my parents died. What happened after I left?"

"Naturally, we searched for you, and those responsible for your parents' deaths," Hono answered in a brittle voice, her polite mask slipping slightly.

"Because they had been assassinated," Shinju said. Hono cleared her throat. "Niece, this is not the time or place to discuss such matters. Your manners have much to be desired after living on that island."

As a little girl, Shinju would have cowered under such criticism. Now, she lifted her chin.

"I've heard many things since I've been back. New samurai. Beatings in the Great Hall."

Hono's stirring faltered even as her face remained neutral, but her motions were enough to tell Shinju that whatever came next was a lie.

"Wherever did you hear that?" Hono asked with a slight laugh.

"Someone told me." Shinju watched her aunt carefully. "They also told me that you said my parents' deaths had been caused by poisoned darts, not the tea."

Hono finally raised her head and looked at Shinju. Her lips were drawn tight, and her face was pale even under the powder and thick kohl around her eyes.

"I thought, of course, they must have been mistaken, for there were no darts when Mother and Father died. How could there be, when the windows to the room were closed?" Shinju waited, but Hono remained silent and ridged.

"What happened, Aunt Hono?" she asked again, growing impatient.

"You don't remember clearly," Hono finally snapped. "You were a child, who had just seen her parents die in her arms, and had fled the castle like a stupid child, worrying us all for years."

Shinju balled her fists. "I remember," she replied in a low tone. "I remember the room, what my parents were wearing, how they smelled, what we talked about. I remember when they began choking, and I screamed and screamed for help, and no one came. Except you."

She leaned forward as she spoke, and Hono backed away on her heels, an expression of fury on her face. Shinju pressed on.

"Why did no one come to our aid that night? Where were the servants, the guards?"

"I do not know," Hono replied, clenching the teapot. Her nails scratched the delicate porcelain. "But I made sure they were punished thoroughly."

"So I have heard." Shinju pressed her hands against her knees, willing herself to remain calm. "Why did you claim that I had put something into the tea that killed them? Why did you tell everyone it was darts instead?"

"What exactly are you insinuating, Shinju?" Hono replied, her voice growing cold. The woman drew herself up, becoming a statue, gazing down her nose at Shinju.

"I am merely trying to find out the truth," Shinju replied, hoping to placate her aunt enough that she wouldn't flee from the room.

"The truth." Hono breathed in deeply through her nose.

"The truth, dear niece, is that you were a foolish little girl, and now you are looking for someone to blame."

Shinju opened her mouth to retort when the door to the room slid open. A servant woman stepped in, keeping her eyes lowered. She carried a platter of sweets, which she lay before them near the tea arrangements.

When she straightened, her face turned towards Shinju.

As if a bucket of frozen water had been dumped over her head, Shinju started with a gasp. Her mind flew back to the day of the festival, long ago, when she had been in the kitchen preparing the tea. This had been part of her memories that had grown fuzzy. Her parents' deaths had overshadowed all else from that day. Until now.

The memory sharpened, breaking through the defenses and created by her mind to cope with her fears and grief. The servant woman. She had assisted in selecting the teas for Shinju.

"You..." she whispered, gaping at the servant, who paused as she reached the door. "You...I remember you...from the kitchen. You..."

Shinju sucked in a breath, her head spinning. "It was you, wasn't it?"

"What are you saying, Shinju?" Hono's eyes darted between them, and she licked her lips nervously.

The servant glanced over her shoulder. She had the same dark eyes, devoid of feeling. They had made Shinju uncomfortable before. They made her skin crawl now.

"It wasn't the darts at all, was it?" Shinju murmured. "It was the tea. And you...you put the poison in the tea, didn't you?"

The servant turned fully, staring at her without expression, before glancing at Lady Hono. "Will that be all, Lady Hono?" she asked in a quiet voice.

"No!" Shinju realized she was now standing, and so was Hono. Raiden remained seated in the corner, watching them intently.

"Enough!" Hono screeched. "You should be ashamed of yourself, Shinju Harigoshi. How dare you utter such lies and bring dishonor to this household?"

"I am not lying! Aunt Hono, this servant, she's the only other person who handled the tea that night besides me! She…"

The tea. If this servant had poisoned the tea, then…

"I was supposed to die too, wasn't I?" she breathed. "I was also supposed to drink the tea, but I didn't, and you had to get me away so that…"

Her hand raised and covered her mouth. Shinju's mind flashed back to that night, reliving it once more, as all the pieces finally locked into place.

She had not died, and when it was discovered that she was missing…

The forest. The men that chased her. They'd been dressed in dark clothing, but in her desperate escape in the boat, Shinju had seen one little detail her subconscious had locked onto.

Emblazoned on their tunics had been the red crescent moon.

"It was you all the time," Shinju gasped, whirling around to face Hono.

"You're delirious with grief!" Hono spat, but her eyes were wide and fearful, reflecting that of a trapped animal.

"Explain, then, how the dart I brought to you yesterday just happens to also belong to an assassin that you hired? Explain how you covered up the poisoned tea by blaming their deaths on the darts? Explain how I was chased by ninja in the forest when I ran away?"

Shinju's chest heaved, and she had moved towards Hono with fists clenched. "Are they not connected?"

Hono barred her teeth at Shinju, then she started to laugh, a high-pitched, cruel sound that caused bile to rise in Shinju's stomach.

"Well, well, perhaps you're not as stupid as I thought, Shinju-chan," she said acidly. "You want the truth? To hear my dirty little secrets?" She gave a horrible grin. Blood thundered in Shinju's ears.

"I planned the whole thing, just as you said," Hono purred, tossing her head and drawing herself up. "I did it to become daimyo."

Her admittance still shook Shinju to the core, rocking her back on her heels in horror. Somehow, she had still held a tiny flame of hope that Akira had been wrong, that it was all a mistake.

Hono smirked, crossing her arms. "I am afraid our time here together will have to be cut short, Shinju-chan. I cannot, after all, let you tell everyone what really happened that night, can I?"

As they spoke, Hono had slowly backed away until she was standing by the folding screen, her hand inching around its side to grab something.

With a screech, she lunged at Shinju with a katana. Shinju quickly dodged, rolling out of the way, and sprung back to her feet. She met her aunt's face, filled with rage and a wild, animalistic expression. Some of her hair had fallen from its updo, curling limply around her face and plastering to her forehead.

"How dare you come back," Hono growled as she slashed at Shinju again. "How dare you ruin everything!"

Shinju continued to duck and dodge each attack, looking for an opening. Her aunt was more skilled than she'd expected. "I? Ruin everything?" She spun, dodging another swipe. "You brought this on yourself!"

Hono answered with a brittle laugh. "Well, you have a point. I should have killed you when I had the chance, rather than have those Otami do it. At least I have the chance to do it now."

"Otami?" Shinju inquired, bewildered. Then she remembered. That had been the name of the ninja clan Raiden told her about when they escaped the Kasuda Clan fortress. Her mind swirled with this revelation. How much deeper did her aunt's deceptions run? What kind of people had she aligned herself with to seize power?

Hono spared a glance at Raiden, who rose to his feet in the corner and continued to watch them with a hardened expression. His eyes grew brighter, but he didn't move until the servant began to sneak out of the room.

With speed unexpected in such a large man, he'd lunged and grasped her arm, pinning it behind her back as he shoved her into the wall. "Not so fast," he snarled as she struggled.

"This is nothing you need to interfere yourself with, Raiden-san," Hono cooed at him.

Shinju used the opportunity to strike past her aunt's defenses and hit her on the mouth. Hono gasped and stumbled back. Her lip was bleeding. Shinju raised her hands into an offensive position. "You will pay for what you've done. Murderer."

Hono cackled, then lunged at her. Shinju continued to dodge every swipe, using what openings she could to land punches and kicks to her aunt's face, abdomen, or legs. Around and around they clashed together in the small room, knocking over the tea set, the screen, the flowers. Hono was good, but Shinju grew more confident as she began to back her aunt into a corner. Hono breathed hard, fire in her eyes, and she expelled too much energy on her attacks.

Her aunt made a quick forceful lunge, and Shinju leapt to the side, grabbed Hono's wrist as it passed by her, and twisted as hard as she could. Hono screamed and the katana loosened from her grasp, falling. Shinju reached down and caught it before it hit the ground, spun and turned to point it at the woman before her. "Yield," she breathed out.

Hono backed away, her hands up in surrender. She looked terrible, makeup now running in wet streams down her face, but Shinju could not tell if it was from sweat or tears. Her aunt cowered in front of her, whimpering.

Anger roiled in Shinju's stomach as she tightened her grip on the katana. All these years, working through her pain and grief, Shinju had always harbored guilt, still believing that it had been her who had played a part in her parents' deaths, no matter what Takumi said, no matter how her heart had longed to heal through his care and assurances.

"How could you do it?" Shinju demanded horsley. "How could you kill them?" She felt as though she might lose the contents of her stomach. Her hand shook as she kept the blade pointed at her aunt.

Hono hadn't just taken the lives of her parents: she had stolen Shinju's innocence by killing them in front of her, and then tricked Shinju into believing it had been her fault. Shinju should have been able to trust her, and that childish faith had been thrown back in her face.

The unfairness of it, the cruelty of it, was enough to send tears to her stinging eyes.

"Why?" she asked again, barely above a whisper.

Hono raised her face, grimacing. "Why?" she mocked, venom dripping from her words. "Because your parents were weak. Because I deserved the position of daimyo. I should have been the one to marry Io, I was the worthiest daughter, but did Father think so? No! At every turn, my right was stolen from me!"

"You wanted it so badly that you killed them for it?" Shinju cried. "We are your family!"

Hono sneered, her eyes turning wild again. "It was worth it. I would do it again. I will do whatever it takes to keep what is rightfully mine."

Shinju shook her head, hardly believing how far gone her aunt was. "You have no right to anything." An unfamiliar emotion intertwined with her anger, and it took Shinju a few seconds to realize what it was: hatred. At that moment, she hated Hono. And it caused Shinju to take a step closer, angling the katana towards a killing stroke.

It would be so easy, she thought, staring down at the sniveling, resentful woman before her. So easy to just swing and end it, to avenge her parents, to free this province from her aunt's lies and cruelty.

Shinju caught sight of her own reflection in the blade, and what she saw frightened her from these thoughts. She felt a shiver of horror quake her hands, and the fog lifted, letting her once again see the situation clearly.

She looked back at Hono, who was now muttering both curses and supplications. Who would Shinju become if she swung that sword?

Another emotion arose within her, engulfing Shinju's anger and desire for revenge.

Pity. She pitied the angry, miserable woman before her. She slowly lowered the sword, blinking as Takumi's voice from long ago echoed in her mind: "*You have much sorrow and guilt in you, child, and if you let it fester, it will consume you.*"

Shinju exhaled, letting the peace she had been taught by the Tsomas replace her wrath. She lowered the katana completely, then tossed it away. Hono started at the sound as it clattered to the floor, and she gazed up at Shinju in confusion. "Y-you're not going to kill me?" she whimpered.

"No," Shinju replied. "I don't want to be like you, Aunt Hono." She watched as a mixture of emotions flitted over Hono's face: rage, shock, then despair, and she crumpled to the ground. Shinju watched in surprise as sobs racked her aunt's body. "I am sorry," Hono groaned.

Shinju narrowed her eyes, not sure if she should believe this sudden change in behavior. "You're sorry you've been beaten, not for what you've done."

Hono continued to wail, crawling on her knees towards Shinju, who backed away in disgust. "I'll do anything you say,

Niece," she begged. "Only, don't tell the Shogun. You wouldn't allow your only living relative to be executed, would you?"

Shinju blanched, thinking about how close she'd come to doing that herself. Out of the corner of her eye, she could see the servant still struggling in Raiden's grasp.

"You've got to be joking," the half-kami snarled, his eyes boring into Shinju's. "You're letting her go? After what she's done?"

Shinju swallowed, taken aback by his outburst. "Raiden-san…"

"She killed your parents, Shinju," he growled. "You have the opportunity to avenge them. Do it!"

Shinju took in the lightning now coursing up his arms, the brighter glow of his eyes and the mask of rage on his face. Something else was driving his passion, but she could not comprehend what. "I cannot do this, Raiden-san," she answered softly. "Why is it important to you?"

He grimaced and turned away, muttering under his breath. Shinju wanted to ask him more, but right now there were more pressing matters. She looked back at Hono.

"Tell me about the thief…assassin…who uses these darts." Shinju bent down on one knee, meeting her aunt at eye-level. "Where is he?"

"I do not know."Her aunt glared at her with red-lidded eyes.

"You asked the Otami to help you, did you not?" Shinju probed further.

"Listen to me," Hono panted, her nails dragging against the wood floor. "It's Lord Hotaka. It was his idea, all of this. He fed me lies!"

A low laugh broke the moment of silence as Shinju digested her aunt's confession. It was the servant.

With a smirk, she managed to turn her head away from the wall. "What a shame to hear you say that, Lady Hono," she rasped. "And here we were getting along so well."

31

SHINJU SPUN TO LOOK at the servant. Niko was her name, she recalled. "You put the poison in the tea, didn't you? What part does Lord Hotaka play in all this?"

Niko simply smirked. "You'll learn soon enough."

Raiden tightened his grip on her arm and shoulder. "The Otami who used the darts," he hissed. "Matsuda, his name was. You know where he is."

She only continued to chuckle, ignoring Raiden's words. Shinju felt her skin crawl at the sound.

The door to the room opened, and Akira stepped in, his brow furrowed. A small man accompanied him, wearing the robes of an imperial advisor. Shinju blinked in surprise. Who was this?

Lady Hono sucked in a breath at his presence and cast accusing eyes towards Akira. "You...you took a vow! You swore to the code of Bushido! You are loyal to me!"

"Yes," he said. "I did take a vow. But I am willing to risk my honor to save Itshino from you and whatever influence Lord Hotaka has over this castle." Akira gestured towards the small man. "Shinju-sama, this is Rikuto, a messenger from the Shogunate. He only just arrived, and I knew he needed to be present."

Shinju nodded slowly, understanding. They now had a direct witness from the Shogun to support her aunt's confessions. Akira might not have been believed, but this man would be.

Suddenly, all the candles and lamps in the room blew out, throwing them into darkness. "So sorry to be late," a deep voice crooned from the balcony. Shinju reflexively moved into a defensive stance. Akira drew his katana and moved in front of her, shielding her and the Shogun's advisor.

As her eyes adjusted, Shinju caught sight of a figure standing on the balcony's railing. He was dressed all in black, and covering his mouth and nose was a long red scarf, its loose end flowing loosely in the air. In the corner of the room, Hono released a breath of relief and stood, her hands groping for the walls.

"Lord Hotaka," she breathed. "At last." Shinju blinked, puzzled. This was Lord Hotaka?

"So, I was right after all," Akira snarled. "You are the leader of the Otami. It was your ninja who infiltrated this castle, posing as samurai."

"Tch, for a samurai, you don't have very good manners, betraying your daimyo," Lord Hotaka commented. "I'm afraid we don't have time to teach you, however." His eyes glinted as a sliver of moonlight in the sky above shimmered down through the window.

Raiden stepped up, lightning beginning to lick the plates of his gauntlets. "I think you're a touch outnumbered, *Lord Hotaka*," he drawled. "Perhaps you overestimate your abilities."

Hotaka shot him a razor-sharp smile. "I think you'll find me more challenging than most, half-kami brat." He stepped down lightly onto the balcony floor. "Perhaps it is you who should be concerned about your numbers."

Raiden smirked. The lightning from his fists cast a glowing blue light in the room and created a ghostly glow against his face.

Shinju tensed as she sensed footsteps in the corridor outside the room. They were in the daimyo's wing of the castle, private rooms that were accessed only by certain servants and samurai. And by the satisfied look on Hono's face, she knew Lord Hotaka was not bluffing.

The Shogun messenger stepped forward. "Cease this assault at once!" he commanded. "You and Lady Hono will feel the full brunt of the Shogun's might if you dare to harm the Harigoshi heir!"

With a start, Shinju realized he was talking about her. "The girl can handle herself," Raiden said with a wave of his hand. He met Shinju's eye and winked. "We've been in a couple of tight spots before, haven't we?"

Akira scowled, his armor clinking slightly as he shifted stance to match the slow movements of Hotaka, who slunk forward slowly like a feline predator. "You heard him, Lord Hotaka," Akira snapped. "Do you really want the Shogun's wrath, and possibly the Emperor's, to fall upon you?"

"Oh, but that will only happen if you all survive," Hotaka stated. "You see, no one knows you are here, except for the advisor." He gave a nod towards Rikuto. "And he's easy enough to dispose of."

Shinju curled her lip at him. "Either fight us or surrender," she said. "I don't want to kill you, but I will do what I must to protect myself and my friends."

"Dear Shinju, you've grown so…spunky," Lord Hotaka chuckled. "I could use someone like you at my side. The Tsomas taught you well."

Shinju froze, staring at him. "The Tsomas…so, you sent the thief to our island?"

Hotaka spread his hands. "As your dear aunt stated earlier, this was all my doing." He reached the corner of the room where Hono leaned against the wall, watching him with an almost religious fervor.

"I tried," she breathed, her voice hoarse.

"I know. And you've done very well for my purposes all these years," Hotaka crooned, smoothing her hair back.

With a perfected speed, he placed his hands on the sides of her head and twisted hard with a sickening snap.

"No!" Shinju screamed as her aunt dropped to the floor. Hono's eyes stared unseeingly across the room, her body splayed out like a doll.

"What have you done!" Shinju cried, curling her fists as she tore her eyes away from Hono and fixed them on Hotaka.

"She was no longer a necessary piece of the game," Lord Hotaka replied calmly, stepping over the body without a glance.

"What game?" Shinju ground out, tensing. "How did you find the island? Why did you take the Kanju?"

Hotaka rubbed his chin, assessing her. "I suppose you deserve the truth before you die." He folded his arms. "I was approached by Lady Hono years ago to assist her in removing your parents from her path to power. In exchange, she promised to give me authority in the province, and unrestrained access to the use of the Black Harbor. We poised as renegades, raiders, attacking villages in the province at random to stir up chaos. That provided the perfect scapegoat for your aunt to use as for your parents' murders."

Shinju's mouth dropped open. More and more clicked into place as she connected his words to what her aunt had said. How could she have been so blind?

"In order to avoid suspicion, my ninja were brought in as samurai. We had a cover to be able to continue our work in the shadows."

His eyes narrowed. "It was quite an embarrassment that you managed to escape my ninja in the forest. I do not plan to make that mistake again."

Shinju gritted her teeth. "How did you find out about the island?"

"Ah, yes. I always believed in the existence of the tide jewels, and I've dedicated many years to searching for clues to their whereabouts. You can imagine my surprise when I discovered ancient texts in the archives of Harigoshi castle referring to the Tsoma family and their connection to the jewels."

Ancient texts? Shinju frowned in confusion. How could there be such a thing? She'd always been told that the Tsomas had disappeared from the mainland with no record left behind. Had they been wrong? Had someone learned what they were charged with protecting and written it down?

"One of my ninja happened to have intimate knowledge of the tide jewels and was able to confirm these texts as truth," Hotaka continued smugly.

Shinju's stomach dropped. No. It couldn't be…

She shook her head. "I don't believe you."

"That is irrelevant," Hotaka answered flippantly. "We have the Kanju in our possession. Your clan failed to fulfill whatever misguided duty they were given."

This was worse than Shinju could have imagined. If what he said was true, her clan had been betrayed. And now this evil man held one of the tide jewels in his grasp.

"What are you planning to do with it?" Shinju asked carefully, trying to keep him talking. "You haven't used it yet. What are you waiting for?"

Lord Hotaka smirked, guessing her thoughts. "I am a patient man, my dear. I have learned long ago to wait until the right pieces are in place."

Shinju studied him warily, thinking over his words. "You need them both," she realized out loud. "You need the Manju too."

He smiled slowly, reminding her of a snake. "You have such a talent for sniffing out the truth. You could be destined for so much more than what that island has to offer you." He extended his hand. "We don't have the Manju yet, but we will soon. All we need is the right guidance. Join me. Be a part of my vision to conquer Horitamo and bring true prosperity to the Empire.

Your knowledge of the jewels would be most beneficial. And in return, you would have anything you wanted."

Her stomach twisting in revulsion, Shinju shook her head. "I would never, *never*, join you."

"Very well then. I hope you enjoyed your brief visit home. You, like your parents, will die here."

There was a loud bang and a flash, and smoke filled the room from the now open doorway. Coughing, Shinju whirled around, raising her arms. In the haze of Raiden's lightning she could make out the forms of other ninja swarming into the room, all clad in black with the red crescent moon emblazoned on their chests.

Niko, still dressed in her servant's garb, stepped forward, shuriken appearing in her hands.

Shinju reached for Akira. "Protect the messenger!" she cried. "He must get to the Shogun!" Akira gave her a hard nod, then stepped forward to meet the sharp blade of a ninja's katana. Another Otami reached Shinju and she quickly dodged his swipe and slammed her fist into his head, then kicked his stomach. The attack sent him backwards, but he was only replaced by another.

It was the escape from the Kasuda Gang once again. Shinju blocked punches and threw her own, spinning to kick and duck to dodge weapons. Raiden's lightning coursed through the room as he fought assailants, and for sporadic seconds at a time, Shinju could glimpse the eyes of the Otami when they drew near enough. They looked at her with no emotion, and somehow that was worse than if they hated her.

It didn't take long for Shinju to realize she was outmatched.

These were no roadside thugs, but skilled warriors, and she was barely holding her own. Maneuvering around the room, she backed out onto the balcony, hoping the space would help her.

Akira's sword flashed through the dissipating smoke, its blade now wet with crimson blood. The advisor had managed to escape through the room's door, and Akira stood before it as he fought to prevent Otami from following.

Raiden roared as he sent a giant bolt of lightning through a cluster of ninja, and they were thrown like rag dolls against the walls, smoking and charred. He was so focused on the next attacks that he didn't see Lord Hotaka approach him from behind.

"Raiden!" Shinju screamed, barely avoiding a flying knife. Raiden turned just as Hotaka thrust a *shinobi* into his side. Raiden shouted in pain, then knocked Lord Hotaka back with a mighty back arm. The half-kami brought a hand to his side, growling as blood began to seep through his lightweight armor.

Shinju's concern for him was pulled away by an Otami that approached her on the balcony, swinging a sword. She grabbed his wrist as he lunged and used the flat of her hand to slam into his face, then quickly chop the arm that held the sword. A trick that usually worked, but the ninja held fast to his weapon and used their proximity to each other to headbutt her.

Shinju reeled back, shaking the stars from her head, and as she clumsily dodged another swipe, the blade sliced through her sleeve and cut into her skin. Gritting back a scream of pain, Shinju twisted, using her body's momentum to deliver a kick to the ninja's chest. He stumbled but recovered within seconds and thrust at her again with a speed Shinju wouldn't have believed possible.

The blade was centimeters from her face when another hand closed over the Otami's arm, and lightning coursed through his body, jolting him into shaking and muffled screams. Shinju braced herself on the balcony railing, staring up at Raiden as he clutched his bleeding side and picked up the fallen blade. "We have to get out of here," she told him.

"Running from a fight? Not really my thing," Raiden rasped, joining her side as more ninja slowly approached them. "I don't think we have much of a choice," Shinju retorted. Her arm was screaming with pain, and she was scared to look at it. The sword must have cut deeper than she realized.

"Akira!" she shouted. "Where are the ronin?"

As the words left her mouth, three *kaginawa* flew up through the air to her right, falling to latch onto the railing of the balcony with sharp hooks. Within seconds, men began climbing up the ropes and jumping onto the balcony, immediately meeting the ninja with drawn katanas.

One of them paused by Shinju. His face was covered, but he nodded to her in respect, before turning to join the fight.

"I guess they are the ronin," Raiden muttered.

Akira raced out to them, cutting down a couple of ninja in his path. "Go!" he told them. "Get out of here and go find the other tide jewel before Lord Hotaka does."

Shinju hesitated, staring into her friend's dirty and blood streaked face. His eyes softened as he met her gaze, and he gave a brief nod. "Do what you must, Shinju-chan," he whispered. "Know that I will defend your home with honor. I will help the messenger reach the Shogun safely, you have my word as a samurai, and a friend."

Shinju ignored Raiden's snort as she strode forward and hugged Akira. "Thank you," she whispered back. "I promise I won't forget you, Akira-kun. I promise that I will come back and help set things right."

He swallowed hard, nodding against her shoulder. Then they parted, and she and Raiden began the climb down from the balcony.

32

THE CASTLE FINALLY DISAPPEARED in the fog. Shinju steered the boat along the swiftly moving river, straining her tired eyes for rocks or fallen trees that might be hidden by the foaming water.

After stopping by Shinju's room to grab her katana and bag, they had escaped the city, fighting off more of Hotaka's ninja, using the eastern gates, left unguarded by the fighting in the castle. Itshino River ran through the province to the southeast, and they had sprinted the half-mile to its banks and commandeered a fisherman's boat.

Taking the river would be their best chance at traveling the mountains and leave no tracks for Hotaka to follow. Hopefully he would be kept busy enough that they had a head start.

Raiden kept silent at the prow, staring out into the night. As before, he was already healing from the stab wound. Shinju thought about how angry he had been earlier by her choice to show mercy to her aunt.

She knew she had made the right decision, but what happened next…Shinju's brain felt jumbled, like a puzzle full of pieces that didn't fit together.

All this time, Lord Hotaka had been behind everything. Her parents' deaths…the attempt on her own life…the theft of the Kanju…

Shinju gripped the oar tightly, ignoring a splinter that dug into her palm. What had happened no longer mattered. All she could do now was go to the location of the Manju and stop Hotaka from obtaining the second jewel.

They drifted along, passing through woodlands and rice fields. The fog eventually lifted, and the moon provided more light on the river. Crickets chirped in their hidden homes among the tall grasses on the banks, and owls hooted as they scoured the ground for nocturnal rodents.

This river would take them to the Kyosho Mountains, which they would need to cross to reach the Port of Kumato, a coastal town where Shinju determined they could secure another boat to take them across the Sea of Stars to Manju Shima.

She hoped they could actually find the island; not even Takumi had known the exact location. Communication between the two Tsoma clans had ceased after receiving the tide jewels and parting ways. Only one message had ever been received by Fushimara from his sister indicating any mention of where her island was. All she had to go by was Takumi's scroll and the dstories passed down by the Clan.

It would have to be enough.

Raiden finally stirred from his spot, glancing at her. Shinju gave him a tired smile.

"I thought you might have turned to stone."

He raked a hand over his face wearily. Shinju could spot a hint of stubble beginning to grow on his chin and cheekbones.

"You asked me earlier why it was important to me," he began, referencing their disagreement. Shinju blinked in surprise but waited quietly.

"What I…am going to tell you, I've never told anyone else," Raiden admitted. His eyes flickered on the long reed he held in his hands, torn from a passing plant.

Shinju swallowed, and stopped paddling with the oar to let them drift along unaided. Only the sounds of the night and the gentle lap of water on the sides of the boat could be heard.

"My mother was my whole world," Raiden started. "She didn't care that I had strange powers, that I was different. She took care of us." A pause. "When I was about six, a messenger for a feudal lord came to our house. He praised my mother's work as a seamstress and claimed that his master wanted her to come to his castle and sew a dress for his new bride."

Shinju held onto every word, barely breathing.

"The messenger said I could not come. My mother turned down the offer, but I encouraged her to go. I would be fine on my own for a couple of days. So she left."

His jaw tightened and he ripped the reed in two. "She didn't come back or send a message. I became worried, so one day I decided I would search for her on the morrow. There was a storm that night, and she returned."

Raiden's hands were trembling, and Shinju found herself

moving closer to him, taking a seat at the prow.

"She had been beaten, and there was a wound in her stomach. Caused by a knife or a blade, I do not know. I begged her to tell me who did this to her, but she died before she could tell me. She died in my arms."

Tears pooled in Shinju's eyes and her heart broke, thinking of the little boy Raiden had once been, experiencing such a horrible moment.

"I became so angry that I called down lightning and destroyed the house," Raiden continued, his voice growing rougher. "I destroyed everything. In the morning, I buried my mother, and made a vow that I would not rest until I had found and killed this lord who murdered her."

It makes sense now, Shinju realized. He seeks revenge…he saw me with my chance to do the same and grew angry when I did not take it.

"Did you find the lord?" Shinju asked gently when several long moments passed. Raiden shook his head. "No. I journeyed to the place where he supposedly lived, but the castle was a ruin. No one had lived there for a long time. It had all been a lie, just to get to my mother."

"Raiden…" Shinju whispered sadly. It felt as though there were no words she could say to comfort him, so instead she reached out and placed a hand on his shoulder.

He almost jerked back, lost in his thoughts and not expecting her touch, but then he leaned into it, giving in. His shoulder was warm and hard under the rough, gray tunic.

"I'm so sorry. What happened to you, and your mother… no one should go through that." She took a deep shaky breath.

"Where did you go after?"

"I wandered the region for a long time before meeting with a group of ronin. They took me in, trained me to fight, but I never forgot my vow. I left when I was older to continue my search."

He glanced at her. "Then I ran into you."

Shinju nodded. They sat without speaking for a few minutes. The moon drifted behind wispy clouds, and far in the horizon, a streak of gray and pink appeared, signaling the coming dawn.

"I understand now," Shinju spoke softly. "I understand why you were so angry."

Raiden turned in his seat to face her. "And I don't understand how you didn't swing that sword," he told her, his voice tight and raw.

Shinju's chin wobbled. "I wanted to. I almost did."

"And?"

"And I decided I didn't want to be like *her.* I was afraid of the kind of person I might become if I followed through and gave in to that moment of hatred." Shinju looked down at her hands, remembering her reflection in the katana with a shudder.

"I didn't want to become someone who killed the only blood relative I had left, no matter what she did. I know it is not what my parents would have wanted. And it would not have brought them back." Shinju felt a renewed sense of peace mingled with sadness spread through her.

"I thought about what Takumi and the Tsomas taught me as I grew up, about forgiving those who wrong you, about not letting grief control and define you. And I made a choice."

She sighed. "I know the truth now. I know that I didn't poison my parents. That truth has freed me, more than Hono's betrayal has hurt me." Shinju watched the sky grow lighter. "That's how I could show her mercy."

"So you would have just let her go?"

"No. I had hoped to hand her over to Akira and the ronin so they could bring her crimes to the Shogunate and let them decide her fate." Shinju let out a breath, watching as it turned to mist in the cool morning air.

"But that doesn't matter now. She's dead. Lord Hotaka killed her."

Raiden didn't respond for a long time. "I don't think I could do what you did."

"I understand." She did. "Whatever happens when you finally face this man, I want you to know something."

This time she reached for his face, some instinct guiding her hand to place it on the tan skin and prickly stubble. His eyes went wide.

"What happened to your mother was not your fault," Shinju told him, gently but firmly. "It was his, and his alone."

He gaped at her, stunned, then closed his mouth and stared at her with an intensity that caused her face to flush.

She dropped her hand to settle in her lap and looked down, suddenly aware of how close they were sitting. One of Raiden's hands slowly uncurled from its fist and tentatively drifted towards hers, as if she was a wild animal he didn't want to startle. Shinju held her breath.

He pulled his hand back and wiped it down his pant leg, clearing his throat.

"Why don't you get some rest," he advised. "I'll paddle for a while."

Shinju wanted to refuse, but her eyelids were heavy and beginning to smart, and so she nodded and moved to sit in the bottom of the boat, leaning her head against her bag, while Raiden took up the oar and sent them sailing faster along the river's current.

He didn't wake her until the sun rose, its rays casting brilliant streaks of gold across the mountains. They were reaching the end of the river, where it would empty out into Lake Goshi.

The river grew wider, filled with more rocks and swirling whirlpools that would crash their boats to bits if they didn't steer properly. The maze of currents reminded Shinju of The Golden Sea and the passage home, and her heart ached. *Soon*, she promised. *Soon I will return.*

Eventually the river quieted and flowed more peacefully, but its depths grew darker. No longer could Shinju see fish or crabs swimming in the shallows. She wondered if the stories about river yokai in this region were true, and she asked Raiden about it.

"I've never seen them, but I've heard the rumors," he admitted. "Best be on our guard. I have a feeling Hotaka and his Otami won't be far behind us."

Soon their boat sailed into the lake, a large bowl carved at the base of the mountain range. Tall, fragrant pine trees grew around the shoreline and speckled up the mountainside, which was covered with boulders and spindly brush. At the far end of the lake would be the Traveler's Pass, the only safe way to cut across the range, and even it was dangerous.

The stories of the yokai that lived in these mountains... Shinju did not have to wonder about them. She knew from Takumi's stories that those were true. If they were lucky, they would encounter nothing but deer or a bear on their journey.

Smoke drifted from rough-hewn houses at the entrance to the pass, the last stop for a traveler to acquire supplies or rest. The pass functioned as a trade route between the eastern coastal towns and villages and the rest of Horitamo, and people often traveled in caravans to avoid getting lost, or for protection against yokai and wild animals.

"We should stop here," Shinju said, nodding at the outpost. "We need things to cross the pass, and you need some rest too."

"I'm fine," Raiden argued, but he looked as tired as she felt.

"No, you're not. You'll need your strength, Raiden-san, half-kami or not."

He twisted his mouth but dropped the subject as they coasted onto the shore and pulled the boat up onto the rocky beach.

At the outpost shop, Shinju sold the boat and used the coin to buy food, camping supplies, and some warm cloaks. The mountain would be cold, even at this time of year, and especially at night.

She met Raiden outside, where he'd been talking to a few of the locals about any recent travelers in the area. "No reports of ninja or large groups coming through," he told Shinju in a low voice.

"Doesn't mean they haven't gone another way," Shinju muttered, fighting off a growing sense of dread. She had never expected this journey to be easy, but it had turned into so much more than she could have anticipated, both physically and mentally.

Would she ever be able to go home again? The island seemed continents away.

They stopped at the tiny inn for bowls of noodles, hot broth, leeks, and wild mushrooms, and dumplings swimming in chili oil. Wonderful, blessed dumplings. Shinju almost cried as she bit into the first one, leaving Raiden snorting at her in amusement.

"Where have you two come from?" inquired the innkeeper curiously as she stopped by to refill their tea. She was a tall, lean woman, with hair pulled back into a tight bun and a sharp but kind face. "Hotake Province," Raiden answered when Shinju hesitated.

"You've come a long way then." The innkeeper nodded. She didn't seem surprised by Raiden's eyes. Perhaps she had seen enough odd things in the mountains that he looked fairly normal to her by now.

"Yes…can you tell us anything about the pass that might be helpful?" Shinju wanted to know in between bites.

The woman put a hand to her chin. "Let's see, this time of year it's pretty mild, but wild animals will have their babies to protect so don't try to mess with any that you see, no matter how cute. Last week a fella was brought back here, his arm torn almost clean off. He'd tried to play with a bear cub. Mama didn't like that."

Shinju gulped. Suddenly the chili oil looked like blood, and she pushed the bowl away to reach for the noodles instead.

"As far as yokai, they usually start trickling down in search of prey at night, so keep a sharp eye out. It would be a good idea to take turns keeping watch when you sleep. Make only a small fire if you must."

"How long is it to reach the other side?" Raiden asked casually.

"Oh, three or four days if you keep a swift pace. Mind you, it's another day or two's walk to the Port of Kumato after that."

The innkeeper moved on to the kitchen, and Shinju set the noodles down with a sigh. "I wish there was a faster way," she said. "Lord Hotaka and the Otami probably have horses. And who knows how far his thief has managed to get."

"Well, we won't know until we get there or they catch up to us," Raiden allowed. "I wouldn't mind, I'd like another chance to fill his gut with lightning." He cracked his fists, and Shinju wrinkled her nose but couldn't help but grin. He seemed to be in better spirits than before…which was saying something for his usually grumpy demeanor.

After eating and dividing up the supplies between them, they walked to the other side of the outpost. "I'll carry the food," Raiden insisted. "If you do, it'll be gone in an hour."

"That is not true!" Shinju pouted. "There aren't any dumplings in there!"

Their shared laughter echoed off the sides of the pass, a strange contrast to the quiet wilderness and outpost. A few sheep in a nearby pen sent them annoyed looks.

"Ready?" Raiden asked, his arms crossed as he surveyed the pass, then glanced at Shinju.

She took a deep breath, fiddling with the strap of her bag. "Ready."

33

IT IS NOT YOUR *fault.* Shinju's words echoed in his ears as they began their journey through the pass.

Never had those words been spoken out loud to him. Not even the ronin who took him in had bothered to tell him such things, wrapped up in their own problems as they were. Raiden had channeled that guilt into his anger until he not only hated his mother's murderer but hated himself too.

He didn't know whether to think Shinju's beliefs about mercy were crazy or admirable. The girl had definitely been taught a lot of foreign concepts on that island: peace, harmony, love, forgiveness. None of those had been a part of Raiden's life after his mother's death.

A part of him wanted to believe they were possible, but he doubted very much that he deserved any of them, especially from Shinju. Who he was supposed to be planning to betray.

The girl walked beside him quietly, her eyes focused on the road ahead of them. Her hair was combed and braided, though shorter tendrils escaped to frame her face. Her skin had been scrubbed clean at the inn, and the late afternoon sun highlighted the scattering of freckles across her nose and cheeks.

She glanced at him and he looked away quickly, mentally scolding himself for behaving like a young boy.

They wouldn't make it very far today, with most of the light already passing them by, but they agreed on leaving as soon as possible. Their footsteps sounded loud on the empty pass. The terrain was rocky and desolate, only shrubbery growing on the sides of the road that had been naturally carved into the land as people traveled through it.

The mountain sides reached high around them, fog circling the various peaks and dark green trees creating the perfect hiding spots for wild animals.

"Have you ever traveled through here?" Shinju asked, breaking Raiden from his thoughts. "No, but I've heard about it from my wanderings." A smirk twitched the corner of his mouth. "They say that yokai creep along the road at night, looking for young women to steal away."

Shinju scoffed at that, yet her eyes searched the shadowy crags of the road warily. "Well, they will have a hard time stealing this young woman away," she confirmed fiercely with a toss of her head.

Raiden hid a grin, then grew thoughtful. He knew she had an adopted father back on the island, but what about someone else? Did she have a boy she liked and hoped to return to?

The mental image of her embracing a nameless, faceless

young man left a bitter taste in his mouth, and he grew silent. Shinju eyed his change of mood curiously but didn't comment. Perhaps she'd grown used to it by now.

Dusk settled over the pass quickly, and they moved off the road to find a spot to settle in for the night. Shinju wanted to keep going, but Raiden advised against it. "You heard the innkeeper. It's too dangerous to travel at night. If we get an early start tomorrow, I think we can reach the half-way point by evening."

She looked torn, but followed him to a outcropping of rock where they could have a bit of shelter. Raiden built a small fire and Shinju began to prepare their dinner, humming as she unpacked some dried seaweed and rice.

"How far is Manju Shima from the coast?" Raiden asked as they munched on the food. "I'm not too sure," Shinju admitted, reaching for the scroll she always kept with her. "Takumi's notes of legend aren't very exact, but they do indicate that the island is east and to follow a trail of stars at midnight."

Raiden frowned. "That's not much to go on. Also, it's the Sea of Stars. All of the water will reflect the night sky. What kind of trail could we expect to find?"

Shinju shrugged. "I know, but maybe something special happens at midnight."

"Wouldn't someone have found the island before this, if there's a noticeable trail?" Raiden inquired.

"You're right. It must not be that obvious," Shinju mused, but he caught the way her voice faltered slightly as she looked over the scroll. It frustrated him that they seemed to be on a fool's errand, but the island had to be real. He bit back another pessimistic comment and settled for adjusting his gauntlets.

Shinju rested the map on her knees and watched him. "Raiden-kun?" she began tentatively. "Who gave you your gauntlets?'

He paused, swallowing hard. Another piece of his life he'd never told anyone about. Well, what did it matter now?

"My father did," he said.

Shinju's eyes widened, and she scooted a little closer to him. In the small space of their campfire, she was near now they were almost touching.

"When?" she asked softly.

Raiden looked down at the gauntlets, turning them slowly so they glinted in the firelight. "When I was a boy, not long after my mother passed. I had been traveling through Kuishi Province, searching for her murderer. I…was so angry that I cursed the Kami and demanded to know why my father had not protected her, or why he never acknowledged me."

Shinju's face twisted with sympathy.

"I struggled with my powers in those days. Lightning burst from my fists sporadically. The air would crackle with static and shock anyone nearby. If I wasn't careful, people got hurt."

"One night there was a lightning storm. No rain, just lighting, twisting across the sky like spiderwebs. I sat out in an open field, blind with my grief, half-hoping I would be struck and killed." Shinju sucked in a breath, placing a hand on her heart.

"What happened?"

"A huge bolt struck the earth near me, leaving a crater in the ground. When the smoke cleared, I found the gauntlets at the bottom."

He raised them up. "When I put them on, I could control my powers better. The silver acts as a conductor."

Shinju's fingers rose and traced the twisting symbols on the gauntlet nearest her, fascinated. The gesture felt strangely intimate, even though she didn't touch his bare skin.

"They're the only gift I've ever received from my father," he confessed.

"That makes them very special," Shinju reasoned. "It means he must care about you, Raiden. A gift from a Kami is not to be regarded lightly."

He snorted. "The Kami are fickle beings. Their desires change like the wind. We're better off without them." She dropped her hand back into her lap, and Raiden turned towards her, resting an arm on the rocks behind them.

"How can you say that?" Shinju asked, exasperated. "Aren't you afraid they might grow angry, hearing you talk so?"

He shrugged, grinning. "Don't tell me you're worried about me. Are you?"

"Well…" She couldn't finish her sentence, and instead glanced everywhere but him, twisting her hands. A faint blush spread across her cheeks.

Raiden leaned closer, studying her with interest.

"You're speechless, for once."

That earned him a glare. "And you're impossible."

"You didn't answer my question."

"Fine! Yes, I'm…a *little* worried."

Raiden chuckled. "Hmmm, only a little. I wonder how we can change that?"

She blinked at him. "You better not do anything reckless!"

"Such as?"

"I don't know…going off into the night to fight yokai?"

He scratched his chin. "That's a good idea, now that you mention it."

Shinju groaned and slapped her forehead. "Men are ridiculous!"

Raiden barked a laugh. "You're too easy to tease. But speaking of men…" He trailed off, fingering a loose thread on her shoulder. "I assume there's some on your island?"

Shinju cocked her head. "Uh, yes, of course. Why?"

He cleared his throat, not meeting her eyes. "You've never mentioned anyone else…besides your adopted father."

She smiled then, her eyes sparkling with laughter. "You're asking if I have a special someone waiting for me?"

She said the words lightly, but they caused an influx of jealousy to pool in the pit of his stomach. The emotion was new, and he felt angry by it as much as he dreaded her answer.

Surely, if there was a boy, he wouldn't have the kind of baggage Raiden carried. He was probably sweet, a pretty boy that all the girls swooned over, and nothing like the grumpy brute Raiden knew himself to be.

Or maybe she preferred Akira. They'd been childhood friends, after all.

"There's no one," she continued softly. He let out a breath, that revelation restoring his confidence.

"Really?" He shifted a little closer, their knees touching now.

Her face grew even redder as she studied their proximity to each other, then glanced shyly at him. "Really. What about you,

Raiden-kun? Do you have someone to go home to after all this is over?"

He rolled his eyes at that. "Do I sound like the kind of guy who has a little wife tucked away somewhere while I scour the kingdom for my mother's murderer?"

She half-shrugged. "Why not? You're…um, I mean, I'm sure lots of women would want to be with you."

"Well, I'd certainly like to meet them," he deadpanned, and she giggled. The quiet sound of her laughter spread a warmth through his chest, and, unbidden, he thought again of how he'd planned to betray this girl.

Raiden knew in this moment as she gazed at him bashfully, her eyes catching his and absorbing their oddity without flinching, that he couldn't go through with this plan.

She had unlocked a part of himself that he didn't realize existed, that he never would have thought possible for someone like him. And it scared him more than anything in the world.

Before he realized it, he had cleared his throat and said, "Shinju, I have to tell you something."

A slight crease formed on her forehead at his change in demeanor. "Yes, Raiden?"

He pulled back, putting some space between them so he could think with a clear head, instead of focusing on the fact that she smelled nice, like jasmine. "I…I didn't decide to help you find the Kanju simply for your clan to reward me."

The girl blinked, tilting her head as she waited for him to say the rest. Raiden winced slightly, trying to find the right way to say what he wanted, and decided to go with being blunt. That was who he was.

"I was going to help you find it, then steal it from you. Once I convinced you to tell me where the other one was, I would leave to go find it too."

Shinju stiffened, her warm smile vanishing like smoke. For a long moment she simply stared at him, then turned towards the fire, bringing her knees up under chin.

"Why are you telling me this now?" she asked.

Raiden blew out a breath, raking his hand through his hair. "Because I changed my mind. I'd rather die honest than live as a liar."

She chewed her lip, considering his words. "You changed your mind," she repeated. "Why?"

He pinched the bridge of his nose, suddenly very tired. But she deserved to know why. After all the compassion she'd shown him, how could he turn her away?

"I couldn't be one more person to betray you," he almost whispered.

Shinju's nails dug into her sleeves, and she tilted her head to look at him with an expression he didn't know how to read.

"You told me all along not to trust you. What has changed, Raiden-kun?"

The way she spoke, so kindly, so completely the opposite of what he deserved…Raiden didn't know whether to pull his hair out or grab her and kiss her just to change the subject. He didn't want to tell her anything more, didn't want to bare the parts of his shriveled heart that had come back to life again after spending time with her.

"Don't you understand?" he growled, clenching his fists and fighting the urge to run.

"I want to," she responded, placing gentle fingers on his arm. He stared at them, wondering how such tiny hands could be so caring and still break a man's nose with ease.

"Whatever your original intentions, you have protected me, and stood up for me, this entire journey," Shinju continued. "You could have joined Lord Hotaka, but you didn't. You chose to keep helping me."

She gave a tentative smile. "No matter what you've tried to become, no matter what you've told yourself, you're a good man, Raiden. You're loyal and brave. These are qualities that I… I admire about you." Her face turned more pink.

Before he could reply, a heavy footstep echoed through the pass ahead. Raiden instantly jumped to his feet and stamped their fire out, plunging them into darkness. Not wanting to draw more attention with light, he quietly drew his sword.

Shinju drew hers as well, seeming to sense this was not a foe she could defeat with hand-to-hand-combat. An eerie silence filled the road; not even the crickets chirped any longer.

A grunting, wheezing noise emerged, accompanied by a giant, hulking shape barely illuminated by the weak moonlight.

"What is it?" Shinju whispered.

The creature paused, gazing around the pass, blinking one huge, yellow eye in the center of its forehead. With the lack of light, the rest of it was difficult to make out, but Raiden recognized enough of the shape and size to answer grimly, "It's an Onihitokuchi."

Shinju stiffened. "An oni that eats and kills humans? Here?"

She had a right to be surprised. Neither of them had expected to encounter such a yokai as this. Raiden thought they might see minor ones such as Onibi or Kappa, who were more mischievous than truly deadly.

What was an Onihitokuchi doing here on a well-traveled pass of Horitamo? They were more likely to appear when a war or famine plagued the land.

It rolled its yellow eye in their direction, and gave a snort, breathing in their scent.

"Lord Hotaka is behind this," Shinju hissed, gripping her katana tighter. "I know it. He must have found a way to lure this thing here to stop us."

"Perhaps, but right now, we need to focus on killing it." Raiden considered whether they should attack first. He could rush it with his lightning, while Shinju could circle around and hack its legs with her sword.

The oni gave a roar and began pounding down the road towards them. The moon eased away from behind the clouds to reveal a twenty-foot monster covered in thick, greenish skin. Dripping fangs protruded from his mouth, and even from several yards away, its rank breath reached them, stinking of decay.

Raiden called on his lightning, feeling the power awaken and course through the air and his body in a familiar dance. He sent the lightning in his right hand to travel up the katana, turning it into both a torch and a more deadly weapon.

"I'll attack it head on," he shouted to Shinju. "You look for openings to stab it with your katana. Don't hold back."

She nodded grimly. "Right!"

When the creature was only a few feet away, Raiden ran to meet it. The oni swiped at him with one giant, meaty arm, but

Raiden ducked and sliced its stomach with his sword.

It roared, a terrible, ear-splitting sound, and backhanded Raiden so hard the air whooshed out of him. He flew backwards, groaning as he felt his ribs crack and bruise. The oni stomped towards him, and Raiden pushed back to his feet, smirking.

"Is that the best you can do?"

Breathing deep, Raiden shot bolts of lightning into the ogre when it raised another hand to strike him. The lightning struck its chest, spreading in a spiderweb over its body. The oni roared with pain and swiped at Raiden again.

He dodged and wondered where Shinju was. He spotted her, not on the road, but on the mountainside. She had used the various outcropping of rocks to climb up, and now she stood on a ledge overlooking the road.

With a running start, she leapt off the ledge and landed on the oni's shoulders, digging her katana into its flesh for purchase. The creature howled and reached back, trying to throw her off.

Raiden distracted it with more lightning, dodging blows to slice at its ankles. The oni stumbled, continuing to roar in anger and pain, but its movements grew faster, as if their attacks were fueling it rather than wearing it down.

Shinju managed to climb farther up its neck and she plunged the katana into the back of its head. With a blood-curdling roar, the oni grabbed her and flung her through the air, where she hit the side of the mountain and rolled down to the ground, limp as a rag doll.

"Shinju!" Raiden shouted. The oni tried to smash him with one of its feet, and rolled out of the way, sending another blast of lightning towards its face. He wondered if he would have to call down a bolt from the sky again: it would drain him even faster, but it was a more powerful attack. Surely this monster couldn't withstand the lightning much longer.

Summoning every bit of his strength, Raiden focused on the sky above, pulling and drawing on storm clouds to gather overhead. He just needed a couple of minutes to concentrate, but the oni made that difficult by continuing to swipe at him with fists the size of boulders.

Shinju's katana, still lodged in the yokai's head, began to do its work. The oni started moving more slowly, lumbering and stepping side to side. Raiden backed up, trying to get a hold on the swirling storm clouds above. His ribs were on fire, forcing him to take shallow breaths. *I must be more injured than I thought.*

With a cry, Shinju appeared, limping but forcing herself to move into a run. She slid between the oni's legs, wielding two *kunai*, and sliced them along the giant ankles. Black blood gushed out like gruesome fountains, and the oni wheeled back, enraged.

"Now!" Shinju shouted, throwing herself to the side. Raiden raised his hands, and with a yell, a powerful bolt streaked down from the clouds, hitting the oni.

A thunderous crack followed, and the oni roared as its body burned from the bolt. It fell to its knees, groaning, then face planted into the road, shaking the ground and the trees around them.

Raiden staggered, holding onto his ribs, and watched the oni warily, half-expecting it to rise again. But it did not move.

Gasping, he turned to look for Shinju. She lay on her back,

close to where their campsite had been. Her eyes were wide and fearful, her face streaked with dirt and blood, but she was alive. Carefully he limped over to her, and they sat together for a long time, catching their breaths.

He didn't even comment when her shaky hand found his and gripped it tightly.

34

For the rest of the night, they slept in a tree. After tending to their wounds and regaining a bit of strength back, Shinju and Raiden climbed one of the towering pine trees and tied them-selves to the branches with rope to keep from falling.

It would have been fun, if they had not just almost been killed.

Shinju's entire body screamed in protest when she moved. No bones were broken, but she was bruised all over and her shoulder had popped out of its socket. That hurt more than the rest combined.

Raiden instructed her to bite down on a stick while he pushed her shoulder back into place. She screamed, almost blacking out as the pain slammed into her with a force equal to that of the oni's arm that hit her. For long moments she lay, shuddering and shaking, before she was able to help bind

Raiden's ribs.

They were cracked, but he didn't seem too worried, only annoyed that they would slow him down. He healed faster than a full human, but even this injury would take time.

He said nothing of the way they'd held hands for a long time after the oni died. Shinju couldn't forget the feeling of his palm, rough and warm, felt, the sense of security and strength that lay within those hands that could summon lightning from the heavens.

She wondered what would have happened if the oni had not interrupted them. His confession about intending to steal the tide jewels had been an unexpected, and unpleasant, surprise. Shinju could have kicked herself for being so naive: of course, Raiden wouldn't be risking his life constantly simply for a reward from the Tsomas.

And yet, as much as she wanted to be angry with him, as much as she wanted to lash out at him for lying to her, she stopped herself. His admittance meant something, and she longed to find out what it was. Did he just feel guilty? Was he trying to trick her into trusting him?

A nervous flutter in her heart wondered if maybe, just maybe, he had begun to care for her, that his affections kept him from wanting to hurt or betray her.

She had been vulnerable with him, and in return he had been vulnerable to her, exposing a side of himself she doubted others had seen. He had accepted her, and stood by her side. Could he possibly care for her the way she was beginning to for him?

Once the thought occurred to her, it took root, and Shinju

became very aware of their interactions, any time they touched, however lightly or casually, or whenever she looked up and caught him watching her.

Settled on her branch, with the rough bark of the tree digging into her back, Shinju glanced over at her companion who lounged on a nearby branch. His eyes were closed, hiding their blue-white glow, and his arms had returned to their usual crossed position.

Shinju sighed and tried to relax, biting back on the pain that still shot through her arm. She'd found some roots in the woods that, once ground to a paste, could be applied to sore muscles. Shinju had spread a thick layer over her shoulder and offered it to Raiden for his ribs.

She blushed, thinking of how he'd lifted his shirt to apply the paste to his side, and she'd caught a glimpse of not only the black and blue ribs, but his well-toned stomach. The image sat with her until the sky grew gray, and eventually an uneasy sleep claimed her at last for a couple of hours.

Raiden woke her with a gentle shake. "We have to keep going." He handed her a wrinkled apple and they descended from the trees, blinking around in the early morning light.

The oni still lay in the road, beginning to smell worse than ever. Flies buzzed around its carcass, and Shinju covered her nose to keep from wretching. They jogged past it quickly and continued down the road through the pass, glad to leave it behind. "I hope there's no more of those," Raiden muttered.

They moved more slowly now, and as the sun crawled higher in the clear blue sky, the heat beat down upon their heads. Shinju wiped sweat off her face with her good arm, wishing for a cool breeze or that a hat would magically appear on her head. The pass had widened, leaving the sparse forest behind, and there was little shade.

A hawk circled lazily overhead, and there were no sounds except their footsteps on the dry, packed earth. Shinju had refilled their water canteens back at the outpost, but they still needed to conserve the precious liquid as much as possible, so she allowed herself only small sips here and there.

"When this is over," Raiden began, his voice dry and raspy. "I'm going to find the coldest, deepest lake and float in it until I'm as wrinkled as an old man."

Shinju giggled, slightly delirious. "I'm going to eat chilled fruit and cream until I burst, then sit under a waterfall with my mouth open."

"That's a good way to drown," Raiden pointed out.

"At least I won't be hot, or hungry!"

"Tch, all you think about is food."

"What else is there to think about?

He laughed roughly. "Right now, I suppose you have a point."

Neither of them had wanted the crushed food in their bags after the oni stampeded through their campsite. The apple Shinju ate that morning might as well have been from days ago, for all it did to fill her stomach.

In an attempt to think of something other than smoked fish and steamed pork buns, Shinju licked her lips and started humming a tune that she'd learned on the island. The song told the story of a boy who went fishing by himself, got trapped in a storm, and was brought home by a large turtle.

Her heart twisted as she thought of home. How long ago had she left? If they found the Manju before Hotaka and took back the Kanju, would it still be too late by the time she returned to the Tsomas?

Her tune trailed off in the wake of these anxious thoughts. Raiden cleared his throat.

"That was nice," he said. "What is it?"

If she hadn't been so distracted, Shinju would have been surprised by his compliment. "Just a song that's popular for children on my island." She smiled wistfully. "They all know the words and demand it to be sung at every festival."

He nodded. "Tell me more about your island."

Pleased by his curiosity, Shinju warmed to her favorite subject, describing the lush jungle, the beaches, the lagoons, and the way of life on Kanju Shima. It passed the time, and kept them both from thinking about the seemingly impossible task that lay ahead.

By nightfall, they reached the half-way point in the mountain pass. A stone hut had been built as a refuge, and according to the sign posted by the door, travelers were expected to leave something behind for whoever stayed there next.

Waiting for them was a pile of firewood and dried root vegetables hanging from the rafters. The hut was small but cozy, with a hearth and brazier, and a few cooking tools.

After eating a meager meal and laying on their bed rolls, exhausted, Shinju stared up at the ceiling, wondering again about how they would protect the Manju and also rescue the Kanju from Lord Hotaka. She had been so focused on beating him to the other island that she hadn't had a chance to think about it.

Doubt clouded her mind. What would the right course be? Could they find the Manju in time? If so, what then? Would she, Raiden, and the other Tsomas be able to defeat Lord Hotaka?

A surge of hopelessness threatened to bring tears to her eyes. *Takumi*, she thought, *I don't know if I can do this. How can I stop an army? A man who possesses one of the tide jewels and will stop at nothing?*

A soft snore drew her eyes to the man sleeping a few feet away from her, his face turned so that she could make out the contours in the dim light of the fire.

I'm not alone, she thought resolutely. *Raiden-kun is with me.*

Two days later, they reached the end of the mountain pass. The road continued onward, winding down from the hill and snaking through the plain of tall, dry grass until it stopped at the Port of Kumato.

From their vantage point, the port was just a small town, barely visible, but beyond it, the Sea of Stars spread out like glass, endless and as far as the eye could see. Boats of various sizes bobbed in the waves near the shoreline.

Shinju clapped her hands and lifted her face to feel the fresh breeze that blew in from the coast. "Thank Ryūjin, we made it!"

Even Raiden grinned, studying the port town. "It's no lake, but it will do."

Throughout their journey, they each tossed around ideas for

securing a boat and sailing for Manju Shima. Shinju didn't want to just steal one, but they needed to keep a low profile, and also make for the island quickly, so eventually Raiden's idea of a little thievery won out.

She squinted, shielding her eyes from the bright sunshine. "Do you see any larger ships that might accommodate Lord Hotaka?"

"No, but that doesn't mean he's not here," Raiden remarked grimly. "We should wait until dark to go down."

Shinju sighed, selfishly wishing that they had time to stop at a bathhouse or an inn to eat some real food. Instead, they found shelter under some scraggly trees, and Raiden told her he would scout the area.

While he was gone, Shinju built a small fire, and wrapped the last of their rice balls and vegetables in leaves, setting them near the flame to warm. "No reason why we can't have a hot meal!" she declared to a beetle, who watched her actions with disapproval.

When Raiden returned, he surprised her with a small, plucked bird, and they roasted it over the fire. "I never want to camp again after today," Shinju confessed after they ate and sat looking out at the glistening sea.

Raiden snorted. "You'll have to on your way home."

"Oh no, I plan to sail home."

"*Nani*? All the way around Horitamo?"

"Of course! I much prefer traversing the ocean to land. It won't take such a very long time." She unbraided her hair from the tight braid, sighing with relief as the tension left her scalp.

Leisurely, she combed her fingers through the strands. "We

will probably meet Lord Hotaka on the sea," she commented. "Whatever he has planned, we will have to be very careful."

Something touched her hand, and she looked down to see that Raiden had leaned forward to finger a lock of her hair. Heat rose through her neck and cheeks, but she didn't dare move as she raised her eyes to his.

For a long moment they stared at each other. Slowly, he leaned forward and brushed his lips against hers.

An explosion of butterflies took flight in Shinju's stomach, and she angled her head to allow him better access. Encouraged by this, Raiden claimed her mouth fully, reaching an arm around her waist to pull her against his chest.

All of her worries melted away in the warmth of Raiden's embrace and the determined press of his lips on her own, and Shinju closed her eyes, allowing the tentative, budding feelings for the half-kami to blossom into more.

For just a moment, all the tasks that lay ahead vanished, only the two of them existed.

35

THAT’S THE ONE.”

“Are you sure?”

Shinju nodded, contemplating the boat chosen to be their vessel. The boat they were going to steal.

She still felt uneasy about taking something so essential to one’s livelihood. The boat had clearly been taken care of: its black paint shone in the moonlight, and at least from a distance, the sail and rigging looked to be in good condition. Most likely it belonged to a wealthier fisherman.

“Okay then,” Raiden breathed, his voice close to her ear. The sound made Shinju’s toes curl in her shoes, remembering their heated kisses from earlier.

Concentrate, Shinju! she mentally scolded herself. *This is no time to daydream about kissing!*

They were taking refuge behind some crates and barrels at

the docks. This late at night, the streets of the port were fairly quiet, everyone retiring for the evening at home, or playing *shogi* at the tavern. Lights spilled from oil lamps in the windows of the stone houses, bleached white from the sun and ocean salt.

The familiarity of it caused a pang of homesickness in Shinju's chest. What she wouldn't give to see her clan's village restored right now.

Sailors and fishermen had long left their nets and the day's catch, and the various boats bobbed quietly in the water, lined up in neat rows with anchors dropped or securely moored. The scent of fish and brine hung heavily in the air; it would have been overwhelming if not for the constant breeze drifting off the sea.

The Sea of Stars earned its name for a good reason. On a clear night, the waters reflected the stars above so accurately that it was easy to imagine yourself sailing through the sky. The beauty of this sea attracted visitors across Horitamo, especially during the Star Festival when the constellations shone brightest, signaling the new year.

Shinju had once dreamed of seeing this sea and sailing its waters, though under very different circumstances.

A lone sentry patrolled the docks, and a few minutes ago he had left his post, probably to change places with another or relieve himself. Checking for any other passerby, Raiden crept from their hiding place, keeping to the shadows. He plucked a wide-brimmed straw hat from a fisherman's stall and plopped it on his head.

"To hide my eyes," he stated to Shinju. "Don't want to draw attention to ourselves, especially if Hotaka has lookouts here."

Following in his footsteps, Shinju crouched low and they circled around the stalls and barrels of fish until they reached the edge of the docks. "You're up," Raiden whispered. Shinju hopped onto the boat, feeling it rock slightly under the movement.

While Raiden untied the rope holding the boat to a pole at the dock, Shinju readied the sail and lines. They wouldn't put it up until they were farther out, to avoid notice. Thankfully there were two oars.

"Definitely a fisherman," she muttered, kicking aside the nets and traps that littered the bottom of the boat. "Not a very tidy one either."

She tapped Raiden's elbow. "We can't take all of this with us."

His mouth twisted, but he nodded, and began grabbing the nets and traps under both arms, setting them onto the dock. "I wish there was another way," Shinju whispered. "Just imagine the look on the fisherman's face when you tell him his boat helped save the empire," Raiden joked in a hushed tone.

They each grabbed an oar once the boat was unloaded and paddled it farther out into the water, staying as low as they could. A solitary lantern swung from the curved prow, but Shinju didn't dare light it yet.

Please, Ryūjin, she thought, *help us find Manju Shima. Help us stop Lord Hotaka.* Nothing answered her save the lap of waves on the sides of the boat, but she felt slightly better.

Every second that passed, she expected to hear cries of alarm, but they drifted on and on without detection, and soon they were far enough away from the port that all she could see were the twinkling of lights and the ghostly glow of the white shops and houses.

After about half an hour, Shinju figured they were enough away, and she unbound the fan-shaped sail. It took to the wind immediately, filling out and pushing them faster out to sea.

Clouds rolled across the sky, and the stars disappeared, throwing the water into inky darkness. Raiden lit the lamp on the prow, and they sat side by side, staring out into the endless night, with land growing further and further away behind them.

Shinju pulled Takumi's battered old compass from her bag and set it on the seat in front of her. The arrow twirled and settled, and she used it to continue navigating the boat towards the southeast.

"You make it look so easy," Raiden confessed, watching her. She smiled, tucking a piece of hair behind her ear.

"Well, Takumi made sure that I practiced sailing a lot over the years, in all kinds of weather. I'll never forget the day he brought me out into a storm. It was terrible! We sailed around in circles for hours."

He chuckled. "Sounds as though you kept very busy on that island."

"Oh yes, idleness is not a virtue," Shinju agreed. "When I'm not training or sailing, I'm fishing, cooking, taking care of the house, tending the garden. Everything has a place and a purpose, with time dedicated to perfecting it."

Raiden nodded. "The ronin who took me in held similar beliefs from their days as samurai, though some of them would hate to hear me say that." He chuckled.

Shinju brought one leg up under her and let the other

dangle, barely brushing the bottom of the boat. "Will you ever go back to them?" she asked.

"The ronin?" He thought about it. "I don't know. Maybe. They weren't exactly like a family, but they are the closest I have to that. I guess it depends…"

He trailed off and glanced at her searchingly. Shinju averted her gaze, blushing, and pretended to be busy with the sail ropes. "Would you ever come visit my island?"

"Am I allowed to?" he questioned, humor coloring his voice. "I thought the Tsomas wanted to keep it hidden from outsiders."

"Well, that's true, but you're different! You're helping to save the tide jewels. I think that makes you an exception."

"I see. And can I expect Takumi-sensei to come out with a katana, demanding to hear my reasons for why I think I'm good enough to kiss his daughter?" Raiden teased, snaking an arm around her shoulders.

"T-Takumi will be very welcoming," Shinju gulped, feeling flustered. "He's a reasonable man."

Raiden snorted. "Every man is reasonable until another man is interested in his daughter."

Could her face grow any redder? Shinju stuttered a response. "I-interested?"

Raiden smirked, though she thought she detected a bit of pink in his cheeks. "Was earlier not obvious enough for you? I'll admit I'm a bit new to all of this."

He cut off her reply with a kiss, and she melted, even loosening her hold on the sail. Right now, she hardly cared if they blew a little off course.

"I've never been kissed before you," she mumbled against his mouth. Raiden drew back slightly, shaking his head. "Those men on your island really need to pull it together."

They skimmed across the dark water for a long time, sometimes talking, sometimes just watching the sea moving and shimmering when the stars could peek out behind the clouds.

"I haven't seen anything yet that looks like a trail," Shinju said after reading the scroll again. "If it's not clear to you, then there's a good chance it's not clear to Lord Hotaka either," Raiden added. "We may have the advantage on him yet."

"I hope so. I can't believe there were ancient documents about the tide jewels hidden in the scholar archives of our castle." Shinju reached her hand into the water, feeling the cold liquid swirl through her fingers.

"My mother would tell me stories about Ryūjin, but I thought they were just bedtime stories until I met the Tsomas." She sighed. "I wish I had paid more attention. Maybe there was something in those that could be useful."

A strong wind suddenly arose, pushing against the boat and stirring up larger waves to smash against the sides. Shinju gripped the lines, trying to keep their direction without putting too much strain on the sail.

"What can I do?" Raiden shouted above the noise of rushing water.

"Tie that down!" Shinju instructed, pointing at the rope attached to the sail's boom. Raiden stepped over quickly, holding the line as it jerked hard in his hand.

After a few minutes of fighting, the wind died again to a gentler gust, and Shinju breathed a sigh of relief. "I hope we haven't blown too far off," she stated, reaching for her compass.

Her hand touched only the wooden seat instead of the smooth round object, and Shinju searched around wildly. "The compass! Where is it?"

Raiden snatched the lantern and brought it back, holding it aloft as she dug through their belongings and felt around the bottom of the boat.

It was nowhere to be found. Shinju groaned, covering her face with her hands. "I can't believe it. It must have fallen out."

There was nothing to be done but to go on. "I'm sorry," Raiden told her, patting her shoulder. "At least you can see the stars now. The wind blew the clouds away."

Shinju sniffled and looked up, studying the expanse of midnight stretched above them, filled with millions of twinkling lights. Her eyes found the familiar shapes of the drum and the mighty hunter, who also looked like the shape of a woman with a long kimono sleeve.

Then she spotted another constellation, and her heart almost stopped.

With a long, curving body and giant claws, the constellation known as the Dragon stood out brightly. His was marked by a large red star, and he seemed to swim or fly. One claw extended back, and the other reached forward.

Slowly, Shinju guided her eyes down from the sky to the water. The Dragon's reflection, shimmering against the waves, pointed due east.

"Of course," Shinju murmured. "The trail is the Dragon."

Filled with a renewed hope, she adjusted the sail and they sped across the sea, heading the direction of the dragon's outstretched claw.

The night stayed clear, but the wind renewed its strength once more, and large waves tossed them around, filling the boat with water. Shinju fought to keep their course while Raiden used a bucket to bail out the water.

Sometimes, a large formation of rock would appear out of the darkness, and Shinju would have to swing the boat wide and hard to avoid a collision. When morning came, they passed some smaller islands, only a mile or so long, but surrounded by reefs or shoals that would be sure to trap them.

Shinju grew exhausted, and her arms and back hurt from the strain of the sail. No matter how often a person sailed, rough waters would always drain one's energy, and the fight to survive came down to how long you could last.

With the stars gone, she had to rely on the sun's movement. Drizzling rain came and went throughout the day, one moment leaving them hot and thirsty, the next leaving them cold and wet and miserable.

During a lag in the wind, which meant the boat barely moved at all unless they paddled, Raiden leaned over the edge, and used a tiny jolt of lightning to electrocute a fish. "Ha!" He snatched it from the water, holding it high for Shinju to see.

"A yellowtail!" she exclaimed. "Oh, if only we had some radishes to go with it."

She used one of her knives to clean and filet it. Trying to figure out how to cook it took some work, but in the end they rigged a little fire under a pan left behind by the fisherman, and added the last of their root vegetables Shinju had taken from the traveler's hut back in the pass.

Night fell once more, and they took turns guiding the boat, led only by the dragon constellation above and the hope that they would soon find the island.

36

DAWN WAS ALMOST UPON them when Raiden pointed out a dark shape in the distance.

"Look!"

Shinju started guiltily from where she'd begun to nod off at the mast. Rubbing her eyes, she peered through the early morning mist that covered the sea. They were approaching something; whether it was an island or not, Shinju could not be sure yet.

The Dragon had faded, his last star winking at them in the dark gray expanse of sky. Fog continued to roll in as they sailed closer and closer to the mass in the horizon, almost completely obscured from view.

"This is it," she whispered. "I can feel it."

Her eyes were dry and her throat felt like sandpaper. Raiden's face was worn and covered with the shadow of beard.

Even the boat seemed exhausted. But at last they had reached Manju Shima, the island home of the other Tsoma Clan and hiding place of the second tide jewel.

The island became more defined through the fog; unlike Shinju's home, this place appeared to be made up of rockier terrain. Instead of soft white sand, the beach was covered with pebbles and stones washed smooth by the surf. Above the beach grew a jungle of dark green plants and moss-covered trees, laced thickly with vines.

The air was still and quiet when they reached the shore and drew the boat up high enough to not be washed back into the sea. Shinju looked around carefully. There was no sign of life except for tiny crabs darting in and out of the pebbles.

"Hmmm, no welcome party?" Raiden mused.

"Perhaps they don't know we are here yet," Shinju added uncertainly. The place felt nearly abandoned, and she saw no other boats along the beach.

"I suppose we should go look for them," she said after a moment. Retrieving their swords from the boat, Shinju and Raiden entered the jungle, following a narrow path that wound through the foliage.

Humidity clung to their skin and clothes, and very soon they were both panting. Shinju felt as though her skin was melting, and she picked up a large leaf to use as a fan.

"Is this like your island?" Raiden huffed. Beads of sweat rolled down his neck and disappeared under his collar. "No, our island has much cooler weather." Shinju couldn't understand it. Wouldn't the presence of the Manju have the same effect here as the Kanju did on her island?

She'd expected a mirror version of the paradise she called home, but instead, this place seemed almost uninhabitable. She groaned and gathered her hair up in one hand, fanning herself with the leaf in the other as they continued to tramp down the path.

"I won't mind if you need to shed a couple layers of clothing," Raiden teased, throwing her a saucy grin and a wink. She responded by playfully launching a tree nut at his head.

"We have to be near their village soon," Shinju commented a while later. Her heart began to sink as they continued to see no sign of life anywhere. Had something happened long ago and forced the Tsomas to move to a different island? Had they been discovered at some point?

She half-hoped that it was true. Any records Lord Hotaka had found would lead him here too, and then he would be as much of a dead-end as they were. Then she could focus on only having to take the Kanju back.

Raiden suddenly thrust an arm in front of her, bringing them to a halt. "Do you smell that?" he asked.

Shinju raised her chin, breathing in the hot air of the jungle, and underneath the soil and plants she caught the smell of something burning. And it wasn't just wood.

Looking up into the sky, she spotted a trail of smoke between the tree branches.

Without waiting for Raiden, Shinju charged ahead, running now in the direction of the smoke. "Shinju!" he shouted. She crashed through the jungle, batting vines and leaves out of her way, until she reached a clearing.

A circle of huts smoldered with thick black smoke and

orange fire, their thatched roofs beginning to cave in. And strewn across the ground were…

Shinju fell to her knees, raising a hand to her mouth as she choked back the rising bile in her throat. Her head spun, tears blurring her vision. "No…no…" she gasped.

The bodies of men, women, and children lay scattered throughout the village. Drying blood gushed from wounds in their heads, necks, or abdomens. Not a single finger or foot moved to indicate any still lived.

Vaguely, Shinju heard Raiden step up behind her. "We're too late," she whispered, frozen by the gruesome sight before. Despite all their efforts, she had been too late. Again.

Not far away, a figure moved in the smoke at the other side of the village, and Raiden instantly moved into a fighting stance, lightning emerging from his fists. Shinju blinked, watching as the figure of the Otami thief appeared.

"You…" she croaked, her hands forming fists.

"Well, well," the thief spoke in a calm, eloquent voice, as if he wasn't standing amongst dozens of dead bodies. "You found us at last. I was worried I wouldn't be able to formally introduce myself, especially after hearing about your little tussle with Lord Hotaka in Itshino."

His face was half-hidden by a black cloth drawn up above his nose, and he wore his hair in a tight bun tied with red twine. His eyes burned with curiosity as he studied Shinju.

"So, you're the little girl who must have shot at me when I stole the Kanju," he mused. "I must say, you're not at all what I suspected."

Shinju did not reply as she slowly stood and drew her

katana.

The thief arched an eyebrow as if amused. "Do you really think that will stop me?" he asked. "Or your friend here? I am not alone this time, you see."

Dark shapes emerged around the perimeter of the village, revealing more ninja armed with shuriken and kunai. "I don't care if you have a legion with you," Shinju snapped. Fury like she'd never known engulfed her, blocking out everything else.

"I won't let you leave this place with the tide jewels. Turn them over now, or die."

"I think we should kill him regardless of whether he turns them over or not," Raiden growled.

The thief clicked his tongue. "Tch, tch, not very Tsoma-like of you, little Shinju. But then again, you're not really a Tsoma, are you?" He moved closer until he was only a couple of yards away.

"How would you know?" she demanded. "How would you know anything about the Tsomas?"

His eyes creased. "Haven't you figured it out yet?"

A pit grew in the bottom of Shinju's stomach. Whispers of a fear, a suspicion that she'd tried to push away reared its ugly head once more.

"You found ancient texts," she replied. "Lord Hotaka told us so."

The thief hummed. "That is true, we did, but they were only helpful to an extent. The rest came from up here." He tapped his head.

An icy shudder swept through Shinju's body. The person with intimate knowledge of the tide jewels, the one Lord Hotaka had mentioned…this was he.

"You're a Tsoma," she breathed.

"Correct! Although I go by the name Matsuda these days." The thief gave a mocking bow.

Waves of realization rippled through Shinju's mind, putting the pieces together. "You came from Kanju Shima. That's how you knew to find the island. That's how you knew where the Kanju was kept."

"Very good, Shinju. Yes, I was born on Kanju Shima, and I'm one of the few who ever left when the ceremony came around."

Shinju tightened her grip on her sword. "Why?" she demanded. "Why have you done this? You've killed innocent people. Your own clan!"

He sighed. "Your naive ideals are rather tiresome. There is more to the world than these quiet little islands. I wanted to do great things I knew I would never accomplish with the Tsomas. So I traveled through Horitamo, and Lord Hotaka offered me the chance to be a part of something grander."

"When I learned that he sought the tide jewels, I divulged to him that I had personal knowledge of their whereabouts. Or at least, for one of them."

"You knew the festival would be happening that night. You planned it all."

"Indeed. I couldn't believe how lax the security became. For something as precious as a tide jewel, the clan disappointed me in their efforts to protect it."

Shinju growled, taking a few steps forward. "You betrayed us!" she shouted. "You killed samurai, and the people in this village. You are a thief, and a murderer. You sought to become something great, but all I see is how far you've fallen."

Matsuda laughed. "Quite a speech! You are a fiery little thing aren't you? But you're missing one more detail. How did we find this place, hmm?"

Shinju's pulse hammered, wondering what else she could possibly be missing. She thought back to her conversation with Lord Hotaka in Itshino. "*We don't have the Manju yet, but we will soon. All we need is the right guidance,*" he'd said.

It hit her like a heavy stone. "You followed us here."

Matsuda clapped slowly. "There you have it. We followed you, keeping our distance, until we were sure of the direction you were heading for. With your help and the clues left in the ancient texts, we were able to find Manju Shima."

Shinju stared in horror. All these people were dead… because of her. She'd led the Otami right to them.

A scream tearing from her throat, Shinju rushed across the clearing, gripping her katana in preparation for a killing stroke. At the same time, Raiden unleashed a myriad of lightning bolts, aiming for the other ninja.

The thief didn't move until Shinju swung her katana. His arm flew up, and her sword caught on the spikes of his bracer. Gritting her teeth, Shinju yanked the sword back and tried again, but the thief was faster.

He blocked the attack with his other arm, then tugged hard. Shinju tried to hold on to the sword, but its hilt slipped from her grasp at his movement, and it fell towards the ground.

The thief kicked it out of the way and lunged at her with a punch. Shinju barely managed to block it, stumbling backwards and trying to regain her footing. Tears and sweat and smoke stung her eyes, and she missed the next hit.

Pain exploded through her face as his armored fist connected with her cheek. Pretending to fall, Shinju used the close proximity to the thief to thrust her knee into his stomach.

He grunted, breaking his stride just enough for her to recover. She backed up, spitting blood from her mouth.

"Hmm, perhaps you're not as weak as I thought," the thief said. "Though you're still no match for me, girl. Why don't you give up, and join us? Maybe Lord Hotaka will let me keep you as a wife."

"I'd rather die a thousand deaths by fire than join you," Shinju spat.

"A pity. You would have kept me amused." He unleashed a volley of jabs and kicks, faster than Shinju had ever faced, and she had to resort to defense, dodging or blocking every move, searching for a moment where she could fight back.

"Perhaps when we use the tide jewels to conquer Horitamo, you will wish you accepted my offer," the thief crooned when his fist connected with her shoulder, the same one that had been popped out of place.

Shinju bit back a scream. In the corner of her eye, she saw Raiden fighting hard against the group of ninja, shooting lightning and punches just as fast. No matter how many he brought down, more appeared from the smoke and the jungle, throwing sharp weapons at him.

She wanted to help him, but the thief circled around, blocking her off.

Keep talking, she thought desperately. *Distract him and use the first opening you get.*

"You will regret using the tide jewels this way," she gasped. "Don't you remember what happens when a human uses the tide jewels for ill?"

The thief cocked his head. "Legends such as the tide jewels are often exaggerated," he stated calmly. "It is common for all kinds of warnings to surround such objects."

"This is true though," Shinju insisted. "Lord Hotaka will lose control of the tide jewels the more he uses them with wicked intent. It's one of the reasons Ryūjin removed the jewels from the humans. Their greed was sending the seas into chaos."

The thief paused, and Shinju kicked him in the neck with her foot. His head swung to the side, and she lowered her stance to send a punch into his stomach again.

She paid dearly for those two hits. The thief swiped at her with his arm, and his bracer cut into her side. She screamed, falling to her knees and blood gushed from her stomach.

"Shinju!" Raiden yelled furiously. Streaks of lightning erupted from his fists, striking all the ninja down. He turned and ran towards her but skidded to a halt when Shinju felt the cold press of steel on her neck.

The thief leaned down, his face level with hers as he held a knife to her skin. "Let's not do anything hasty, Raiden-sama," he said pleasantly.

"Let her go," Raiden snarled, still channeling lightning.

"You weren't nearly so compassionate the last time we worked together, Raiden. I wonder what has changed?" The thief trailed a finger down Shinju's face.

"Was it this one? I must admit, I rather envy you. She's

certainly…unique."

"Matsuda," Raiden hissed. "If you kill her, you know there would be nothing stopping me from killing you. And I would make sure it's as slow and painful as you can imagine."

The thief chuckled. "Oh, I know. That's why I have something else in mind."

Shinju blinked, trying to decipher his words through the haze of torment from the wounds in her side.

"You're a capable man, Raiden-sama," the thief continued. "I will give you a proposal: join us, and help us conquer Horitamo with the tide jewels, and I'll let you in on a little secret."

"Nothing you say could possibly interest me," Raiden scoffed, carefully edging closer.

"Oh? Not even the identity and location of the man who killed your mother?"

Raiden froze, and Shinju sucked in a breath. *Don't believe him*, she pleaded to her companion with her eyes. *He's trying to trick you.*

The half-kami's face turned a dark shade of red and he clenched and unclenched his fists. Lightning licked up and down his arms, sparking and snapping.

For a brief moment, Shinju feared he might take Matsuda up on his offer. She knew what this meant to him, what it was like to finally learn the truth. *Could I blame him?* she thought. *He barely knows me, and this is about his mother.*

Swallowing her misery, Shinju looked straight into his eyes and hoped he could read what she expressed to him. *I won't hold you back.*

Raiden's gaze burned back, fierce and strong, and he

seemed to resolve something within himself. "No."

The single word echoed loudly between them. Relief swept through her, and she would have collapsed if it had not been for the blade still held to her throat. "Pity," the thief replied.

"You won't get away with this." Her words brought the thief's attention back. "Ryūjin will rise from the depths of the sea and stop you, just like he did the last time someone misused the jewels."

"Ryūjin," the thief hummed. "Oh, you mean the great dragon who no one has seen in hundreds of years. My dear Shinju, I'm surprised you actually believe he would act on your behalf." He leaned closer to her ear. "In fact, I'll bet he's dead. He lay in his palace at the bottom of the sea and disintegrated into foam, and no one knew. How terribly tragic."

Shinju clenched her jaw, contemplating shoving her elbow into his stomach and risk being cut by the blade at her neck, when another ninja approached. "The tide jewel is securely onboard," he told Matsuda. "Lord Hotaka commands us to return to the ship immediately."

"Looks like playtime is over," the thief crooned in Shinju's ear. "I actually hope you survive long enough for us to see each other again."

"It will be your death if we do," Shinju rasped, barely breathing to avoid the sharp steel at her neck. Matsuda chuckled. "We will see, won't we?"

He suddenly gave a sharp whistle, and out of the trees flew a volley of arrows, aimed at Raiden. At Shinju's cry of alarm, he swiftly turned and threw up a scattering of lightning towards the arrows, but two managed to slip through his defenses.

One struck his leg, and the other struck his chest, sharp enough to pierce even the lightweight armor he wore.

Raiden cursed and fell, gritting his teeth. "No!" Shinju cried. The thief pushed her down, and she crawled towards Raiden, gasping at the sharp agony in her stomach.

"Come," she heard Matsuda say, and then they were alone. The ninja left as quietly as they'd arrived, and to Shinju, it felt as though they'd taken everything with them.

37

THE DISTANCE TO RAIDEN seemed a mile long. Shinju half-crawled, half-ran to his side where he lay, growling as he broke off the shafts of the two arrows.

"Are you okay?" Shinju gasped. Tears fell down her cheeks as she examined his wounds. "Never better." He grimaced when he saw her own injuries. "You're worse off than me. We need to stop that bleeding."

"And you need to get those arrows removed!" Shinju countered. "What if they're poisoned?"

"I can take it," he insisted. "I'm more angry at myself. I can't believe I didn't sense those damn arrows." He tried to rise to his knees but stumbled and had to catch himself. Shinju raised her other hand to her mouth, unable to hold back sobs.

"This is all my fault," she cried. Everything was gone. The tide jewels. Her clan. Her family. Akira. And now, Raiden could be taken from her too.

"Hey." Raiden put a hand on her shoulder. "We'll figure it out, but right now, we have to make sure we don't bleed out here. I don't feel like dying today." He swallowed hard, moving his hand to cup her cheek gently. "I don't want you to either."

Shinju wanted nothing more than to lie down and keep crying, but he was right. She sniffled and gazed around at the village. The fires had died down, stopped by the stonework of the huts, and now just smoldered with black smoke.

"Maybe there's some medicine still left," she croaked. Her throat felt dry and stung when she spoke. Leaning on each other, they managed to limp towards one of the huts that showed the least damage.

Her heart hammering, Shinju picked through the belongings they found, trying not to think about the fact that it had been someone's home, and now they were dead. Because of her.

In a basket she found some crushed herbs and in a tiny clay pot there was a small amount of salve. She also found a needle and thread. Raiden nodded in approval. "Let's rip up some of that cloth over there, we can use it for bandages."

They set to work. Shinju retrieved her bag from the edge of the village and uncorked the canteen of water, wincing as she poured it over the gashes in her waist. Raiden examined them while she blinked rapidly at the sky.

"They're not too deep," he told her. "But you'll need some stitching." "Your arrows first," Shinju told him firmly. He started to argue, then groaned when he moved his shoulder. "Fine, take out one of your daggers. We'll have to dig them out."

He slowly removed his armor and outer tunic, dropping

them to the floor. Shinju blushed and lowered her eyes; it was the first time she'd seen him completely bare-chested.

Pull yourself together, she scolded herself. From the knowing grin on Raiden's face, she knew he'd seen her blush.

Shinju held the knife over a flame, then settled on her knees next to Raiden when he lay down on a mat in the hut. "Could really use some sake right about now," he muttered.

Shinju leaned down and kissed him briefly, and he sighed. "Hmmm. I think I should get a kiss for every stitch."

She smiled in spite of herself. "I'll see what I can do. Now, hold still as best you can."

With the tip of the knife, she began digging out the arrowhead in his shoulder. Raiden's fingers dug into the earth as he snarled. Sparks shot from his hands. "Keep going," he ground out when she paused.

Little by little, both arrowheads were dug out of his skin. Shinju stitched them up, then poured more water on his wounds, then applied some of the salve. "That's enough," he told her roughly. "I'll heal fast enough without all that. Your turn."

She shed the outer layer of her tunic, then rolled the undershirt up just below her breasts. If she hadn't been in such excruciating pain, she might have been a little more self-conscious. Raiden gently touched her abdomen.

"It's going to hurt," he warned her, holding the needle over a small flame in an oil lamp. "I know," she whispered, staring at what was left of the hut's roof. After a moment, the needle pierced her skin, and she choked back a shriek, gripping the sides of the mat.

"I'm going to kill Matsuda," Raiden told her in a dangerously calm voice as he worked. "Then I'll summon him from the grave and kill him over again. He'll regret ever laying a finger on you."

Shinju squeezed her eyes shut, trying to focus on anything but the searing fire of her wounds. She latched onto his words, an anchor to keep her from floating away as the pain continued, seeming to never end.

"That's my girl," Raiden whispered, pausing in the stitching to smooth back her hair. "Just a little more."

Finally, her cuts were sewn shut, and Raiden applied the salve, then helped her wrap the bandages around her waist.

"I don't know why I thought I could do this. Why I thought I was somehow chosen for this." She shook her head, tears dropping onto her pants. "All I've done is fail, over and over."

"It's not your fault," Raiden told her softly.

"If I had come here sooner, I might have been able to prevent this, to warn the village of what had happened with the Kanju." Shinju trembled, staring at her hands which were dirty and scraped from her fight with Matsuda.

"You should have taken him up on his offer."

Raiden's hands stilled where he had been tying off her bandages. "Why would you say that?"

"You had a chance to find the man who killed your mother," Shinju whispered.

Raiden let out a breath. "Do you really think I would have left you?"

"Everyone else has," Shinju argued, her voice cracking. "My parents, Takumi, the Tsomas." She bit her lip hard, trying and failing to hold back a fresh wave of tears. "Everyone around me comes to ruin. Maybe I'm cursed."

Raiden moved around to sit in front of her. "Listen to me. Before I met you, I didn't care about anything except finding that man. I didn't care if I lived or died, or what I did to survive." He reached out a hand and wiped her tears from cheeks.

"Then you come along, this young, bright-eyed, determined little thing, with all these strange ideas of honor and mercy and forgiveness. You've been through so much, and yet at every turn, you continued to do exactly the opposite of what I would have done. It's exasperated me to no end."

He drew closer so that their noses almost touched. Through the blur of tears, Shinju found herself drowning in the blue-silver glow of his eyes. "If you think I'm ever leaving you, Shinju Tsoma, you're quite mistaken."

Shinju leaned her forehead on his, letting the words wash over her and sooth some of the ache in her heart. He was solid, and real, and here with her, and he hadn't left.

"Maybe we should just run away," she mumbled. "Go somewhere, just the two of us, and leave everything behind."

Raiden grinned, but it faded as he smoothed her hair back. "As much as I like the sound of that, you know what we have to do."

Shinju pulled back slightly, gazing into his face. "What *can* we do?" she asked. "Lord Hotaka has a ship, and both tide jewels. If he figures out how to use them, they could be halfway across the sea by now, ready to attack the imperial city and begin his conquest of Horitamo."

Saying it out loud made her feel even more lost. What could

the two of them do against such an impossible threat?

"So you would just give up?" Raiden questioned slowly. "What about your clan?"

Shinju's shoulders drooped. "I think it's too late." She rubbed a sleeve across her nose, wishing she would awaken from this horrible nightmare. If only she had been stronger, or had magic, or…

"I don't think you really believe that," Raiden interrupted her thoughts. "You told me that you were the only one from your clan untouched by the island's magic, that you had somehow found your way there as a child in a boat, alone. And then we met. We both happened to be in the same prison. I knew of Matsuda and his poisoned darts, which led us to your home, which led us here."

He raked a hand through his tangled hair, grown longer now and passing his shoulders. "I never believed in fate, or destiny, or that there's something bigger than all of us, bringing everything together in some kind of plan. But you do. And I can't deny that it seems like this has all happened for a reason."

Shinju stared at him in surprise. "You said we were meant to meet," he continued. "That it was no coincidence that a half-kami would help you recover the Kanju." He crossed his arms. "Well, it also doesn't seem to be a coincidence that the only Tsoma who has a chance of stopping Lord Hotaka is you."

She swallowed, allowing the words to sink in. He was right, she realized, clarity shining through the haze of her despair. But what if it was all a mistake? How could she go forward, when every time she tried to save those she cared about, disaster struck?

Seeming to sense her conflict, Raiden stood and left the hut, returning a few minutes later. He squatted before her and placed Takumi's katana on her lap.

"You said you couldn't lose your family again," Raiden reminded her, echoing the phrase she'd told Akira back in Itshino. "Remember who this is for. Remember who you are."

Her fingers curled around the hilt, its familiar design awakening a longing for Takumi, for his words of wisdom and guidance. She thought about the Tsomas, about all the people Hotaka had killed, and all those who were about to be destroyed because of his wicked plan to use the tide jewels to conquer Horitamo.

She had failed before, but this wasn't the end. It couldn't be.

Somehow, some way, there was still a purpose for her, and she had to keep going until she figured it out.

"You're right," she whispered, standing. "I won't forget my clan." Her chin lifted, and Raiden stood as well. "I am Shinju Hagiroshi, *and* Shinju Tsoma. I'm a protector of the tide jewels, and I will do what must be done." Then she sighed heavily. "I just wish I knew where to start."

"Well, we still have a boat." Raiden pulled her into a hug, both of them careful of their injuries. "And you're forgetting something else."

Shinju raised her head to look up at him. "What?"

The corner of his mouth twisted into a wicked grin. "I'm the half-kami of lightning and storms, aren't I? Lord Hotaka is sailing on a ship, out in open water."

Understanding dawned over her. "Of course! Raiden-kun, you're wonderful!"

"I knew that already," he replied, but a light shade of pink tinged his cheeks as Shinju hugged him as tight as she dared. A faint spark of hope stirred within her. Maybe…maybe they still had a chance.

38

THE SKY HAD DARKENED when they left the hut. A murky blanket of gray clouds spread overhead, and the island looked drained of color. The vibrant green of the jungle faded to a brown, and the earth cracked and turned to dust under their feet.

Shinju sighed sadly. "This is similar to what happened on my island." She gazed around at the bodies of the other Tsoma Clan, the protectors of the Manju. They had been going about their daily lives, unaware that this morning would be their last.

Together, they dug a large hole in the ground and carried the dead into it. This was slow, hard work, made more difficult by their injuries. Shinju's head pounded as she tried to arrange the bodies in a proper burial manner, whispering prayers over them.

She wanted to cry, but all of her tears seemed to have dried up.

After salvaging what supplies they could from the village, Shinju and Raiden trekked back through the jungle to the little stretch of beach. Their boat was still there, rocking back and forth in the water. The tide had come in; the waves were darkening and growing wilder in the fading sunlight.

"We have to hurry." Shinju dumped her bag into the boat and readied the lines, then she and Raiden pushed off. Using the oars, they paddled as quickly as they could out into open water, using the waves to boost their momentum.

"Do you think he's already using them?" Raiden asked. "I'm not sure," Shinju answered. "I've never seen the Kanju's power before. The Tsomas always taught that the tide jewels should never be used except under the direst of circumstances."

The wind picked up so much that they had to tie down their belongings. Shinju wished she could put the sail up, but as the wind continued to change directions, she worried that the sail might be ripped away. They would have to keep paddling.

"They got a few hours head start on us," she called to Raiden. "But the water is changing. See? The tide is pushing us towards the direction of the imperial city. It's like…it's like the sea knows what's happening and wants us to help it."

"I hope you're right," Raiden said. "Keep your eyes peeled on that horizon. As soon as we see their ship, I can begin making trouble for them."

Shinju heaved a lungful of air as she paddled hard with her oar. "Even from so far away?" she asked.

"It's been a long time, but yes, all I'll need is a target to focus on." He wiped sweat off his forehead and winked at her. "I hope you're ready for a good show."

Shinju answered with a shaky smile, warmth spreading through her at his attempt to cheer her up. *I am not alone*, she thought, repeating the words to herself. *Raiden is with me. The Tsomas are with me. And Ryūjin is with me. I refuse to believe that he has abandoned us completely.*

Manju Shima grew smaller and smaller behind them, until was a lonely speck on the ocean. Shinju sighed mournfully. No one would know what had happened there, except the rest of the clan. She could not fail them; their sacrifice had to count.

For hours they paddled across the sea, stopping here and there to rest. Eventually Shinju could put the sail up and they moved faster, but the growing thunderclouds above concerned her.

"Another storm," she commented. "It will slow us down."

Raiden leaned back, looking straight up into the sky. He breathed deeply, then shook his head slightly. "I don't smell rain. This is a lightning storm." As he spoke, a streak of purplish light flashed across the sky, followed shortly by a deep roll of thunder like a drum.

Shinju watched as Raiden's face grew serious but thoughtful. "Is it…Raijin?" she dared to ask carefully.

He gave a short nod. "Yes. But it's nothing to do with us." Raiden returned to paddling, his face closed off. Shinju held back the questions burning on her tongue.

Evening fell, and the first few stars peeked out bravely through the brewing mass of black clouds. As Raiden predicted, there was no rain, but lightning and thunder followed them. Shinju grew more worried that they wouldn't reach the city in time.

"You need to drink some water, and eat something," Raiden told her. "Rest. You won't be able to fight if you pull those stitches out."

She took his advice and settled in the bottom of the boat, applying more salve and healing herbs to her wounds, then looked at Raiden's. They were already almost completely closed.

"How do you feel?" She took her time rebandaging his shoulder, enjoying the feel of his warm skin under her fingers. "Well enough to strangle Matsuda with my bare hands," Raiden replied darkly. "He's going to pay for touching you."

Shinju's heart gave a funny leap. After all they'd been through, it was still new and strange to hear him talk about her this way. It thrilled her, but also made her nervous too. Their… relationship was very unlike any of the courtships she'd witnessed on the island.

"What are you thinking about?" Raiden asked, and she started, realizing she had begun staring off into space. "Oh, um, about us." She sat down quickly, keeping her hands busy with the lines.

Raiden leaned forward, his eyebrow raised. "About us, hmm?" He placed a finger under her chin so she would turn her head to look at him. "Care to elaborate?"

Shinju flushed and met his eyes shyly. "Well, everything has happened so fast. And differently. On my island, if a man and a woman begin courting, it's a long ritual. Flowers, walks on the beach, tea with the family. They might kiss only after the engagement is agreed upon."

Raiden thought for a moment. "Do you want that?"

Shinju chewed her lip, considering. She liked kissing him, and…well, they had been thrown into unusual circumstances. None of this was normal, and yet, she wouldn't trade it for anything.

"Every girl likes to be romanced," she admitted, "and I want to do it all properly. But I also like the way we do things. It's right for us. Don't you think so?"

Raiden swallowed, blinking a couple of times and clearing his throat. "Yes." Then he gave her one of his old, mischievous grins. "Romancing huh? I have a few ideas about that."

Something caught the corner of Shinju's eye, and her response died in her throat. There, on the horizon, was the tiny figure of a ship. "Hotaka!"

"What? Where?"

"There!"

She leaped to the prow, pointing. Her eyes had not tricked her. A ship with black sails moved swiftly through the water, almost disappearing from their sight again.

"Let's get closer," Raiden growled, and he paddled while Shinju worked the lines, silently urging the wind to push them faster. As if heeding her plea, the wind picked up speed and the currents worked in their favor.

They fairly flew over the water, getting closer to the ship ahead. "Look!" she cried. Unnatural waves spread out on either side of the ship, larger than they should be for the weather. "He's using the tide jewels. Probably practicing." Renewed urgency and fury filled her.

"If they haven't spotted us yet, they will soon," Raiden cautioned. He dropped the oar and stood, reaching his arms up.

"It's time." The already murky clouds above them moved rapidly, gathering in speed and turning black. They blocked out the weak sun; it was as if a giant's shadow had passed over them.

Thunder rolled, deep and ominous, and if she had not been with the half-kami of lightning, Shinju would have been fearful. To be trapped on open water in such a storm would be nothing short of life-threatening.

The wind whipped at their faces and clothes. Shinju's braid came undone, her hair flying into her face. Raiden wore a wild grin, his eyes brighter than she'd ever seen them. Lightning coursed through his arms, reaching in flashing tendrils towards the sky.

They were close enough now to the other ship that Shinju could make out the people running back and forth on the deck. Canons fired, and a ball hit the water in front of them. Raiden laughed. "Is that all?" he shouted. The clouds swirled and formed a mass above the ship. Purple-white light flashed in their depths.

Taking a deep breath, Raiden swung his arms down, clenching his fists. A second later, dozens of lightning bolts rained from the sky, striking Hotaka's ship. They were so bright that even at a distance, Shinju had to blink and cover her eyes, but that didn't stop her from catching a good look at the brilliant display of white and purple and blue energy pouring from the heavens.

When they ceased, the ship smoked, and the unnatural waves slowly receded. The black sails were shredded, and one of the masts was on fire.

Raiden slumped, breathing heavily, but he was grinning. "I

think that should keep them busy. With any luck, I managed to hit Hotaka and Matsuda."

Shinju climbed back up to the prow of their boat and studied the ship. The wind continued to carry them along, bringing them closer.

All at once, the water beneath them surged, and an enormous wave rose up with alarming, abnormal speed to loom over them. "Look out!" Shinju cried, grabbing hold of the lines, as the wave's curl overshadowed, then smashed upon them. Instantly her eyes and ears and mouth were flooded with water, and she was raised up and tossed about in the surge.

Only her hands gripping the rope kept her from being washed away from the boat.

When she emerged from the wave, gasping for breath, she searched wildly for Raiden, and found him holding on to the mast, grimacing and coughing. "Guess he's figuring out the tide jewels," he rasped.

Their boat teetered back and forth, bobbing like a toy in a tub, and water had filled the bottom. Their sail had ripped and flapped almost uselessly. The wind began to change again, swirling in different directions, as more giant waves began to throw the sea into turmoil.

Lord Hotaka had taken a hit, but it wasn't enough to slow him down.

39

TRYING TO KEEP THEIR boat afloat and catch up to Lord Hotaka, Shinju and Raiden began a fight with the sea. Waves crashed upon them, nearly sweeping them away and capsizing the boat. Saltwater stung Shinju's eyes and filled her throat, and she coughed, retching from swallowing so much.

Raiden roared furiously and began bringing down more lightning bolts onto the Hotaka's ship. The winds and brewing clouds and waves did not seem to bother him as he took hold of the mast with one hand and summoned lightning with the other. His face and eyes glowed with an otherworldly light that Shinju had never seen; the son of the thunder Kami had truly emerged in this moment.

He collapsed, breathing heavily and drained. Sparks snapped and shivered along his gauntlets. His hair hung limply in his face. Shinju started to go to him, but he held out a hand.

"Don't touch me yet," he whispered. "I'm too full of energy, I'll shock you."

She swallowed and nodded. "Are you okay?"

"I will be, I just need to recover." He struck the side of the boat with his fist. "I can't hit him!" he complained. "Hotaka. Something is protecting him from my attacks."

Shinju had been so focused on their boat that she didn't realize how near they had come to Hotaka's ship in spite of the waves. She looked up, and could see him now, standing on the upper deck with the tide jewels. The Kanju he held in his hands, and it glowed blue-ish, the Manju answering with a purplish glow from its place on a pedestal.

"It's the tide jewels," she told Raiden. "They are protecting him with their magic." She looked back at Hotaka as their boat drifted closer, taking advantage of the currents and a momentary reprieve from lack of magical waves.

He doesn't really know what he's doing yet, Shinju realized with a start as she caught the expression of frustration on Hotaka's face. He was glaring down at them, concentrating. *He isn't using them properly.*

By now he should have been able to wash them far away. But the lightning had done its damage, and dead bodies littered the deck, while Hotaka tried to regain control.

Their eyes met, and for a moment Shinju thought she saw a hint of fear pass over his face. Then it twisted with a cruel smile, and he picked up the Manju so he could hold both jewels in his hands.

He began saying something, and suddenly the sea went still. An eerie silence filled the air, as if even the wind held its breath in anticipation of what was to come. "What now?" Shinju gasped.

The water beneath their boat receded, sucking backwards, and a colossal wave built up higher and higher, filled with struggling fish and plants and sediment from the sea floor. Water dripped down on them, and the curl of the wave pulled at their boat until they were almost falling backwards.

Raiden rushed forward and wrapped his arms around Shinju as the wave paused a moment, then crashed down. The impact stole Shinju's breath away, tearing her from the boat and Raiden's arms.

She turned over and over, head over heels, a mere doll in the midst of the wave's power. She couldn't breathe, couldn't think, and had no control over her limbs. Something hard smashed into her arm and she yelped, her voice drowned by swirling, dark water.

Shinju's lungs burned, desperate for air, but she couldn't seem to right herself. Water filled her nose and eyes, an endless stream. I can't drown! she thought, trying to kick and use the momentum of the tide to push herself towards the surface. I can't go like this!

A brief light glimmered in the darkness above her, and Shinju headed for it. Her head pounded and her stomach heaved. The lack of oxygen made her chest feel like it might explode, but she pressed on until she broke the surface of the churning water.

She took a gulp of air, almost choking on it. Coughing and spluttering, she searched around her. "Raiden!" she called, but her voice only sounded like a croak. The remains of their boat floated on the tumultuous water, and she managed to seize onto one of the larger pieces, digging her nails into the slick wood.

To her left she could see Lord Hotaka's ship, and for a brief second she wondered why he lingered, rather than continuing on to the Imperial City, but her more pressing concern was Raiden.

Peering through the darkness and the murky, churning waves, she floated on the wood, kicking and trying to maintain her position. If Raiden was nearby, she wanted him to be able to find her.

No matter where she looked, the half-kami's familiar glowing eyes and black hair were nowhere to be found. Panic rose in Shinju's chest as she called out for him again, not caring if Hotaka and the Otami heard her.

"Raiden!" Her voice was still raw, breaking under the strain of her shout. Tears flooded her vision, and she let them pour out over her face, not daring to loosen her grip on the precious wood that kept her afloat.

Where was he? He couldn't have drowned. Shinju refused to believe it. Please, please, she begged, searching the darkness with all her might. *I can't lose him too.*

Something flashed above a swell of water, and she kicked towards it, propelled by a surge of hope.

Raiden hung off another broken section of their boat, coughing and gasping for air. He blinked, his eyes unfocused, until he saw Shinju. Her name crossed his lips, inaudible, but Shinju knew what he said.

They managed to swim towards one another, kicking and holding onto their own pieces of boat wreckage. When she reached him, Raiden's arm immediately reached around her shoulders and pulled her to his chest. "I thought I lost you," he choked.

Shinju nodded, shivering. "I thought I lost you too," she croaked. "I was so afraid." She gripped his shirt and held on to him, his body becoming an anchor as they both kicked to stay afloat. Relief filled her, but not enough to scatter the severity of their predicament. They couldn't stay here like this.

Then she noticed his arm. "Raiden…" She pivoted her head to look at the other arm wrapped around her. "No…your gauntlets!"

He nodded grimly. The silver, intricately crafted gauntlets were gone from his forearms.

"When the wave hit, I was sucked under the boat as it broke apart. The straps had already come loose during the storm, and I foolishly put off tightening them." He heaved a weary sigh. "They are probably at the bottom of the sea by now."

Shinju closed her eyes, her heart aching for him. The gauntlets were the only things he'd ever received from the Kami Raijin, and now they were lost. "I'm so sorry, Raiden-kun," she whispered.

"It's done," he replied in a hard voice, signaling he didn't wish to talk about them anymore. "We need to figure out what to do now."

Lifting her head, Shinju looked back at the ship. Now she could see more clearly the damage Raiden's lightning had accomplished. Gaping holes filled the hull, and a mast had split in half, still smoking, with the sail completely burned away. Splintered wood littered the deck; Otami scurried about the deck, shouting.

No one seemed to have noticed them yet.

"W-we can still stop them," she whispered hoarsely. "If we ride the tide, we can float to the ship and climb up."

Raiden gazed at her with concern. "You're hurt, Shinju. Your injuries—" "I'm fine," she insisted. "We can't stop now. We have to keep going!"

"I'm not going to let you kill yourself!" he argued. "You have no weapon. We almost drowned, and you're still injured from the fight yesterday. It will be a miracle if your stitches are still holding."

Shinju spat out a mouth full of water as a wave lifted up and over them, sloshing against the wood. "I'm not going to give up," she told him. "We are so close!"

"And what do you expect to do?" Raiden demanded harshly. "Walk up to Hotaka with no resistance? The second you step foot on that deck you'll be shot by arrows or struck down by a sword."

He was right, and Shinju knew it. Despair clouded her mind as she gazed back at the ship. It was starting to move away, limping along across the water. Perhaps Lord Hotaka did not want to risk damaging it further by using the tide jewels.

An idea came to her mind. "Listen," she said. "Do you think you could keep up with the ship on your own?"

Raiden frowned. "On this?" He eyed the distance between them and the ship and nodded slowly. "Yes, I think so. I can feel my energy returning already. Why would I be on my own though?"

"I have a plan."

Shinju explained her idea, and his frown grew deeper. "Shinju, I'll get my lightning back soon, but without my gauntlets...my powers will be unpredictable. I don't want to hurt you because I couldn't control them."

His dark eyes were filled with uncertainty, and Shinju's heart swelled. She took his hand, lacing their fingers together. "You can do this, Raiden-kun. I believe you are strong enough without the gauntlets. You won't hurt me."

He sighed again, shaking his head. "Are you sure about this?"

"Yes. Raiden, it will work, I promise."

He studied her for a moment, then looked back at the ship, thinking. "Alright. I could reach the back of the ship, where that little ledge is there, and climb up. Do you see it?" Shinju did.

"Wait for my signal." She paused, then raised a hand to nestle in his wet, dark hair, and pulled his head towards her to capture his lips in a deep kiss, pouring all of her fears and longings and wishes into it.

When they parted, Raiden breathed a chuckle. "We better survive this, Shinju Tsoma. I'm going to want another kiss like that before I die."

40

"HELP!" SHINJU CRIED, WAVING her arm wildly in the air. With the other she held onto the driftwood, what had once been part of the hull of her boat. She kicked hard, trying to catch up to the ship.

"Help!" she cried again, glad that her voice sounded stronger than before, despite all the seawater she'd swallowed. Someone peered over the ship's railing and spotted her. He turned and shouted to the other Otami, and more joined him at the edge.

"Please!" Shinju cried, hoping she looked as pathetic as she felt. "Please help!"

A familiar figure joined the group. "Cast a line, bring her up!" he ordered. Shinju paddled closer, and a rope was thrown in her direction. It splashed into the water and she grabbed the line, relief coursing through her. "I've got it!"

The men pulled the rope back, bringing her closer to the ship. Waves splashed into her face, and the wake threatened to pull her under if she let go of the rope. A small boat lowered, carrying two Otami, dressed in their signature black. They didn't speak as they grabbed her by the shoulders and hauled her into the boat like she was a fish.

She sat, shivering, as the boat was raised back up and leveled with the deck. Hands grabbed her, pulling her roughly from the boat and tossing her to her knees onto the deck.

A pair of boots entered her line of vision. "Well, well, so we do meet again," drawled a voice that made Shju's skin crawl. "I must admit, I rather like you this way."

"She had no weapons, sir," one of the Otami reported. Shinju, shivering and tensing, raised herself to her knees to look up at Matsuda, whose eyes twinkled at her from his black-clothed face. "Where is your lightning friend? He gave us quite a bit of trouble earlier. I would like to return the favor."

Shinju sniffled and wrapped her arms around her torso. "He's gone," she whispered. "The wave…"

Matsuda nodded. "Ah. I suppose not even a half-kami could withstand Lord Hotaka's mastery of the waves, though it is quite a miracle that you did."

Shinju did not reply; her side was screaming in agony now that she had finally grown still, and the cold made her teeth chatter.

"What should we do with you now, hmm?" Matsuda hummed. He crouched down to her level and gripped her chin with his gloved hand. "All your fire has been washed away. But I sense you still have some fight in you yet."

Shinju clenched her jaw and met his gaze straight on, determined not to look afraid. "Lord Hotaka seems to be having some trouble with the tide jewels," she responded. "Wouldn't his mastery have brought you to the imperial city by now?"

Matsuda's grip on her chin tightened painfully. "Oh, do not worry, my pet. Lord Hotaka is simply reserving his powers until we reach the city. If you behave yourself, perhaps he will let you survive long enough to watch him conquer it."

"And then what?" Shinju jerked her chin from his hand. "Once you've conquered and laid waste to Horitamo, what comes next?"

"That's Lord Hotaka's decision. No doubt he will begin to look to the lands beyond our seas," Matsuda informed her cheerfully. He eyed her wet, torn clothing with a leer that made Shinju feel as if she wore nothing at all.

"Matsuda," an Otami approached, giving a quick bow. "Lord Hotaka commands you to bring the girl to him."

Matsuda sighed, then grabbed Shinju's elbow, forcing her to her feet. Her muscles screamed in protest, and she fought to keep her footing on the slippery deck. "No doubt he will want to punish you for damaging our ship," Matsuda told her. "I hope he leaves enough of you for me."

Shinju spat in his face, and after a moment of surprise, Matsuda backhanded her, hard. She fell back to the deck, pain lacing through her bruised body and now her sore face.

"Matsuda!" A deep voice called from above. Shinju, groaning, raised her head to see the imposing figure of Lord Hotaka, standing on the upper deck. He was clothed in a fine black tunic and pants, looking hardly rumpled. Even his steel-gray hair was pulled back neatly, and he no longer wore the same face cloth as the rest of the Otami.

"This is not how we treat our guests," he continued, folding his hands in front of him. "Bring her here."

Matsuda obeyed with a bow, then snatched Shinju's arm again and dragged her up the stairs to where Hotaka waited.

She had time to glance quickly at the pedestal where the tide jewels rested before she was forced to her knees again. "Bow before your future Emperor," Matsuda told her.

Shinju squared her shoulders and sat back up, staring at Lord Hotaka with barely concealed disdain. "So, you caught up to us," he said quietly. "I'm impressed you haven't died yet. Perhaps you're more useful than I thought."

He gestured to the tide jewels. "These truly are remarkable objects. It's no wonder your clan wanted to keep them for themselves."

His words angered her. "That's not true. The Tsomas protected the tide jewels, so they wouldn't be used by evil men like you."

Hotaka chuckled. "And yet, here we are. Your clan is dead and I have the tide jewels. A new era is about to begin." Shinju snorted, tossing her wet hair over her shoulder. "So you say. And what will you do when the tide jewels no longer obey you?"

He frowned slightly. "What are you talking about?" She smiled sweetly, glancing at Matsuda. "He didn't tell you?"

"She's lying," Matusda interjected. "The tide jewels obey you, Lord Hotaka. They obey whoever holds them."

"For now," Shinju argued, examining her nails. "But eventually, if you continue on this path, they will turn against you. You won't be able to contain them." She paused while Hotaka and Matsuda looked at each other. "Perhaps your thief, nor your ancient texts, tell you everything."

Matsuda growled and grabbed her hair, yanking so her head fell back. He held his bracers to her throat, the spikes gleaming dangerously close.

"Remember these?" he snarled. "Just because I find you amusing doesn't mean I won't slice your pretty neck open."

Hotaka blinked with an expression of mixed boredom and annoyance. "Calm yourself, Matsuda. I want to hear what she has to say."

Matsuda growled and pushed Shinju away. "She's only making things up so that you doubt yourself, my lord."

Hotaka silently considered Shinju. She suppressed a shudder as she looked into his eyes. They reminded her of the eyes of a shark: cold and calculating. "The tide jewels respond to my commands," he said at last. "If they try to rebel, I will bend them to my will."

Shinju couldn't resist responding with a grim smile. "Are you really willing to risk Ryūjin's wrath?"

Hotaka scoffed at that. "The great dragon has abandoned this world. He didn't arise from his palace to help your clan, did he?"

He turned away, walking over to where the jewels rested, glowing with an otherworldly, luminescent light. "It's time we take these powers back into our own hands and decide what they'll be used for, not an old, decrepit beast of legend."

Now, Shinju thought. "We will see about that," she retorted, then pursed her lips together to release a sharp, high whistle.

Strands of lightning erupted from the back of the ship, stretching over the stern and hitting Otami. The lightning was faster, ferocious, and more erratic than before.

Shinju twisted in place and jerked the katana from the belt of a nearby ninja who stood frozen with surprise. She rolled away and jumped to her feet, blade raised. Only Hotaka stood between her and the jewels.

Matsuda started towards her, but Hotaka held out a hand. "Go find our half-kami friend," he ordered. "And make sure he's really dead this time."

Shinju grinned. "You underestimate him. And you underestimated me." She moved into a stance, feet placed a part and the sword raised over her head.

"Foolish girl," Hotaka snarled. "You're as stubborn as your aunt. Do you really think I will lower myself to your level?" He sneered. "You are afraid. Even now, your hands shake. You are not as courageous as you are trying to be. Give up."

"It is because I am afraid that I can have courage at all." She gripped the sword's handle, never straying her gaze from his. "I have something worth fighting for. Something I am willing to die for. You have nothing."

Shinju lunged at him. Hotaka's sword was out and meeting hers, steel on steel, in a flash. She grit her teeth as the swords screeched together. "You think very highly of yourself. But you're not the Emperor yet."

He smirked, the shark eyes missing nothing. "Perhaps not, but I am the Master of Tides now."

Shinju swung her sword again, meeting him strike for strike, pushing off, pushing forward. He deflected her swings easily, playing with her, almost lazily. But her goal wasn't to beat him.

"There's only one Master of Tides," she said. "And his powers don't belong to you."

Behind her, she could hear Otami yelling. The air filled static, and lightning streaked across the deck. Raiden stood on the other side of the ship, wind whipping at his clothes and hair as he fought off ninja and their weapons. "You will die here," Hotaka growled. "And I'll make sure he watches." He moved forward, swinging his katana towards her. Shinju ducked and spun, knocking off his attack, and purposely bumped into the pedestal.

It teetered, and the jewels bounced against each other with a loud clack, then rolled off onto the floor. "No!" Hotaka shouted, lunging for them. He snatched up the Manju, but Shinju had thrown herself down and wrapped her hands around the Kanju.

They jumped to their feet, facing each other, both holding one of the legendary tide jewels. The Kanju hummed and pulsed in her grasp, and Shinju could not ignore how surreal this moment was. She had never even touched it before, and yet, the power that filled the jewel called to her, reached for her.

"Intoxicating, isn't it?" Hotaka tightened his grip on the Manju as he began to step to the side. Shinju moved as well, keeping him in her sights. "You can feel it, can't you? The magic, the power of the tides calling to you."

As he spoke, the Kanju glowed even more, and Shinju's fingers trembled. She held the power to recede the tides, to control the flow of the mighty sea, just with her will. Gazing into the pearlescent orb, she could almost make out movement, like waves themselves.

"You think you have the strength to use such a tool, girl?" Hotaka snarled. "Let's see what you can do." He held up the Manju and focused on it, planting his feet. Suddenly the ship jerked, leaning forward, as the sea rose up behind them. The waves grew larger, carrying them along.

Shinju lost her balance and fell back, managing to grab onto the railing and hold on to the Kanju, but she lost her katana. To her right, she could see that Raiden and the ninja had also been thrown off balance.

Gritting her teeth, Shinju concentrated on the Kanju. *Please,* she thought, *I need your help. Recede these tides, change the water.*

The Kanju pulsated, glowing brighter, and the ship lurched again, moving backwards, and waves crashed over them as the jewels now fought against each other, trying to obey different commands.

Shinju struggled to her feet, bracing against the railing, and placing her other hand on the Kanju. Hotaka scowled at her and pushed back with the Manju's power. The ship began to toss to and fro as the currents battled for dominance. Water washed some of the ninja off the ship, but Hotaka did not seem to care.

Shinju spared a glance in Raiden's direction. He was gripping a rope near the other mast, looking up at her in awe. He met her gaze and he nodded. Raising up his free hand, he shouted, and called down lightning to where Hotaka stood.

The blinding white light struck down with a crash, and Shinju couldn't help but cry out and fall to her knees, clutching the tide jewel to her chest.

She peeled her eyes open and looked towards the spot

where Hotaka had stood, expecting to see nothing more than a burnt corpse. Horror filled her.

Hotaka stood, smirking, completely unharmed. "Did you think I wouldn't be protected with only one jewel?" he mocked. "I'm afraid you'll have to do better than that." Taking advantage of her surprise, he lifted the Manju and spoke to it.

The waves began pushing them once more, and the ship slid sideways. Wood broke off and fell into the sea. Shinju managed to hang on to the railing as she too asked the Kanju to move the waves.

The ship kept moving sideways, and with a start, Shinju realized they were moving in a circle. She chanced a glance over the side of the ship and realized that they caused a gigantic whirlpool to emerge in the sea. The ship sailed around its outer edges, hopelessly caught.

"Hotaka! This is madness!" she shouted at him. "Give up the Manju! Neither of us can control them!"

"Never!" His eyes were wild, chaotic depths of black ink. He was drunk on the power of the jewels, and Shinju realized that if they didn't stop him, the entire ship would be lost to the whirlpool.

The pedestal, which had been sliding back and forth across the deck earlier, suddenly fell towards her. The heavy oak crashed into her arm and broke the railing at her back. Shinju cried out in pain and fear as the Kanju slipped from her grasp, and then she was falling, falling weightless into darkness. Her pulse thrummed in her ears as she briefly heard someone shout her name before the cold water enveloped her with icy fingers.

41

TIME STOOD STILL EVEN as she was sucked deeper and deeper down into the swirling water. Unable to breathe, unable to swim, unable to do anything but wait for death beneath the crushing strength of the sea.

She'd barely managed a lungful of air before hitting the water when she fell, and now that precious oxygen was gone. Her chest and lungs burned, and water surged up her nose, filling every part of her body. She was drowning.

In the span of seconds, Shinju's life flashed before her eyes. Her childhood, her parents, Takumi, the Tsomas, even Peiku's furry face. And Raiden. Raiden, with his endless eyes that saw the depths of her soul, and arms that kept her safe. She would never see him again.

They'd spoken briefly of the future. She'd started to dream about introducing him to Takumi. To guide him around her island home and showing him all the things that made her happy. Of loving him and easing the scars and burdens they both carried, together.

Her future had completely vanished in an instant. This was where her life ended. There would be no more second chances. As the pressure tugged at her, and black spots clouded her vision, Shinju wondered if she would see her parents again in the next moments.

The water around her slowed, and she hung in the midst of it, weightless, floating. Shouldn't she be dead by now? Drowning happened quickly. Then the current began to move once more, this time pushing her urgently along in one direction, paying no attention to her feeble kicks.

Shinju gasped, then realized she no longer needed to take a breath. Had she truly died then? Was this the final journey to what lay ahead in life beyond this world? She hadn't imagined that it would be underwater.

Downwards and forwards she shot, flying through the sea like a bird in the sky. She passed colonies of coral reefs, brightly colored fish gaping at her. Sharks darted away, their tails zigzagging and leaving trails of bubbles behind.

This can't be real, she thought.

The depths grew colder and darker, only a faint glimmer of light piercing the dark water, coming from the early morning sun. Had it really been a day and a night since they left Manju Shima to track down Hotaka?

Shinju blinked slowly, watching the sea floor pass her by. Her vision blurred and cleared, and she continued to breathe freely. The currents dragged her along as if she were nothing more than a clump of seaweed towards an endless depth of midnight blue.

This felt familiar, Shinju thought with a jolt. She had seen this…she had been here before. Panic gripped her as the memory of a dream, distant and faint, trickled to the forefront of her mind.

Her dream about the thief had come true. Could it be possible that the dream about meeting Ryūjin was also coming to pass?

Shinju's heart thumped wildly as she tried to get a better look at her surroundings, but even when she tried to slow herself down, the water paid her no heed. This had to be the work of magic, she realized. She was not dead, nor dying: something else had seized her.

A glimmer flashed in the distance. Shinju swallowed, both intrigued and fearful, hardly daring to believe what she would see if her dream had truly become reality.

The gleam grew closer, and took the form of spires rising up from a great palace, sunk deep into the sea floor. It was *so* bright that Shinju had to squint and blink, waiting for her eyes to adjust the sudden light after being thrust through dark water for so long. Seaweed waved lazily in long, tall towers, surrounding the palace. Shinju could see the walls and spires were covered with shells and pearls and colorful coral.

Schools of fish swam in patterns through the palace towers. A sea turtle floated by, his eye fixating on Shinju for a long moment, before he turned and paddled away, returning to his business.

As Shinju took in the dazzling sight before her, she felt like an intruder. *I shouldn't be here*, she thought. *I don't belong here.* The palace was peaceful and beautiful, unlike any place on land that Shinju had seen, and yet there was also a great presence, something hidden within its walls that watched her.

Why am I here? She wondered, gazing at the palace. What had brought her all the way from the Sea of Stars to the palace of Ryūjin beneath The Golden Sea, across the continent?

Her heart stuttered as she floated forwards, the current finally depositing her in front of the palace. She gazed into the gaping gateway to the great dragon's home. He had been depicted in all the stories as miles long, a gigantic being that defied imagination, yet none of those stories felt adequate to prepare her for this.

All her thoughts vanished as two eyes appeared in the dark haze, blinking at her. They were green and blue and gold, and the black pupils were shaped like slits. Steam, visible even underwater, rose from between the eyes.

A shudder passed through her as a voice, deep and ancient as the sea itself, spoke her name. "*Shinju Tsoma.*"

If she could have bowed, Shinju would have thrown herself to the sandy floor below, but instead she remained floating, rigid, her heart pounding so hard she thought it might erupt from her chest.

Slowly emerging from the entrance to the palace, the snout of the great dragon appeared, then the rest of his face. In contrast to his brightly colored surroundings, Ryūjin's scales were the color of the sea itself on a clear day: deep cerulean, with a sheen that cast him in a faint glow. The dragon's angles were sharp and yet fluid at the same time, as if his face surged and moved with the sea.

Two massive black horns curled up and back from the top of his head, and as he breathed, steam spiraled up from his nostrils and through the water in tendrils larger than Shinju.

For a long moment they stared at each other: human and dragon laying eyes upon the other for the first time in perhaps centuries. Shinju realized she was shaking all over, and words seemed to have escaped her completely. Could she even talk underwater?

Ryūjin blinked again, slowly, and his voice thundered through her mind, even as he barely opened his jaws. "*What do you seek, child?*"

Shinju licked her lips nervously and floundered to find something to answer. "I…Did you bring me here, Ryūjin-sama?" She could have slapped herself for such a ridiculous question; it distracted her from realizing she could speak.

The dragon barely reacted. *"I am the sea, and the sea brought you here."*

Shinju nodded. Her brain felt scrambled. Had Ryūjin himself really saved her from drowning?

"Great Dragon, Ryūjin-sama," she began again haltingly. "I need your help. Please…the sea is in danger. The Empire is in danger. Lord Hotaka is using your tide jewels to do terrible things. I tried to stop him, but…"

Her mouth trembled. The sea turtle from earlier, accompanied by several schools of fish, swam closer, watching. "I couldn't do it. I can't do it alone. Raiden and I tried, but…we need you now."

The dragon said nothing but continued to look at her with

fathomless eyes. "Please," Shinju begged as tears pricked her eyes and trailed down her face, not washed away by the water surrounding her. "I don't know what else to do."

"Long have I guided your steps, Child," the dragon murmured. *"You have not been alone."*

Unbidden, a memory returned to her, of the night she had fled her home in Itshino, taking the boat out onto the sea. She'd lain in that boat, terrified, as a storm rolled over the ocean, and a great form had appeared near the surface of the water, pushing her boat along.

She'd thought she'd seen scales, and even a great eye, but then she'd fallen asleep, exhausted with fear, and had awoken on Kanju Shima in Takumi's home.

That memory…she'd thought she'd dreamed the whole thing. But it had been real. Ryūjin, the dragon ruler of the sea, had protected her as a child and brought her to the Tsomas.

The weight of this revelation nearly tore her heart open. Who was *she*, that this Kami would intervene in her life?

"You remember," the dragon rumbled. Shinju could only nod, too overwhelmed to answer.

Ryūjin's head stretched farther out from his palace, moving closer to where Shinju floated. The gathering of fish, turtles, and now even jellyfish, did not flee at his approach. He loomed over her, able to kill her with one snap of his enormous jaws that housed rows of razor-sharp teeth, but Shinju no longer felt fear.

"You have asked for my help. Why?"

Shinju gazed into those ancient, green-yellow eyes. "Because," she answered firmly, surprised that her voice did not shake this time. "You are the Master of Tides. You are the only one who can stop Lord Hotaka now. Because…I believe that you will not let calamity fall upon these waters again."

The dragon raised his head, gazing up at the endless length of sea that lay between them and the surface. *"Be at peace, child,"* he rumbled. *"You have called, and I will answer."*

Joy rushed through her at those words. "Oh, thank you, Ryūjin-sama!" She managed an awkward little bow, bringing her palms together at her forehead.

The dragon began to move, the rest of him leaving the palace. The sea shook as the enormous length of his scale-covered body emerged, looping smoothly and gliding through the water as easily as any sea creature. The movement stirred the water, pushing Shinju out of the way.

She watched in amazement as Ryūjin brought his head near her and stopped, while the rest of his body still flowed out of the palace.

"Grab on, little human," Ryūjin commanded. Shinju found she could now swim, and still breathe, and she hurried to obey. She approached the enormous face with a renewed mixture of awe and fear and clung to the base of one of his giant horns.

"We are in The Golden Sea," she wondered aloud, "How will we reach the Imperial City in time?" Surely they were hundreds of miles away.

A deep rumble echoed in the dragon kami's throat as he began to rise to the surface. *"I will show you."*

42

THE PLAN HAD BEEN working. While Shinju drew the attention of Matsuda and Lord Hotaka, Raiden had made his way to the ship, taking advantage of the distracted ninja to climb up the slick wood planks, listening for her signal.

It seemed to take a long time.

The loss of his gauntlets had been nothing compared to the moments he'd thought he'd lost Shinju to the wave's wrath. When they'd reunited in the water, he'd silently promised himself to never let her out of his sight again.

Only minutes later he had done exactly that. As Shinju pleaded with him to agree to her plan, Raiden had wanted to rage, to grab her and bear her away somewhere safe, no matter how she resisted. But he'd committed to helping her, to seeing this through, and stopping Hotaka had become personal.

Mostly because of Matsuda. How Raiden longed to inflict

pain upon the thief for every hurt of Shinju's.

He'd crouched on a small ledge of the ship used by sailors when the hull needed repairs, listening and barely breathing. He vaguely heard Matsuda's voice, then Hotaka's and he bristled, training every sense towards Shinju. She was right: they'd kept her alive to rub their victory in her face.

Then the signal: a sharp, clear whistle, and Raiden sprang to life, unleashing lightning over and across the ship. He'd aimed blindly but knew the short enough burst would cause the intended chaos, and be far enough away that he wouldn't hit Shinju by mistake.

Oddly enough, it felt good to use his powers without the gauntlets. It had been so long since he'd even practiced without them, that it felt as though something deep inside him unleashed what had previously been reigned in.

Ninja descended as he climbed to the railing and jumped over to the deck, but he'd welcomed their attacks. He was angry and knew how to put that anger to good use.

Still keeping a hold on his powers as best he could to reserve energy, Raiden fought his way through ninja and hired pirates, wondering how many more of these fools could possibly be in the ship. Men he'd already killed with lightning bolts lay strewn across the deck, yet more kept coming.

Across the ship, he saw Shinju engaged in combat with Hotaka, the jewels within her reach. Then his eyes caught on Matsuda, walking towards him with a katana drawn.

He smiled, slow and cruel, as he shot lightning through three more men before turning to Matsuda. "Surprised you had the courage to face me," he growled.

Matsuda chuckled. "Oh, Raiden, you truly have been an interesting opponent. I can see now why she cares for you. You're quite persistent."

Raiden narrowed his eyes, sizing up the thief. He was average height, but his build was evidence of years of hard training. When Raiden had worked with him years ago, Matsuda had been both cunning and deadly. Even with his powers, Raiden knew he would need to be more vigilant with him.

"Then you must know I plan to kill you very slowly," Raiden answered, "for daring to lay a finger on her."

Matsuda pulled his mask down, giving Raiden an arrogant smirk. "I plan to do much more than that if she survives this little spat with Lord Hotaka."

Fury overcame all other emotions, and Raiden flew towards him, roaring. Lightning sprang from his fists, wild and fast, but missing their mark as Hotaka jumped out of the way, twisting to throw a shuriken he'd hidden in his hand.

Raiden batted the knife away and pulled back on his lightning, considering. Without the gauntlets, he'd lost the ability to command his lightning exactly where to hit. He could feel his powers raging within him, pulling at both the air and his body, hungry to be unleashed.

"Fine," he muttered, and sent a surge through his fists, keeping the lightning there so that his hands were now filled with deadly electricity. Matsuda lunged at him with his katana, and Raiden dodged, grabbing Matsuda's wrist and sending a punch of lightning into his stomach.

The ninja screamed and fell to his knees, shaking as the surge covered his body. Raiden kicked him in the face, watching with satisfaction as the ninja collapsed, groaning.

The ship lurched and Raiden lost his balance, grabbing on to the rigging as he slid by. He looked up to the upper deck where Shinju was, and saw that Hotaka held one of the jewels… and so did she.

More ninja tried to approach him, but the ship continued to lurch crazily, swaying back and forth. Waves raised and raised over the deck, washing away anyone not holding onto something. Raiden spotted Matsuda trying to crawl away, and he grinned, unleashing a spark into the water.

It traveled up Matsuda's legs and through the rest of his body, and he shook uncontrollably, flesh burning.

Raiden let out a breath and turned back to where Shinju stood.

She leaned against the railing, holding onto it with one hand while her other held a tide jewel. Gritting his teeth, Raiden started to stumble his way across the tilting deck, bracing himself when water crashed over the ship.

He reached the unbroken mast and met her eyes.

They were wide and dark, the light of the jewel reflecting on her face. With her hair unbound and waving wildly behind her, Raiden thought her almost transformed, a goddess descended upon the earth to unleash judgment.

When he had summoned the bolt of lightning to hit Hotaka, his heart had soared as it found its mark, and for a few seconds he thought, *This is it. It's over.* They would take the jewels and go back to Shinju's home, and then…well. He wasn't sure what would come next, but as long as this fiery, passionate girl was with him, he didn't much care.

But the tide jewel protected Hotaka, its magic still enough to shield him from Raiden's lightning. Shouting in frustration, he started to move away from the mast, intending to reach Shinju, but the ship lurched again, and the world began to spin.

He slipped on the wet deck, catching himself just in time to look up and see the pedestal crash into Shinju, breaking the railing, and sending her toppling over the edge.

"NO! Shinju!"

A blinding fear like he'd never known took hold of him. The wave had been one thing, but this…the jewels had created a treacherous storm, and she had just fallen inside it.

She was gone. The only person he cared about, the girl who had drawn him from the brink of darkness to start believing in light once more.

Raiden's fingers dug into the deck as he turned his gaze towards Hotaka.

"You," he breathed, fury gathering within him. The clouds overhead reformed, black and filling with the roll of thunder. "You…you killed her…"

He staggered to his feet, breathing heavily as he dug down deep into his well of energy, willing it to fill every pore of his body, to overcome the last remaining fragments of control he had over it. Nothing mattered anymore; there were no more reasons for him to hold back.

Hotaka walked to the broken railing and looked down into the sea, then he met Raiden's eyes with an expression of contempt. "You're a hard man to kill, Raiden," he remarked. "Like a cockroach, you just don't know when to quit."

Now that there was no longer a battle between the jewels,

the waters calmed slightly, and the battered ship began to right itself. Raiden smirked grimly. "If you think those jewels are going to protect you from me for much longer, think again. I've killed Matsuda and most of your ninja. It's just you and me now."

Hotaka raised an eyebrow, as if mildly disinterested. "I'm afraid you're quite mistaken, Raiden." He swept an arm to the side, pointing towards the horizon.

Raiden glanced over and saw three ships sailing towards them, bearing the sails of the pirates of the Black Harbor. Beyond them, he could see a sliver of land. They were closer to the Imperial City than he thought.

Raiden snorted. "In case you haven't noticed, they're far enough away that I still have plenty of time to peel the flesh from your bones," he growled. Static, wonderfully sharp and piercing, filled the air, raising his hair. Good. His powers were renewing.

Hotaka cocked his head. "You have that look," he reflected. "The same one she did. I noticed it the first time you and I met."

Raiden frowned in annoyance. "What are you talking about, old man? The first time we met, Shinju wasn't there. Perhaps the magic of those jewels has addled your brain."

The Otami leader smiled cruelly. "I'm not talking about Shinju."

He let the statement hang in the air like bait, waiting for Raiden to bite. Thunder echoed again overheard, the clouds churning faster. Soon, Raiden thought. In the distance, he could hear the faint shouts of the approaching pirates. Gnats. He would wipe them all out. Everyone responsible for Shinju's death would fall.

"I had wondered if we would ever meet," Hotaka continued conversationally, as if Raiden were not seconds away from blasting him. "Your name became well known, as well as your powers, over the years. I kept waiting for you to find me."

Those words eclipsed Raiden's movements, stilling him as his mind lurched to the edge of discovery. Realization grasped at him with unforgiving claws, and shock poured through him as Hotaka confirmed it with his next sentence.

"You're the demon welp of that little seamstress. Oh yes, I remember her very well." He sighed, as if recalling a happy memory. "She was fun while it lasted, but of course her temper got her into trouble. A family trait, I think. Tell me, did she make it home before she bled out on the road like an animal?"

Raiden gaped at Hotaka, frozen by the casual admission of guilt. The man he'd hunted his whole life, the man he'd vowed to destroy, the man who had taken everything from him, stood right in front of him. And he'd recounted his crimes against Raiden's mother as if she were nothing.

Pure, red-tinted fury exploded from Raiden as he screamed. He threw his arms up, and unleashed a torrent of lightning bolts, more powerful than any he'd summoned before. They slammed into the ship, breaking through the wood as easily as a sword through paper.

Pieces of the ship blew into the air, and water began to pour in. Raiden barely noticed. He only had eyes for Hotaka, who stood beneath the lightning attacks, holding the jewels and bracing himself as they enveloped him in a magical shield.

Snarling, half-mad with vengeance, Raiden stepped towards

him. His only thought was to kill, to avenge his mother. Shinju. Their faces flashed before him; their voices asking him why he hadn't saved them, why he hadn't done more.

Shinju had found the strength to spare her aunt. Hotaka would receive no such mercy. Raiden did not care if it damned his soul.

He raised one arm up, then down, then the other, bringing lightning from the sky down onto Hotaka, giving it all that he had. His energy would fade eventually; this might even kill him. He had never pushed himself so hard before. The power ripped through him, unyielding, hungry, and bottomless.

Hotaka spoke, and a wave as tall as a castle rose up beside them. Raiden drew closer, pressing against the wind and roar of a water, determined to find a hole in Hotaka's armor.

The wave slammed into him with the force of a tsunami, knocking him to his feet and breaking his concentration as water filled his throat. The lightning stopped, and all he saw was swirling water, unforgiving and relentless, battering him side to side and sweeping him out to sea.

Using the last of his strength, Raiden pumped his arms, heading for the surface, fighting against the tide as it pulled him farther away. He could hold his breath longer than an average human, and he'd never been so grateful for that particular gift until now.

He burst out of the water, gasping, and turned immediately towards the direction of the ship. Or what was left of it. A chunk of debris floated by, and he grabbed onto it.

The ship had broken in two, and both halves were sinking. Hotaka stood on a wave, the water holding him above the wreckage. In his hands he still held the tide jewels.

Just as quickly as Raiden's fury had overtaken him, it extinguished, leaving him with nothing but empty despair. He'd used so much power that now he felt as shaky as a newborn lamb, weak and unable to do more than watch as Lord Hotaka remained in control over the seas.

Black spots danced in his vision, and Raiden rested his forehead on the floating wood. "I'm sorry, Mother. Shinju." *Shinju.* He blinked slowly, allowing the image of the girl he loved come to mind. If he was to die, it would be with her in his last thoughts.

Beyond the wreckage of the ship, past Hotaka the tower of water that he stood upon, an eruption of water rose up to the gray sky. Even from a mile away, Raiden could feel the shower of droplets upon his face.

He watched, stunned, as the form of a dragon, great and dark and dreadful, emerged from the sea, bearing a girl on its head.

43

Ryūjin carried them to the surface of The Golden Sea, breaking through the water and into the sky. Shinju held on for dear life, hardly able to keep her eyes open as water, then wind, rushed around her as they launched through the air.

The dragon curved, soaring for a long moment like a bird in flight. Glancing down, Shinju noted with a start that they were miles above the sea's churning waves. From her place on Ryūjin's head, she could see the rest of his body, winding and thick and powerful as it suspended in place.

His scales shimmered in the early morning light, brighter than all the finest, exquisite jewels in Horitamo. Under the sunlight, she could now make out flecks of gold amongst the cerulean blues of the plates.

Two front legs, ending in massive claws, pawed through the air in climbing motions, bringing them higher even as Ryūjin curved down. Were they going to fly? Shinju wondered incredulously. Could the lord of the sea fly in the sky as well as through the waters he ruled?

She looked down his long back, watching as a thin emerald-colored dorsal fin, like that of a sailfish, opened and closed, folding as if testing the wind.

Then suddenly they were falling, diving headfirst back into the sea. Shinju gripped the black horn and dug her heels into his scaly head as best she could, bracing for the impact that would surely tear her from her seat, but they entered the water as smoothly as a knife through butter, barely budging her from her seat.

Ryūjin began to soar—for that was the only word Shinju could think of to describe it—through the water, moving faster than any other sea creature that lurked in the depths below. He kept near the surface and occasionally, without warning, he would arch once more and they would fly up into the air, only to crash back into the sea moments later.

Whatever magic Ryūjin possessed, it kept Shinju from drowning as they journeyed. When they ascended into the sky, Shinju began to gaze around them, trying to see land. Several times she glimpsed the tiny islands that stretched around the mainland's western coast, and even fishing boats.

Ryūjin did not speak to her again, but Shinju found herself content enough to simply hang on for the ride. The sinking hope in her heart renewed with each passing second, and she felt certain that with Ryūjin himself coming to their aid, and at the rate they were traveling, surely, *surely*, this would be enough to stop Lord Hotaka.

Her thoughts shifted to Raiden. He would be so worried… and angry, she knew. She could only pray he had either stopped Lord Hotaka somehow or had escaped and would be waiting for her somewhere on the sea.

How long had it been since she'd been taken to the palace beneath the sea? Based on the location of the sun, it would seem hardly any time had passed at all. But how could that be? Her journey through the water had felt like hours…

Within minutes, she realized they had rounded the northernmost tip of Horitamo. Miles away to her right, as they emerged from the water once again, Shinju thought she could see the Imperial City, small and glistening even in the mist, where the Palace by the Sea stood in eternal sunshine, surrounded by cherry blossom trees that never wilted thanks to the Emperor's magicians.

Then Ryūjin dived again, and this time he swam deeper than before, shooting straight as an arrow. Fish, whales, and sharks fled before him. Shinju's heart hammered into her chest and she gripped his horn even tighter. They must be close, she thought. Nothing else could ever cover such distance in so short of time, except the lord of the sea.

"*We are here, child*," the dragon's voice spoke, loud and clear. "*Let us see this human who claims to master the tide jewels.*"

In the next moment, Ryūjin dashed upwards, giving a final push through the water, and exploded out of the sea. Shinju blinked, wiping the spray from her eyes.

Below, waves churned in a hypnotic rise and fall. Gasping, Shinju surveyed the sinking wreckage of Lord Hotaka's ship. Where was Raiden? He couldn't be…

She searched the sea desperately, looking everywhere for the half-kami's familiar figure or glowing eyes. Instead, all she saw was Hotaka, using the power of the jewels to stand upon a tower of spinning water.

Shinju climbed to her feet on shaky legs, staring down at the man who had ruined her life, who had done unspeakable acts in his pursuit of power. *Let him try to fight Ryūjin-sama*, she thought triumphantly.

Hotaka, to his credit, recovered fairly quickly from his initial shock and horror at seeing Ryūjin, Kami of the Sea, Creator of the Kanju and Manju, who helped formed the kingdom of Horitamo, emerge from the depths to challenge him.

The great dragon peered down at the Otami daimyo, a deep, rumbling growl reverberating through the air. Hotaka grimaced, clutching the jewels before him. "I see you have finally awakened from your slumber, Ryūjin," he mocked. "I suppose you are here to scold me for stealing your precious tide jewels."

Shinju scowled at his words but kept silent as she waited for Ryūjin to speak.

"*You have caused great evil to fall upon my seas, human*," Ryūjin boomed, his voice even louder and deeper than when they'd been underwater. "*You must return the tide jewels, and answer for your crimes.*"

"I shall do no such thing," Lord Hotaka retorted. "I am the Master of Tides now, serpent, and you will submit to my authority!"

Gritting his teeth, Hotaka began focusing on using the tide jewels' powers. The waves around them stirred, as did the wind, but nothing else happened.

Shinju could see Hotaka begin to panic slightly, sweat dripping down his brow as he tried to summon the power of the tides. "What-what is this?" he seethed.

"Did you think that the jewels are more powerful than I?" Ryūjin's question rumbled like a roll of thunder. *"I am the sea. I created these tide jewels for humans to use for good, but they truly answer only to me."*

"No!" Hotaka shouted, sounding like a petulant child. "This magic is mine! I've used them, and they answered. I can feel their power within me still!"

"You have used the Kanju and the Manju for wicked deeds, and that wickedness will be repaid to you," Ryjuin answered.

"Oh? You might be a Kami, but you are not invincible!" Hotaka shouted. He turned, still using the tower of water, and moved closer to three ships that sailed close by. Shinju blinked in surprise as she took in the pirates that occupied the decks.

"Fire!" Hotaka yelled. With answering booms, the ships launched cannon fire into the air, aiming at Ryūjin. Shinju cried out, clutching at Ryūjin's horn. The great dragon calmly leaned out of the way, the cannonballs flying past them harmlessly.

"Closer!" The men far below on the decks scrambled to obey Hotaka, who snarled and tried to use the jewels again, succeeding only in stirring the waters into a frenzy.

Ryūjin growled, a sound that frightened Shinju even though she knew it was not directed at her. The waters trembled, and the great dragon's tail surged up from the depths. It rose high into the air, turning to the side until it hovered over the ships, then crashed down.

The ships flew to pieces, no match against the strength of Ryūjin's tail. Men screamed and dived overboard, and some were sucked down into the sea. The water boiled white and black, and Ryūjin swept his tail through the remnants of the ships once again.

Shinju swallowed, her mouth dry, and felt slightly dizzy. She had believed Ryūjin to be powerful, but to witness his strength up close was intimidating. And she knew this to be the least of what he could do.

"Shinju!" a voice called far below her. Shinju dropped to her knees and peered over the edge of Ryūjin's head and saw Raiden. A small boat had escaped the wreckage of the ships, and he had commandeered it.

"Raiden!" Relief flooded her, so strong that tears leapt into her eyes. His face, anxious, relieved, and fearful all at once, stared up at her.

Ryūjin suddenly lowered his neck, bringing it level with the water. His chin brushed the tops of the waves, blocking them from Hotaka's view. And suddenly Shinju was stepping off the great dragon's scaly head and into the arms of her half-kami.

Raiden held her as if he'd never let her go. "Are you alright?" he asked, his voice shaking. Shinju could only nod, closing her eyes and burying her face into his chest, breathing him in.

She felt him shift, lifting his face from her hair, and she looked up. He was staring up at Ryūjin with an expression of awe and respect. "Thank you," he told the great dragon softly.

Ryūjin answered with a slightly rumble in his throat. *"At last we meet, son of Raijin."* Then he raised his enormous head to serve back to Hotaka.

The Otami Lord had been trying to use the jewels, and a few

waves rose up for him, splashing feebly against Ryūjin's side.

The great dragon opened his jaws and roared. The deafening sound reverberated through the air, stirring the water and raising waves of his own. The wind blew with the force of a hurricane, spinning Shinju and Raiden around in their boat as they clutched each other.

The roar lasted for several seconds, and Shinju managed to peek out from her place against Raiden's chest. Ryūjin reared his head back, then plunged forward, his open mouth revealing rows of mammoth teeth, sharper than any shark's.

Hotaka barely had a chance to react as the dragon's jaws clamped over him, and the Lord of the Otami disappeared into the maw. The tide jewels fell from his hands into the water.

Ryūjin dived into the sea, sending renewed waves to beat against their boat, coasting them along the surface. The rest of his body and tail rose up in a great arc, then they too disappeared into the deep.

Immediately, the sky cleared, and the sea became calm, smooth as glass. Sunlight tentatively shone out from behind a scattering of white clouds, and all grew still.

Panting, Shinju searched the water, waiting with bated breath to see if Ryūjin would reappear. She could barely believe what she'd just seen.

"That," Raiden spoke in a hushed voice, "was incredible."

Shinju gripped his tunic, her eyes never leaving the water. "Is it…is it really over?" It seemed too good to be true. She felt Raiden's lips press against her forehead, and he answered, "Yes, I think it is."

44

SHINJU SHIELDED HER EYES as sunshine sparkled on the waves. She was almost home.

Ryūjin carried them across the seas, seemingly undisturbed by an additional human riding on his head. Raiden did not look entirely comfortable, as if half-expecting the dragon to suddenly turn his head and swallow them both.

"Do you see it?" he asked Shinju. "Not yet, but we are close. I recognize these waters." She smiled, glad to be back in a familiar sea.

After sending Lord Hotaka to his doom, Ryūjin had returned to Shinju and Raiden on their little boat and presented both tide jewels to Shinju. The blue-green and purple glowing orbs floated through the air, coming to a halt before her. She took them both in hand hesitantly.

"You have one more task ahead of you, child," Ryuin spoke. *"And*

I will bring you there."

Home. The word had never been sweeter. And it was not the castle in Itshino that Shinju now pictured in her mind as home, but Kanju Shima, the island lost on The Golden Sea.

"Ryūjin-sama?" she asked timidly. "Returning the Kanju to the island…it will help the Tsomas, won't it?"

The dragon merely looked down at her silently, with the benevolent patience of a parent to a questioning child. Shinju sighed. *I guess we will find out when we get there.*

The jewels shimmered where they now lay in her lap. Shinju traced a finger over the Kanju, remembering the first time she had ever seen it. Takumi had brought her to the shrine when she had been newly welcomed into the clan, so she could see for her own eyes what they protected.

Even as a child, she'd understood the jewel was something special, sacred. It had never occurred to her that she might hold it one day, let alone use it.

Please, she thought, *please restore the magic to my island. Please help the island give up its hold on my family.*

Ryūjin sped across the water, remaining this time at the surface rather than diving in and out. Dolphins and fish occasionally swam beside them, leaping out of the sea as if to rejoice at the presence of the sea Kami.

Shinju glanced at Raiden. He sat close to her, his knees drawn up, and had been very quiet. "Are you alright?" she asked. He shook his head and blinked, as if scattering thoughts away.

"I'll tell you later," he answered lowly, and managed half a grin.

Shinju squeezed his shoulder. Perhaps he was nervous

about meeting Takumi and the rest of the Tsomas.

"Look!" she exclaimed, pointing towards the horizon. "There it is!"

The island rose to greet them, dark and silent under brooding storm clouds. Shinju trembled, her initial joy at spotting her home replaced by worry. What if she was too late? What if the return of the Kanju wouldn't be enough?

She had been so sure that this would work, that she had refused to even consider the possibility that it wouldn't, not since Raiden first asked her that question so many days ago it felt like years.

They drew closer, and Shinju gasped. The island's trees and plant life had withered, turning black and sickly gray. The beach had lost all color, driftwood scattered across the sand. A terrible smell emitted from the island, of rot and death.

"Oh no." Shinju choked back a sob. It looked worse than before, and the fear that she was too late raised its ugly head. Could she really have come all this way only to fail again?

Ryūjin swam up to the shore and Raiden jumped off onto the sand, then turned to look back at Shinju expectantly when she did not move from her perch.

She clutched the jewels, hesitating. The moment she stepped onto the island, she would learn whether or not the return of the Kanju, and the additional presence of the Manju, would revive the island. Fear kept her rooted to Ryūjin's scaly brow, fear that in the end, none of this would matter.

"It is time, child," Ryūjin told her. His voice rumbled, vibrating the water and the shoreline. A wind began to blow, stirring the dry palm trees.

Shinju took a deep breath and nodded, then jumped off onto the sand.

Instantly, the Kanju began glowing, brighter than it ever had, and a shockwave of bluish-green light emitted from the jewel, spreading out and over the island.

Beneath their feet, the ground began to tremble, lifting the sand and causing the driftwood to slide. Trees shook, dropping palm fronds and coconuts. Shinju heard a strange sound, as if the entire island gave a deep sigh.

Then, slowly at first, the angry clouds above them dispersed, allowing soft rays of sunlight to shine through. With the sun's arrival spread a nearly invisible ring of magic, and wherever it touched, color returned to the island.

Bowed trees straightened and bloomed, turning full and green again. The decaying plant life revived, filled with flowers. The sand returned to warm tan, and far above them, the magic spread up the mountain, changing its gray pallor to lush emerald.

Birds began to sing and return from wherever they had been before. Dolphins splashed near the shoreline, playing. The air became sweeter and fresh, like it had always been.

Shinju's knees shook and her eyes filled with tears. "It worked," she breathed. In the distance, the sound of voices reached their ears.

Shinju gasped.

Takumi. The Clan.

Raiden suddenly reached over and carefully took both of the tide jewels from her. "Go," he told her with a smile, nodding in the direction of the voices. Shinju thanked him with her eyes, then turned and ran up the beach.

Over the grassy knoll and up the familiar path she sped, hardly daring to believe her eyes. The village had been completely restored by the Kanju's magic. Not a single home had been forgotten. But best of all were the people Shinju saw gathered around just outside it.

"Look! It's Shinju!" someone cried, pointing. The Tsomas turned, gasping and murmuring with surprise, and began moving to meet her on the path. But one figure broke away from them, sprinting as hard as he could.

Tears blurred Shinju's vision as she crashed into Takumi, his arms coming around to hold her so tight that she could barely breathe, but she did not care. "Takumi," she sobbed into his shirt. He kissed the top of her head, then pulled her back slightly to look at her.

His mouth trembled as Shinju memorized every line and crease in the facc that was so dear to her. "You did it, Shinju-chan," he whispered. "I knew you could. I am proud of you, Daughter."

They barely had time for another word before the rest of the Tsomas descended upon them, exclaiming excitedly and asking a thousand questions. Shinju laughed and wiped away her tears, barely believing that her people had been restored to her.

Then she remembered Raiden and Ryūjin down at the water. "Everyone!" she cried, holding up her arms. "Please, you must come with me down to the beach, there is someone you need to see."

She broke away from the group and began jogging down the path, leaving them no choice but to follow her.

At the sight of Ryūjin, waiting patiently in the water as waves lapped around his large body, the members of the Clan cried out in shock, then many of them began throwing themselves down onto the ground. "Ryūjin-sama!" they exclaimed. Others stood frozen, gaping at the dragon, then at Raiden, who still held the jewels.

Shinju bit back a smile, glancing at Raiden, who watched with some amusement as well.

Yuudai, still in his ceremonial robes and not a hair out of place, stepped forward, accompanied by samurai who had immediately taken up their old positions. Bracing himself on his walking staff, Yuudai approached the great dragon, his face pale but set with a respectful joy.

He bowed to Ryūjin, who lightly inclined his head in returning, bringing it lower so he could be more level with Yuudai.

Takumi stopped at Shinju's side, placing a hand on her shoulder. His face effused an almost child-like wonder as he stared at Ryūjin. Shinju smiled, remembering all the stories Takumi had told her about the dragon; how surreal this must be for him now.

"Great Kami, Ryūjin-sama, you honor us with your presence," Yuudai said by way of greeting. "On behalf of the entire Tsoma Clan, we thank you for delivering us from the darkness that befell us with the theft of the Kanju." The old man's shoulders shook slightly. "I-I am afraid we have failed you, Ryūjin-sama. Forgive us."

The great dragon blinked slowly, then looked over to where Shinju stood with Takumi. "*I do not see failure,*" he rumbled. "*You did not know the purpose, but you adopted an outsider into your midst, raising her as your own, and she was here for such a time as this, to redeem what was stolen."*

Shinju blushed, feeling everyone's stares on her. Takumi squeezed her shoulder and stood straighter, showing them all that he was proud of her.

Yuudai bowed again, humbly accepting Ryūjin's words.

"You have upheld your vows to protect the jewels for hundreds of years," the dragon continued. *"But I believe it is time for me to take them back beneath the sea. It is clear to me that as long as they exist in the mortal realm, there will always be some who seek to use them for their own purposes."*

People gasped in dismay. Shinju felt a jolt of shock. She had not expected this. Takumi stiffened at her side.

"Great Ryūjin," Yuudai responded with an even shakier voice, "You are wise in all things. You have every right to take back the jewels; they belong to you. However, we beg you to reconsider. The magic of these jewels has sustained our island for centuries. We are bound to it, as you know. If the Kanju is removed again, will we not lose our home once more?"

"Be at peace, Yuudai Tsoma," Ryūjin answered. *"The magic of the jewels will be near enough under the sea that your home will not suffer in their absence. You do not need to fear."*

Relief spread in whispers through the gathered clan. "We thank you for your generosity," Yuudai managed to answer after clearing his throat.

Ryūjin turned his long neck to look at Raiden, who stood by silently. "It is time, son of Raijin," the dragon announced. Shinju slipped away from Takumi's side and approached the half-kami.

He gave a brief nod of his head, then handed the Kanju to Shinju.

Taking the Manju in both hands, Raiden stepped up the dragon's face, lowered to his eye-level, and placed the jewel against Ryūjin's forehead. With a brilliant light that caused a collective gasp amongst the humans, the Manju became absorbed into the dragon's head, completely disappearing save for a small circle of purple above his right brow.

Raiden backed away. Shinju bit her lip and walked up to Ryūjin. An emotion she could name fluttered in her chest as she gazed into the ancient eyes of the Kami.

"Are you going away again?" she asked. "I must return to my own realm," answered the dragon. "But do not be sad. You will see me again." Warm breath tickled Shinju's face as Ryūjin bent his head closer, and the scent of salt and wind and bamboo gently caressed her senses.

Shinju smiled and placed one hand on the giant snout, a gesture she was quite sure no human had dared to do before, as even the dragon looked slightly startled. Then she lifted up the Kanju and pressed it into his forehead, blinking as it too burst into a flash of blue light, and absorbed into Ryūjin's forehead above his left eye.

A brief wind ruffled the trees. Ryūjin raised his head towards the sky, closing his eyes. For a few seconds, his entire body glowed, the scales turning into prisms of light, shining multicolored beams over the water.

Taking a few steps back, Shinju felt Raiden at her side, and she reached between them to touch his fingers. He glanced down, grinned, and laced his hand with hers.

Together, they watched as Ryūjin bade them farewell, then the Kami turned and glided quickly back into the sea. For a few moments they could see the dragon's long, winding body curving beneath the surface, and finally fade from view.

After a few minutes, Yuudai turned and walked slowly over to Shinju and Raiden. The people around them murmured, drawing closer. They stared at Shinju with mingled awe and respect; for Raiden, they held curiosity and some suspicion.

Shinju released Raiden's hand to place her palms together and bow to her daimyo. "Yuudai-sama," she murmured.

"You saved our lives, Shinju," Yuudai responded. "We owe you a great debt." He placed his palms together and bowed to her; the rest of the clan followed suit, even the children.

Shinju felt her face warm and she gripped the sides of her pants nervously. "Please...don't," she begged. "You don't owe me anything. I'm just glad to have my family back."

She caught Takumi's eye, and a lump rose in her throat at the tears she saw there.

"You must have quite a story to tell," Yuudai continued. "We would very much wish to hear it."

Shinju nodded, feeling a little lightheaded. Sweat broke out over her forehead, and her hands shook. "Yes...of course..." She swayed, then her feet gave out and she fell.

Strong arms caught her, and Shinju heard her name being called, but the voice was far away. Darkness clouded her vision, and she knew no more.

45

The moment Shinju answered the daimyo, Raiden stiffened, looking at her closely. She had grown pale, and trembled as if cold. When she collapsed, Raiden grabbed her quickly, preventing her from hitting the ground, and called to her, but her eyelids only fluttered.

Almost instantly, an older man with iron-gray hair and a concerned expression on his kind face arrived at Shinju's side, bending over her with familiarity. From Shinju's previous proximity to the man, Raiden assumed this must be Takumi, her adopted father.

"She's dehydrated, and exhausted," the man said quietly after examining her for a few seconds. Raiden nodded. "We haven't slept in days." His chest hurt, looking at the girl in his arms who normally held such a quiet strength, and now looked so delicate.

The rest of the clan had begun to gather around, murmuring worriedly and seeming to put aside any hesitancy they may harbor for Raiden's presence among them.

"Come, let us bring her home," Takumi instructed, straightening. "She needs water and rest." Raiden dipped his other arm under her legs and scooped her up. She was so light.

He followed the man through the crowd and up the path to the village. Raiden barely registered the beauty of the island around them; cherry and peach blossom trees had burst into bloom, despite it not being their season. The plants were much greener and the flora more vibrant than he had ever seen.

The path consisted of a worn-down track through the ankle-high grass, soft underfoot. They reached the village shortly, and it was exactly as Shinju had described it to him: white stone and wood, multi-colored lanterns swinging from lines that crisscrossed through the main road, wind chimes made of shells that emitted music with every brush of the wind.

Takumi led him to a house a ways off the main row of buildings. They climbed the three steps up to the simple porch, and through the opened door into a calm, tranquil common room. "This way." Takumi gestured to a smaller room down and to the left.

Raiden had to stoop to enter inside. Shinju stirred slightly in his arms but continued sleeping. He watched as Takumi quickly unrolled a soft *shikibuton*, then laid Shinju carefully on top of it.

"I will fetch some water and tea," Takumi told him, and padded out of the room. Raiden let out a breath and sat down, rubbing a hand over his face. He didn't blame Shinju for fainting; he didn't feel quite himself either.

So much had happened in the past few days. Both of them survived off adrenaline and urgency, and now that it was all over, he could feel the weight of all they had experienced begin to take its toll on his body.

Takumi returned bearing a tray of soft cloths and a bowl of water. He rolled one cloth and dipped it into the water, then gently lifted Shinju's head and pulled her mouth open so he could squeeze water into it.

Shinju murmured and managed consciousness long enough to drink more, then Takumi lowered her head again. He dampened another cloth and laid it on her forehead after wiping away some of the dirt from their travels.

Raiden stayed out of the way, letting Takumi assume fatherly duties, and glanced around the room. Various flowers and scrolls and weapons were stacked around the edges. He smirked. Shinju wasn't very neat, apparently.

Takumi left again and returned shortly with steaming tea. He offered a cup to Raiden, who accepted it even though he didn't care for the brew. He took a sip and was surprised at the warmth that spread through his tired limbs. It had a minty, flowery flavor, and it reminded him of Shinju for some reason.

For a long time, the two men sat in silence, drinking the tea and watching as Shinju slept.

"Ryūjin-sama called you the son of Raijin," Takumi stated in a quiet voice. Raiden shifted, moving to sit cross-legged. "Yes. My mother was human," he answered.

Takumi blinked. "How unusual," he murmured, without any of the revulsion Raiden was used to hearing from most people when they learned what he was. "Well, any friend of

Shinju's is a friend to the Tsomas. You may stay as long as you wish."

Raiden swallowed and bowed his head, summoning manners he forgot he had. "Thank you."

"I am sure you would like to rest as well," Takumi added. "There will be plenty of time to talk later."

Raiden hesitated, casting his gaze back to Shinju. She seemed to be dead to the world, resting more peacefully than he'd ever seen her. "I will watch over her," Takumi said softly. His almond-shaped eyes crinkled kindly, but with a knowing glint.

Normally, Raiden would have scoffed at the other man's hospitality and insisted on staying where he was at Shinju's side, but this wasn't some peasant in a no-name village. And Raiden had to admit that he was far too drained to put up any kind of resistance.

Accepting the offer, Raiden finished his tea and followed Takumi back into the main room of the house. Takumi slid open a door, and inside was another small but comfortable room, with a *shikibuton* already unrolled and waiting, as well as water for drinking and washing.

"We live simply here," Takumi explained, "but please let me know if you need anything."

Raiden swallowed again, feeling awkward. He was a stranger to this man, who had the same quiet strength that Shinju exhibited, and instead of interrogating Raiden on who he was and what he had to do with his daughter, Takumi treated him as a guest and assumed the best.

Now I know where she gets it from, he thought with a chuckle as the door slid shut.

Raiden splashed water on his face and neck, then lay down on the soft futon. The little house was quiet, though he could pick up on the murmur of voices outside in the village. More than likely, the daimyo, his samurai, and the village elders would be descending upon Takumi to inquire about Shinju and the stranger with glowing eyes.

Before he realized it, Raiden drifted into a sleep more restful than he'd had in years.

Shinju slept for three days, waking only at brief moments to drink water and the medicinal tea that Takumi brewed. Her father doctored her wounds and kept a close eye on the slight fever she'd gained.

Whenever Raiden went outside, a small furry creature would dart under some bushes, peering out with glittering black eyes. Raiden wondered if it was Shinju's pet tanuki, but his attempts to lure the creature closer went unanswered.

A funeral was held for the fallen samurai at the shrine of the Kanju, and the clan, though happy to be alive, grieved the loss of their warriors and spent the day in a somber mood. That night, a thunderstorm rolled in, and once a bolt of lightning struck the ground.

Raiden went out to see it; when he returned to the house, Takumi looked at him curiously, but asked no questions, much to Raiden's relief.

For the first time in many years, Raiden had nothing to do. He sat by Shinju often, and looked after her when Takumi left the house. But there did not seem to be much else that he could really contribute to. He wasn't used to being idle, and he didn't know what to make of his new-found free time.

Takumi was a quiet, resourceful, purposeful man, which Raiden found he respected, and the two men shared some brief conversations, tentatively learning of each other.

On the third day, Takumi asked Raiden if he would accompany him to visit the village elders. They were all very anxious to learn about Shinju's journey, and as Takumi refused to wake her before she was ready, Raiden was the only other person they could turn to for answers.

Raiden assented, and that evening he followed Takumi through the village and up the winding path to a larger home surrounded by gardens and peach blossom trees. The property crawled with samurai; Raiden thought wryly that they must have felt deeply offended by the murder of their brethren and so wished to not make the same mistake again.

Introductions were made in a small room sparsely outfitted with sweet-smelling wood walls, tatami mats, and low cushions for seating. Only the daimyo, Yuudai, Takumi, and a handful of the other elders were there. Raiden nodded to them and took a seat, folding his arms out of habit.

He met each of the men's gazes; he knew his glowing eyes were unsettling, and most people could not look him straight on. But these elders seemed relaxed, if not mildly curious, and gazed calmly back at him. The female elder, a tan, wizened woman with hair still black as a raven's wing, gave him a slight smile of encouragement.

"Raiden-sama," Yuudai began, "I trust that your stay with us has been comfortable?"

"It's just Raiden, and yes. Takumi has been more than gracious with my presence in his home."

"That is good. And you know why we requested you to come here tonight?"

"Yes." Raiden paused. "I think some details would be better if they were told by Shinju, but I will tell you what I can."

He told them how he and Shinju met, and that he had agreed to help her on her mission to find the thief of the Kanju. Unsure of how much Shinju would want them to know about her past just yet, he skirted around her connection to Lady Hono, and merely said that the trail led them to Itshino Province, where they encountered Lord Hotaka and the Otami.

"It was from Lord Hotaka that we learned he had sent the thief and was hunting for the Manju as well. We tried to beat him to the other island, to warn the Tsoma Clan there, but…we were too late."

The elders murmured sadly amongst themselves. Shinju had told Raiden that communication between the islands had been lost many years ago, but they were still connected by blood and purpose. The clan had suffered many losses in a matter of weeks.

"We followed Lord Hotaka out to sea. I struck his ship with lightning, but the jewels protected him from harm. He used the jewels to create a wave that destroyed our boat. Shinju and I almost drowned."

He swallowed hard, thinking back on that moment when he

had surfaced in the churning, black water and had not seen Shinju anywhere.

"We concocted a plan of distraction. Shinju convinced them to bring her on board, and she maneuvered herself close enough to Lord Hotaka to attack him, while I snuck aboard and fought the rest of the ninja, including the thief."

His audience leaned forward, clinging to his every word. He continued to tell them of how Shinju had managed to capture one of the jewels and use it against Hotaka, but in the end, she had been thrown overboard.

"I thought she was gone then," Raiden admitted, clenching his fists and trying very hard to keep any surges from appearing through his hands. "I attacked Hotaka with everything I had left, but the jewels protected him again, and he swept me off the ship with another wave."

No need to tell them of his own connection to Hotaka; Raiden himself was still processing that revelation. He finished his tale by describing the way Ryūjin had appeared with Shinju, and defeated Lord Hotaka.

The elders' expressions varied once he fell silent. Raiden knew he had left out much from the story, when he glanced at Takumi, the man's thoughtful but shrewd eyes told Raiden that he knew it.

"Much of what you have told us is troubling, Raiden," Yuudai finally said. "These ancient texts you spoke of…I fear they may fall into the wrong hands once more. And the fate of the Tsomas on Manju Shima is grave indeed."

"Even with the tide jewels back in the possession of Ryūjin-sama, our way of life is threatened," another elder added. "More people may try to find this island, seeking the jewels."

"So stop them if that happens," Raiden cut in. "You have samurai. Shinju told me you have some knowledge of magic. You have the means to defend yourselves, even against a battalion. Seems to me that you've grown soft after so many years of living untouched by the outside world."

His words aroused angry protestations from the elders until Yuudai lifted his hand for quiet. "He is right," Yuudai agreed. "Despite all our preparations, a lone thief was able to steal past our defenses. We have much to improve upon."

He turned back to Raiden. "Thank you, Raiden, for enlightening us on what has happened, and giving us a great deal to discuss concerning our clan's future." It was a dismissal. Raiden bowed and stood. To his surprise, Takumi rose as well and accompanied him out to the front of the daimyo's home.

They stopped outside the gate. Farther down the pathway, Raiden could see the lanterns lit in the village, orange glows gently swinging in the dusky haze of the evening. He wondered if Shinju was awake yet.

"There is something I would like to know, Raiden," Takumi spoke softly. Raiden waited as the other man looked off into the night, beyond the groves of palm trees and to the sea beyond. "The thief…he was one of us, wasn't he?"

Raiden nodded. "Yes."

Takumi let out a rush of air. "I thought it might be so. The elders will be even more displeased at that news. But what has happened has happened. All we can do is decide how to move on, yes?"

Raiden shifted his feet, unsure of how to answer. Takumi

patted him on the shoulder, then turned and went back into the house.

Raiden walked slowly back to Shinju's home, checked on her, and sat for a long time on the back porch, staring out into the forest.

46

SHINJU CRACKED HER EYES open, blinking blearily at the ceiling. Her throat felt dry and her head spun as she pushed herself up, groaning.

Golden morning light spilled into the room through the paper windows, casting a glow on the polished wood floor. She rubbed the heels of her hands into her eyes, then blinked again, trying to focus on her surroundings.

A cup of water sat on the floor next to her, and Shinju almost knocked it over in her haste to drink it. The cool liquid soothed her throat and she sighed in relief. Then she finally realized where she was.

This was her room. In her home, on the island. "Ohhh…" Shinju breathed out a quiet sigh of relief as she gazed around the space. Her belongings were just where she'd left them, as if nothing had ever changed. Had her whole journey for the tide jewels been some strange dream?

She moved again, and the stitching in her side pulled smartly. Not a dream, then. She looked down at herself; her dirty, worn clothes were gone, replaced with a familiar clean, simple kimono. Her wounds were freshly banaged, and she could smell the lingering scent of Takumi's medicines in the air.

Shinju managed to rise to her feet and shuffle across to the door, sliding it open.

In the common room, Takumi looked up from where he sat at the table. "You're awake!"

In moments Shinju found herself enveloped in his arms, then he helped her over to the table to sit.

"How long have I been asleep?" Shinju asked. Her head still felt groggy. "Three full days," Takumi answered, pouring her a cup of tea. "Today is the fourth morning."

"Three days?" Shinju could barely believe it. She accepted the tea and sipped it mechanically, her mind reeling. "What has been happening? Where is Raiden?"

"Raiden has barely left your side," Takumi answered with a knowing grin. "He stepped out just a little while ago; I expect he will return soon. As for the rest…it can keep. What you should focus on is regaining your strength."

"Have I been ill?" Shinju asked, taking another sip of the tea. She could already feel it fortifying her. "Not ill, exactly, simply exhausted." Takumi stood and approached the hearth, where a pot of something that smelled heavenly simmered.

"Try to eat as much of this as you can." He poured a healthy portion of the soup into a bowl and gave it to her. Shinju obeyed and ate, pausing in between mouthfuls to ask more questions.

When Takumi decided she'd eaten enough for the present, he suggested that she go down to the springs and have a proper bath. "That would be glorious," Shinju sighed. "I can hardly believe I am home again." She searched Takumi's face. "I have so much to tell you."

"I can see it in your eyes," Takumi answered. "This journey has changed you."

Shinju felt a lump in her throat grow as she cast her mind back over all that had happened since she'd left the island. "Yes. You always said I would face my past one day, and I did."

She gazed past him towards the open back door, watching as the bamboo swayed and creaked in the breeze. "Takumi, I haven't been honest with you and the Tsoma elders about who I am…where I come from…"

Takumi reached across the table and placed a warm, calloused hand on hers. "Please, Shinju-chan, you do not need to tell me this until you are ready."

Shinju shook her head. "I am ready now. I must tell you or I think I will burst."

He gave an assenting nod. "Very well."

Shinju steadied herself and took another sip of tea. Once she started, she could not stop the flow of words. The dam had burst, and she no longer felt the need to hold back, to hide the parts about herself that she'd kept behind the door for so long.

She told him everything: how she was the daughter of the daimyo of Itshino Province, how her parents had died, how she had blamed herself for years about her parents' deaths, harboring a guilt that ate at her soul. How, upon her return to Itshino, she had faced her aunt and learned the horrible truth that Hono had killed Airi and Io, and allowed the takeover of Lord Hotaka and his Otami legion.

When she finished, Shinju felt again a wave of exhaustion, but relief. Dragging the truth into the light hurt, but it was a good pain.

Takumi rose from his seat across the table and came to kneel beside her. Shinju realized tears were streaming down her cheeks, and she wiped at them absently.

"I could always tell that you were holding something back," Takumi said gently. "But I had no idea it was all of this."

"I am sorry I never told you," Shinju confessed. "At first, I was afraid you might send me back, or that I would be kicked out of the Clan for doing something as horrible as what I believed I'd done. After a while, it became easier to just…hide it away and try to put it behind me."

"And I am sorry I let you bear this burden alone," Takumi told her sadly. "Perhaps I should have pushed you to open up more, but I thought…with time…"

"No," Shinju disagreed. "You and the elders did all that was right. The problem was me." She released a shuddering breath. "I grew to trust you all, but I didn't trust myself to expose what had happened to me and try to face it much earlier."

She spun the empty teacup between her fingers. "I am glad I now know the truth, though it came at a price."

Takumi placed a hand on her shoulder. "I am glad you told me. I see that look in your eyes; I am not angry with you, Shinju-chan. I am proud of the young woman you've become."

Shinju nodded and smiled at him. "I am thankful for you,

Takumi. You are a good father."

They sat in silence for a while, letting the confessions and revelations of Shinju's journey wash over them and settle into the past, where they would be replaced by peace and healing for the future.

"Now, go on with you. There's someone who's been lurking around this house, eager to see you."

Shinju grinned and stood, padding over to the back door and looking out into the garden. "Peiku?" she called. A reddish-brown blur of fur darted out of the bushes, bounded up the steps and launched itself into her arms.

"Peiku! I have missed you, my friend!" Shinju laughed as the tanuki licked her face and nuzzled her neck. "Thank you for looking after everything while I was gone."

She kissed his fur and scratched his stomach like he loved. The tanuki purred and gave several little yips before he began snuffling at her pockets for treats. "Ha! Some things never change. No treats this time," Shinju told him.

Peiku followed her all the way to the springs, where she took a very long bath in the steaming water, scrubbing every inch of her skin until it felt raw and smooth. Her thoughts drifted towards Raiden as she rinsed her long hair. What had he been up to while she slept? Did he like her island home? Had the Clan been welcoming to him?

The urge to stay and soak in the rejuvenating hot spring was strong, but Shinju finally roused herself to stand and dry off so she wouldn't turn into a wrinkled prune. She wrapped a freshly washed kimono around herself and slipped on a pair of sandals, then headed back up the path to her house.

Shinju was surprised not to run into any of the villagers; perhaps they were doing their best to give her and Takumi space before descending upon them with questions.

When she reached home, she sat on the back porch and worked her hair with her favorite comb carved from a tortoise shell. She hadn't been able to find it in the destruction before she left on her journey, and she sighed with pleasure as the gentle teeth ran through her tresses.

Peiku lounged beside her, basking in the sun on the warm wood planks. His ears twitched forward and he sat up, staring off to the left. Shinju glanced over and her heart leapt.

Raiden stood at the far corner of the porch, a hand resting on one of the posts as he watched her. A grin tugged at the corner of his mouth, but his eyes bore into hers with the same intensity as when they first met, sending a fluttering through her stomach.

"You look like a bird, preening your feathers," he said softly. For a moment neither of them moved, and then Shinju jumped to her feet and crossed the few feet between them to launch herself into his arms.

He immediately enveloped her in a hug, holding her in a way that made Shinju feel safer than she ever had. "I missed you," she whispered. "Three days seems like an eternity."

Raiden chuckled. "That it did. Waiting for you to wake up was excruciating."

Shinju pulled back slightly to look at him. "How have you been? Where did you go? What's been happening since I fainted?"

He glanced at the house, then set her gently on her feet. "If you're up for it, do you want to go for a walk?"

"Oh, yes! I'll grab my boots."

Once ready, Shinju rejoined Raiden outside and together they started down a path that ran parallel to the rest of the village. With Peiku at their heels, Shinju pointed out some of the scenery to Raiden, excitement infusing her at the opportunity to show him her home, even though she was sure he had seen much of it at this point.

Birds chirped in the trees, and monkeys chattered overhead as they strolled beneath the canopy of lush foliage. Shinju ran her fingers gently over flowers and bushes, sighing with contentment. Seeing her island whole and well again comforted her.

As they began to climb farther up towards the mountain, Raiden gestured to another direction. "Let's go this way," he said. "I want to show you something."

Shinju acquiesced, simply happy to be with him. He told her that he had spoken to the elders about their travels, and that he had kept mostly to himself the past few days, though the Clan had been welcoming to him.

"I hope you are rested enough, because tomorrow they are going to throw a party in your honor," he chuckled. Shinju nearly stumbled. "A party? Oh *no*," she groaned, slapping her forehead. "What are they thinking?"

"I'm sure it has something to do with the fact that you saved the entire island, and the empire as well," Raiden replied slyly.

"It wasn't really me," Shinju pouted.

"Look on the bright side. I have reliable information that hundreds of dumplings will be served."

"There better be," she grumbled.

He led her into a clearing and stopped. Looking around, Shinju could see a small waterfall trickling down the side of the mountain, and also the sparkling waters of the sea through the tangled growth of the jungle. Back the way they came, the village was visible down below the winding path.

All around them bloomed hibiscus flowers and banana trees. A few birds tittered overhead, observing the presence of humans.

"This is a beautiful place," Shinju commented admiringly.

Raiden walked to a clump of bushes and reached beneath them to pull out an object wrapped in cloth. "When you left me and Ryūjin on the beach, the dragon gave me these."

Raiden unrolled the cloth, and Shinju gasped. The silver gauntlets shone up at them, undamaged from the sea. "Oh, Raiden! How wonderful! They are not lost after all!"

"He commanded the currents to bring them here," Raiden added, his voice still holding some awe at the Kami's power. "I hid them before the Clan arrived and relocated them here after you were settled at home."

Shinju cocked her head. "Have you decided not to wear them anymore?"

"Perhaps. He took a deep breath. "I would like to not rely on them to control my powers. Since coming here, I have not had any outbursts or surges I could not command. I don't know what to think."

Shinju tapped her chin. "It could be that the magic in this island is more attuned to your powers and provides a different environment where the lightning is not as uncontrollable. Have you spoken to Takumi about it?"

Raide shook his head. "No. But maybe I will. I am not used to sharing these things with others."

He sounded a little lost, and Shinju gave his arm a squeeze. "One step at a time, hm?"

47

THE FOLLOWING DAY, SHINJU felt almost entirely normal again, and agreed it was time for her to see the daimyo and elders. Accompanied by Takumi and Raiden, she approached the village on the main road, and immediately gasped at the preparations for the night's celebration.

It would be just as grand as the Festival of Lanterns, she thought. Hundreds of colorful lanterns had been strung between homes and shops, and freshly painted banners and ites waved from every window and doorway. Even now, the smells of the feast were hanging deliciously in the air.

They were, of course, stopped many times by Clan members wishing to greet Shinju and express their delight that she had recovered, and how grateful they were for what she had done for them. Children followed, gazing at Raiden with large eyes and whispering behind their hands about his eyes.

Shinju met all this with some embarrassment, and could barely answer as gifts and food were presented to her. "Alright, off with you all!" Takumi finally ordered good-naturedly. "Shinju-chan must see the daimyo now."

This announcement cleared their way, though children continued to tag along, abandoning their chores.

"Are you really kin to Raijin-sama?" they asked Raiden. "Can you make storms? Why do your eyes glow? Have you ever seen Raijin-sama?"

Shinju could not help but giggle at Raiden's perplexed expression. "Go on, tell them!" She nudged his arm and winked, while he threw her a scowl.

"Yes! Tell us!" the children exclaimed.

Raiden sighed in resignation. "Fine. Stand over there." The group of children practically shoved each other to the ground in their haste to obey. Raiden lifted one arm, and ribbons of lightning flashed and flickered up and down his hand and wrist. He'd worn one of the gauntlets today, not quite sure if he could trust his powers around large groups of people.

The children gasped in delight and clapped. "What else, what else?" they cried.

Raiden glanced at Shinju and Takumi. "I'm not sure I should show you now. Maybe later."

"Awww!"

"Away with you rascals," Shinju laughed, shooing them back to the village. "We have important things to do."

The rest of the morning was spent with the council. Shinju described the details of her journey to them, even the parts about her family, which she could see surprised Raiden and even

Takumi. But she was tired of hiding.

By the end, Yuudai and the elders had many questions, which she tried to answer as best as she could between sips of ginger water and bites of pineapple and coconut, which had been laid out for them to enjoy.

She learned that not everyone in the village was satisfied with the outcome of the Kanju's theft. Some people, especially the younger ones her age, wanted to leave the island now that the jewel was no longer under their protection.

"What about you, Shinju?" Yuudai asked quietly. "You have another life waiting for you, if you choose."

Shinju didn't answer right away, trying to gather her thoughts. "This is my home," she finally stated softly. "This is where I belong. But…I cannot ignore the chaos my aunt and Lord Hotaka poured out on the people of Itshino. With the council's permission, I wish to return there and help set things right."

She fingered one of the flowers that adorned the platters of fruit. "I made a promise to a friend that I would not forget them. I do not intend to stay and rule as daimyo," she added quickly, "but perhaps my presence will bring some hope to a broken province."

Yuudai nodded his head in agreement. "You have the council's permission, though you do not need it. May Ryūjin guide you on your journey to restore your family's honor."

He bowed, and Shinju bowed in response. "Now, why don't you go enjoy the preparations for tonight. You have certainly earned it."

Shinju gratefully accepted, feeling as though she might want a nap after the long morning. Outside in the hall, she turned to Takumi. "Are you upset that I chose to leave, *Otousan*?"

The older man placed his hands on her shoulders, gazing at her with pride alight in his eyes. "How could I be upset when my daughter chooses the right path? You are fulfilling a promise, and bringing peace to the memory of your parents. Go, and I shall be here when you return again."

Satisfied with his answer, Shinju turned to Raiden, who had remained pensive throughout the meeting. "Well," he remarked, "I guess it's a good thing I'm getting used to sailing."

Shinju laughed. "You'll come with me, Raiden-kun?"

"Of course. You think I'm staying behind? Someone has to be the voice of reason," he replied drily, earning a grin and an eyeroll from her.

That afternoon, Shinju refreshed herself with ginger water and experimented with her hair, while Peiku lolled across the floorboards, occasionally thumping his tail. He had been hard to seperate from Shinju since she'd awakened, unless Raiden was nearby. The tanuki had not yet warmed up to the warrior.

Shinju finally gave up any intricate braiding and decided to let the long mane of black hair fall to her waist, only gathering a small section at the top of her head into a bun, where she placed her old jade brooch.

She dressed in the blue kimono she'd worn for the festival only a few weeks ago, marveling at how much had changed in such a short time. She was thinner, and her eyes held a startled sort of look in them, like a deer's. *I am not the same girl I was*, she mused. *But I am still me, all the same.*

When Shinju entered the main room, Raiden and Takumi

stopped their quiet conversation and stared at her. The half-kami's eyes grew wide as he looked her up and down. "What, did I put this on backwards?" Shinju teased, gesturing to her outfit.

"Not at all, my dear," Takumi answered with some amusement. "Raiden, why don't you escort Shinju into the village? I'll be along."

Raiden got quickly to his feet and stepped around the table to Shinju, almost knocking over the oil lamp hanging from the ceiling with his head. He wore new clothes too, plainer than hers but still dyed in the Tsoma blue. She wondered where they'd come from, as he was much taller than the other men in the village.

"You look beautiful," he told her, his cheeks turning slightly pink. "You too," she told him a little breathlessly as she became lost in his eyes.

Takumi cleared his throat, snapping them out of their moment. "Shall we?" Shinju asked, biting back a smile.

They walked together to the village center, which was alite in reds, oranges, and golds. Candles and lanterns provided joyful warmth to the dusky evening, and music had already begun. Shinju lifted her nose to sniff the smells of food wafting from the stalls.

Her friends Haru and Izumi stopped them to talk. Izumi had already met Raiden a couple of days ago when she'd stopped by the house to bring an orchid plant to Shinju, but the others hadn't.

"We are so glad you are safe!" Izumi gushed, taking Shinju's hands. "I can't believe you returned with Ryūjin-sama! I want to hear all about your journey!!"

"Yes, the elders haven't told us much of anything yet!" Haru complained.

They continued walking and chatting, Shinju pausing at the temporary food booths to gather a bowl of her well-deserved dumplings swimming in chili oil, noodles mixed with leeks and cabbage, and a little bag of almond cookies.

"Some things never change," Haru commented. "Shinju, you're always thinking of your stomach!"

"I'm hungry!" Shinju protested around a mouthful of dumpling. "Raiden-kun and I haven't eaten this well in so long."

Her friends eyed the half-kami curiously, but Raiden merely stared back in neutrality, quietly munching on a fish skewer.

"He's a bit serious, isn't he?" Izumi whispered to Shinju.

"A little, but I don't mind," Shinju mumbled, shoving noodles into her mouth with a pair of chopsticks as her cheeks glowed with embarrassment.

"Ugh, clearly you lost your manners on your adventure," Izumi groaned.

The festivities continued, including dancing and even a play that the village children had put together to act out Shinju and Raiden's heroic journey to save their island.

In spite of herself, Shinju laughed and clapped her hands at the paper dragon and ill-fitting costumes; Raiden looked as if he didn't know whether to be amused or uneasy.

Hours later, when the celebration began to reach its natural end, Shinju slipped away to the beach. Her cheeks hurt from smiling and she'd begun to tire of telling her story over and over. As much as she loved her Clan and was beyond grateful to have them back, she could take only so much attention.

The beach was peaceful. Waves rolled gently against the shore, and the fresh, salty air pulled at Shinju's hair. She breathed deeply, and watched as Peiku, who had lurked nearby throughout the party, rolled in the sand and sniffed at a crab.

Shinju gazed out across the water, searching for any sign of Ryūjin out of habit. She wondered what the great dragon had meant when he'd said she would see him again.

"I thought you might be here," a deep voice spoke behind her. Shinju glanced over her shoulder as Raiden stepped down off the grassy ledge and onto the sand, his feet barely making a sound.

She smiled. "The beach is where I've always gone to think or have some time to myself."

Raiden paused, and she hurried to add, "Of course, you can join me, Raiden-kun."

She sat down on a log and patted the space next to her. Raiden obliged, and Shinju couldn't help but giggle a little at how tiny he made the log seem compared to his size.

"I see you've got some admirers," she said. "The children are quite impressed with you."

Raiden snorted. "They're alright. Here." He thrust something at her, and Shinju took it carefully. It was an intricately folded dragon, made from blue and gold paper. Shinju's chest swelled with warmth.

"It's beautiful," she said. "You made this?" He gave an affirming nod.

"Thank you, Raiden." Shinju traced the spine of the dragon with a fingertip. "Who knew that the great Raiden-sama was capable of creating something so delicate?" she teased.

He rolled his eyes and folded his arms. "Don't tell anyone, I have a reputation to maintain." The side of his mouth quirked.

Shinju grinned and leaned against his shoulder, and they sat in silence for a while, watching the waves.

"You were right about this place," Raiden said. "It is… peaceful. There's something about it that calms me in a way I've never felt before."

She raised her head to look up into his face, which had turned thoughtful.

"Remember the place I showed you yesterday, where I had hidden my gauntlets?"

"Yes."

Raiden cleared his throat. He suddenly looked bashful, an expression so unlike him that Shinju furrowed her brows. "I was thinking it was a good spot for a house," he added.

"A house?" she echoed in surprise. "You mean…oh, Raiden! Are you really going to stay then?"

He ran a hand through his hair, both pleased and embarrassed by her reaction. "Yes, well, it's better than anywhere else I've been. And…you're here."

Shinju leaned her head back on his shoulder. "I'm so glad. But, why did you pick that spot? It's a bit far from the village."

"Exactly. I still want my solitude. I don't need nosy neighbors poking their heads in my door every few seconds," Raiden grumbled. Shinju giggled, imagining how irritated the half-kami would be if that were to happen.

Then she sobered. "Raiden, I want you to stay, of course. But…what about your search for that man? Are you going to give that up?"

He was silent for a long time. "The search is over," he answered hoarsely. "I found him."

Shinju drew back, startled. "You did? But…I don't understand. When did this happen?"

Raiden clenched and unclenched his fists, staring off into the jungle towards the sea. "It was Lord Hotaka. He told me so, after you fell into the whirlpool."

Shinju's mouth dropped open in shock. "Lord Hotaka?"

Would that man's evil deeds never end? she wondered hopelessly. How many lives had this man hurt and destroyed in his search for power?

"I'm so sorry," she whispered. "Are you…are you angry that Ryūjin-sama killed him?"

Raiden sighed. "I was at first. I had tried to kill Hotaka, you know. After he told me who he was, rage like I've never felt before, even when my mother died, consumed me and I unleashed all the lightning I could upon him. It's how the ship finally broke apart. But the jewels protected him, and he sent me overboard with a wave."

His shoulders shook slightly. "I had spent all these years searching for this man, and he was right there. And when at last I had the chance to destroy him…I couldn't. And now he's gone."

Shinju stayed silent, her heart grieving for him.

"But," he continued, "I've had time to think. And…I am glad it happened this way."

He looked down at his hands. "This path of revenge was taking me to a place where I didn't care about anything but fulfilling my vow. I lost myself."

Shinju swallowed as Raiden lifted his face to her. "All these years I've been shrouded in darkness. It wasn't until I met you that I realized my life could be different."

He blinked hard a few times, and Shinju could feel her own eyes moisten as she drew closer to him. "What you have…what this Clan has…do you think it is possible for someone like me to have that too, even with what I've done?" Raiden asked, almost whispering.

"Yes," Shinju affirmed gently, raising a hand to slide her fingers into his hair. It had grown since they'd started on their journey. "Yes, I think it is possible."

He cleared his throat and nodded, his whole body relaxing as if a weight had been lifted from him.

"We're quite a pair, aren't we?" Shinju slipped her fingers into his hand, loving how much bigger his palm was. "Who would have thought?"

He grinned and lifted her chin so he could kiss her. "Indeed."

EPILOGUE

AKIRA SHIELDED HIS EYES as sunlight glinted brightly off the tiled roofs of the palace. He was wandering amongst the gardens, lost in thought and barely noticing the beauty around him: cultivated gardens, peach blossoms floating in the breeze, calming fountains and pools topped with lily pads.

Shinju had been closeted with the Shogun and members of the Imperial Court for hours. It had been almost a month since her return and abrupt departure from Itshino, and in that period of waiting, Akira worried he'd never see her again.

Her and Raiden's arrival at the gates of the Imperial Palace a few days ago had been met with relief on his end, even though he'd been less than thrilled to see the hulking half-kami still at her side.

Akira, Rikuto, and the handful of ronin who had agreed to come to the palace were able to vouch for Shinju's identity.

Those in the Court who remembered Io and Airi were enthusiastic about Shinju's return and desired to immediately establish her as the new daimyo, while others argued that she was not fit to step into her father's place after being absent for so long.

This would not be resolved quickly.

Dismissed from the discussions, Akira found himself prowling the hallways of the palace like a ghost, feeling equal parts anxious and hopeful. Despite what Shinju told him about her decision to not take up the mantle of daimyo, he still believed that she was the best option. Especially now that her duties with the Tsoma Clan seemed to be fulfilled.

He cast his mind back to their conversation two nights ago.

"We heard reports of a sea battle, of the tides changing oddly, and a storm brewing out on the coast," he'd said. "Sailors also claimed to have seen a…a Dragon, rising above the waves."

Shinju smiled, her eyes distant as she sat picking at a thread on her dress. "All true. Ryūjin…he really came and destroyed Lord Hotaka and his fleet of ninja and pirates. The tide jewels are back where they belong, in his palace. And my family…the Tsomas, they've been restored."

Akira blew out a breath, shaking his head a little. "I can hardly believe it…but I'm glad you're safe. You know…I was worried you wouldn't be coming back."

His old friend arched her brow, feigning offense. "You thought I wouldn't keep my promise?"

He swallowed. "No…I thought you might have died. Again."

She'd sobered immediately. "I'm sorry, Akira. I've caused you a lot of trouble, haven't I?"

"Well some things never change." He smirked. "You were always trouble when we were children."

"If I recall, you were always very eager to be my partner in crime," Shinju threw back with a grin.

They shared a laugh, thinking about summer-filled, blissful days when lessons and playing samurai were the most of their worries.

"So…now what," Akira asked after a few moments. "It's all over right? You'll be meeting with the Court tomorrow." Shinju glanced at Raiden, who had been sitting silently in the corner with his arms propped behind his head as they reminisced. His eyes cracked open at the change of subject, their blue glow meeting Shinju's gaze.

"We will choose a new daimyo for Itshino Region," Shinju finally answered. "Then, Raiden and I will return to Kanju Shima."

Akira's heart sank. "Are you really okay with someone else occupying your family's home? Removing your heritage?" he questioned. Shinju shifted. "It won't be like that."

"Yes, it will. That's how any new daimyo would be; they will want to establish their rule in the region and be known as the dominant family."

He could see that she didn't believe him, and he restrained himself from arguing. Akira could only hope that the Shogun and the court could talk some sense into her.

"You know, wearing the tiles down won't make it go by any faster," a low voice rumbled, interrupting Akira's thoughts.

He whirled to find Raiden emerging from beneath an archway into the gardens. "What else can I do?" he muttered. "I've been barred from the discussions, and Shinju won't see that she's the best fit for daimyo."

The warrior cocked his head. "Are you sure you're not just trying to make her someone you want her to be?"

Anger filled him. "I want what's best for her. I always have. She is the last Harigoshi, and her place is with her region and family. It's what she was born to do."

Raiden shrugged. "People change. Shinju has a new life now. It's time you accept that."

Akira wanted to knock the smug expression off Raiden's face. The other man had a knack for wearing down Akira's patience, for pushing him to anger…to action.

"Don't act like you know her better than I do," Akira snapped. "I grew up with her. We may have been separated for ten years, but she is still the same girl I spent every day with as a boy. And you just met her weeks ago."

Raiden folded his arms, assuming a confident stance. "And yet, I'm the one she wants to go back to her island with."

Akira couldn't help it. He was not allowed to carry his samurai swords with him while on palace property (technically he was still a questionable subject to the court), but those weren't his only weapons.

He swung his fists at Raiden with all his strength, knowing the other warrior could take it. Raiden dodged the punches, grabbed Akira's wrists, and threw him aside, knocking him into a wooden screen.

"Looking to get another beating, boy?" Raiden prodded. "I guess you didn't get enough last time we fought."

Akira growled and lunged at him again, this time managing to at least meet Raiden's arms as he threw them up to block his attacks.

"Last time was three years ago," Akira snarled. "I've learned more since then."

Raiden smirked. "I should hope so, Ghost of Itshino."

The two sized each other up, then came together again in a

flurry of fists and kicks. Akira poured all of his worry and anger into the fight, growing more and more annoyed with every passing moment. Just one hit, enough to knock that look off of the half-kami's face, would satisfy him.

A throat cleared, pausing their movements. Raiden had grabbed him into a headlock while Akira was pounding him in the stomach. They glanced up at Shinju, who stood watching them at the entrance to the garden.

"Well, I'm glad to see you two are bonding in some way," she joked weakly.

Raiden released Akira and they moved away from each other, the latter quickly wiping the trickle of blood from his nose.

"I wouldn't go that far," Akira mumbled, shooting a dark look towards Raiden, who merely looked amused. He turned his attention back to Shinju as she drew near.

"The court…have they reached a decision?"

Shinju hesitated, then nodded. Akira held his breath, trying to read her expression.

"Raiden-kun," the young woman began gently. "Could you give Akira and I a few moments, please?"

"Sure." The half-kami nodded and slapped Akira on the shoulder. "You're getting better, kid." He stalked off, not before giving Shinju a tweak on the chin. Akira scowled. He would never understand what she saw in that brute.

"Shall we walk?" Shinju suggested, and the pair began to circle the bubbling fountains.

"Please tell me," Akira said after a minute.

"It's good news," she began. "The court and the Shogun

have agreed to establish a new daimyo for Itshino. Hideki Kurosawa. He's a distant cousin of my mother's; a good man. I was able to spend some time in conversation with him."

It *was* good news, but Akira still felt unhappy by the decision. He sighed. "I suppose it is a good thing the province will remain with the family. Though I still think it should be you."

"I know. I'm sorry I've disappointed you, Akira." Shinju turned to him and took his hand. "You've always believed in me, pushed me to succeed, even as children. Your loyalty…please do not think I do not care about that."

Akira swallowed and nodded, trying to ignore the way the touch of her hand on his sent goosebumps up his arm. "I suppose it is time for me to accept that you're doing what you think is best," he admitted.

It irked him, but maybe Raiden had a point. He'd spent so much time building Shinju up as one kind of person in his mind, that he had been ignoring who she really was, what she wanted.

"So, you're really going to leave now," he added glumly.

"In a couple of days, yes. We will stop by Itshino on the way to settle some things with Hideki."

Akira sighed. "I wish you safe travels then. And…even though I cannot stand him, I hope you will be happy with Raiden-san."

Shinju chuckled, her cheeks growing pink. "Thank you, Akira-kun."

She stopped by a small pool, where little orange and black speckled fish eagerly probed the surface for handouts. "There's more," she continued. A scroll appeared in her hand.

"I made some more negotiations. Maybe I'm not going to

be daimyo, but my parents' and Osamu's lessons are still in here somewhere." She tapped her temple with a grin.

Akira eyed the scroll curiously. "What is it?"

Shinju's eyes watered unexpectedly. "It's for you."

His confusion growing, Akira unrolled the scroll. His eyes darted over the carefully written words, and surprise caused his mouth to drop open.

"It's…from the Head Imperial Scholar," he breathed.

Shinju nodded. "Yes. They are offering you a place among them." she placed a hand on his shoulder, squeezing lightly. "You can finally pursue your dream, if you wish."

Akira's head spun as the news sank in. He had never imagined, never even considered, that this path could open for him again.

"I-I don't know what to say," he stammered. "Shinju… thank you."

"Be happy, Akira. Go and take your place in the Palace by the Sea. And I expect very long letters telling me all that you're learning." Her voice wobbled slightly, and Akira too found himself blinking back tears.

"You'll come visit?" he asked, desperate for this not to be goodbye.

"Of course, though I do not know when." A breeze caught her hair, loosening strands from the simple updo. A tinge of salt flavored the air, and he could see her eyes grow distant as she looked out in the direction of the coastline, out past the walls of the city. His friend had indeed changed.

"I'll look for your boat on the sea then."

GLOSSARY

Arigato gozaimasu – thank you

Code of Bushido – the principles of the samurai, emphasizing honor, courage, skill in combat, and loyalty the daimyo above all else

Daimyo – a feudal lord of the warrior class who ruled different provinces or regions; reported to the Shogun.

Gomen – sorry

Hōō – a legendary bird from eastern mythology, similar to that of a phoenix

Jinbei – light, casual top and bottom clothing set

Kaginawa – a type of grappling hook

Konbonwa – good evening

Kunai – a multi-functional, hand-held blade shaped like a spearhead

Nani – "what?"

Oba – aunt

Oni – a large, fierce yokai similar to an ogre

Otousan – father

Okaasan – mother

Shikibuton – traditional Japanese futon bed

Shogi – Japanese chess

Shogun – the title of the military dictators of Japan, appointed by the Emperor and usually the de facto rulers of the country

Shuriken – a small but deadly concealed blade, usually taking the shape of a throwing star

Sumimasen – an apology

Tatami Mats – woven straw mat used in Japanese flooring

Umi nyōbō – a dangerous yokai that lives in the ocean, can take the form of a human woman, with scaly skin, webbed feet and hands, and teeth like a shark.

Yokai – supernatural beings from Japanese folklore, can take many different shapes as monsters, etc.

Yukata – a light, casual kimono

Honorifics

-san – commonly used with those you don't know well; a title of respect similar to "Mr."or "Mrs."

-chan – used with people you are close to, mostly associated with young women or children.

-kun – mostly used when addressing young boys or young men, can also be used by females when addressing a male with whom they have a close friendship or other attachment

-sensei – used to address teachers or other authority figures, to show respect for someone who has achieved mastery in some art

-sama – most formal, used to address those of a very high status or the kami.

ACKNOWLEDGEMENTS

Five years ago, I bought a little black notebook and began jotting down ideas for a novel. Bouncing back and forth between a shaky outline and writing whatever came to my head, it was a draft that I would put on the back burner, only to return to it months later with renewed vigor.

For a long time, I doubted myself. Writing a book is hard, no matter what genre it is, and I was intimidated by writing a fantasy that incorporated elements of a culture and language so different from my own. In 2020, I finally pulled the trigger and made a serious goal of self-publishing this story that craved to be told.

Shinju was partially born out of a love for samurai and martial arts movies I consumed in my childhood. With my dad and brother, I would watch Jackie Chan, Jet Li, and many others, completely awed by not only the fighting technique but the storytelling as well. I've always held a fascination for mythology and fairytales, and the more interested I became in Japanese art, culture, and legends over the years as I grew up, those elements eventually came together to influence this story.

Many, many revisions later, my first book now exists. It is a dream that at last has become reality.

It's hard to believe that I made it this far. I always wondered what I would write in my acknowledgements were I to publish a book, and my heart is full as I think of how many people, in both large and small ways, contributed to this moment in my life.

Firstly, I give all the glory to my Savior, Jesus Christ. Every good gift, every perfect gift, comes from Him alone, and it is from Him that I received this insatiable desire to write and tell stories. It is my hope that the themes discussed in this story, and all my future books, will serve as a compass to point readers to Him, who provides perfect peace no matter who you are or where you've been.

I'd like to thank my husband, Nolan, for his support, love, contribution to the creation of this book's map, and reminding me that writing should be fun and not a chore.

To my parents, who instilled in me a love for reading and writing at an early age and taught me many valuable lessons that have in turn been woven through this book. Thank you.

To my friends who have been my cheerleading squad throughout the process of writing this novel: Ellen Stiling, Adrianna Lucas, Asia Johnson, and Seraine Berube.

To my amazing, talented cover artist and formatter, Benita Thompson, for designing the book of my dreams and being very patient with my indecisiveness and one million questions. You're a rockstar.

To my street team and beta readers, thank you for your support, encouragement, feedback, and assistance in putting my novel in front of more eyes. This book is what it is because of you! I'm forever in your debt.

To the fellow indie authors and writing groups on Instagram who have inspired me every step of the way, I wish I had the room to name you all. Each of you are incredible and I love that we are on this journey together of writing and sharing the stories near and dear to our hearts. Special thanks to Brittany Howard, Victoria Lynn, Brian McBride, Olivia J. Bennett, Mckayla Eaton, and Lindsey Robison (who is the ultimate Raiden fangirl and I love it).

To the teachers and professors from my youth who encouraged me to keep writing and only scolded me sometimes for reading ahead in the assigned texts, thank you for the insight and critical thinking skills you cultivated in the classroom and beyond.

To the brilliant authors and creators who changed my life and shaped my imagination: C.S. Lewis, J.R.R. Tolkien, Jane Austen, Louisa May Alcott, Lewis Carroll, L.M. Montgomery, George Lucas, J.K. Rowling, and Walt Disney.

Last but certainly not least, to my Papa, Robert Mayer, to whom this book is dedicated. You were my writing buddy, my role model for self-publishing, and the one who told me to never give up. And I never will.

ABOUT THE AUTHOR

Charisa Norris is an indie author from Southwest Florida. Since childhood, she has dreamed of writing stories that inspire others the same way her favorite books have inspired her. She holds a particular fascination for fairytales, mythology, and folklore. When she is not writing, Charisa enjoys hanging out with her husband, reading, going to the beach, and traveling. *Shinju and the Master of Tides* is Charisa's debut novel.

CPSIA information can be obtained
at www.ICGtesting.com
Printed in the USA
LVHW042136061222
734732LV00027B/547